"Having served with Rick Crawford on the House Intelligence Committee, I've heard firsthand some of his amazing stories about his service as an Army Explosive Ordnance Disposal soldier. Rick has drawn on these unique experiences to craft a first-rate spy thriller."

—Devin Nunes, CEO of Truth Social and former chairman of the U.S. House Intelligence Committee

"I commend Congressman Crawford for his authentic story about an event during America's efforts to help Afghan forces fight off Soviet troops as they invaded their land in the '80s. Since he was there as an Army EOD soldier, his novel rings with reality and intrigue. Once you start, you'll be propelled to the end. *The Stinger Proxy* is a must read!"

—LTG (RET.) Jerry Boykin, EVP Family Research Council, and author of *Strong and Courageous*

"My friend and colleague Congressman Rick Crawford's smashing debut novel *The Stinger Proxy* combines his patriotic experience of boots on the ground service in uniform with his legislative leadership in Congress. *The Stinger Proxy* grips the reader from the first page with a racing plot, humble characters, and deeply human relationships all while shining light on an important chapter of our military and national security."

—Elise Stefanik, U.S. Representative, House Republican Conference Chair

"Congressman Rick Crawford's *The Stinger Proxy* is a must read for all who admire covert operators, intrigue, and authenticity. Writing from experience, former U.S. Army EOD tech Crawford spins a spine-tingling novel about what happened behind the scenes of what eventually became America's longest war. I highly recommend *The Stinger Proxy*!"

—LtCol Oliver L. North USMC (Ret.), bestselling author, CEO of Fidelis Publishing and Fidelis Media

"Quick, insightful, and brilliantly written. A perfect blend of history, culture, and fiction. The plotting is thick and yet fast-paced. The characters feel so real (because some of them are real!) and fascinating. I challenge anyone to begin reading this book and then try to put it down."

—Congressman Chris Stewart (R-Utah),
House Intelligence Committee
and *NY Times* best-selling author

"Congressman Rick Crawford has had an amazing career in service to our country both in uniform and out. His new novel, *The Stinger Proxy*, draws from that experience and creates an environment for us to see conflict, war, and intelligence through the eyes of an author who experienced all of that. I sat beside Congressman Crawford on the House Intelligence Committee and traveled to South America with him on congressional business. He is humble, talented, and has earned our attention."

—Trey Gowdy, former Congressman,
author, Fox News host

"My friend Rick Crawford has written a gripping tale of political-military intrigue that combines the best of fiction and historical events. Rick draws upon his own military experience to show the reader the harsh realities faced by small teams of elite American soldiers deployed overseas to defend our nation. These warriors often fight on an ambiguous battlefield and find themselves a part of stranger-than-fiction events. I recommend *The Stinger Proxy* to any reader interested in the insights of an American patriot who has served both on our front lines and inside the innermost halls of power in Washington."

—Senator Tom Cotton (R-Arkansas),
combat veteran, author

CONGRESSMAN

RICK CRAWFORD

A NOVEL

THE STINGER PROXY

Fidelis Publishing ®
Sterling, VA • Nashville, TN
www.fidelispublishing.com

ISBN: 9781956454215
ISBN: 9781956454222 (ebook)

The Stinger Proxy
A Novel

Note to readers: A list of characters has been placed at the end of the book. Real people are indicated by an asterisk before their names in this list. A single asterisk represents a real character. A double asterisk represents a real character whose name was changed.

Order at www.faithfultext.com for a significant discount.

Cover designed by Diana Lawrence
Interior design by Xcel Graphic
Edited by Amanda Varian

Manufactured in the United States of America
10 9 8 7 6 5 4 3 2 1

Fidelis Publishing, LLC
Sterling, VA • Nashville, TN
fidelispublishing.com

This book is dedicated first to my family. My beautiful wife, Stacy—who has listened patiently to my stories for almost thirty years—was the one who continued to say this was a story I needed to tell. And to my two awesome kids, Will and Delaney. They've known me all their *lives, but as I tell them, they haven't known me all of* my *life. It's my hope this story gives them a little insight into some of what made me into the man who would become their father.*

And to the EOD community, and that includes my dad—some of the finest people I've ever known—this book is for you. I learned, and continue to learn, so much from the exceptional people who comprise its elite ranks. I am blessed for having been able to serve alongside these unique warriors who do perhaps the most dangerous job I can think of with such dedication and professionalism.

To all of you—thank you for helping me tell this story.

CHAPTER ONE

ISLAMABAD, PAKISTAN
APRIL 10, 1988
1210 HRS.

The mid-day call to prayer could scarcely be heard over the wailing sirens. Explosions shook the city and rockets flew in every direction as citizens ran in panic for cover. First responders swam against a veritable flood of humanity in their efforts to reach the site of a fire and continuing explosions. The closer to the epicenter, the clearer the devastation. Lifeless human bodies became more plentiful, along with the odd horse or donkey. People bloodied by the blasts, clutched their children, their wounded family, friends—even strangers—and sought shelter without any idea where they would find it. Debris flew in all directions and buildings were damaged—some piles of rubble. A black mushroom cloud hung over the city, rising hundreds of yards into the sky, a stark backdrop against the streaking rockets and the frequent plumes of white phosphorus falling back to earth. Hospitals overflowed in every quarter of the city.

The military camp, surrounded by two major metropolitan areas, was the site of the ongoing devastation. As the detonations persisted, and rockets whizzed overhead, the pandemonium continued unabated. The first blast to break the mid-morning silence set off a wave of frenzied speculation adding to the confusion. Was it an earthquake? Was India attacking for some unknown reason? Could it be the Israelis? And what about the Soviets? Perhaps the war in the neighboring country to the west was spilling over into their own. The camp was known to have been a weapons depot at one time. Could that be at the root of the problem? Nobody knew for certain what was happening. What the people did know was their president was out of the country attending an Islamic culture conference, and the response to this conflagration would fall at the feet of their prime minister.

FT. INDIANTOWN GAP, PA
APRIL 10, 1988
0247 HRS.

Will Carter awoke abruptly, startled. He was an early riser, but the alarm clock seemed particularly annoying this morning. The loud, unexpected sound echoed through the small barracks room, his home at Ft. Indiantown Gap, Pennsylvania—affectionately referred to as "the Gap" by those stationed there. When he focused finally on the bright red numbers of the clock, they displayed 2:47 a.m., then he realized it was the phone ringing rather than his usual 5:30 alarm. He dutifully picked up the phone and before he could say, "hello," the voice demanded, "Carter, I need you at the unit—now." He recognized the voice quickly—it was Master Sergeant Steve Jackson, the first sergeant at his unit.

"What's going on?" Will inquired. "Is everything okay?" he asked.

"Everything's fine," Jackson replied.

"Is it my family?" Will pressed.

"I can't talk about it over the phone," Jackson replied, "just get your ass down here."

He wasn't scheduled for 24-hour response duty, so Carter knew something was wrong. If needed for an Explosive Ordnance Disposal response, Jackson would have told him straightaway. Carter was unsatisfied, however, with his assurances that everything was fine. Jackson was a straight shooter—direct, even abrupt at times—so it was no surprise he would want to speak to Carter face-to-face; but surely he would not have left him in the dark either. Will tried to reassure himself that if there were a family problem, someone in his family would have the good sense to call him directly rather than call the unit. It had been his observation, though, often in an emergency, good sense didn't always prevail. And what if his parents were in trouble? Someone may have news about them and didn't know how to call him directly.

These were the thoughts running through Will's head as he jumped into his pickup truck—a four-wheel-drive Ford Ranger he bought the year before—and quickly headed for the 56th Explosive Ordnance Disposal Detachment.

The unit was only a couple miles from his barracks; but even with no traffic at about three o'clock in the morning, the short, pleasant drive seemed slow as Will's trepidation grew. Finally, he arrived, coded into the security system, proceeded through the heavy front door, and headed straight to the orderly room where Jackson's desk was located. When he walked in, Sergeant Carter saw Jackson was standing with his back to him, intermittently reading something in his hand and glancing up at the big unit roster and calendar on the wall. It was the clear, laminated kind, and there were several entries scrawled in a variety of colored grease pencils, each color having meaning. Even with all the negative thoughts racing through his mind, Will couldn't help but marvel at six-foot-seven Jackson; his height still capturing his attention though he had served under him since his arrival at the 56th some three years earlier.

When Jackson turned and spoke in his baritone voice, he simply said, "Have a seat."

Will could feel the reverberation of his words and quickly followed the instruction. Once seated, he inquired, "What's going on, Top?"

Jackson took his seat behind his desk, looked Will in the face, and said bluntly, "Pack your s**t, you're going to Pakistan."

"What—Pakistan?!" Will replied, confused.

"That's right, Pakistan," Jackson said. "Here's a list of everything you'll need." He handed Carter a "DF"—a disposition form the Army used for a variety of purposes. For example, in this case, instructions to a soldier for the kind of tools he might need to take with him on a deployment to Pakistan. The DF was straightforward with no hints of why he was going to Pakistan. It mostly ordered him to have his demo kit, Kevlar helmet, flak vest—the usual tools of the trade for an explosive ordnance disposal (EOD) technician.

At this point, Jackson began his brief. He had an unusually hard look on his face, and although he was a plainspoken Vietnam veteran from Michigan, ironically, he wasn't what one would consider a hard man. That's why his look caught Carter's eye; it added a level of unexpected gravity. Will was barely twenty-two years old and pinned on sergeant stripes only four months before. Still, he was a confident young man—if only slightly cocky.

"An ASP went high order," Jackson explained. "Big f***in' mess," he added, referring to an ammunition supply point, or ASP. "A lot of casualties and the place is still on fire—rounds still cookin' off," he said. "This is still very close hold, so you'll get a full brief at Dix," he continued, referring to Ft. Dix, New Jersey, home to Will's command unit. "Looks like Combs got the duty, so he'll drive you over to Dix. You'll need to be ready in an hour, so hurry up," he instructed.

"Who's going with me?" Will asked.

"Just you from the 56th. You'll hook up with the rest of your team at Dix. And by the way," Jackson added, "no calls home or to your girlfriend or anybody—this s**t's classified."

Will pondered the high order detonation of an ASP in Pakistan. Since the Soviets invaded neighboring Afghanistan years before and a raging war was happening, could this be related? Pakistan was next to Afghanistan. Details were scarce, but he thought the ASP could have been a staging point for munitions bound for Afghanistan. Jackson had a similar experience in Vietnam, and he knew what was in store for the cocky young blond sergeant, who stood before him. That could explain the dour look on his face when he made his pronouncement. Jackson, at this point, didn't know any more than Will did, but his experience as an EOD tech in Vietnam told him the young sergeant was about to have his hands full.

Jackson liked Carter. Will had respect for him too, even though some months before they fell out over an assignment Will was excited about. He was on orders to Greece—a dream assignment for a single twenty-something. But Jackson wanted to keep him at the Gap. Paradoxically, if he hadn't thought so highly of Carter, he would have more than likely let him go, but Jackson arranged to make him stay. Will didn't take that as a compliment, and it affected his attitude toward his first sergeant for a while. But not for too long: As a reward for not going to Greece, Will was sent to the E-5 board and Jackson, a member of the board, awarded him maximum points. Will pinned on sergeant stripes three weeks before his twenty-second birthday.

In the moment, Will forgot about the worry he had for his family. But Jackson's admonishment of no contact with family or friends brought it rushing back. He was close to his mom and dad and called them every few days. He knew they would be worried when they didn't hear from him, but he had to stay focused. Will was a second-generation EOD tech, and his dad—a Vietnam vet with twenty-four years of service—would understand any silence. It was his mom he worried most about. She lived through multiple deployments keeping the home fires burning for Dad, and to him, it seemed unfair she would have to go through it again—this time with little or no information to ease her concerns. Will could contact family only when given the okay—that was the Army way.

Will returned to his barracks and began packing, which took little time because he had such a short list of things to bring and he needed to hurry. As luck would have it, he had been to the Post Exchange, or "PX" as it was called—a general store type establishment common on Army posts—the day before and stocked up on two items he considered essential: Big Red gum and wintergreen Certs. He carried little in his pockets from day to day but was seldom without gum and mints. He didn't think he was obsessive compulsive; he was simply conscious of the need to maintain fresh breath. This added a strange uncertainty to his thoughts: he wasn't sure how long his supply would last, since he had no idea how long he would be gone.

It occurred to Will he needed to get his finances in order before he traveled. He only had three monthly bills to pay—his truck insurance payment, a Visa card with about a two-hundred-dollar balance, and his phone bill. He took his dad's advice to set up a direct payment for his truck note so that took care of itself. His plan was to leave his checkbook and the key to his mailbox in the hands of his trusted friend, Dan Hildegard. Will hated to wake him up so early, but under the circumstances, a fellow soldier would understand. He knocked on the door and Hildy quickly opened it and responded with a very abrupt, "What the hell?!"

"Sorry, dude," Will replied. "I need some help." When he explained the situation, a serious expression replaced Hildy's sleepy look.

"Yeah, man," Hildy replied. "Whatever you need." Will signed about a dozen checks—still unsure that would be enough not knowing how long he'd be gone—and left Hildy with instructions to open the mail and "just keep me current."

Hildy was a solid-built redhead from the Upper Peninsula of Michigan. When he arrived at the Gap, it struck Will that they now had two from Michigan in this eleven-man EOD detachment. *What were the odds*, Will thought. He and Will became fast friends and spent a lot of off-duty time together. Hildy had little in common with his fellow Michigander, Jackson, who was a motor head and kept as many as six cars at a time out behind the unit. Jackson spent most of his free time under the hood of one those vehicles, which he bought from a local auto auction. He bought the castoffs nobody seemed to want, fixed them up, and sold them off at a little profit. In fact, one of the first things Hildy did when he came to the 56th, was to buy one of those cars from Jackson. He didn't necessarily regret the purchase, but he did note Jackson was oddly more concerned about the car than he was. "Top's always on my ass about this car," he said often, referring to Jackson's frequent lectures about good preventive maintenance—a topic he could expound on endlessly if given the opportunity.

"I wish I was going with you," Hildy said. He didn't have a clue where Will was going or why, yet there was no doubt he meant it. Will felt the same way. Such was the bond they had as young soldiers, who had each other's backs. Will didn't even know yet who his teammates would be. He had no doubt they would be competent owing to the very thorough training received in becoming badge-wearing EOD techs, but they weren't the brothers-in-arms he knew and served with at the 56th. Still, the urgency of the situation didn't allow much time for discussion—even between friends—and Hildy could do little more than shake Will's hand and say, "Be safe, man, see you when you get back."

With his finances more or less in order, Will quickly returned to his barracks room just across the hall from Hildy's. No sooner had he walked in the door, the phone rang. "This is Carter."

"Change twenty-eight," said Jackson facetiously, referring to the latest update on the situation. "Get rid of your uniforms," he said. "This is gonna be civilian clothes now," he explained.

"What? So, what am I supposed to pack now?"

"S**t, I don't know," Jackson said. "I guess, that means civilian clothes only—figure it out," he added. "By the way, Control says a 30- to 40-degree temperature range, so think about that," he advised, referring to the weather information he received from their parent unit, the 542nd EOD Control Center at Fort Dix. "Combs is on alert too, he may be going with you," he added. "Hurry up."

This latest information complicated things. Uniforms would certainly have been much simpler, just grab and go. Will didn't have a lot of time to plan a wardrobe, so he just gathered the basics—underwear, socks, T-shirts, a couple pairs of jeans, a few shirts, and one particular pair of pants that made him stop and think for a moment. This pair of olive drab jungle fatigue pants was one of his favorites because they were his dad's, who wore them in Vietnam. In that instant, it struck Will as odd that this single pair of government issue OD green jungle fatigue pants would go with another Carter on another deployment some twenty years later. In his mind that had to be good luck though; and because they weren't camouflage, he reasoned they could pass for civilian clothes and threw them in his duffel bag.

On the drive back to the unit, Will continued thinking about the civilian clothes order. What did it mean for the assignment? He couldn't answer his own question, so he stopped thinking about it. Finally, he arrived at the unit and parked out back. He usually parked in front, but because he would be gone for a while, he thought it would make more sense if he could squeeze in somewhere amongst the many vehicles Jackson kept out back. The soldiers of the 56th referred to the lot out back as "Jackson's Used Car Lot." When Will walked into the orderly room, Jackson was at his desk.

"Mind if I leave my truck on your lot, Top?" Will asked.

"That's fine, go ahead," Jackson replied.

"I'm gonna hide my keys though so you don't sell it before I get back," Will joked. Jackson chuckled, which was the best Will could expect since he was not a jovial man. He then instructed Will to give him the keys so Top could start it up periodically and make sure it was properly taken care of. Will could think of no one better qualified for the task. He placed the keys on Jackson's desk and said, "It's due for an oil change in a thousand miles." A broad grin broke out on Jackson's face, and he appeared almost delighted at the prospect of having yet another vehicle to mess with. Will was only joking about the oil change, but the truth was, he would not have been the least bit surprised to return and find his truck in better shape than the day he parked it on Jackson's Used Car Lot.

Will walked down the hall toward his office to await the arrival of Sergeant Combs. The unit was a converted firehouse and had a big bay in the front with two huge overhead doors. At the end of the hall, two steps led down into the bay, which had once housed two fire engines and was big enough to accommodate at least one basketball goal had the soldiers bothered to place one in there. Off the bay was a retrofitted sensitive compartmentalized information facility to accommodate the unit's classified materials. Will's desk was in this so-called SCIF, and it was his responsibility as the Security NCO not only to ensure the physical security of the facility, but to secure all classified publications—which consisted primarily of military ordnance technical manuals, periodic classified messages, and updates from the FBI Bomb Data Center. The other desk in the SCIF belonged to Combs, the Maintenance NCO who would be arriving soon.

T.J. "Teej" Combs was one of the three other sergeants stationed at the 56th. He walked in, bags in hand, wide-eyed in anticipation. He was eager to deploy. Most of them felt that way: they joined the Army to do something, to see action. Serving in an EOD unit gave them a lot of opportunity for action. They worked with all levels of civilian law enforcement. They served on presidential protection details with the Secret Service. Many responded to bomb threats at schools, banks, abortion clinics, etc.—often encountering live improvised explosive devices. Of course, there was the occasional call to pick up an antique grenade or other vintage ordnance as families sorted out the estates of their deceased WWII veteran fathers and grandfathers. And they were always busy responding to the routine—if you could call it that—unexploded ordnance calls invariably accompanying the myriad training exercises conducted on the sprawling Ft. Indiantown Gap in the Blue Mountains of Pennsylvania.

This was different; an overseas deployment, one about which they knew little. While the Cold War continued through the 1980s, what was going on in Afghanistan was anything but cold. Hot as it was though, most Americans knew little, if anything, about the violent struggles of the Afghan Mujahideen, battling to expel the Soviet invaders from their country. These self-styled freedom fighters had been warring with the Soviets for close to ten years, the fighting unseen by most Americans. If what Will surmised about this assignment was correct, he was soon to get a much closer view.

Will and Combs threw their bags in the back of EOD-1—nothing more than a military Chevy Blazer—and prepared to leave. The noise of the diesel-powered Blazer made conversation difficult, but that usually didn't stop them from talking. This uncertain trip was obviously different, so they were unusually quiet. They arrived at Control in just under two hours as the sun was rising over Fort Dix.

FT. DIX, NJ
APRIL 10, 1988
0625 HRS.

Apprehensive, Combs and Carter walked into the orderly room at the 542nd EOD Control Center. It was early, but clearly Major Aquino and Sergeant Major James Scott had been up all night. Scott was nursing a cup of coffee and reviewing some handwritten notes.

He was on the phone most of the night communicating with various units under the 542nd.

"About time," he said with a hearty laugh, knowing of course, they made excellent time, given the circumstances. "Grab some coffee if you want," he offered. "Wiley will be here shortly with some donuts if he's not lost." He was referring to Staff Sergeant Wiley Adams, certainly a capable soldier, but one whose personality also lent itself to derisive comments, like the one by the sergeant major.

Wiley had been in the Army for around sixteen years and languished at the rank of E-6. He appeared happy as a staff sergeant, content to play a supporting role. He had to be good in that role, otherwise Scott would have gotten rid of him. Stationed in Hawaii early in his Army career, Wiley took up surfing. He wasn't necessarily a good surfer, but he did like to look like a surfer. Even in winter at Ft. Dix, New Jersey, it was common to see Wiley wearing shorts, flip-flops, and a Hawaiian shirt in his off time, as though he were on his way to Waimea Bay. It was a type of behavior provoking scorn and amusement.

Scott, on the other hand, was a jokester. He loved to laugh loudly, often at other people's expense. He was immensely likable and fun to be around. Yet he could be all business too and had close to three decades of service, including two tours in Vietnam. A young soldier would do well to learn from him. Sergeant Major Scott would be the senior NCO leading the team to Pakistan, a comforting thought to Will.

"The donuts are here," Scott said, pointing to the door. Wiley walked in with a dozen under each arm. True to form, he was wearing a Hawaiian shirt and flip-flops, though his jeans, instead of shorts, were a slight change.

"Surf's up I guess, eh Wiley?" Will joked.

"Huh?" he replied, the comment floating right by him.

"How's it goin'?" Will asked.

"Oh, good," he said, as he placed the boxes of donuts on the table close to Major Aquino. Combs watched without comment, grinned, shook his head, and stifled a chuckle.

Major Aquino was poring over some messages he received about the incident igniting the pending deployment. He was prepared to deliver his brief but delayed it while he awaited the arrival of the full team. Major Aquino, the commanding officer of the 542nd, was a quiet man, who paired well with his more boisterous senior NCO, Scott. The major was a West Point graduate, so he carried himself in a formal military manner. He was courteous to fellow officers, NCOs, and the enlisted ranks but also spoke plainly. He typically did not engage in bull sessions and if he had occasion to speak, it was usually to relay something official. He was a private person and shared little about his personal life. You could count on mission focus from him.

What Will gleaned from Scott was Major Aquino would not be leading the team. That task was reserved for Captain John Halstead, who was en route to Ft. Dix from Ft. Meade, Maryland. Captain Halstead was another Vietnam vet, with whom Will was only slightly acquainted. Halstead had been an evaluator at a field training exercise that Will's unit underwent the year before. Will only had a brief conversation with him. The captain was complimentary of Will's performance though, and even mentioned it to his commanding officer. The captain was given free rein to choose the members of his team. That could only mean Will, along with the other members of the team, must have made a good impression on the captain. Their selection was not random.

The rest of the team began to arrive, starting with Shane Hutchinson, a second term staff sergeant from the EOD unit at West Point. He was a tall, blond from a small town in east Tennessee. He was not equal to Sergeant Major Scott in rank, but he was every bit his equal in bluster. He was loud and loved to talk. He was quick with a joke, not necessarily the smartest guy in the room, but a very capable EOD tech. "What's up, f***ers?!" Hutchinson exclaimed as he walked into the orderly room, unaware Major Aquino was present. Scott shook his head and shot him a look, to which Hutchinson replied sheepishly, "Oh, sorry sir." Hutchinson would serve as a team leader along with Sergeant First Class Ed Morgan, who served at the working EOD unit at Ft. Dix, and who was next through the door.

Sergeant Major Scott, Sergeant First Class Morgan, Staff Sergeants Hutchinson and Adams, and Sergeant Carter, along with Sergeant Combs on standby, waited for the rest of the team. They were expecting two more E-5s and, of course, Captain Halstead.

Combs was hot to go and the look of deflation on his face when Major Aquino, who had been on the phone, ordered him back to the Gap, reflected utter disappointment. The major hung up the phone and bluntly said, “Combs, the team is full, go on back to your unit.” As much as Combs was disappointed, Will was relieved. They were close friends, and when Will wasn’t spending time with Hildy doing single guy things, he spent a lot of time over at the Combs’s house with T.J. and his wife, Dana. Will shook TJ’s hand and said, “Take care of Dana, Teej.” He just smiled a disappointed smile and said, “Roger that, see you when I see you.” And with that, Combs turned and went through the door toward the Blazer that brought them from the Gap, only to return there alone.

About this time, Captain Halstead arrived. Will noticed immediately his countenance was different than it was when he first met him during the field training exercise. Despite the seriousness of the mission before him today, he appeared fully prepared for the task, without apprehension, and ready to go. His only concern was his wife and two dogs at home. The Halsteads had no children, so their dogs—Irish setters—filled that void, if there was one.

The team was almost complete. Sergeants Chad Campbell and Tom Thiessen were traveling down from Ft. Devens, Massachusetts, about a five-hour drive and were expected within an hour or so.

When Captain Halstead walked in, he noticed Will sitting at a table with a Coke in one hand and a donut in the other—he was yet to take up the habit of coffee, opting for his caffeine consumption in the carbonated form—and he walked right up to Will, smiled, and said quietly, “Glad you could make it.” As Will stood to salute, he winked and said, “Keep your seat.” He walked over to Major Aquino on the other side of the room, saluted dutifully, then shook the major’s hand. The two fell into serious conversation.

Will’s selection made him proud, but was coupled with trepidation that he had better not screw up. He was given a special opportunity and needed to make good on it. Deployment as a member of Captain Halstead's team was indeed a welcome change from the daily routine at Ft. Indiantown Gap.

Campbell and Thiessen walked in together, at which point Hutchinson loudly announced, "Better late than never."

"Not too damn late," Campbell said. "We made it in less than five hours."

"Well, it was four hours and forty-seven minutes to be precise," Thiessen said. "About 278 miles," he added with a heavy Wisconsin accent. Very nasal in tone, with a distinct inflection on the Os, which was characteristic of his region. Tom was meticulous and felt the need to communicate the exact details of the trip, lest anybody become confused about when they left, and when they arrived.

"Whatever," Campbell added. "We're here."

Chad Campbell was a straight-up, no-nonsense scrapper from western Kentucky. He was not a big guy—barely five foot seven with his boots on—but you would want him on your side if you were ever in a fight. He was stout built and did pushups and sit-ups for fun to help pass the time.

With the entire team finally assembled, all took a seat in the orderly room and awaited the major's brief. The Pakistani Army used an installation found between the capitol city of Islamabad and the city of Rawalpindi—home of the Pak Army—to store weapons bound for Afghanistan. The two cities combined had a population close to two million people. Somehow— the intelligence was not clear yet—there was a detonation that triggered a chain reaction within the stored munitions. There were more than one hundred estimated dead at this time, with over a thousand casualties reported—and rising. The fires were still burning. High order detonations were being reported with rockets going ballistic and live fused ordnance being kicked out over an estimated twelve-mile radius.

The weapons were stored improperly which led to the chain reaction causing the devastation. The Pak Army was not skilled in operations of this nature and would require U.S. help. A three-man Navy EOD detachment from the USS *Enterprise* was deployed and on the site. The Army team would meet with them, collect the necessary intelligence, and relieve the Navy team. They should expect to find U.S. weapons, such as Cobra, Tow, Redeye, and Stinger missiles. In addition, there would be a variety of other munitions from multiple countries. The team would find and secure as much U.S. ordnance as possible, and record serial and lot numbers before disposal operations began. They would also collect as much technical intelligence as possible on any foreign ordnance found. Render safe procedures—RSPs—would be performed only to save lives. Otherwise, after the technical intelligence data was gathered and recorded, "blowing in place" would be the preferred method of disposal whenever and wherever possible. Captain Halstead and the sergeant major were experienced in these types of operations, and the Pak Army assured them they would defer to these two experienced leaders.

With that, the major turned the brief over to Captain Halstead. "The sergeant major and I did this kind of s**t in 'Nam," he said. "It's tedious, it's dangerous, and it's slow going," he added. "We have to take our time and do what we're trained to do. Pay attention and keep your head outta your ass, and you'll be fine," he said. "Sergeant Major."

"Yes sir," Scott said. "Heads out of your asses at all times. The s**t will be real out there. This is not a training exercise," he emphasized in his thick Georgia accent. "You will follow safety procedures to the letter. You will help your teammates. This is a hot zone—literally," he said. "It's still on fire, for *****t's sake. Y'all do what we tell you and you'll be fine."

"Any questions?" the captain asked.

The team wasn't bashful, but no one wanted to speak first. Finally, Hutchinson, who hadn't been blessed with a well-developed sense of self-awareness, broke the silence with a very loud and raucous pronouncement, "Sounds simple enough," he said. "We'll wrap this thing up in a week," he added.

All heads turned in unison toward Hutchinson. "Were you listening at all to any of this, Hutchinson?" the sergeant major loudly inquired. "The captain just said keep your head outta your ass and that starts now," he added. "Now pull yours out and pay the f*** attention!"

That also got everyone else's attention. They began to rethink the wisdom of asking any questions now, but after a long and awkward silence following Hutchinson's rebuke, Will decided to begin. "Sir, it looks like we have a pretty good handle on our own stuff," he said referring to the Dragons, Tows, and Stingers Major Aquino mentioned, "but do we have anything on the foreign stuff we'll be running into?" The one thing about working on military ordnance was the level of predictability it offered—at least for U.S. ordnance. With American ordnance they knew what they were up against and knew what to expect. It was the unknown foreign ordnance that was potentially more lethal.

"Well, that's the sixty-four-thousand-dollar question," the captain responded. "There's very little we know at this point about the foreign s**t they had stored," he continued, "but the Navy team has been on the ground now for a couple of hours and they'll obviously have more for us when we get there."

As if on cue, Major Aquino walked in the room. "Just got a little more intel from the embassy," he said. "Looks like there have been multiple reports of casualties consisting of white phosphorus burns—a lot in fact," he added.

That set off a general murmur among the team. They began speculating about what had to be a sizable cache of white phosphorus ordnance—sufficient to cause reports of a sizable number of WP burns—though they still didn't have any idea what the ordnance was or its country of origin.

White phosphorus, or "Willie Pete" as it was commonly known, was nasty stuff. It was used mostly for signaling since it produced copious amounts of smoke on contact with oxygen. So much smoke it could also conceal troop movement. It burned extremely hot and the only way to stop it was to cut off its oxygen supply. WP boosters were used as igniters in napalm tanks, as seen during the Vietnam War. It was said if you placed a piece of white phosphorus in the palm of your hand, it could burn straight through before you could get the oxygen cut off to stop it burning. *Nobody was crazy enough to test that theory*, Will thought, but it did force caution on the part of anyone handling the stuff, even under ideal circumstances.

"Why would they be storing that much Willie Pete in one place?" Morgan pondered aloud. "You don't usually see enough of that in one place to cause that many casualties."

They still didn't have hard numbers but began learning there were well over a thousand casualties, and the major did cite a figure north of 30 percent that were WP-related injuries.

"Well, this just got a whole lot more messy, didn't it, sir?" Scott said, directing his comment to the captain.

"It did for a fact," the captain replied solemnly.

Following their briefing, the team went to the clinic. Not everyone was current on their shots, so most of them received several injections to prevent any number of illnesses common in Pakistan—typhoid, yellow fever, hepatitis A and C, measles, encephalitis, and certain others. The most memorable was the "catch-all" gamma globulin shot—which had the consistency of what felt like cold Karo syrup. That raised a knot in Will's hip that lasted a good forty-eight hours. Finally, the medical staff distributed tetracycline and doxycycline pills for daily use starting at once to help ward off malaria and dysentery.

"That last one was a b***h," Campbell said, rubbing his right butt cheek.

"Looks good, feels great," Morgan responded with a chuckle, referring to the double Gs in the GG injection.

Next stop, McGuire Air Force Base, where a plane was being loaded with a huge supply of C-4 explosives and everything else they would need to perform a challenging task.

CHAPTER TWO

MCGUIRE AFB, NJ
APRIL 10, 1988
0850 HRS.

By the time the team made it out to the flight line, the C-141 Starlifter cargo plane that would carry them to Pakistan was close to fully loaded. The crew was performing final pre-flight checks and all that remained was for the team to board. As Will stepped onto the plane, he overheard the loadmaster inquire of Captain Halstead, "Where are you guys goin' with all this Class IV?" referring to the placards affixed to the sides of each pallet of explosives.

The captain smiled and replied, "As far as you can take us."

The crew of this Air Force Starlifter knew nothing of the team's mission. All they knew was they had a planeload full of C-4 accompanied by eight guys in civilian clothes, and that was all they would know about who they were and their destination. They would fly the team to Saudi Arabia where they would refuel and change crews, and at that point, their contribution to this mission would end.

It would be a long ride to their first destination—Dhahran, Saudi Arabia—so each soldier staked out a little space of their own to settle in. There were jump seats on either side of the plane, and with only an eight-man team, there was plenty of room to stretch out and catch some sleep during a 16-hour flight. The space between the pallets of C-4 and the jump seats was tight, but one person could pass through easily enough if he kept one shoulder forward and the other back as he walked. Will was situated at the front of the cargo bay on the left side of the plane.

As Will was arranging his gear, Captain Halstead stepped around from the front of the first big pallet of C-4 and moved toward him. He handed Will a set of earplugs and asked if he was wearing his dog tags. Will nodded and the captain said, "Let me have them, you won't need them," offering no further explanation. "They'll just get in your way." Will handed them over. "I'll give these back to you later," the captain said.

Captain Halstead moved a little further down the left side of the plane where Thiessen had temporary residency. Over the engines of the Starlifter, Will could barely hear Captain Halstead when he was standing right next to him—he had to shout his instructions—so he certainly couldn't hear what he was telling Tom. But he could see Tom was doing as he had done, accepting the earplugs the captain offered, removing and handing over his dog tags.

The process was repeated with Hutchinson and Campbell before Captain Halstead disappeared behind the last pallet of explosives and started up the right side of the aircraft.

Falling asleep proved a challenging task. For one thing, Will's right buttock continued to ache from the GG injection. The jump seats, which were like Army cots, were even less comfortable than Army cots, which was saying something. But Will, so keyed up, could not have fallen asleep if the crew had provided him with a feather mattress.

After an hour or so of random thoughts, Will's heavy eyelids finally yielded and he dozed. He woke up suddenly to the roar of jet engines. He had been deep in dream and it took a moment for him to come to himself in the unfamiliar surroundings. It felt to him like he had been out for days instead of about three hours.

Will couldn't go back to sleep so he thought he'd stretch his legs. He got up and walked around the front of the explosive-laden pallets to the other side of the plane. Captain Halstead had his Walkman on and was singing along—loudly. As Will got a little closer—the captain was singing so loudly that despite the engine noise, and his earplugs, he could make out the words. In truth, he was yelling more than singing. Will could just make out the song the captain was yelling to—“Missionary Man” by the Eurhythmics. Every fourth or fifth word he would get right, but the rest was pure gibberish. He never missed a beat as Will walked by. He just nodded, smiled, and kept on with his musical yelling. Seated further down on the right was Scott. As Will got closer, he saw he was trying to read a book in the faint light. Will walked up to him, and the sergeant major smiled and closed his book.

“How ya gettin’ along?” Scott inquired.

“I’m good,” Will said.

“My ass is still throbbing,” he said referring to the GG shot. “Couldn’t sleep if I wanted to.”

“I caught a little nap,” Will said, “but I’m still feeling it too.”

To be heard, you had to practically yell, so real conversation was exceedingly difficult.

Wiley Adams was immersed in a riveting game of solitaire. He positioned himself in such a manner that he was hanging over the side of the jump seats with his cards laid out in front of him on the floor of the plane. He didn’t look comfortable, but also didn’t seem the least bit deterred by it and played on.

Morgan was sound asleep at the far end of the right side of the plane and had been since just after takeoff.

By this time, Captain Halstead was working on a new song as Will walked back by him; “In the Air Tonight” by Phil Collins. Lyrics were not his strong suit. Will thought to himself, *If only Phil could hear this*, but he just smiled and gave the captain a thumbs-up as he passed. The captain responded with a nod as he launched into an epic air drum solo.

As he made his way back toward his space on the jump seat, Will nearly bumped into a crew member as he rounded the first pallet. He was taken aback to discover it was a young blond senior airman and he was unaware she was on the plane. Ordinarily Will would have started flirting with an attractive girl like her, but it hardly seemed appropriate under these circumstances.

“Enjoying the flight?” she asked.

"What?" Will replied loudly compensating for the noise.

"I said, are you enjoying the flight?" she repeated.

"Oh—yeah," he answered. "Everything's fine."

"Did you guys bring anything to eat?" she asked.

Of course, they hadn't, and Will was hungry. In fact, the mere mention of food at that moment brought the sensation to the fore and he began to lament the fact he hadn't had the foresight to even grab a bag of jerky or something else to snack on.

"There's some box lunches up front," she said, pointing to a storage compartment. "Sodas too, and some juice, I think."

Will was trying to be as polite as he could be and not appear too eager to shovel food down his gullet, but now, knowing food was just a few feet from him, he felt famished. It must have been obvious to her as she let out a slight laugh and said, "Help yourself."

Will smiled, thanked her, and reached into the storage compartment. There were stacks of white boxes, each marked with the contents of the box—ham, turkey, cold cuts, etc. He didn't want to appear overly picky, so he just took the first one off the top—it was "cold cut trio." *Dang*, he thought to himself, *this sucks*. But he didn't verbalize it not wanting to appear ungrateful. A second look revealed an ample supply of soft drinks, so he grabbed a Coke and sat down on his jump seat.

There was nothing particularly exceptional about a salami, pastrami, bologna, and provolone cheese sub under normal conditions, but at that moment, it was a culinary delight. It only got better from there. Will found a bag of Lay's sour cream and onion chips in the box along with a Grandma's peanut butter cookie—a twin-pack. He couldn't believe his luck. The crowning glory of this gastronomic success was the accompanying Coca-Cola. The sound it made when the pop-top released its fizzy contents was joyous and that first gulp was—burn and all—so satisfying he could scarcely contain the resulting audible, "ahhhhh." Will couldn't have been happier if a waiter had suddenly appeared with a succulent ribeye steak cooked to a perfect medium-rare with a baked potato slathered in butter and sour cream. It was the little things in life he tried to take pleasure in.

If it was difficult to hear on the plane, it must not have been difficult to smell. From all the way in the back Hutchinson came to life. He must have caught wind of the salami as he made straight for Will. "What the hell," he said. "Where'd you get that?"

Hutchinson was ravenous. Will motioned to the storage compartment, and Hutchinson began to rifle through the boxes, not content to pull from the top and take his chances, as Will had. After a thorough perusal, he produced a box, held it up, and announced with great delight, "Roast beef!"—like he'd won the box lunch lottery. As Campbell and Thiessen—also roused by the scent of food—stepped up for their turn, Hutchinson said, "Good luck, b***hes!" And he punctuated the remark with a sinister "Heh!"

Tom stepped up to take his turn. He looked and looked. He started to select one of the boxes only to replace it and continue his search. "What the f***," an exasperated Campbell said. "Just take one and go—s**t, man!" Undeterred, Tom selected one, eventually. He took an equally lengthy time selecting his drink before spotting a bottle of cranberry juice. He held it up and said, "Wisconsin." That statement prompted a puzzled look from Campbell. He had no idea what that meant and made the mistake of asking, "What's that supposed to mean?"

Tom took the opportunity to expound on the fact that Wisconsin was home to a significant amount of cranberry production and, as such, it was his duty to support the industry. Tom loved his home state and would talk incessantly about topics related to it. The Packers, cheese, the Badgers, cheese, the Brewers, cheese, beer, whatever. Campbell immediately regretted asking the question as Tom continued to drone on about the virtues of cranberries. Chad rolled his eyes and returned to his space on the jump seats.

By now, the rest of the team had queued up for a box lunch—except for the sergeant major—with Captain Halstead bringing up the rear dancing his way over to the storage compartment, his Walkman headphones still firmly in place. He grabbed a box and a drink in time with the music and returned to his spot. They couldn't quite make out what he was listening to at first, but speculation ended when he belted out a line. It could only be Fleetwood Mac's

"Secondhand News." The captain added the unmistakable series of "bow, bow, bow, bow, chika bows" confirming their suspicions.

Throughout the trip the team passed the time playing their own version of "Name That Tune" with Captain Halstead. They would all try to guess what he was listening to, which was a considerable challenge given his propensity to butcher lyrics. If he was aware of their little game, he never let on and continued to give them plenty of material to work with.

Hutchinson, Thiessen, Wiley Adams, and Morgan were standing around close to the storage compartment with the box lunches, eating, drinking, and casually conversing. Since Will found his spot on the jump seats at the front near the storage compartment, he was privy to the conversation as well.

"Did you guys check out that flight chick?" Hutchinson asked the group in general. "She's hot."

"Flight chick?" Morgan asked. He was the last of the group to get in line for a box lunch and was unaware of the assistant loadmaster, to which Hutchinson was referring. "What's a flight chick?"

"Dude, she's the one who gave us our lunch," Hutchinson replied. "She looks good too," he added. "I'd like to—"

"Hutchinson!" the sergeant major screamed. "You better lock it up! That's strike two, a**hole," he added. "One more and this'll be a short trip for you!"

No one saw Scott walk up just in time to hear Hutchinson's remarks about the "flight chick." It was a good thing too, because right about that time, Senior Airman Johannson reappeared to inquire about lunch.

"Did everybody get something to eat?" she inquired.

"We're good to go," the sergeant major responded, reaching for a box lunch while shooting a sharp look at Hutchinson. "Thank you, Airman," he added.

"No problem, sir," she replied. "We've got plenty."

Ordinarily, Scott would have taken umbrage at being addressed as "sir," but since they were in civilian clothes, he didn't expect her to know his rank and offered no correction. He nodded to her politely and looked at each team member as a reminder he was watching. Of course, he was primarily concerned about Hutchinson, but he gave them each a piercing look as a warning.

In turn, the team returned to their spots. Will was trying to read a magazine, *Western Horseman*, which had been a favorite since he was a kid in New Mexico. But he was having difficulty reading it, with a thousand thoughts popping up in his head, chief among them, thoughts about home.

Just after Will's third attempt at reading the same page, Senior Airman Johannson circulated again. "You doing alright?" she asked.

"Oh hey. Yeah, sure," he said. "I'm good." "How 'bout you?"

"Fine," she said. "This is a long haul," she added. "We've been doing hops back and forth between McGuire and Mildenhall."

"Oh, yeah—I used to live there," Will said. "Not Mildenhall, but right next door at Lakenheath."

"I love going there," she said. "We only get to spend a day or two at a time though, when we do get to stay," she added. "Most of the time it's just quick turns."

She smiled and said, "I'm Beth," and politely offered her hand.

"Nice to meet you," he said, standing, and shaking her hand, "I'm Will." She had a firm handshake, which Will attributed to good upbringing and a sense of confidence. He had already noticed her name was Beth Johannson. She was wearing a sage green flight suit bearing the insignia of the 438th Military Airlift Wing out of McGuire Air Force Base. Aircrew wings embossed the black patch on the front of her uniform along with her name and rank.

"This is an unusual cargo," she said, as close to prying as she would get.

"Yes, it is," Will replied lamely. He didn't expound.

There was a brief, awkward silence. "So, I guess you were an Air Force brat if you lived at Lakenheath," she inquired.

"Yeah, I lived there almost four years," Will replied. "Fourth through most of seventh grade."

"I'm an Air Force brat too," she said. "My dad finished up at Offutt," she added, referring to the Air Force Base at Omaha, Nebraska. "I went in the Air Force straight out of high school, and here I am."

Beth was friendly and attractive. She had long blond hair, lengthy enough to wear in a neatly tucked bun. Her eyes were a lovely shade of blue, and she had a fair complexion. Will's guess, adding up her name, eyes, hair color, and complexion, was she had Scandinavian heritage.

They fell into conversation, and Will learned they had a lot in common. Both were Air Force brats, following family tradition, who wanted to go to college, joining the military for college money. They talked for the better part of an hour before the conversation was interrupted when the flight engineer appeared from the cockpit and motioned for her.

"Duty calls," she said lightly, and disappeared.

Will returned to his *Western Horseman* taking up where he left off. He began to nod and positioned himself on the jump seats more comfortably. Before long, he was asleep again.

CHAPTER THREE

DHAHRAN, SAUDI ARABIA
APRIL 11, 1988
1155 HRS.

Will awoke to the sound of chirping tires on a runway. They finally arrived in Saudi Arabia. He was looking forward to stretching his legs. They taxied in and waited for the crews' instructions. Flying on a military cargo plane was a lot different than flying on a commercial airliner, but the one thing they had in common was you didn't do anything without the crew's instructions. There were strict safety protocols to follow.

Once the plane parked, Senior Airman Johannson appeared and made her way to the door. From his vantage point on the jump seats closest to the front door, Will was the first to see her. As she moved toward the door, she announced, "Finally."

"That was a haul," Will replied.

"Looks like you got a little sleep after all," she said.

"Sure did," he said. "Feelin' pretty rested."

The team began moving toward the door. One thing was clear, they were ready to get off that plane; most of them needed to hit the latrine. To no one's surprise, Shane Hutchinson was the first to verbalize exactly that.

"I gotta take one healthy s**t," he said.

Will cast an apologetic glance Beth's way but said nothing. She just smiled and looked forward, awaiting the order to open the door. With the order finally given, she opened the door, and they proceeded down the steps, onto the tarmac, and into the terminal.

As the team walked toward the terminal, Morgan stepped up next to Hutchinson and said, "Damn, Hutch, you just say whatever pops into your head, don't you?" in reference to his excitement about his imminent bowel movement.

"Well, hell," he said. "When you gotta go, you gotta go."

"Totally understandable," Morgan replied, "but the rest of us don't need to know about your s**t schedule, so how 'bout keeping that to yourself?"

The sergeant major heard the exchange between Morgan and Hutchinson from the beginning of Hutchinson's comments at the door. He had it in mind to dress Hutchinson down again, but hearing Morgan address the situation, he didn't feel the need to pile on criticism, so he let it be. He was conscious of the fact he had already been on Hutchinson's case twice less than a day in and didn't want to give the impression of singling him out. Besides, he felt Morgan did an excellent job addressing the issue discreetly, in line with the Army's latest guidance on proper workplace conduct.

Morgan had only intervened because of the presence of a female. In an all-male unit, it was common for soldiers to make crude comments about bodily functions, and a lot more. But with the modern military and an ever-increasing number of female service members, it was necessary to adjust what was once considered acceptable parlance. Indeed, Morgan had recently processed a new female soldier into his own unit—the first female assigned there—and was integral in helping to retool a cultural environment previously exclusively male.

The team went inside the terminal and availed themselves of the facilities. They would not be on the ground long. Campbell took the opportunity to knock out a hundred pushups, while the rest sought other, less strenuous diversions. There was coffee available, but little else in the way of refreshment. It was approaching midnight local time and they still had about a three-and-a-half-hour flight to Islamabad ahead of them. The timing of the flights would allow them to land in Islamabad before dawn. They were on schedule but would need to leave soon if they were to keep to it. They would have to refuel and re-crew, then be promptly on their way.

The crew who got the team safely to Dhahran filed into the terminal. Captain Halstead made his way over to them and shook the pilot's hand. They talked briefly before Captain Halstead turned and motioned to the sergeant major. "Saddle up," Scott instructed. Will lingered, hoping to at least get a chance to say goodbye to Beth. "Hurry up, Will," Morgan shouted as he exited the terminal. "You don't want to get left behind here."

He looked back in time to catch a wave from Beth who mouthed, "Good luck." And that was it. Will would never see her again.

"Did you get her number?" Tom asked. "No, I didn't," Will replied, feeling stupid for letting the opportunity pass.

"Hell, you put in the time, son," Hutchinson said. "I'm gonna have to coach you up, dude."

"You're a married man aren't you, Hutch?" Will asked. "I figure you're pretty rusty by now."

"Married, yes," he said, "but I ain't dead," he added. "I sure as hell wouldn't let something like that get away, and that's a fact."

"You better watch yourself, man," Campbell advised. "Carly doesn't strike me as the type who puts up with that kind of bulls**t," he added, referring to Hutchinson's wife.

"Oh, I've never cheated on Carly," Hutchinson said. "But I do still like to look," he added. "Besides," he continued as he started to climb the steps to board the plane, "it don't matter where you get your appetite, as long as you eat at home." With that little chestnut, he stepped inside the plane.

"Yeah, I'm sure his wife would be delighted to know her husband's out here building up his appetite," Will added, which prompted a general chuckle.

In short order, they were all aboard and taxiing for takeoff to Pakistan.

While the shortest leg of the trip, it seemed to take forever—like that last hundred miles of a thousand-mile drive, when you just want to be home. Will was anxious to get to Pakistan, even though he had no clue what to expect. He was on the precipice of what could be a big adventure. At twenty-two years of age, he was eager to begin.

Will was the only member of the team not married and the youngest and lowest ranking. There were two other sergeants on the team for a total of three E-5s. There was an unspoken structure of seniority. Captain Halstead was obviously the officer in charge with the sergeant major being the senior NCO. Sergeant First Class Morgan was next in line following the logical Army rank structure. He had seventeen-plus years in and was counting down to retirement. He and his wife, Linda, were from south Jersey, so requesting assignment to the 63rd EOD was not an accident. He planned to retire when he hit twenty years, and Ft. Dix would be his last duty station before pursuing his second career as a member of the Atlantic City, New Jersey Police Bomb Squad—at least that was his plan.

The two E-6s on the team, Adams, and Hutchinson were separated by years both in time in grade and time in service. Hutchinson had been in the Army eight years, promoted to staff sergeant a year before. In contrast, Adams had been serving for just over sixteen years, his most recent six as a staff sergeant. Wiley was capable in most respects, but he was not a leader. However, he was a good follower, and was particularly loyal to the sergeant major, having served under him at Ft. Bragg prior to arriving at Ft. Dix. What he lacked in initiative, he made up for in reliability when set to task. Once he was given direction, Wiley generally performed efficiently, requiring little supervision, seldom ever offering a complaint—traits highly valued by Scott who had little regard for "whine bags." Chronic complainers made things more difficult for themselves and those around them. Adams spent six of his sixteen years in the Army under Scott.

That left Campbell, Thiessen, and Will—in the descending "pecking order." Chad was nearly a year into a second term, after re-enlisted the previous year. Thiessen outranked Will by about three months based on time in grade. He got acquainted with Tom back at EOD school. He was in the class ahead of Will and they had occasion to socialize from time to time while they were at Indian Head.

A good ten hours passed since he ate anything, so Will looked in the storage compartment containing the box lunches from the first leg of the flight. As luck would have it, there were some boxes left so he quietly partook while the rest of the team slept. Will wondered about their mission. He knew little about Pakistan except it was situated between India and Afghanistan, and it was once a part of the British Empire—a fact he learned while living in England as a child. He would occasionally ride his bike down to the British Post Office at Lakenheath, which was managed by a pleasant Pakistani gentleman, who immigrated to Great Britain some years earlier. Will loved Cadbury's chocolate and orange squash—uniquely British treats—and visited the BPO often, sampling the wide selection of goodies found on the shelves. Mr. Malik was always friendly and talkative, which is how Will learned how he came to live in England, and a little of the history between the two nations, which is to say more of his personal history. Mr. Malik was from an area he called the Kashmir region, and he talked about the ongoing problems his people had with Indian government. That didn't mean a lot to an eleven-year-old American kid who was more interested in sweets than a cursory lesson in geopolitics, but Will assumed the situation must have been bad enough he wanted to leave. Mr. Malik now considered himself English, and as Will saw it, he was. Mr. Malik became a devoted fan of football—what Americans call soccer—which was particularly English of him. He talked often about his two favorite teams, Ipswich Town, a Division One team from a small city close to Lakenheath and, of course, the English national team. Will became a Leeds United fan, a city further north of his home at Lakenheath, for reasons still unknown to him. The two had spirited, but friendly, debates on who supported the better team.

Will finished his sandwich and chips, felt completely rested, and surprisingly only a little nervous given the danger ahead of them.

CHAPTER 4

CHAKLALA AIR BASE
RAWALPINDI, PAKISTAN
APRIL 12, 1988
0535 HRS.

Will was now moments away from getting his first glimpse of a country which, up until less than twenty-six hours ago, he gave only a passing thought to after brief conversations with a migrant postmaster. The team was on schedule and preparing to land. Through the small window of the forward door on the other side of the plane, Will could make out the faint red line of the horizon. That meant two things, it would soon be dawn and they were approaching from the south. Of course, he didn't have to be Ferdinand Magellan to figure that out, but Will liked to know where he was, and where he was going at any given moment. Soon, the plane touched down. Whoever planned this pre-dawn landing in Islamabad nailed it. By the time they taxied, and parked, they could see the sun beginning to rise.

The crew began opening the huge cargo doors at the rear of the Starlifter and the ramp began to lower. What struck the team first was the rush of warm air quickly filling the cargo bay. Will was prepared for 30–40 degrees Fahrenheit, as Jackson advised, before leaving the Gap. What they found out was 30–40 degrees meant *centigrade*—not Fahrenheit. At that moment they felt a blast of air about 80 degrees Fahrenheit, and it was only a little before 06:00. None of them had bothered to consider the difference between Fahrenheit and centigrade before leaving. Now, it was the primary topic of conversation. Everyone began to grumble, and the sergeant major said, "S**t, this ain't 30 degrees!"

"No, and it's not the States either," the captain added. "Damn, we should have known to convert, but I sure wasn't thinking about that."

As the sun began to rise in earnest, some of them started to think about how they could modify their wardrobes to adapt to the unexpected heat.

"Don't worry about that s**t now," Scott instructed. "Here comes our contact," he added, pointing to a small white SUV heading toward us leading a caravan of two white passenger vans and three large cargo trucks.

The white SUV pulled up close to the team and their staged gear to await the arrival of this motorcade. The vans fell in behind the SUV and the trucks positioned close to the ramp of the plane. The first person emerged from the front left door of the white SUV. It was not the driver of the SUV since vehicles in Pakistan had the steering wheel on the right side of the vehicle—like in England. The man appeared to be an American, based on his complexion, and he gave a wave and a big smile as he approached the team. He was dark-headed with some signs of gray showing through. He wore a white Guayabera shirt—the kind you might see worn by men in Latin American countries—and khaki trousers. He looked for all the world like a tourist and lacked only a 35mm camera strapped around his neck to complete the ensemble.

The tourist look was deceptive; he turned out to be Army Brigadier General Herbert Wassom, the U.S. Defense Representative in Pakistan. He approached the team in a very friendly manner. "Good morning, gentlemen," he said. "Welcome to Pakistan."

The captain stepped up and introduced himself as he shook the general's hand, not saluting as they were all in civilian clothes. The sergeant major followed suit. The captain had a lot of questions, and he was preparing to pose the first one when the general lightly raised a finger and politely said, "One second, captain, I'd like to meet your team."

"Of course, sir," the captain replied. He turned on his heel sharply, motioned the general toward his team, and they proceeded in their direction. Morgan watched all this unfold, and he sensed the gentleman in the touristy clothes was, in fact, someone important. He came to his feet and discreetly called the team to attention.

"I think this is our guy," he said, slightly above a whisper. "Attention."

They quickly came to attention in line as if they were in formation preparing for inspection and awaited the reviewing officers headed their way. "Relax, gentlemen," the general said. "I just wanted to introduce myself while we're waiting on the Paks to arrive."

"I'm General Wassom," he said in an easy Southern drawl. "I'm the defense rep here in Pakistan," he added, as he reached out to shake hands with Morgan.

"Sergeant First Class Morgan, sir."

"Glad you're here, Sergeant, where ya from?"

"South Jersey, sir."

"Outstanding."

This process repeated itself with each member of the team, the captain maintaining pace with the general, two steps behind.

Will was last in line, and as the officers approached him, the general began to smile. He reached out to shake hands, placing his left hand on Will's shoulder, and said with a grin, "Son, are you old enough to be here?" Will was a little taken aback, but before he could respond, Captain Halstead said, "This is Sergeant Carter, sir."

"Sergeant? How long you been in, young man?"

"Three years, sir."

"Three years?" the general said, almost incredulous. "Well, you've done well for yourself, son—outstanding," he added. "Glad to have you here."

It was true Will had a baby face. He could easily go two or three days without a shave, and no one would notice. As he looked down the line of his teammates, it occurred to him why he stood out. It had been nearly two days since any of the team employed a razor, and they were all beginning to sport the makings of a beard. Will, on the other hand, was still smooth by comparison.

"At ease, gentlemen," the general instructed. "Here come the Paks," he said, pointing toward a line of military vehicles headed their way.

The general had a very calm way about him and spoke in a reassuring manner. He was not an especially big man, but he was lean and fit. More importantly, General Wassom was a hardened warfighter with close to thirty years in the Army and a tour in Vietnam to his credit. After graduating Western Kentucky University, General Wassom entered the U.S. Army. He was an artillery officer and saw his share of fierce fighting in Vietnam, the bloodiest taking place in the A Shau Valley, the site of the infamous battle of Ap Bia Mountain—commonly referred to as "Hamburger Hill" by the soldiers who fought there. As a battery commander, his unit was integral in providing fire support to the infantry units who were fighting a fierce North Vietnamese force. He certainly saw far worse than what awaited the team at the still smoking Pak Army garrison a few miles from where they had just landed.

The sun was up by this time and the light revealed they landed on an airstrip of a military installation. A secure-looking fence was visible off to the east less than a half-mile away. The vehicles the general spotted were passing through a gate and leaving behind them spires of dust slowly settling to the ground as they sped toward the awaiting plane.

As the vehicles came to a stop, a man dressed in a crisp military uniform exited from the front door of the passenger side of the first truck—the Pak version of a Jeep. His fatigues were khaki in color and the legs of his pressed trousers neatly bloused at the top of his well-shined boots. He had an array of colorful ribbons affixed to his uniform above the left breast pocket of his neatly tucked shirt. The epaulets on his shoulders bore his rank—with which the American team was of course unfamiliar. He had Pakistani Army insignia patches on each of his sleeves, which were rolled neatly above the elbow. He wore a black beret with a regimental crest, which presented a striking contrast to his one unique feature—a long white beard, unusual for an officer. He reached back into the cab of the truck and produced a riding crop which he placed under his left arm. He matter-of-factly stepped toward General Wassom, stopped about a pace in front of him, audibly snapped his heels and rendered a formal salute.

General Wassom did not return the salute. Instead, he politely extended his hand for a handshake. "Good morning, Brigadier," General Wassom said. "Our team has arrived."

General Wassom turned, directing the Pak general toward Captain Halstead. "Brigadier," he said. "This is Captain Halstead. He's the officer in charge of our team."

"Very good," the Pak general said. "I am Brigadier Javed Nasir, engineers." He shook hands with the captain but didn't offer any other further salutation.

"And this is Sergeant Ma—" General Wassom began, before being bluntly interrupted.

"Forgive me, General," Nasir interjected, "but there is little time for these pleasantries. We must proceed to the garrison most urgently."

"Of course," said General Wassom. "Ready, men? If you'll load up in the vans, we'll follow along behind the brigadier."

"Sir, if I may," the captain inquired, "we'll need to secure our explosives. We can't just drive off without maintaining custody."

Brigadier Nasir raised an eyebrow when the captain made that request. He thought that suggested the American EOD team lacked trust in his men and their ability to transport and store the explosives. Of course, that concern was not unfounded given the reason the team was there; Nasir offered no objection.

"Absolutely," the general said. "We've already made arrangements to have your cargo transported to a secure location. We're under a tight time constraint here, so we'll need to move quickly."

"Outstanding, sir," the captain replied. "I was just wondering if you would be averse to one of my team staying behind to oversee the transport and storage."

"That sounds like a pretty good idea," the general agreed. "Who did you have in mind?"

"Sir, if you'll give me just a minute to talk to the sergeant major, we'll have a recommendation for you."

The captain stepped over and huddled briefly with Scott after which he returned to the general with his plan.

"Sir, we'll leave Sergeant Campbell behind to oversee the offloading of the plane and the transport of the explosives, if that's alright with you," the captain offered.

"Are you sure we shouldn't have a more senior NCO handle that task?"

"Well sir, we considered that," the captain began, "but our senior NCOs will be team leaders, and they'll need to get eyes on, and receive the direct brief themselves. Campbell is our senior E-5 and we're certain he is more than capable to handle this task."

"That makes sense," the general agreed. "Good enough for me. Let's move out."

The sergeant major gave the order for the team to secure their gear and place it in one of the vans that was part of General Wassom's motorcade. The captain and the sergeant major took Campbell to the side and explained his orders to him.

"Do any of these guys speak English?" Campbell inquired.

"None of these guys here do," replied the captain, "with the exception of the Pak general, but he'll be with us."

"Well, this should be interesting," Campbell said.

"Don't worry," the captain said. "They tell us there's a platoon of Pak soldiers on their way here, and the platoon leader speaks English. He'll handle his men, and you can handle him."

"Yes sir," Campbell replied.

"Here," the sergeant major said, handing Chad a manila envelope, the contents of which had a manifest and inventory of the four huge pallets they spent the last twenty-four hours or so traveling next to. "Check the inventory coming off the plane, going onto the trucks," Scott explained. "You'll need to check it again when it comes off the truck for storage," he added. "We've gotta manage this real tight—we'll be doing this s**t every day—got it?"

"Roger that, Sergeant Major," Chad replied.

With that, the captain and the sergeant major moved toward their respective vehicles. The captain rode with General Wassom, which would give them the opportunity to exchange information at a higher level. The sergeant major jumped in the first white van behind the general's SUV, where Will was seated along with Morgan and Thiessen. Adams and Hutchinson brought up the rear seated in the third van, which held all the team's gear.

The platoon of Pak soldiers, which would handle loading and unloading the explosives onto and off the trucks, cleared the gate and passed by Will's van on the righthand side and continued toward the airplane.

As the team drove toward the airfield gate, Tom remarked how an unusual scent hung in the air. "Yeah," Will said, "I smell it too." It wasn't a particularly offensive odor, but it was a distinct aroma, nonetheless. It turned out, nobody else could place it either. The conversation about the unusual scent continued, with the sergeant major relating a similar experience from his time in Vietnam, until they passed through the gate and began to negotiate a roundabout—what Americans might call a traffic circle—that would direct them onto a much more heavily travelled thoroughfare leading to the smoking garrison.

The traffic was exceptionally heavy on the roundabout on this particular morning—people heading to work, or markets, or wherever—and as the vans merged into the flow of cars and trucks, Thiessen and Will simultaneously gasped at what they saw next. A large commercial truck—similar to what the military might describe as a deuce and a half—mowed down a man who, for an inexplicable reason, was walking on the inside lane of the roundabout. The truck never slowed and continued its way, the driver either unaware he had just plowed over a pedestrian, or unconcerned. What happened next was shocking. The driver of the car just behind the offending truck, slammed on his brakes and two men quickly jumped from the car. The two men hastily grabbed the lifeless body of the unwary pedestrian and casually tossed it into the tall grass of the roundabout median only to return to their car and speed away. The whole incident unfolded in the span of just a few seconds, barely disrupting the flow of traffic.

"Did you seed that?!" Tom exclaimed.

"Holy s**t?" Morgan added, his jaw agape in disbelief.

"No way that just happened," Will added.

While everyone in the van was stunned, the Pakistani driver who worked for the U.S. Embassy appeared unfazed by the whole thing. Their motorcade continued as if nothing happened.

"Well, boys," said Scott, "I guess we're not in Kansas anymore."

CHAPTER FIVE

CAMP OJHRI
RAWALPINDI, PAKISTAN
APRIL 12, 1988
0715 HRS.

By the time they reached Camp Ojhri—the epicenter of the huge explosion that was the reason for their Pakistan deployment—the sun was high enough to have raised the temperature to a stifling 90 degrees, which was surprising given it was only mid-April and not yet eight o'clock in the morning. They went through the gate of the garrison and parked in an area secured for them. They prepared to proceed on foot from there to inspect the damage—which they could already see was extensive—and assess the situation of the unexploded ordnance strewn about. From the perimeter, columns of smoke were visible, spiraling upward, dotting the landscape before them. A network of firehoses crisscrossed the garrison.

The team assembled in front of the vehicles and prepared to make their way into the morass of munitions. "Before we proceed, I must advise you to be very cautious," the brigadier blithely advised, adding oddly, "if you put your foot wrong, God help you."

The glib tone of the Pak general took the team by surprise. The captain and the sergeant major looked at each other in disbelief. But the brigadier only continued.

"Captain, I realize this will be a hazardous operation, and we expect you may lose some men. However—"

"Let me stop you right there!" the captain interjected, his tone rising. "Yes sir, these operations are inherently dangerous and, believe me, I'm quite familiar with them," he continued sternly. "But we intend to conduct this operation in a very deliberate manner with safety as our primary consideration. We're here to help prevent any further loss of life. It's my understanding, sir, that you and your officers would be deferring to our team's expertise, which means we will be leading this operation in accordance with our considerable training and experience. And one other important detail, Brigadier," he said, "I intend to leave here with my whole team—complete and unharmed—and if you have any ideas to the contrary, sir, we'll stop right here and head back to our plane."

The captain spoke in a respectful, but forceful tone; as respectful as he could muster in his shock caused by the Pak general's nonchalant and awful suggestion that the captain would lose a member, or members, of his team. General Wassom saw the whole exchange but was silent at first. However, at this point he weighed in.

"The captain is right, Brigadier. These men are experienced, and they know what they're doing. You indicated to me not more than twenty-four hours ago that you would be turning this operation over to our team. If that's not the case, Brigadier, we need to know that now."

"This is most irregular, General," Nasir said.

"No, Brigadier," the general replied. "It would be most irregular to proceed any further without a very clear understanding of what these men are here to do, and how they intend to do it."

"Very well, General," Nasir acquiesced. "We shall proceed under the captain's direction. But understand, I will not take responsibility for any unforeseen circumstances that may arise."

"That's fine, Brigadier," General Wassom said. "If we proceed under the captain's direction, you won't have to."

In that moment, there was a gamut of emotions as the team watched their captain dress down this arrogant Pakistani general. There was an element of relief knowing who was in charge. There was a high degree of reassurance knowing their general backed the captain—his expression of support could not have been scripted any better. They felt a sense of pride as American soldiers. This was a defining moment for the entire team, galvanized by the leadership of two American officers.

In contrast, the behavior of Brigadier Javed Nasir showed a callous disregard for human life. The team was briefed about the methods employed by the Pak soldiers to address the unexploded ordnance littering the garrison. Officers ordered enlisted soldiers downrange armed with nothing more than a three- to four-foot stick. When the soldier found a piece of ordnance, he would flip it over. If it didn't explode, the soldier would pick up the ordnance, carry it to a wheelbarrow to a "safe area" for destruction. If the ordnance did explode, the result was usually fatal. The Pak Army had already lost several soldiers in this operation supervised by Nasir, using the flip-and-pray method—or more accurately, pray first and then flip. When a Pak soldier died flipping and praying, another would replace him with the same orders. This process continued under the direction of an unconcerned Nasir.

Brigadier Nasir certainly stood out among the Pak Army soldiers. His long white beard was not regulation; he was given special dispensation to wear it based on religious considerations, although most, if not all, the soldiers of the Pak Army were Muslims too. Being the only general in the Pak Army given permission to wear such facial hair earned him the moniker "White Beard."

White Beard introduced himself as an engineer—which, by education he was, having graduated from the Pak Military College of Engineering some thirty years earlier. Indeed, he served in various engineer units throughout his career as an Army officer. What he neglected to mention, however, was the fact he was currently serving in Inter-Services Intelligence (ISI)—the Pakistani counterpart of the American CIA. The team didn't know this at first, but it wouldn't have made much of a difference anyway. However, White Beard's position as the deputy director of ISI would later fuel rampant speculation about just how this explosive incident came about, his role in it, and the disposition of certain sensitive ordnance the team was there to recover.

The confrontation between the captain and White Beard now behind them, they went toward the garrison center and the stored munitions. It could have been a dangerous trek—a variety of unexploded ordnance was visible in all directions—but the captain suggested they stop and formulate a plan before entering such a hazardous environment. After some discussion with the sergeant major and Morgan, the captain began to communicate his plan of action.

They would lay out the garrison in quadrants and position a team on the perimeter of each quadrant, moving toward the garrison's center. As each team moved inward, any unexploded ordnance encountered would be marked and photographed, with all relevant visible data recorded for further intelligence evaluation. They would not be performing render safe procedures on the ordnance they found. RSPs would be superfluous in this environment. There had already been untold numbers of detonations, and the Paks evacuated the garrison and surrounding area. On the smaller pieces of ordnance, the best course of action would be blowing in place. Given the damage already inflicted, small, controlled detonations using the M112 blocks of C-4 they brought with them, would be minimally disruptive. Of course, they would cut the M112 blocks into quarters, making the shots unnoticeable given what this area already experienced.

As the captain was completing the plan, a Pak Army Jeep pulled up. The vehicle, driven by a Pak soldier, carried three passengers. As they got out of the Jeep, it became clear this was the Navy team with whom the Army team was to connect. The men were wearing civilian clothes, but their tool belts gave them away. Among other items on their belts, each carried a Ka-bar knife and a set of M2 blasting cap crimpers—common and essential tools for EOD technicians.

Lieutenant Dale Johnson led the three-man team, a tall, skinny man wearing jeans, a polo shirt, jungle boots, and wire-rimmed glasses. Lieutenant Johnson hailed from Medford, Oregon, and had been in the Navy about six years. Johnson and his team had been assisting in de-mining operations in the Persian Gulf.

Two "salts"—a term often used to describe sailors who had been on multiple cruises—accompanied Johnson: Senior Chief Brent Sonberg and Petty Officer First Class Tony Wyndham. The Navy team had been on the ground for some thirty-six hours, spending most of their time responding to calls to address unexploded ordnance—what they called running incidents—in and around the

Islamabad/Rawalpindi metro area. Indeed, the U.S. Embassy—a full twelve kilometers north of Camp Ojhri—sustained two impacts from 122mm rockets that went ballistic from the fire. The good news was the rockets were unfuzed, meaning a RSP would be slightly less hazardous. The bad news was the rockets were filled with high explosives and the kinetic energy of the impact damaged them severely. The two rockets proved difficult to extract, particularly one that lodged in the wall of the embassy compound. Difficult as it was, both rockets were safely extracted, transported, and destroyed at a range designated for just this purpose, several miles north of Islamabad. Oddly enough, the U.S. Embassy was not the only American structure damaged. The International School, about nine kilometers west of the garrison—attended by the children of American diplomats, and a considerable number from other countries—suffered a hit from one of the stray rockets as well. Fortunately, there were no injuries sustained from the rockets at either the school or the embassy.

The Navy team was visibly relieved by the arrival of the Army team. Driving up in time to watch the last part of the tense exchange between the captain and White Beard, they were too far away to hear what was said, but it was clear there was tension in the air, along with the dust their Jeep stirred. Lieutenant Johnson assumed Captain Halstead was the officer in charge based on what he had just seen. After acknowledging General Wassom, he approached the captain and politely introduced himself. The two shook hands and Johnson began to share the information his team gathered since their arrival.

"We've been humping since we got here," Johnson said. "We gave the garrison a quick look, but the kickouts were a much more pressing issue," he added, referring to the ordnance the blast sent into the surrounding metropolitan area. "This is a pretty heavily populated area," Johnson continued. "We've run into a considerable number of 122mm rockets, a bunch went ballistic and got into a residential area a pretty good ways away from here. Two hit our embassy, and one even hit a school—those are both miles away in two different directions."

"That's what we heard," the captain said. "Also heard you guys have run into a bunch of Willy Pete."

"Yes, we have," Johnson said. "That s**t's all over the place, on the garrison and all over town. I'd estimate about a third of what we've run so far has been WP, the hospitals all over town are covered up with burn victims."

"How are you handling those WP rounds?" the captain inquired. Of course, he'd had plenty of experience dealing with WP when he was in Vietnam, but that was in rural and remote areas.

"Well, none of the stuff we've run into so far has been fuzed," the lieutenant began, "but those WP warheads are thin, as you know, they break open easy when they impact."

"We've been keeping buckets of mud handy in case we run across smokers, which we have—plenty," Johnson explained. "We just pack 'em off with mud and transport 'em as quick as we can. This area is full of people; you can't blow anything in place and you couldn't BIP Willy Pete rounds anyway."

"The problem is," Johnson continued, "they get bounced around in the back of these big trucks, and by the time we get out to the range, some have started smoking again and that makes 'em tougher to handle."

"Think we can get our hands on some fabric of some kind?" the captain inquired, addressing his query as much to General Wassom and White Beard as to the Navy lieutenant. He turned slightly to include them in the conversation. "Burlap would work great," he recommended. "Pack those open warheads with mud, like you're doing now, wrap 'em in burlap, and hit 'em again with a little more mud," he added. "This heat'll bake 'em dry by the time we get 'em ready to load. That should make 'em a lot safer to transport and handle."

Under ideal conditions, the procedure the captain described was carried out the same way using plaster of Paris instead of mud, and gauze rolls instead of burlap strips. The procedure was used to address leaking chemical munitions. But these weren't ideal conditions, so the field expedient method of mud and burlap would suffice.

"Brigadier, how 'bout that burlap?" General Wassom asked.

"That seems a reasonable request," the brigadier responded. "We shall make the necessary arrangements."

"We're gonna need a lot, Brigadier," Johnson advised. "We've got WP all over the place."

"We shall make the necessary arrangements," White Beard repeated, arrogantly showing disrespect toward the two EOD teams, deployed to help him and the Pak Army.

The brigadier's arrogance reflected his opposition to U.S. military support. He insisted he could oversee the operation himself without any outside intervention, particularly from Americans. From the time the Navy team landed, he was uncooperative, and his attitude only worsened with the arrival of the Army team.

White Beard undoubtedly acted hastily in his response to the detonation at the garrison and hadn't given much consideration to safety, evinced by the number of Pak soldiers killed after being ordered downrange to address unexploded ordnance, to say nothing of the unnecessarily rising toll of civilian casualties in and around the twin cities. He was also keenly aware his superiors were watching him closely, and they were unimpressed thus far. The brigadier displayed a sense of urgency, bordering on desperation. But desperate for what? Given his hostile attitude, certainly not for Americans' or his superiors' praise. Quite possibly, he hated Americans. But there had to be more to it. Whatever it was, neither of the teams—nor the American general—would tolerate his reckless disregard for basic safety. EOD teams worked under adverse conditions and understood the need to work quickly but would never trade speed for safety. That was exactly what White Beard was doing, trading speed for safety and his haste was costly. In fact, he had already expressed his frustration to General Wassom with what he considered the slowness of the Navy team.

"These soldiers are simply not moving fast enough, General," he said, errantly referring to the Navy team as soldiers. "We must move much more expeditiously," he added, his exasperation rising.

"Well, I'll tell you what, Brigadier," General Wassom responded. "These men are extremely well trained and experienced, so if they tell me they're moving at the correct speed, then I'm going to take their word for it."

The general's folksy, Kentucky tone did not appeal to the brigadier, and General Wassom knew it, which is why he was inclined to pour it on thicker any time White Beard became rude, which was happening more often of late. The general found White Beard simply insufferable. His position as U.S. Defense Representative required him to maintain a high degree of diplomatic professionalism, which he always afforded his Pak counterparts. Still, the general saw no need to extend any added courtesies to White Beard.

While the high-level parley was taking place with the officers, the two Navy NCOs came over to get acquainted with the Army team. Senior Chief Petty Officer Brent Sonberg was a wiry fellow from Montana. He was wearing Wrangler jeans, jungle boots, and a white T-shirt—which by the end of a remarkably busy day was almost light brown caused by a mixture of dust, dirt, smoke, and sweat. He had sandy-colored hair and sported a Fu Manchu mustache, which was common among sailors but would never pass Army muster. Sonberg correctly identified Sergeant Major Scott as the senior NCO of the Army team since he appeared older than the rest of them.

While the sergeant major was not directly involved in the conversation, he was watching intently as the officers conversed. He could clearly see White Beard was not happy about something, but he wasn't sure why.

Senior Chief Sonberg introduced himself to Scott and the two shook hands cordially. "That Pak general is a piece of work, isn't he," the sergeant major said, safely out of earshot of the convened officers.

"He's a piece of something," Sonberg replied. "I told the L-T that mother f***er was gonna get some guys killed if he kept on, and sure enough, he did," Sonberg added. "We got to the garrison yesterday to scope it out, and he was sending guys in to flip rounds and pick 'em up."

"He's been treating these Army privates like remote tools," Petty Officer Tony Wyndham added, stepping up to shake hands and introduce himself. "We saw two poor b*****ds get blown up right in front of us."

"Yeah, he's been in a big hurry," Sonberg said. "He's lost at least four guys we know of, two since we've been here. The L-T had to go to our general and let him know how unsafe he was being, and there doesn't seem to be any love lost between General Wassom and that bearded son of a b***h."

"Uh-huh, I could sort of sense that," Scott replied.

"We looked at the garrison real quick, but it was still mostly on fire, so we've been running incidents in town," Sonberg explained. "The Paks have been stretching hoses all over the garrison to put out the fires, but rounds have been turning up all over town."

Sonberg briefed the team, reiterating what the lieutenant shared with the captain. The Navy team spent the bulk of their time collecting unexploded ordnance in heavily populated areas surrounding the garrison. They reasoned that would give the Paks time to put the fires out on the garrison, which was exacerbating the problem of the UXO—the abbreviation for unexploded ordnance—scattered about. Then they could help formulate a plan of attack to deal with the garrison when the Army team arrived.

At this point, the officers began to complete their plans which, much to White Beard's irritation, would begin first thing the following morning. He was upset at the delay but offered no further comment. He pushed as hard as he dared, at least for today. Tomorrow, the full-scale operation to clear the garrison would begin. With a plan in place, White Beard saluted the American general smartly, took a seat in his Jeep, and left the garrison.

"Captain," the general began, "your team has been traveling for about twenty-six hours or more and these Navy boys are all but worn out," he said. "How 'bout we get y'all settled in at the hotel, you boys can get cleaned up and catch a little rest, and we'll meet for a briefing before dinner this evening?"

"Well, that sounds like an excellent idea, sir," the captain replied.

"How'd that be with you, L-T?" General Wassom said.

"Absolutely," the lieutenant agreed, without hesitation. He and his team were dog tired. A shower and a nap were just what they needed.

As they prepared to leave for their hotel, it occurred to Will there didn't seem to be any other Pak officers present besides White Beard—only enlisted men—from the time he met them at the airfield, until the time he left the smoking garrison. That was odd.

When the brigadier arrived at the garrison and got out of his Jeep, his soldiers stopped what they were doing and came to attention. They all seemed to expect an "at ease" or "carry on," but the order never came. They stood at attention as best they could under the circumstances—some holding fire hoses with water still coursing, some holding shovels or other tools—all appearing somewhat vexed by the disruption of their work.

Will was certain the enlisted ranks of the Pak Army were not bilingual and had no way of knowing exactly what Captain Halstead and the brigadier were saying but if they could read simple body language, it should have been abundantly clear White Beard was not happy. His abrupt departure from the garrison punctuated that sentiment and added to the confusion of the weary soldiers. The brigadier came and went without saying anything to, or even a glance at the soldiers working diligently to fight the fires hampering cleanup efforts. On White Beard's exit, the Pak soldiers seemed perplexed by their brigadier's behavior, and oddly enough, appeared to look to the captain for some guidance. The captain did his best to gesture kindly for the soldiers to carry on, which they did with a sense of relief and bemusement.

"You'll like this hotel," General Wassom said, as they started to leave the garrison. "This is where most of the visiting dignitaries stay, the few who we get here," he added. "We have had a few VIP types since I've been here and one particular congressman from Texas who comes fairly frequently." The general didn't elaborate. The team loaded into their respective vans and went out the garrison gate into the heavy city traffic toward the Grand Islamabad Hotel.

GRAND ISLAMABAD HOTEL
ISLAMABAD, PAKISTAN
APRIL 12, 1988
0855 HRS.

Expectations for their accommodations were uncertain—they had few notions of what a Pakistani hotel might be like—but this place did not disappoint. The hotel had an exceptionally large and ornate entryway leading to the front desk. A cadre of bellhops met them at the revolving door and offered to take their bags. Will was unaccustomed to such treatment and instinctively declined politely.

Once they were checked in, the general informed them they had a couple more people to meet. "Here they come now," he said, motioning toward the door. Two gentlemen were walking through the entrance, headed their way. The men looked American and wore casual clothes. Nondescript for sure, but certainly a contrast to the shalwar kameez, the traditional garb for Pakistani men.

"General," the men each said.

"Good morning, gentlemen," the general said, "our team has arrived."

"Yes sir," one of the men said. "Glad they made it in okay." He appeared to be the senior of the two, and he turned to us and began his introduction. "I'm Brad Miller, Planning and Outreach," he said. "And this is my colleague, Cory Leftwich."

The two men shook hands all around and made it a point to thank each team member for being there.

"Sir, I imagine these guys are pretty tired," Miller said. "If it's alright with you, we'll let them get settled and a little rest, and then we'll hook up with you back at the embassy later."

"Sounds like a plan," the general said. "Let's say fifteen hundred?"

"Copy that, sir," Miller replied with a nod, and the two turned and made their exit.

Will's room was on the fourth floor; so was Morgan's. As they walked down the hall together to their rooms, Will asked, "What's Planning and Outreach?"

"What are you talking about?" Morgan replied. "Planning and Outreach?"

"Those two guys down in the lobby," Will said. "I assumed they were from the embassy, and he said, 'Planning and Outreach.'"

"Oh, yeah, they're CIA," Morgan said matter-of-factly. "They just don't come out and say that in public, so they use the whole 'Planning and Outreach' thing to attract less attention. We'll get a bunch more details from them this afternoon at the embassy."

There was nothing more to do but settle in and await the upcoming visit to the embassy. They were to meet in the lobby at 1430 (2:30 p.m.), so Will figured he had a few hours to rest. But first, a nice shower would make the pending nap even more refreshing. Under normal circumstances, a shower was a fairly straightforward proposition. But the "Planning and Outreach" guy in the lobby told them not to drink the water, which complicated things as Will had to make a conscious effort to keep his mouth shut in the shower. Nevertheless, he finished showering, confident he avoided ingesting any water.

He unpacked, called down to the desk for a wakeup call and laid down for a nice nap. He thought that would be simple enough too, considering how tired he was owing to the jet lag. But the conversation with the gentleman on the phone at the front desk was unsettling. The desk clerk was perfectly polite and obliging, but his English wasn't the best, which left Will unconvinced he would receive a wakeup call at the correct time. While he laid there worried that he would doze off and miss muster in the lobby, he dozed off anyway. To his relief, however, the phone rang at two o'clock, just as he asked.

It's strange to wake up in unfamiliar surroundings, and Will had to remind himself the events of the last thirty-six hours happened, he had not imagined them. He was waking—somewhat disoriented—in a hotel on the other side of the world from home, far from the safety and security of his humble barracks room at Ft. Indiantown Gap, Pennsylvania. He allowed himself plenty of time to get ready, brush his teeth, change clothes, and prepare for the rest of the day. He was so excited at the prospect of going to the embassy he completely forgot the admonishment about not drinking the water. He hadn't, but he brushed his teeth and likely ingested some water in the process. He would pay for that later.

CHAPTER SIX

GRAND ISLAMABAD HOTEL LOBBY
ISLAMABAD, PAKISTAN
APRIL 12, 1988
1420 HRS.

Will stepped out of his room and saw Chad Campbell emerging from his room. He noticed Will was walking out his door and waited as he walked down the hall.

"What's up?" he asked casually.

"Hey, man," Will responded. "You're back," he added, referring to Campbell's mission to secure their explosives. "How'd everything go?"

"Well, we got it done," Campbell said. "But those guys were pretty slick. They tried to move faster than I could count, so we had to slow 'em down—a bunch," he explained. "They were trying to keep me from getting a good count."

Of course, the team knew what they brought with them and the inventory was unaltered in flight, but it was important they make an overt show of accountability from the beginning. They knew there would be frequent attempts to steal as much of their explosives as possible, should they not exercise a high degree of security. That would be difficult. They could inventory everyday—and did—but if they were the least bit complacent, their explosives could fall into the wrong hands. Since there were only eight of them, they would have to rely on their daily inventories, and the ongoing surveillance provided by their friends at Planning and Outreach. The Paks knew they were being watched closely, so any attempts on their part to steal any explosives, even a small quantity, would have significant political risk.

Chad mentioned he did have a little help. No sooner than the offloading of the plane began, a man drove up in a little Suzuki SUV. He got out of his vehicle and walked up to the plane and looked inside. The dark-haired, dark-complected man dressed in khaki was wearing a light tan vest—the kind with lots of pockets. He had on a pair of horn-rimmed glasses and sported a long beard. He looked like he could have been a photographer or part of a news crew. He spoke briefly with one of the senior enlisted soldiers who was overseeing the transfer of explosives from plane to truck, and based on that exchange, Chad supposed he was some sort of Pak official.

The short, bearded man approached Chad and First Lieutenant Bhatti—the platoon leader in charge of the Pak soldiers—and greeted the lieutenant in Urdu, to which Bhatti responded. He then turned to Chad extending a hand, and said, in perfect English, "Good morning, Sergeant, welcome to Pakistan."

His perfect English was closer to perfect American, with a distinct Texas drawl. Chad was shocked, almost silenced, but managed a handshake and a bewildered, "Mornin'."

"My name's Jeb," the man said. "I'm here to help you make sure all this stuff gets where it's supposed to get," he added. "Can't be too careful," he said casting a slight glance and a wry smile Bhatti's way.

Jeb's arrival couldn't have been better timed. First Lieutenant Bhatti spoke English well, having completed an engineering degree at Purdue University, but was playing coy with Chad, who was trying to slow down the transfer process long enough to get an accurate count. Bhatti, although very pleasant, feigned broken English in a transparent effort to delay, if not undermine, Chad's work. When Jeb arrived and spoke to Bhatti in Urdu, it was clear he could no longer employ that tactic, and he dropped all pretense of a communications gap.

With Jeb on site, the plane-to-truck transfer proceeded smoothly, and all conversation with Bhatti was conducted in English. However, Jeb did occasionally go over and converse with the senior enlisted soldier—a sergeant major—out of earshot of Pak officer. These exchanges made Bhatti visibly nervous, based on his body language, but he said nothing.

Jeb was a mystery to Chad. He looked every bit as Pakistani as the men he was working with, but when he spoke to Chad, his accent confused him. Adding to the mystery was how this guy knew to refer to Chad as sergeant, given the fact Chad was in civilian clothes. His interactions with the Paks indicated he was a man of experience in this country. Adding his personal knowledge of Chad, the two obviously having never met before, and Campbell could only conclude Jeb must be a spook of some kind.

The man never mentioned where he was from, what or who he represented, but Jeb's American accent provided a great degree of comfort to Chad. Indeed, Jeb's presence added an element of accountability to the operation, and they completed the task surprisingly quickly. The trucks loaded, they proceeded north to a secure storage site.

"You can ride with me, Chad," Jeb instructed, again surprising Chad, he had never told Jeb his name. He was happy to ride with Jeb but couldn't help being a little nervous given how much Jeb knew about him already. Chad half expected him to mention something from his past. For now, all Jeb appeared to know was he was Sergeant Chad Campbell.

After securing the explosives at a military installation north of Islamabad—Jeb assured Chad this location was a safe and secure storage site—they went to the Grand Islamabad Hotel. Chad received the same instruction from Jeb as the rest of the team, meet in the lobby at 1230.

After Campbell's quick update, he and Carter went down to the lobby to await the rest of the team. One by one, each member appeared. By about 2:25 they were all assembled, waiting for the vans from the embassy. To everyone's surprise, General Wassom walked in. No one expected him to come for them, but it was clear the general was taking a keen interest in the operation.

"Afternoon, boys," the general said, casually. "Everybody ready?"

"All present and accounted for, sir," Captain Halstead replied.

"Well, let's get going," said General Wassom.

Wassom appeared to enjoy being around the team. They were a small unit, not in uniform, but it seemed to please the general to be around soldiers. He was very casual toward them, but the captain maintained a sharp military bearing with him, even though they were in civilian clothes, and the general appreciated it. He earlier remarked that it was "good to be around soldiers for a change," although he was careful not to make that remark in front of their sailor counterparts. There was even a detachment of Navy Seabees at the embassy, and of course there was a full complement of Marine guards, but soldiers, as the general mentioned, were sparse.

It was an estimated thirty-minute drive to the embassy, but the traffic was so heavy, Will didn't think they could get around the block in thirty minutes, much less the eighteen kilometers to the embassy. The drivers of the vans in the motorcade seemed to know what they were doing. They navigated the heavy traffic with relative ease, dodging and weaving with great skill, seldom stopping unless traffic lights or signs directed them to. For Will, it felt like a ride at an amusement park, rocking back and forth, although it wasn't amusing.

UNITED STATES EMBASSY
ISLAMABAD, PAKISTAN
APRIL 12, 1988
1515 HRS.

After about a forty-minute easterly trek through the congested Islamabad traffic, the team arrived at the U.S. Embassy. They found it comforting to see the Marine guards standing their post at the embassy gate, and as they passed through security, they felt safely at home as the gates closed behind them. The vans dropped them at the front door of the embassy and they went through another security check before following General Wassom up a few flights of stairs, down a couple hallways, and into a secure conference room.

There were some light snacks, coffee, and soft drinks on a credenza to one side.

"Help yourself," the general said. "We'll get started in just a few minutes." With that, Wassom departed.

Even though they arrived at the embassy a little behind schedule due to the heavy traffic, the team still had to wait a few minutes for the briefing to begin. That was fine with them, more opportunity to take advantage of the snacks and drinks. Will grabbed a Coke and a twin pack of Hostess chocolate cupcakes. That would have to tide him over until something more substantial could be procured. The rest of the famished team made short work of the refreshments too.

"I could eat the ass out of a dead skunk," Hutchinson said, stuffing a Twinkie in his mouth.

"Damn, Hutchinson," the sergeant major said, although he was just as hungry as everyone else.

"I guess that means you're hungry?" the captain inquired, sarcastically.

"Yes sir," Hutchinson replied. "It's been a few hours since that sandwich on the plane," he continued, "I'm running on empty."

"Well, if you can control yourself for a little while longer, Hutchinson, I think they have dinner set up for us after this brief," the captain said.

That was welcome news for all of them. They wondered when they'd get to sit down to a meal, but no one asked about it until Hutchinson's crass comment broke the ice. This time everyone was glad of it.

With the snacks all but consumed, the team began to get visibly antsy, though no one said anything. When the door opened, there was close to an audible sigh of relief.

General Wassom walked in followed by Brad Miller, Cory Leftwich, and another gentleman the team hadn't seen before. Will thought the man looked Pakistani but learned he was wrong when Campbell, who stood near Will, leaned over, and said quietly, "That's Jeb."

He looked exactly as Chad described him earlier. There were only twelve chairs around the conference table, so Will stood to one side along the wall with Thiessen and Campbell, the three of them being the junior NCOs. The general sat at one end of the table with Jeb seated to his right and Miller and Leftwich, respectively, to his left. At the other end of the table, Captain Halstead took a seat with the sergeant major on his right and Lieutenant Johnson to his left. The rest of the team filled in around the table, and as everyone took their seats, the general began.

"Gentlemen, this is a very fluid situation," he began. "I know you received a brief prior to your departure, and you've been to the site, so I won't waste time going over what you already know."

"However, there are some important details we haven't shared with you for a couple of reasons."

"One, this is compartmentalized information, it's purely need-to-know." He added for effect, "You didn't need to know until you got here."

"Second, this is a developing situation, the nature of the intelligence we're about to share doesn't leave this room—everyone clear on that?"

"Yes sir," the entire team responded in unison.

"Outstanding," the general replied. "I'm going to turn it over to Hawkeye here to give you more details."

Jeb stood up and began to speak. Will turned to Campbell and very discreetly inquired, "I thought you said that was Jeb?"

"Yeah, I did," said Campbell. "That's what he told me anyway."

The introduction of "Jeb" as "Hawkeye" added another puzzling element to the mix, but Will needed to concentrate on the presentation. Still, it was curious to him.

"First, let me thank y'all for being here," Jeb said. "This is a pretty hairy situation and we're gonna keep you busy."

"As the general said, there are some developments we need to read you in on. We've been assisting the Paks with weapons and material going into Afghanistan for some time now, and it has gone relatively smoothly for the last eighteen months or so—until this incident."

While the United States played a prominent role—primarily financial—in support of the Mujahideen's efforts to expel the

Soviets from Afghanistan, the only direct material support in country had been the provision of Stinger missiles. The U.S.-supplied Stingers first saw action in September 1986. A three-man fire team of Mujahideen rebels took down three Soviet Mi-24 Hind helicopter gunships at a Jalalabad airfield. That was a game changer for the Mujahideen, and a steady supply of Stinger missiles began to flow into Afghanistan through Pakistan.

The material and munitions bound for Afghanistan were staged at the Pak Army based at Cherat—home of the Special Services Group—in the foothills above the Peshawar valley. The S.S.G. or "Maroon Berets" as they were known, were an elite special operations unit with a mission set, and skill set, modeled after the U.S. Army Special Forces. Going back as far as the early 1950s, the S.S.G. were trained by U.S. Army Special Forces. The S.S.G. even wore the Green Beret for a time—an homage to their American counterparts—before adopting their own iconic maroon beret. In addition to the S.S.G. headquartered at Cherat, there were elements of the ISI on the installation as well. Cherat also offered a superior position with regards to its proximity to the city of Peshawar, a key location just inside the Pak border where Afghan refugees had been congregating for some years to escape the fighting in their homeland.

For a variety of reasons, it made sense for Cherat to be integral as a staging point for material support of the Afghan freedom fighters. What didn't make sense to Jeb though, was why the Paks diverted the shipment in question to transit Camp Ojhri—an installation in the heart of a major metropolitan area—as opposed to the remote location of Cherat. Jeb was not satisfied with the explanation he got from White Beard dismissing the mishap as just a storage error. Jeb was intimately familiar with the handling of munitions and material bound for Afghanistan. He was a key enabler in getting the Stingers and other weapons into the right hands. For reasons he attributed to White Beard, Jeb was excluded from the conversation when the decision was made to re-route this shipment through Ojhri.

For close to three years, Jeb played an integral role in the training and equipping of Afghan rebels. He went back and forth between

Pakistan and Afghanistan, traversing the famed Khyber Pass, more times than he could recall. He fostered relationships with key figures in the Mujahideen leadership on one side of the border, and critical elements of the Pak government on the other, including essential S.S.G. and ISI assets. He was troubled by his omission from the decision to ship through Camp Ojhri. He knew he could no longer trust White Beard and would have to play things very close to the vest where he was concerned. That was why he took a personal interest in monitoring the transfer of explosives from the plane to the trucks and being properly secured.

His relationship now compromised with White Beard—ISI's number two—he would have to be extra cautious. Although the conflict with White Beard had so far remained unspoken, Jeb knew eventually it would come to a head. It also meant he would have to be careful with other ISI contacts and the Pak military. Paks, whom he had placed a high degree of confidence in, he must now keep at arm's length.

"We know what this shipment of ordnance was supposed to contain," Jeb explained. "There were a good number of Stinger missiles among a bunch of foreign ordnance. I know you've run into a bunch of 122mm rockets already. We expected those, they're Egyptian-made BM-21s." The BM-21 was an Egyptian version of the Soviet-made truck-mounted multiple-launch rocket system of the same nomenclature. The Soviets were using these against Afghan targets to devastating effect. The Egyptian models weren't exact replicas, but they were proving extremely helpful. These, along with the AK-47 Kalashnikov rifles, and of course the U.S. Stingers, were the real difference makers for the Mujahideen.

"There's a significant number of 82mm mortar rounds and some recoilless rifle rounds as well," Jeb said. "What the Navy guys have run into thus far is primarily the 122mm rockets, I think those far-ranging kick outs are largely due to the rockets going ballistic as a result of the fire," he added, looking at Johnson, who was nodding in agreement.

"The problem we're running into on the garrison is, for some unknown reason, some of those mortar rounds were stored fuzed," he continued. "In the blast, some of them apparently armed, and that's why these Pak privates are getting blown up when they go downrange."

It was clear a sizable number of at least the mortar rounds were inexplicably stored with fuzes installed. The team would have to assume all the ordnance was fuzed and employ the highest degree of safety. The mortar rounds looked like Egyptian copies of Soviet ordnance. The Soviets employed very few safeties on their artillery and mortar rounds, which made them dangerous to handle, even under the best conditions. Adding to the danger in this case was the fact Egyptian-made weapons incorporated even fewer—if that was possible—safety features than the Soviet models.

The minimal safety features on foreign-made ordnance was a stark contrast to U.S.-built weapons systems. Designed to be as safe to handle as possible, the high number of safety features found in American-made ordnance, at times, even worked to their disadvantage. In Vietnam, for example, Viet Cong and North Vietnamese Army soldiers often used American "dud" ordnance against them. Sometimes they would extract the explosives from large unexploded 250- and 500-pound bombs that littered the Vietnamese countryside and use them in improvised explosive devices against American targets. In other cases, dud American 81mm mortar rounds were used in Vietnamese 82mm mortar tubes. If an American soldier neglected to remove one of the safeties before dropping a round into a mortar tube—which happened often—he was effectively sending ammunition downrange for the enemy to re-use against Americans. Despite this high dud ratio, the American military chose to err on the side of caution in protecting the safety of their own troops in combat.

That was certainly not the case here where safety was given little consideration in this weapons cache. The kinetic energy of the Camp Ojhri blast could have been sufficient to arm the fuzed ordnance, which would account for the high number of casualties in the outlying areas of the garrison. In effect, the blast launched a shower of mortar fire in a radius of several hundred meters around the garrison. The tail booms affixed to the 82mm mortars would orient the rounds point down as they fell back to earth, meaning the fuzes, most of them the point-detonating variety, could function with high order detonations. Many of the rounds did function as designed and inflicted major damage and casualties. However, many of the rounds didn't detonate and lay scattered about the garrison and littered the urban landscape beyond the garrison's gates. The remaining unexploded ordnance had to be treated as live, fuzed ordnance and handled with extreme caution.

Jeb was not an EOD tech, but he knew weapons. He responded promptly to the blast, and after an inspection of the garrison's damage and surrounding area, recommended a deployment of EOD soldiers quickly to help the Pak Army. He further noted White Beard was in an even greater hurry to act, disregarding safety in his haste.

"I advised against any hasty action," Jeb told us. "But the brigadier insisted on beginning cleanup operations as quick as he could. Hell, there were still rounds going high order all around us, and he was sending guys into that mess," he added. "It was bad enough as it was, but he cost a lot of lives unnecessarily."

An evacuation perimeter was established based on the total explosive weight estimated in the weapons shipment, but Pak officials were still having difficulty pushing people back, despite the devastation surrounding the garrison. People were choosing to hunker down in many cases, over the uncertainty of leaving their homes.

There was still the question of the Stinger missiles, how many were there, and what happened to them? Jeb was not entirely forthcoming. He didn't give the team a number, but he did acknowledge there "were supposed to be" Stingers in this shipment. At this point, there was no evidence of any Stingers, he said. Clearly, he was unhappy with that key intelligence but didn't elaborate.

In his first meeting with the Navy team after a few hours of running incidents, Jeb inquired about what the team encountered. "We've been mostly running into 122mm rockets," Johnson informed him. "Mostly high explosive, but a pretty good number of WP warheads."

Lieutenant Johnson informed Jeb they had not run into any 122mm rockets thus far that were fuzed, which was encouraging. However, the news about the white phosphorus struck Jeb as unusual, and he felt the need to run that up the chain as soon as possible as an added precaution. But he was still vexed by the lack of information on the Stingers. He made a quick trip to the embassy to update the intelligence reports about the white phosphorus and met back up with the Navy team. This time he asked them directly, "Have you run into any Stingers?"

"No sir," Johnson replied. "Nothing like that. Mostly these 122s. A good number of 82mm mortar rounds closer to the garrison, and a few 'reckless' rifles," he continued, "all foreign so far."

"Well hell," Jeb said.

There was still a possibility there could be some Stingers on the garrison, but so far, it was too dangerous to attempt a recon. There were still fires around the camp, and with ordnance scattered everywhere, Jeb knew it would be better to wait on the EOD team to help secure a path in to determine the disposition of any Stingers.

Jeb continued with his brief, avoiding any further talk about Stingers. Instead, he focused on the unusual number of white phosphorus rounds. "Based on what the Navy guys have told me, and what we can glean from Pak officials regarding the nature of the casualties," he said, "we estimate about 15–20 percent of the 122mm rockets were WP.

"Of course, I don't have to tell y'all, that adds an additional safety concern," he added. "We've set up a demo range for you up north with pretty much no limit," he explained, referring to the maximum allowable explosive weight per shot. "That's where they've been transporting the 122s for destruction."

One thing was certain: the lack of Stinger missiles weighed heavy on Jeb, or Hawkeye as the general introduced him. They were the most effective weapon so far against Soviet aircraft wreaking havoc on the Afghan countryside. Jeb was in Peshawar at an Afghan refugee camp when he got the news of the first Mi-24 Hind helicopter shot down by the Mujahideen. He was enjoying dinner with one of his many contacts in Afghanistan, a then twenty-five-year-old hardened war fighter named Muhammadin who was visiting his family at one of the many refugee camps covering the border landscape.

A young Afghan freedom fighter carrying an AK-47 walked into the family tent and whispered something in Muhammadin's ear. A smile broke out on Muhammadin's face, and he quickly shared the information with Jeb. Jeb was so excited by the news he abruptly stood from the low dinner table where he had been sitting cross-legged, and hastily departed. He risked offending his hosts, but Jeb knew he had to let his superiors know quickly.

Jeb was anxious to get into the garrison and conduct a full site exploitation. He was feeling much less confident that the Stingers would be present but hoped he could find some evidence of why they weren't there, and who might be responsible. He knew they were still days, if not weeks away from an environment safe enough to offer him an opportunity to assess the situation fully. He also knew he had to be patient and had no plans to hurry the team along, knowing well the human cost of hasty actions.

Another complicating factor Jeb discussed was that it appeared everyone in Pakistan knew his Army team was there. As the sun was rising just after the C-141 landed, there were at least five major metropolitan newspapers in Pakistan reporting on their front pages the arrival of an American EOD team in response to the "Camp Ojhri blast." What worried Jeb the most—and the whole EOD team once they found out—was the detail of the information shared. He attributed this to the Soviets. Their embassy was within sight of the U.S. Embassy, fully equipped with an array of signals intelligence hardware—clearly visible from the U.S Embassy—that might have intercepted traffic from Forces Command back home at Ft. McPherson, Georgia. While this was an issue, the bigger problem was how the Soviets—if it was them—acquired this information. And if they knew about the team, and what they were doing in Pakistan, it made sense they knew even more information that had nothing to do with their mission. This set off a firestorm of speculation inside the embassy, not to mention back home at Langley and Ft. Meade, the homes of the CIA and NSA, respectively. Intelligence community officials set about identifying the gaps allowing this to happen, and the steps necessary to prevent it from happening again.

Another concern was what if it wasn't the Soviets who acquired the sensitive information? Who could it have been? Was it possible the information was gleaned from a human source? If so, who? And how? The tension between White Beard and Jeb—and General Wassom for that matter—escalated. Could there be more to it than just the Camp Ojhri blast contributing to the deteriorating relationship Jeb and the general perceived? How could this impact the EOD team? And the bigger picture going forward was, how could this impact the ongoing efforts in Afghanistan? Could White Beard be working multiple sides? So many questions were unanswered.

"Needless to say, you'll have a lot of eyes on you," Jeb explained. "We expected the ISI to be watching, but now the Soviets will be watching very closely too. Not sure at this point who else might be in the mix, but you guys can just focus in on the technical stuff," he continued. "You've got an important job to do, and I'll make sure you can do it without any security issues or disruptions."

Jeb spoke authoritatively, which was reassuring. Still, the intelligence he gave about sensitive information in Soviet hands troubled Will and the others. It made the point that the team was now in a hostile country, ally or not. The only meaningful interaction they had with the Paks until now was with the annoying and unfriendly White Beard. It made sense some of his officers and men would share his views—First Lieutenant Bhatti was one example. Of course, the Soviets were openly hostile, and having them watching the team's operations only added to the tension.

Jeb concluded his brief. He was anxious for the team to begin but also acknowledged Captain Halstead as the officer in charge. He would defer to the captain's experience and expertise and allow him to manage his team and the operation. For his part, Jeb knew he would have to run interference with White Beard, who would continue to be irritating and demanding. This would keep him busy for as long as they were in Pakistan.

CHAPTER SEVEN

As Jeb wrapped up the brief, the general inquired, "Anybody hungry?"

"I bet we could eat, sir," the captain replied.

Exuberance buzzed around the room and the general responded to it. "I believe they've got us set up down this hall." He walked down the hall as the team fell in behind him. The closer they got to the dining room, the more they could smell food. As they approached the dining room door, the general stepped aside, as a stampede of hungry soldiers and sailors moved past him. The captain appeared slightly embarrassed by the display, but the general just smiled as he waved them past. The captain was just as hungry as everyone else but made sure he was the last member of the team to go through the door, deferring to the general. "After you," said General Wassom, and Captain Halstead went into the dining room to a table.

After a satisfying meal, dessert, and the requisite coffee talk, the general advised that transportation was ready for the trip back to the hotel. Fully fed, the only thing the team needed now was to be fully rested. Tomorrow would be a long day. They made their way out to the waiting vans and back to the Grand Islamabad Hotel.

The drive back to the hotel was much less stressful than the trip out to the embassy. The traffic at this hour was considerably lighter and they made it back to the hotel in about twenty minutes walking through the revolving door around 8:00 p.m. Will got to his room just in time to deal with sudden digestive turbulence. As he walked in the door, he lunged quickly into the bathroom to direct a case of explosive diarrhea toward the toilet. After a good ten minutes of gastric violence, the onslaught abated, and he went to bed.

Intestinal problems would bedevil the EOD team during their stay in Pakistan. While Will suffered like everyone else, he was never sidelined. Every other member of the team spent a day or two in their room waiting out intestinal uproar, unable to work. Eventually, everyone got to a manageable point, but no one on the team could say they had a solid bowel movement in Pakistan. Embassy staff told them there was a lab on the grounds staffed by two lab techs whose job it was to analyze stool samples so chronic dysentery suffered by U.S. personnel could be controlled. An elusive goal, and the reason the embassy asked team members to bring stool samples in for analysis.

It was easy enough to learn to keep your mouth closed during a shower, but brushing your teeth was a different story. The team didn't have bottled water, and the hotel didn't offer any. Fortunately, they had their canteens. They filled them at the embassy, and then used the water sparingly, including while brushing their teeth. It struck Will as ironic they were staying in this very modern, well-appointed hotel, yet couldn't drink the water without getting violently ill.

Will was sleeping deeply when there was a sudden wailing outside his window. He sprang upright in bed, unsure what he was hearing on a PA speaker around midnight. He learned later the wailing was the Muslim call to prayer—the Salat. He had never been in a Muslim country, so was unaware of this custom, which occurred five times a day. After the shock, he continued his sound sleep until a little before the morning call to prayer, just before sunrise. He was an early riser and was wide awake when the morning call sounded.

A quick morning shower—being careful to keep his mouth shut—followed by brushing his teeth with canteen water: the morning routine was now in place. Will reasoned the shorter the shower, the less opportunity there would be to ingest bad water.

Jeb was curbside waiting on them when the team exited the door of the hotel. "Let's load up, gentlemen," he instructed. As they boarded the vans, they noted the presence of several coolers. They held ice water, filled at the embassy.

"Y'all are gonna want to fill your canteens, and keep them filled," he advised. "Make sure you stay hydrated—we can't afford any heat strokes," he said.

There were also a few thermos bottles containing hot coffee, along with Styrofoam cups and a couple boxes of snack cakes. "Grab some coffee and some grub," Jeb said. "We can eat on the way to the garrison."

The strong coffee made Will think of his days working on New Mexico ranches during high school. He wasn't a coffee drinker then, but when that was all there was available, he could force himself. Just like on the ranch, the coffee was strong and black. There was no cream or sugar to take the edge off. The coffee paired well with the little snack cakes though, and by the time he was finishing his last bite of a second cinnamon cake, the vans were pulling into the gate at Camp Ojhri.

The Navy team would continue running incidents, as they had since their arrival. There were several more reports of a variety of unexploded ordnance in areas beyond the gates of the camp, scattered about the city. They were given the coordinates of their first stop and departed in the company of two Pak soldiers.

The captain began designating teams and outlining the details of the plan. To no one's surprise, White Beard drove up and immediately began issuing instructions. The captain tactfully informed White Beard the team was briefed on the situation and would execute a well-formed plan. The captain acquired a map of the area and plotted points from which each team would enter the camp. They would start by spotting and marking unexploded ordnance (UXO) and determining the disposition of each item. EOD work is inherently dangerous and there is no "safe" way to handle UXO—just a least dangerous way. The captain had years' experience and would quarterback this operation. An unsettled White Beard acknowledged it to General Wassom. White Beard could not be prevented from voicing his opinion, regardless. The captain endured his input patiently, and respectfully demurred whenever an unworkable suggestion was offered, which wasn't easy because most of White Beard's suggestions were dangerous.

The first thing the captain did was to stop sending Pak soldiers downrange on pray-and-flip missions. This did not sit well with White Beard, but he said little. The plan was to station teams at multiple points around the perimeter of the camp and "sweep" their way into the center of the garrison. This would require the help of Pak soldiers. They knew the camp and could help find the routes in and keep the teams on course.

The biggest problem would be language. Almost none of the enlisted men spoke English. The team would need at least one officer to accompany each assisting squad. Most of the Pak Army officers were Western educated—having attended college or graduate school in either Great Britain or the United States—and spoke English well, if not fluently. Assigned to each EOD tech was a squad of Pak soldiers to aid him. They each received the coordinates on the perimeter of the camp from which they would begin their sweep. Outside of White Beard, there was only one other officer present, a surly major educated in the States, though he never said where. Once the captain laid out the plan, the major began barking orders. The enlisted men formed up in squads of eight, and each EOD tech directed to a squad. Once they assembled with their squads, several trucks made their way through the gate. They each boarded a truck with their squads and left to their assigned starting points on the perimeter.

"An officer will be dispatched to each squad directly," White Beard informed the captain.

"Very good sir," the captain replied. And he watched as each truck departed through the main gate.

CHAPTER EIGHT

CAMP OHJRI
RAWALPINDI, PAKISTAN
APRIL 13, 1988
0815 HRS.

The squads rode in trucks called a deuce-and-a-half—a two-and-a-half-ton truck that had long been a staple of the U.S. Army wheeled vehicle inventory. Will jumped in the back of one the trucks with a squad of Pak soldiers none of whom spoke English. They exited through the main gate, turned right, and made their way around to the south end of Camp Ojhri. Nothing was said on the bumpy ten-minute ride, just an exchange of awkward smiles and head nodding.

Will's squad arrived at their designated entry point and jumped out of the truck. There was a building that looked to be a barracks. It didn't appear to be damaged, but was unoccupied. There was a dirt circular drive in front of the building and a grassy area to one side. There was a grove of trees providing a nice shady spot over the grassy area, a welcome relief from the glaring morning sun. As they exited the truck, Will motioned for the Pak soldiers to assemble in the shade. The soldiers encircled him with anxious looks, awaiting his next direction. Since he didn't have any idea when to expect the arrival of his assigned officer, Will sat down in the shade on the grass and gestured for the soldiers to have a seat with him. They did and seemed relieved—if not surprised—for this brief break from what was a demanding pace under White Beard's direction.

As they sat cross-legged in a circle awaiting the arrival of an English-speaking officer, they began to smile at each other. The smiles intensified and, for reasons Will didn't understand, they all began to chuckle. Still not sure what they were chuckling about, he reached into his pocket and produced a pack of Big Red gum. Not knowing how long he would be in country, Will decided to ration the gum, so he peeled the foil wrapper back, tore it in half, placed the remainder back into the pack, and put the gum in his mouth. The soldiers were watching his every move. He pulled out another piece of gum and offered it to the soldier next to him. He was obviously the senior man in this squad. He was the only soldier wearing chevron stripes on his sleeve, so Will knew he was at least a sergeant, like him. However, he was clearly older than Will.

He accepted the gum with a smile and imitated Will, tearing the piece in half, re-wrapping the rest and placing it in his shirt pocket, then putting the gum in his mouth. As he began to chew, he smiled, and then opened his mouth and fanned as if to cool his mouth from the spicy gum. This incited further laughter from the soldiers. As the laughter began to subside, a young soldier stood and approached Will. The soldier pulled a tin from his pocket and offered Will some of the contents. The tin contained a green, powder-like substance not unlike the consistency of Copenhagen. Although Will was not a tobacco user—he had certainly tried Copenhagen and Skoal in the past since most of the cowboys he ran with as a teenager were seldom without a can—so he accepted the offering, mostly out of courtesy. The soldier smiled. Will placed the green stuff under his lower lip as one would place a dip of snuff. He regretted it at once. The moment his tongue touched it, he began to cough and gag, and his eyes ran. Courtesy or not, he had to spit it out or risk choking. The soldiers could not hide their amusement and went from laughter to full-on hysterics. As Will continued to gag and spit, he reached for his canteen and rinsed repeatedly. Spitting profusely, he wiped his eyes, and joined in the laughter.

The arrival of Captain Abed, the Pakistani officer who would go with Will's squad, could not have been better timed to calm things. He drove up as Will was rinsing and spitting, with his soldiers laughing hysterically. He barked sharply at the sergeant and then turned to Will. "It appears my men are having some fun at your expense," he said apologetically. "I am Captain Abed."

"Not at all, sir," Will replied. "We were just getting to know each other a little," he said, wiping his eyes and smiling at the sergeant, who was smiling back. Several of the soldiers were still snickering, and Captain Abed shot them a sharp look. Will didn't know what that green substance was, but from then on, he made it a point to avoid putting unknown green, powdery textured substances in his mouth.

"I'm Sergeant Carter," Will said.

"Very nice to meet you, Sergeant," the captain replied. "I will be assisting you with this squad."

"We have a big job ahead of us," Abed continued.

"Yes sir, we sure do," Will agreed. "How 'bout we get started?"

"Indeed," Abed replied.

Will outlined the plan to the captain who made no objections at all. On the contrary, he appeared very conciliatory and willing to work with Will. In sharp contrast to what the team experienced from his colleagues, Captain Abed was pleasant and helpful. His attitude was contagious. His men seemed much less apprehensive and noticeably more relaxed than they were on the ride over in the back of the deuce-and-a-half. Their apprehension was understandable. Several soldiers died in the first stages of the cleanup operation, and Will could only assume there were friends of those dead soldiers among this squad.

Captain Abed assembled the men and relayed the instructions of the plan. As he spoke, he gestured and, although Will certainly didn't speak Urdu, he could clearly understand the captain was letting them know they would no longer be flipping UXO with sticks, as Will instructed him. The sense of relief was palpable, visible in their eyes.

Will began to gear up, which consisted of donning his Kevlar vest and helmet and securing his tool belt around his waist. He noticed the squad had no safety gear. Nothing but their uniforms.

Will questioned Captain Abed about the availability of safety gear for these men. "This is all we have available," Abed explained.

"I'd sure feel better about it if we could at least get these guys some steel pots," Will said. It may not have mattered much if they had any, but Will couldn't shake the feeling of unfairness. He was asking them to support this effort while he was wearing a helmet and flak vest, and they had nothing.

No sooner than that thought entered his mind, there was an explosion. Will turned quickly toward the direction of the noise. He saw a column of rising smoke that looked to be about a mile or so to the northwest. That was close to the staging area at the north gate.

"Captain, I need to get over there fast!" Will exclaimed.

Abed yelled at his driver and motioned for Will to come with him. They ran for his truck, quickly jumped in, and headed out the gate. They obviously couldn't drive straight toward the explosion. UXO littered the ground throughout the garrison; so they wound around the perimeter of the camp to the north gate. They arrived at about the same time as Captain Halstead, followed by Hutchinson and Thiessen.

Each of his EOD teammates drove over with their assigned Pak officer. They exited their vehicles to a grisly sight. A Pakistani soldier lay dead on the ground about twenty feet back from a smoking hole. Worse, White Beard was standing over him. There were two other men standing there with White Beard—the surly major they met that morning, and a senior enlisted man.

The captain proceeded toward the site, which was situated over a hundred yards to the west from the north gate. The brigadier and his men stopped talking when they noticed the Americans were approaching.

"We have suffered another casualty," White Beard said matter-of-factly.

"Yes, I can see that," Captain Halstead responded sternly. The dead soldier was clutching what was left of a long stick, so it was clear what happened.

"Brigadier, I thought we were very clear on this operation," Captain Halstead began. "I thought we agreed to stop sending our men downrange with sticks," he said firmly, his voice rising in volume. "This should not have happened."

"WE are not sending OUR men downrange, Captain," White Beard said. "I am sending MY men downrange."

As if on cue, Jeb arrived. He drove through the gate in his Jeep right up to where the men were standing. He got out of his vehicle, walked over to the dead soldier. He knew immediately what happened. He promptly turned toward White Beard and said sharply, "All due respect, Brigadier, but what the f***!"

The brigadier's eyes opened wide, and his jaw dropped. "Do not address me in such a manner!"

"We've been very clear about this, Brigadier," Jeb said. "We will direct this operation," he added forcefully. "This was entirely unnecessary."

Jeb stepped back for a moment to confer with the captain. One by one, the rest of the Army team arrived on the scene. They all stood by watching the exchange between Jeb and the brigadier.

"This s**t's gonna stop or we'll just blow this whole f***in' s**t hole in place," Jeb said to the captain. "This a**hole is impossible to work with."

"Well, I guess his guys just waited 'til our teams fanned out and started doing things his way again," the captain surmised. "Something else bothers me we didn't think about 'til today. "These guys don't have any safety equipment at all—not even a steel pot."

Will was relieved to hear the captain address that issue. Jeb was immediately responsive. "Well, that's an easy fix," Jeb said. "I'll get on the horn and take care of that quick."

"I'm gonna have to head back to the embassy and talk to General Wassom about this s**t anyway," Jeb added. "I'll add that to my list of things to do. Let me deal with this a**hole for now."

Jeb collected himself and approached White Beard again. "Brigadier, I'm going to ask you, if you would please, sir, to attend to your fallen soldier and then stand down."

"Very well," White Beard responded, "but I am not pleased with the pace of this operation."

"Noted," Jeb replied. "One other thing, Brigadier," he continued. "My team is going to assist the Navy team in collecting and destroying the UXO outside the wire and suspend operations here on the garrison for now."

"Come again?" White Beard said, aghast.

"Your men are not properly equipped," Jeb explained. "I'm going to make arrangements to get some proper gear here for these soldiers who are assisting my teams. We'll continue operations here at the garrison after we get the gear here," he continued. "In the meantime, we'll halt all operations here on the garrison."

"What gear are you suggesting?" White Beard inquired.

"Basic gear they should have already had," Jeb said. "Helmets and flak vests."

"I hardly think a flak vest or helmet would have made any difference to this chap," White Beard said pointing to the dead soldier. Indeed, there were several wounds visible on the man's body, the most severe of which was a large, jagged gash in his neck just above the collar bone. It must have been the fatal blow as it cut about halfway through his neck.

"Maybe not, Brigadier," Jeb said. "But we'll never know now, will we?"

CHAPTER NINE

After the exchange with White Beard, the team headed north of Islamabad to a remote location. The Navy team had been busy amassing a significant amount of ordnance at the range Jeb set up for them. They would spend the day preparing the collection of UXO for destruction. It consisted mostly of 122mm rockets, but there was the odd 82mm mortar round, and some recoilless rifle rounds as well.

Jeb advised the team he would connect with them at the range after he stopped off at the embassy. He was sure White Beard wouldn't stand down as he was instructed, but there were many eyes on the garrison to alert Jeb to any activity requiring him to act quickly. He paid a brief visit to General Wassom and told him what happened that morning at the garrison. The general was not pleased.

"That son of a b***h is going to get us all killed," the general said. He recognized White Beard was likely to be an ongoing problem and he would probably have to bring this matter to the attention of the ambassador, if he couldn't get it resolved at a lower level—and soon.

"There's maybe one or two individuals I could visit with about White Beard," the general suggested. "Maybe they can redirect him and keep him out of your way. Failing that, I may have to loop the ambo in," General Wassom said. "I hate to do that, but it may be our only option if he keeps on."

Jeb nodded in acknowledgment. "One other thing, sir," Jeb said. "We need Kevlar vests and helmets for these Pak soldiers. I'm not sure a flak vest would have helped that poor b*****d who got killed this morning," he said. "But they need a morale boost as much as anything. It looks bad for our guys to be wearing vests and helmets, and these guys don't have s**t," Jeb added.

"How many do you think you'll need?" the general asked.

"Well, I think we'll need at least fifty, maybe more," Jeb said. "But fifty would be a big help."

"I'll ask for a hundred as long as I'm asking," the general said. "You know how the Army works."

"Roger that, sir," Jeb said. "The sooner the better. I've got the teams on the range for now, but we really need to get back into that garrison as quick as we can and check it out."

There was a reason White Beard was so intent on being present at the garrison, and Jeb knew it. White Beard wanted to be the first one in. Jeb assumed it was either to remove evidence or maybe plant some. Jeb needed more insight into exactly what happened, how and why. Although he hadn't yet apprised General Wassom of his assessment just yet, Jeb dismissed any chance of recovering any Stingers. The best he could hope for at this point was to determine if there were any Stingers at all at Camp Ojhri in the first place. It was obvious to him the Stingers were removed either before or after their arrival at Camp Ojhri. The question was how, and by whom? And Jeb also understood White Beard was going to make the job as difficult as possible. He was confident his assets at the garrison would keep an eye on White Beard and his aides and alert him of any trouble, but he was puzzled why the ISI Deputy Director would be so personally involved in this incident. He could have easily delegated this, as most in his position would do. That told Jeb all he needed to know. White Beard knew more than he was saying, and it was highly likely he was involved in the disappearance of the U.S. Stinger missiles. White Beard was playing dumb though, and so would Jeb—for now.

DEMOLITION RANGE
NORTH OF ISLAMABAD, PAKISTAN
APRIL 13, 1988
1155 HRS.

Jeb arrived at the range right about noon. The teams had been busy preparing the UXO for destruction, and there was a lot of it. More than the Navy team brought out. It turns out the Paks had been picking up UXO all around town leaving only the fuzed ordnance behind for the Americans to deal with. The rockets in the outlying areas were a good distance from the garrison for a reason—many of the rocket motors ignited in the blast causing the rockets to go ballistic. Many of them were severely damaged from the impact. The Paks left those for the Navy team. There were no fuzed rockets found, however, so the Paks set about picking up the rockets near the garrison and transporting them north to the range.

While the collection of the rockets and other UXO certainly sped up the operation, the Pak soldiers had not been briefed on proper handling of white phosphorus rounds. Not only that, the rockets that went ballistic still had live rocket motors. In the blast, some of the rocket warheads were separated from their motors so the Pak soldiers were picking up fully intact 122mm rockets—some of them with WP warheads—along with separate warheads and rocket motors. They were unwittingly exposing themselves, and civilians around them, to grave danger not being properly trained on how to handle the ordnance. It was just their good fortune there were no further casualties in the course of this gross mishandling.

Adding to the workload was the fact the Paks had not sorted the UXO in any discernible fashion. Everything was mostly piled up randomly. Will imagined that's how the ordnance was stored in the first place, which is why this whole thing was such a mess. He and his teammates sorted high explosive rockets from WP, spent rocket motors from unspent, 82mm mortars, and recoilless rifle rounds. The Paks thought it was unnecessary since they were just going to blow everything up, but there was a right way to go about it, and the Paks were woefully unfamiliar with it. The WP rounds had to be blown up, into the air, to allow for the WP to be consumed. Blowing it down, into the ground, would just drive it into the dirt. At some point that could be a problem. It could potentially stay put for a long time and create a major fire hazard long after everyone forgot about it. You wouldn't have wanted to be the poor sucker walking on the range who inadvertently unearthed some shallow, unseen WP.

The high explosive rounds on the other hand were blown into the ground to minimize fragmentation. The unspent rocket motors required special attention as well. Applying sufficient explosive was necessary to consume the rocket motors and prevent them from going ballistic.

Another consideration was the damaged WP warheads. Their Navy colleagues did an excellent job addressing the issue, but several of the rounds the Paks handled were beginning to smoke. Fortunately, Jeb made arrangements for a water truck to be on hand. The team could make all the mud they needed, so they kept the buckets handy. Anytime someone spotted smoke, they would holler. Being the junior man, Will had the dubious honor of being the first mud bucket runner. He spent a good part of that first day mixing and toting mud. It made setting the shots a little messy since they had to place the explosives beneath the WP warheads, but they managed.

The various ordnance was organized into smaller stacks for multiple, smaller shots as opposed to a single big one. This caused some consternation among the Pak soldiers. They reminded the Americans there was essentially no range limit, so why go to the extra effort of setting up all these shots? The team spent a little time educating the Paks on the different techniques required for each type of ordnance, and why it would be safer—and necessary—to execute multiple shots. Each would still be sizable given the amount of UXO being destroyed. The size of each shot would also require significant standoff. The safe area was at least a half mile away, and the team didn't have radio-controlled firing devices or blasting wire. What they did have was a lot of time fuze and plenty of M2 igniters, so they used non-electric firing trains. It required a little extra time and math to calculate the burn rate of each roll of time fuze, but it was necessary to determine how much to cut to allow a comfortable return to the safe area.

The team sent all extraneous personnel and vehicles back to the safe area, apart from three trucks that would carry them back once they pulled their igniters. They positioned those trucks about a hundred yards up range and left them running with a driver waiting.

Morgan was in charge. Hutchinson, Thiessen, Campbell, and Will would pull the igniters for each shot on his command. Each of them were positioned by one of the first four of six shots, spaced sufficiently to prevent a sympathetic detonation, awaiting Morgan's direction, who had his eyes on his watch. Since Will was the junior man, it was his job to yell "fire in the hole," which he did, in three directions, at the top of his lungs.

"Pull!" Morgan said and pointed at Hutchinson. "Smoke," Hutchinson replied, after pulling his igniter and verifying the presence of smoke from the time fuze, which happened almost immediately. This process repeated itself for each of them on thirty second intervals at Morgan's command. Hutchinson leapfrogged down to shot number five, with Campbell doing the same for number six. They walked briskly back to the trucks, loaded up, and headed for the safe area.

The safe area turned out to be just over three quarters of a mile to the west of the demolition area. Their trucks traversed a dry creek bed on a well-worn road and up a steep rise to an elevated area that gave a good vantage point. They allowed themselves seven minutes for a safe return and made it back in a little over four. As they exited the trucks, Morgan looked at his watch and announced, "Two and a half minutes." It seemed like an exceptionally long two and half minutes as they anxiously awaited that first shot.

The first two would be WP. Will had only seen a WP shot once before in training and was excited to see these. Morgan looked down at his watch. "Five, four, three, two, one . . ." With only a slight delay they saw, and then heard, that first shot—spectacular! A huge plume of white smoke shot hundreds of feet into the sky before spreading out like the limbs of a giant willow tree and burning out as they fell back to earth. Right on cue the second shot detonated less than a second after Morgan said, "Now!" Another stunning display more impressive than any fireworks Will ever saw. The remaining shots fired not more than a second off Morgan's audible cues.

The Pak soldiers stood in stunned silence, many with jaws agape. Whether it was the explosive display they saw, or the precision of execution, they appeared awestruck. The truth is everyone was amazed. No one on the team had done anything like what they just experienced. Still, they tried to play it off as just another day at the office with the Paks looking on. That was a defining moment. From that point on, the Pak soldiers looked at them differently. There was a palpable change in their attitude toward the American EOD team. The Paks clearly viewed them as experts—although they knew not to get comfortable with the term "expert" as it applied to their work—and had a new and immediate level of respect for them.

Jeb, who joined the team on the range about an hour earlier, did not miss the precision of the detonations either. "That was pretty damn impressive," he said. "S**t—non-electric . . ." he added, trailing off. He had nothing but respect for his EOD team, in contrast to the Paks. But this display went further in confirming his trust in them. He also sensed further that the Paks elevated him, since he was integral in bringing the American EOD teams to Pakistan. From then on, it was clear to the Pak soldiers who was in charge. Even the Pak officers, except for White Beard, showed a greater deferential tone.

Captain Abed and the other squad officers arrived at the range by the time the team returned to the safe area. Abed approached Will and shook his hand just seconds before the first WP shot went up. He stood speechless until all the shots fired off. "Congratulations, Sergeant Will, that was most impressive, most impressive indeed," he said effusively, while shaking Will's hand vigorously. He and his fellow officers were all amazed.

CHAPTER TEN

It was only about 2:00 p.m., but Jeb felt this would be a suitable time to return to the embassy. The six shots cleared all the UXO awaiting destruction on the range. There was still a lot left around town—they hadn't even begun to fully address the garrison—but Jeb thought a little R&R to finish the day would be in order.

"Well, it's still a little early," Jeb said, "but let's head back to the embassy. I asked the general for some helmets and flak vests and I need to get back and check on that," he added. "Plus, y'all can grab something to eat and lay around the pool for a while."

That sounded great to the team. Although the idea of swimming brought up the issue of their wardrobes. Nobody brought climate appropriate clothes, and there was certainly no consideration given to the possibility of swimming.

"I guess we could just swim in our pants," Thiessen said.

"Maybe they wouldn't mind if we swam in our skivvies," Campbell said, prompting a general chuckle.

"The hell with that," Hutchinson said. He produced a pocketknife and immediately began to modify the jeans he was wearing. Some of the others on the team followed suit and set about cutting the legs off their pants.

"At ease with that s**t," Morgan instructed. "You can take care of that when we get back to the embassy—damn!"

Everyone put away their knives, most having made not much more than small incision. Hutchinson was the only one who completed the task. He was in such a hurry he didn't properly calculate the length of what were now short-shorts.

"Damn, Hutchinson," Morgan said. "Did you get those short enough?"

Everyone turned and looked at Hutchinson and broke out in laughter.

"What?" Hutchinson responded.

"You best be careful when you sit," Campbell advised. "Those things ain't keeping no secrets."

Wiley was having problems of his own. He had quickly shortened one pant leg and was about to start on the second when Morgan put a stop to the field expedient tailoring. Wiley closed his knife and returned it to the sheath on his tool belt. He looked even more pitiful than usual standing there in half a pair of shorts.

Will happened to be standing next to Senior Chief Sonberg when all the wardrobe alterations were taking place. They were laughing at Hutchinson's too-short shorts when Morgan's admonishment brought the tailoring to an end.

"Guess I'll just swim in my pants for now," Will said.

Sonberg reached into his backpack and produced a pair of UDT shorts—the kind that had for years been standard issue for the "frogmen" of what were the old underwater demolition teams—hence the name UDT shorts. Now they were basic issue for Navy divers, Navy SEALS, and Navy EOD techs.

"I don't want to take your shorts," Will said.

"Don't worry about it," he said. "These are spares," he added, handing Will the shorts.

"Besides," he continued, "I think we're about to head back to the *Enterprise* pretty soon anyway, I've got more on board."

"Oh, I didn't know you guys were leaving," Will said.

"Yeah, we were only supposed to be here 'til your team got here anyway," he said. "I think you guys can handle it from here," he added, smiling.

He was only kidding of course, but there was something to the sense of superiority Navy EOD techs projected over the other branches. They all went to the same school of course, but the Navy students—being second-class divers—went on to a very exhaustive block of training in underwater ordnance the other branches didn't receive. Adding to their superior air was the fact most of the mobile units to which Navy techs were assigned were also airborne designated—many providing support to SEAL teams—so in addition to being divers, they were also jumpers.

Ignoring their cockiness, Will respected the Navy EOD mission. He went through most of EOD school at Indian Head in a Navy class—parting ways when they reached the underwater ordnance phase—so he was accustomed to the extra degree of cockiness that was part of the Navy EOD community.

The blast at Camp Ojhri disrupted some important work the Navy team was doing in the Persian Gulf, and they were eager to return to it. Their dispatch to Pakistan was never intended to last more than a few days. They were a quick response force to stand in the gap until longer term reinforcements arrived; that was the Army team. The Navy team performed splendidly and would soon return to their home away from home aboard the USS *Enterprise*.

As they were preparing to leave the demo range, Jeb approached Hutchinson.

"I don't want to see you in those shorts after today," Jeb instructed with a sharp tone.

"Bulls**t," Hutchinson replied. "It's hot as a mother—"

"Get on the bus, Sergeant—now!" Jeb interjected before the expletive could leave Hutchinson's lips. He motioned to one of the two white vans that brought them out to the range.

Hutchinson complied and Jeb quickly followed him onto the van.

"You can't work around these people in shorts like that, Sergeant," Jeb explained. "They're very conservative and that's highly offensive."

"Well s**t, it's a hundred and hell out here," Hutchinson said.

"I don't give a s**t how hot it is, soldier," Jeb said, his temper flaring. "Your d**k is practically hanging out for *****'s sake!"

Hutchinson looked down and immediately turned red when he realized how exposed he was. He wasn't endowed with a keen sense of self-awareness, but he was well-endowed in other ways. In his haste, he cut his pants way too short, inadvertently exposing himself. Making matters worse, he opted to go "commando" that day due to the heat.

"Well, hell," Hutchinson said. "I guess I did cut 'em a little close."

"A little? It's a wonder you didn't severely injure yourself."

"Well, I guess I'll just swim in these then," Hutchinson conceded.

"You misunderstand me, Sergeant," Jeb said. "I don't want to see you in those shorts at all the rest of the time you're here—understood?"

"Roger that," Hutchinson replied, curtly.

Jeb was particularly attuned to the culture of the people in this part of the world, and his concern for their sensibilities on matters of apparel were well informed. He was sensitive enough though, to order Hutchinson into the van before laying into him about the inappropriateness of his new shorts to spare him any further embarrassment in front of the Pak soldiers. The confrontation—although quite stern—was necessary and discreet.

Hutchinson took the legs of the pants he had just converted into shorts, pulled them back over his legs, and began using his roll of electrical tape to reattach the legs of the pants. He was mostly doing it to try to get a rise out of Jeb, but Jeb viewed it as less of a stunt, and more of a prudent move.

The result was a mess. Hutchinson in his taped-together jeans looked ridiculous but it served as a visual reminder of how not to cut the legs off your pants.

Will was beginning to have second thoughts about wearing the UDT shorts Senior Chief Sonberg gave him since they were short as well, but he hadn't even tried them on yet, so he chose to wait until he got back to the embassy before making that decision. At the very least he could swim in them, which he was eagerly looking forward to as the temperature soared to over a hundred degrees.

On the ride back to the embassy, Hutchinson began to stew about the confrontation with Jeb. He wasn't exactly sure who Jeb was or who he worked for and bristled at being spoken to so sternly.

"Who the f*** is this Jeb anyway?" he questioned aloud. "He sure thinks he's in charge, don't he?"

"That's because he *is* in charge, dumbass," Morgan replied. "He's Special Forces, Sergeant Major says he's a colonel."

"Well s**t, why didn't he say so from the get-go," Hutchinson asked. "That might have been good to know."

"I'm not sure we're supposed to know," Morgan said. "Sergeant Major said he found out from the captain, but we're supposed to ignore that and just keep referring to him as 'Jeb.'"

"Well, he damn sure doesn't look Special Forces," Hutchinson said.

"What are Special Forces supposed to look like?" Will inquired.

"Well hell, I don't know—not like that I guess," Hutchinson responded. "Every Green Beret I ever saw was pretty damn STRAC" he said—using the common acronym meaning "strategic, tough, and ready around the clock"—"And a lot bigger than this dude."

"Well, I'm sure they are pretty STRAC on the garrison," Will replied. "But I always thought they were supposed to blend in when they were on a mission."

On that score, Jeb succeeded masterfully. He certainly blended in and would be hard to pick out in a crowd of Pakistanis on the street in Islamabad.

"Ahh, what do you know about it?" Hutchinson said.

That was a valid point. Will had never been around any SF soldiers before, so any idea of how they appeared or operated was influenced by Rambo movies. However, he had to acknowledge this Green Beret was making quite an impression.

"Whatever he is," Thiessen chimed in, "he's got some balls on him. I thought that Pak general's head was gonna explode when he got on his ass this morning."

"Yeah, I'd say he hasn't been spoken to like that before," Morgan said, chuckling. "But he had it coming."

"Hell, yeah he did," Campbell agreed. "Jeb cares more about these Pak soldiers than that bearded mother f***er does."

Everyone agreed.

CHAPTER ELEVEN

Arriving back at the embassy the team was greeted by a staffer who everyone assumed was with the State Department. Her job was to show the visiting team around and familiarize them with the amenities the embassy had to offer.

"Hi guys, I'm Tara." She raised her hand slightly with a welcoming wave. "I work in the Office of Protocol here at the embassy. General Wassom asked me to show y'all around a little."

Will wasn't paying much attention to what she was saying because her appearance proved a major distraction. So much so he scarcely recalled anything about the orientation she gave. She was quite attractive and appeared to be in her mid-twenties. She was tall with long sandy-blond hair. She spoke with a slight Southern lilt, which was music to Will's ears. As it turned out, she hailed from Johnson City, Tennessee—a tidbit of information Hutchinson extracted in his banter with her. He had no shame and, married or not, could not be prevented from flirting with any female he deemed attractive—as Tara certainly was.

"Well, hell," Hutchinson said, in his usual boisterous tone. "Another Tennessean, please tell me you're a Vols fan."

"Well, I was raised to be a Tennessee fan," she said, "but I went to Vanderbilt."

"Aw hell, sweetie," Hutchinson said. "You're breaking my heart."

"Yeah, my daddy says the same thing," Tara replied as she walked them to the next stop.

The tour moved to the cafeteria, which would have been fortuitous had it not been for the obvious fact the cafeteria stopped serving lunch at 2:00 p.m. and the dining room didn't open until 6:00.

Tara was unaware they hadn't eaten any lunch, so when she found out—the result of Hutchinson's complaining—she escorted them over to the commissary where they could pick up a snack until the dining room opened.

"Sorry about that, guys," she said. "This probably would have been the best place to start," she added with an apologetic smile.

"Do we have time to grab a quick snack?" the sergeant major asked.

"Oh, of course," Tara replied. "Take your time, I'm in no hurry at all."

The whole team filed by, and Will was the last in line, which he planned, hoping he might have the opportunity to introduce himself.

"Tennessee, huh?" Will said with a smile.

"That's right," she said, smiling broadly right back. "How 'bout you? Where are you from?"

"Well, all over, I guess," he replied. "I'm a military brat but I have an aunt who lives in Memphis if that counts for anything," Will added in the hopes it would prolong the conversation as much as anything.

"Well of course it does," she said. "We're practically neighbors," she added with a slight giggle. Of course, Memphis and her hometown were some five hundred miles apart so the notion they were neighbors was ridiculous, and they both knew it. Besides, Will only visited Memphis on a few occasions and had little that could be considered any real connection to the state. Still, she seemed to be enjoying the brief interlude and Will certainly was. That is, until Morgan interrupted.

"Hustle up, Carter," Morgan said, approaching from the door of the commissary. "They're getting ready to close."

"Oh crap," Will said. "Oops, sorry about that," He added sheepishly after the inadvertent slip.

Tara laughed. "I hear much worse than that around this place."

"I guess I better get in there before they close on me."

"Sure, I'll just wait right here."

They finished their commissary transactions and proceeded outside to continue the tour. Again, Will brought up the rear so as not to appear too anxious. He also didn't want Tara to see him devour the Reese's peanut butter cups and Pringles. He was always a fast eater, so they were both quickly consumed. Tara walked them by some clay tennis courts, and what she called a baseball field. It was a softball field, but they were surprised to find one in Pakistan. It looked well kept.

They continued and walked by the lab they knew about. Tara pointed it out referring to it simply as "the Lab," but didn't elaborate on what "the Lab" did.

Finally, they arrived at the swimming pool. It was a nice pool, the kind you might see at an American country club. It was big enough so you wouldn't feel crowded. There were a few people lounging beside it, which made it appear even more inviting, the idea of laying around the pool with nothing else to do was appealing.

Just then, something else caught their eyes. "Guys, check that out," Will said. Just beyond the fenced area of the pool there was a volleyball net set up. Volleyball was mandatory in the EOD community. As a child Will sat and watched the guys in his dad's EOD unit play volleyball. They played almost daily at EOD school. And of course, every EOD unit Will knew of had their own volleyball court.

"Nice," Wiley said.

"Game on," said Thiessen.

As hot and tired as they all were, they were still up for some volleyball.

"Um, ma'am," Will said, directing an inquiry to Tara. "Do you know where we might get our hands on a volleyball?"

"It's Tara," she replied, "but you know that, Sergeant," she added with a smile. "And yes, the Marines have one. I'm surprised they're not out here," she continued. "There's usually a few out here playing this time of day."

"All right!" Hutchinson exclaimed. "Just what I wanted to do, spank me some jarheads in volleyball."

"I wouldn't be so sure," Tara said. "They're pretty good—they play a lot."

Will was still trying to figure out how Tara knew he was a sergeant. He hadn't introduced himself as a sergeant. Come to think of it, he hadn't really introduced himself at all. *Maybe it was just a guess*, Will thought. *Or maybe she saw a roster or something with their names and ranks. Or maybe she asked someone*. Will wouldn't worry about it for now. He took it as encouragement though, and just decided to continue the conversation. He liked how this day was shaping up.

"Well, *Tara*," Will said, being particularly careful to enunciate her name for effect. "Uh, we play a lot of volleyball ourselves, and it's Will, by the way," he continued as the team listened on and began to chuckle. "Maybe the Marines might like a match at some point?"

"Oh, I'm sure they would," she said. "They're pretty proud of their volleyball skills. I'll ask them if they're up for it."

"Oh yeah, bring 'em on," Hutchinson said. "Bring 'em on!"

"I tell you what, Tara, we're going to take a swim—cool off a little, ya know, hang by the pool," Will said. "And if the Marines are up for it, we'll be ready anytime."

"Well, okay *Will*," she replied, with a particular emphasis on his name. "If I run into any Marines, I'll let them know y'all are just 'hanging by the pool,'" she added, gesturing air quotes as she said it. "And that you're up for a little volleyball. How would that be?"

"Well, that sounds just right," Will replied.

Will knew he was coming off a little cocky, but her tone indicated she was enjoying the playful back-and-forth as much as he was. He was less concerned about the Marines showing up and more concerned about getting a chance to interact with Tara again.

"I'll leave you gentlemen to it. And I'm sure I'll be seeing you around," she said, looking at Will flashing a big smile.

After she walked away, the team set in.

"Nice work, Carter," Morgan said. "I'm proud of you."

The sergeant major shot Carter a foreboding look over the top of his glasses. "Easy, son," he said. "You keep that mule in the barn," he warned.

"Well hell, Sergeant Major," Hutchinson said. "I doubt his little mule has ever even been out of the barn before anyway—it won't know what it's missing."

The whole team, even the captain, got a big kick out of that one. Will had to admit, Hutchinson was quick with the jokes, but it was always better to laugh with him. So he joined in the laughter too.

"Don't you worry about young Will here, Sergeant Major," Morgan said. "He's a good boy. Isn't that right, Will?"

"Oh, well of course," he replied, playing along.

"Not that good. I heard all about that fat redhead he hooked up with back at Indian Head," Thiessen added with a wry laugh.

Of course, it was a pure fabrication, but Will knew better than to protest and add credence to the joke. So he just chuckled along with everybody else.

"What about it, Carter?" Campbell asked. "You ain't sayin' much."

"Well, I learned a long time ago," Will said. "Admit nothing, deny everything, and make counter accusations." And with that, he made his way to the men's locker room to don his newly acquired UDT shorts for a relaxing swim.

"Words to live by," said the captain, chuckling.

CHAPTER TWELVE

The others followed along and began to make alterations to the pants they were wearing. All except Hutchinson. He took Jeb's warning to heart about never wearing those shorts again. He didn't bother removing the legs of his jeans he taped back together. Instead, he just removed his shirt, boots, and socks and dove into the pool with the hopes his tape job would hold. It held, for now. Hutchinson swam down to the shallow end of the pool and shot upward out of the water like a breaching whale.

"Woooo-eeee!" Hutchinson yelled. "Man, this water does feel good!"

The rest of the team emerged from the locker room and dove in. Will and the Navy guys were all wearing UDT shorts. His Army teammates were all sporting modest-length field expedient swim trunks so as not to incur Jeb's wrath.

They swam for a bit and most of them were content to loll about in the shallow water. Tony Wyndham, however, began doing "crossovers"—swimming from one end of the pool to the other and back on a single breath. This would have been accomplishment enough from anyone else, but Tony was short-legged and a little on the paunchy side, making the feat seem that much more impressive. He didn't have the long and lean build most people would associate with swimmers, but Wyndham had been a Navy diver for a while and was obviously quite capable.

Wyndham surfaced about halfway through his third trip down. He seemed barely out of breath and was content to float around having what he considered sufficient exercise for the day.

He timed it exactly right. They saw three Marines walking toward the volleyball net, one with a ball under his arm. The Marines were not in uniform—they were wearing gym shorts and T-shirts—but their high and tights gave them away. If that wasn't enough, they all wore some variations of red and yellow—the signature colors of Marine Corps physical training gear.

"Look," Thiessen said. "The Marines have landed."

"Let's go, boys," Hutchinson said, anxious to hit the court. "It's game time."

They all got out of the pool and headed for the court.

The court was sand, so they were about to get filthy—a sacrifice they were all ready and willing to make for the sake of a good game.

As they approached the court, one Marine spoke. "We hear you guys might like to play a little v-ball." The Marine in question was Sergeant David Brown—a tall, wiry kid.

"Well, hell yes," Hutchinson replied with a smile. "What took you so long?"

"Well, we wanted to give you guys plenty of time to rest up first," Brown said with a chuckle. "You're gonna need it."

His fellow Marines got a chuckle out of that too. One of them was a Corporal Ruiz. The other was another sergeant, Chris Shelton. He was a big guy and obviously spent considerable time in the gym. All three of them seemed amused at the prospect of taking on what they considered to be an interloping team of volleyball upstarts.

"Oh, I think we're plenty rested," Will told them. "Ready when you are."

"Jungle rules," Hutchinson informed them.

"Jungle rules?" Shelton asked. "What's 'jungle rules'?"

"That's where you try not to get hurt," Hutchinson said with a big grin. "We get pretty physical."

"We like physical," Shelton said.

The captain and the sergeant major were watching all this unfold. Neither of them had any intention of joining in the fun, opting instead to watch from the sidelines. However, they did express some concern about the possibility of injury.

"Hutchinson's gonna f*** around and get somebody hurt or maybe himself," the sergeant major said to the captain. "I guess I better rein him in a little."

Hutchinson was a big guy and could be a little aggressive when it came to volleyball. He was pumped and ready for action.

"Well, that one Marine's almost as big as Hutchinson," the captain replied. "That looks like a pretty even matchup."

"That's what concerns me, sir," Scott said. "I could see those two tying up out there."

He yelled for Hutchinson and waved him over. Hutchinson trotted over to the sergeant major seated on the second row of a little set of bleachers beside the sand volleyball court. It was clear volleyball drew a crowd at the embassy.

"What's up, Sergeant Major?" Hutchinson asked.

"Take it easy out there, Hutchinson," Scott instructed discreetly. "We don't need you starting any s**t, getting anybody hurt or anything."

"Hell, Sergeant Major—you know me," Hutchinson said. "This is gonna be a nice, friendly game," he added with grin.

"Yes, I DO know you. That's why I mentioned it."

"Got it, got it," Hutchinson said, anxious to get the game started.

"HEY, I'm serious," the sergeant major said. "We're here to do a job, and we can't afford someone getting injured—particularly in a volleyball game."

"Do you copy?" Scott asked.

"Roger that, Sergeant Major," Hutchinson replied. "Lima Charlie," he added, indicating he understood the sergeant major's instruction "loud and clear."

"Will you and the captain be playing?" Hutchinson asked.

"I'm too old for that s**t," the captain said. "I'll leave the volleyball to you guys."

The captain actually loved volleyball as much as any other EOD guy and would have enjoyed playing, but he recognized the need to keep some distance between himself and the team. He knew the embassy staff would be watching and decided it would be prudent to refrain from the type of activity typically associated with the enlisted ranks.

"What about you, Sergeant Major?" Hutchinson asked.

"Hell no," he replied. "Just get out there." He too liked a good volleyball game as much as the next guy but thought it would be wise to follow the captain's lead and remain a spectator.

While Hutchinson and the sergeant major were engaged in their little confab, three more Marines arrived.

"I guess we'll go six on six," Will said. "Who's in?" he asked, inquiring about their starting lineup.

Wyndham was still floating around the pool, and Lieutenant Johnson and the senior chief took seats on the bleachers and were talking to the captain and the sergeant major.

"The squids ain't playin'," Campbell said. "It's an all-Army team today."

"Good enough for me," Hutchinson said.

As the Marines huddled up for some last-minute strategizing, the Army players fanned out and took their positions. Hutchinson took his post up front on the left side ensuring he would have as much time at the net as possible as they rotated positions. Campbell was in the middle with Wiley on the right. It made for a very uneven front line as Wiley was almost as tall as Hutchinson, and Campbell was a lot shorter than both of them. Morgan, Thiessen, and Will took the back.

"Visitors serve," Brown said, rolling the ball under the net. Campbell picked it up and tossed it to Will since he was positioned in the back on the right, and would be first to serve.

"Serve it up, Carter," he said.

Will picked up the ball, bounced it a time or two and asked, "Everybody ready?" There was a chorus of affirmative responses from both sides of the net, and he bounced the ball a few more times to build the anticipation.

"You gonna play with yourself all day or what?" Shelton asked, "Serve it up—s**t!"

"You sure you're ready?" Will asked sarcastically.

"Hell yes," responded one of the Marines in the back. "Serve it up!"

With one more bounce, Will pronounced, "Service!" He delivered a hard overhand jump serve that cleared the net by about an inch, landing on the other side of the court, untouched by any of the Marines. They were caught flat-footed, not expecting the overhand jump delivery. One Marine in the back made a diving effort at the ball but came up short.

"Alright, alright," Brown said. "I see how it is now," he added. "Don't expect to get away with that s**t again."

Will didn't. He knew that might have been his one chance at an ace, so he took it early. He would have to be much more careful in the future. He was the only one on the team who employed the jump serve. Everyone else was content to just put the ball in play—underhand from some—and take it from there. Will was more aggressive on serves. There were pitfalls with that approach though. When it worked right, as it just did, the jump serve was a thing of beauty. But it could just as often go bad, blocked at the net or sailing out of bounds with the opposing team choosing to lay off. When that happened, not only did they lose their serve, but Will would also suffer the scorn of his teammates, who frowned upon the jump serve and would take every opportunity to point out his failure.

That first serve set the tone though, and Will was able to help take the Army out to a three to zero lead early on before the back and forth ensued. The first game lasted about twenty minutes with multiple lead changes and just as many good-natured barbs traded between the Army and the Marines. It was all wholesome fun. About midway through the second game, the bleachers began to fill. It was after quitting time, and word of the match spread. Embassy staff filed out to watch. This was a bit of a novelty for them. They saw the Marines play regularly, but this new team was elevating the level of play and it was worth watching.

The Marines took the second game in a hard-fought effort. That meant they would need to play a rubber game to settle this match. The bleachers—though not big—were nearly full, adding to the excitement. Much to Will's delight, Tara was among the spectators. They played game three to near darkness, finishing in twilight with a victory for the Army EOD team. The onlooking crowd, though clearly aligned with their Marine guards, were very appreciative of the Army team's efforts and paid them off with a rousing ovation. In a show of great sportsmanship, the Marines went over to the other side of the net and offered up congratulatory high fives.

"Let's do this again," David Brown said to Will.

"Count on it," Will replied, sealing the pact with a handshake.

They were all famished by this time, so they cleaned up and headed to the dining room.

The dining room was like any nice restaurant you might find in any American town. There was a maître d', starched white tablecloths, candles, and a piano bar. Will sat at a table with Thiessen and Morgan, making conversation—mostly rehashing the volleyball match with the Marines. There were couples seated here and there, with a family or two interspersed among the diners. As he sat there awaiting dinner, it struck Will how odd it was to be in this benign setting, when just outside the comparative safety of the embassy walls, there was a hard, dangerous world with a war going on less than 200 miles from where they were seated. Odder still was the random way in which their team became part of it, if only on the periphery. *Life is like a river* Will thought, *never knowing what's around the next bend.*

CHAPTER THIRTEEN

CAMP OHJRI
RAWALPINDI, PAKISTAN
APRIL 14, 1988
0730 HRS.

Jeb didn't feel comfortable going back into the garrison until the Pak soldiers were adequately equipped, so the next day was spent running incidents around town. The number of calls decreased, but so did the number of teammates. Half the Army team fell victim to the Islamabad water and were holed up in their hotel rooms fighting off what they assumed was dysentery. The healthy Army team members met the Navy team at the north gate of the garrison. Carter paired up with SFC Morgan while Tom Thiessen worked with the captain. Each team departed the garrison in the company of their Pak Army guides and proceeded to work.

The torrid heat continued unabated refusing to offer even the slightest breeze to help cool the busy teams. They encountered a variety of UXO with a number of white phosphorus rockets continuing to turn up. Whoever procured this shipment of munitions clearly had a penchant for "Willy Pete." The good news was, they encountered no smoking WP rounds and only two items among the other ordnance were fuzed requiring that they be blown in place. All told, the three teams finished an active day completing a collective thirty incidents around the perimeter of the garrison and beyond. The UXO was transported to the demolition range for destruction and the day was complete.

ISLAMABAD, PAKISTAN
APRIL 15, 1988
0530 HRS.

Will rose the next morning and went through what became routine. He met the team down in the hotel lobby as he did the day before. On this morning an embassy driver met them, who directed them to the vans outside. They were driven straight to the embassy where they met Jeb. He walked the team down to the cafeteria for breakfast. It was Friday morning, and they were prepared for another busy day. As it turned out, Friday was the Muslim day of worship, and out of respect for the host nation, the embassy also observed Friday as the day of worship. The team would have the day off. Jeb's frustration was building, but he held it in check. He would have gladly continued working on Friday as he would any other day but he did not want to press his Pak counterparts.

So they spent the day lounging around the embassy intermittently playing volleyball and swimming. The best part of the day came late in the morning. Tara appeared at the pool. It was her day off too and what better way to spend it than poolside? Of course, there were other embassy personnel present—even a few families with small children—but all heads turned when Tara arrived. She was tall and striking, and impossible to ignore, particularly for a young Army sergeant like Will Carter.

"Good morning, gentlemen," she said cheerfully, as she walked past them on her way to a vacant chaise lounge at one end of the pool.

Will and Tara's eyes met briefly as she passed, and he made a conscious effort not to look like a lovesick puppy. She was wearing a flowered cover-up of some kind over her swimsuit, and she carried a big white towel in one hand and a boom box in the other. When she arrived at her chaise lounge, she placed the towel and the cassette player on the chaise, stepped out of her flip flops and let the flowered cover-up slip from her shoulders revealing a modest one-piece swimsuit. She was beautiful. She walked over to the pool, delicately touched her toes to the water, then stepped back and dove in. She disappeared briefly and rose in the shallow end of the pool. She emerged from the water with her head back allowing her long hair to fall down the back of her neck.

Had it not been for Campbell, I'm sure she would have caught Will standing there with his mouth wide open as she surfaced. He noticed Will was absently gawking at her. He was in the shallow end of the pool, and Chad was standing close to him.

"Dude—dude," he said, trying to discreetly get Will's attention. "Be cool, man."

"Oh—uh, yeah, yeah," Will said. In that moment, he was thankful it was Campbell, not Hutchinson, who noticed he was gazing at the young beauty. Hutchinson would have been merciless in his teasing.

"Hey, guys," Tara said as she swam over and seated herself on the edge of the pool next to Will. "Enjoying your day off?"

"Oh yeah," Will replied. "I sure didn't expect anything like this when they told me I was going to Pakistan."

"Expect what?" she asked.

"Um, well, uh," he stammered feebly. Will began to feel his face get hot. He knew he was blushing, which always came easy for him, particularly in the company of pretty girls, like the one sitting next to him. It was a perfectly innocent question. What was he expecting? Tara sat there with a patient smile as Will tried to collect his thoughts and form a complete sentence. She seemed perfectly at ease and in no hurry for him to answer.

"I guess I didn't expect to be relaxing in a pool right about now," Will said, trying to appear cool. "Especially with someone like you."

Yesterday's witty repartee came much easier for some reason as she showed the team around the embassy. Now, it was just Will and Tara, and he was at a loss for words. In the meantime, Campbell quietly swam away, leaving the two to talk.

"Someone like me?" Tara asked

"I have to say, you're pretty easy on the eyes," Will said.

"Well, I could say the same about you too," she replied with a smile.

The two fell into conversation, and Will began to learn a lot about Tara, mostly about her family back in Tennessee. She was the oldest of three sisters. The youngest was a junior in high school back in Johnson City, and her middle sister was finishing her sophomore year at the University of Tennessee. Tara's parents were teachers back home, and both coached basketball. Tara played basketball in high school too, she was certainly tall enough. Will estimated her height at about five feet ten since she stood almost eye to eye with him while she was wearing flats. She always thought she'd end up teaching school, like her parents, but she stumbled onto a different path.

She attended Vanderbilt on an academic scholarship, the result of high achievement in high school; she graduated as the salutatorian. That was very intimidating to Will having not attended college yet. She majored in political science and only went into the foreign service by accident. She attended a career fair at Vanderbilt where she met a recruiter from the State Department. The idea of serving overseas appealed to her. No one in her family spent much time overseas, except for her grandfather who served in the Army in WWII and of course her dad, who was a Marine in Vietnam.

It was the State Department brochure at the career fair that caught her attention. Inside the brochure there was a photo of an embassy—she couldn't recall which one—showing a Marine standing guard. The Marine in the picture made her think of her dad. It reminded her of a photo on the wall in the hallway near her mom and dad's bedroom. It was a picture of her dad in his dress blue uniform. That photo was there in the hallway for as long as she could remember. She was standing there in front of a little kiosk at the career fair, lost in her memories of home prompted by a photo on a brochure, when the State Department recruiter approached her. "And that," she explained to me, "is how I got started at State."

Tara had an affinity for the Marines. Not in the way a groupie has an affinity for a rock star. Hers was a reverence. She held them in high esteem. It was a feeling she had because of her father's service. It was curious she felt so connected to the Marines. Her father rarely, if ever, spoke of his time in Vietnam. All she really knew about his time as a Marine was based on that photo in the hallway. But that State Department brochure triggered something deep down inside of her that brought out the profound respect she now had for the Marines.

For their part, the Marines in the embassy viewed her like a sister. Beautiful as she was, none of them ever made an untoward advance. She was not an object of their affection in any romantic sense. Rather, they were very protective of her.

As they talked, it became clear Will was hungry. His stomach growled audibly.

"Excuse me," he said apologetically. "I'm so sorry."

Will was highly embarrassed, but Tara just giggled and said, "I'm hungry too, let's get some lunch."

They went to the cafeteria. Will found the food at the embassy satisfying, but there was something lacking. He noticed they had pizza on the menu, but no meat toppings. Tara explained why. Because it was a Muslim country, they did their best to follow the local customs; particularly where meat and pork was concerned. But she added, they offered things like ham sandwiches, that weren't on the menu—you had to ask for them. Complicating the request even further was how few of the Muslim cafeteria staff would handle pork products. There were only two non-Muslims in the kitchen. They were both Catholic, although they were Pakistani, and since it wasn't Sunday, both were on hand to make a ham sandwich. There was an extra charge added to pork products too. Given the hassle and added cost, there weren't a lot of requests made for them.

It seemed easier to stick with the basics at lunchtime, so Tara and Will continued their conversation over cheeseburgers and fries. The more he learned about her, the more intimidating Will found her. After joining the State Department, Tara spent a year in DC learning Russian. She was highly intelligent, but she was equally charming and nothing about her suggested pretentiousness. She was warm and friendly, and Will found they had more in common than he would have thought given her education, experience, and position. She was a small-town girl and hadn't forgotten it.

She confided in Will that one of her guilty pleasures was country music, a vice they both shared. She received a cassette tape from her little sister back in Johnson City every couple of weeks or so. Her sister recorded two or three hours of a local country radio station back home—commercials and all—and then sent the tapes to Tara. She loved to play them by the pool on her days off. It helped her keep up with the latest country music, and the DJs and commercials reminded her of everything going on at home. She played the tapes on a boom box and, surprisingly, no one objected. It was like listening to any radio station back home and had a comforting effect on listeners around the pool.

They made their way back to the pool and, sure enough, Tara played her radio tape. The first song was "Always Late" by Dwight Yoakam. They enjoyed the music, the ads, and even the news, although it wasn't current news any longer.

Before too long, the team—half of whom had just recovered from bouts with diarrhea was hollering for Will to get over to the volleyball court. Despite their recent infirmity, they couldn't be dissuaded from more volleyball. Will made his way over and Tara came along. She took a seat on the bleachers, and Will removed his shirt, folded it neatly, and laid it carefully on a bush next to the bleachers.

"Kind of a neat freak, aren't you," she said, smiling.

"Well, I wouldn't go that far," he replied. He did like things to be orderly. But the truth was simpler: he didn't have a lot of clothes and was concerned about when he'd get a chance to do his laundry. He was also starting to become a little self-conscious about how poorly dressed he appeared compared to the embassy staff. Will was doing the best he could with what he had, but he began to worry about the impression he was making on Tara with his limited wardrobe. She didn't seem the least bit bothered by it though, so Will tried to forget about it and just enjoy her pleasant company.

As they were wrapping up an active day of swimming and volleyball, Jeb reappeared and gathered the team for another briefing. It looked like he never took any time off. They assembled in the conference room where they received their first briefing. Notably absent was the Navy team who flew out before dawn on a C-2 bound for the USS *Enterprise*. The Army team, now alone, had to complete the operation. The captain and the sergeant major seemed anxious to get back to work.

"Our flak vests and helmets just arrived," Jeb informed us. "We're going back into the garrison tomorrow," he continued, "and we're going to get after it."

"We'll get these Pak soldiers better equipped," he added, "and we'll be able to move a little quicker and safer."

CHAPTER FOURTEEN

Jeb gave the team the time off, and he showed no sign of regret for the decision, or resentment toward them. He felt they needed it. Yet, he was sure White Beard was not taking any days off. Even though he hadn't received any reports from his Pak assets at the garrison, Jeb knew White Beard would have been poking around and more. He began to suspect the Stingers—and maybe other items—were removed from this shipment, and the remaining ordnance deliberately sabotaged. Jeb didn't believe there was intent, necessarily, to inflict extensive damage on the metropolitan area. More than likely, it was a poorly executed sabotage plan. Whoever was responsible obviously miscalculated the amount of ordnance and the poor storage, which set off the chain reaction leading to the carnage on Camp Ojhri and the surrounding twin cities.

While Jeb knew it was essential that they get back to work as soon as possible, he had no intention of making the operation any more hazardous than it was by unnecessarily pushing the team. Captain Halstead was relieved to hear the flak vests arrived. He never verbalized it—at least not within earshot of any junior team members—but he was bothered by the poor way White Beard used the Pak soldiers from the time they first stepped onto Camp Ojhri. The captain's primary responsibility was his own team, but he would do what he could to make things as safe as possible for everyone involved. He was encouraged by the willingness of both Jeb and General Wassom to supply flak vests and helmets to the Paks. Now that they were being better equipped, he felt confident they could move forward with the garrison plan.

Jeb resigned himself to the cold hard truth that he would not be recovering any Stingers. From this point, Jeb was on a fact-finding mission. He would work closely with his team, assisting in every way possible. The mission before them was the primary impediment to Jeb's ability to reconcile the facts surrounding the events leading to the Camp Ojhri blast.

Astute in his observations, Jeb was cautious by nature when it came to drawing conclusions. There were certain things he knew though. First, Stinger missiles were a highly valuable commodity on the global arms market. Second, a man with the contacts like White Beard had, could do well for himself with such a supply. And third, White Beard was not to be trusted. There was considerable evidence to Jeb's mind suggesting White Beard was a suspect. Yet, he couldn't rule out the Soviets or even the Iranians, who were engaged in a lengthy war with Iraq and could benefit from Stinger missiles too.

Over the last few years, many more Iranians made their way into Pakistan. The reasons why weren't entirely clear, but Jeb knew they were not there for innocuous reasons. The more he thought about it, the more he came to believe White Beard, while central to the plot, if there was one, was not acting alone. Perhaps he was serving as a facilitator for one, or even more, other parties. The Soviets would surely have an interest in preventing the Stingers from reaching their destination in Afghanistan; the missiles were a game changer in the hands of the anti-Soviet Mujahideen. But the Soviets, anti-capitalist as they purported to be, were not above dabbling in the arms trade if it presented a profit-taking opportunity. After all, their decade-long siege of the Afghan countryside was proving to be a drain on their finances, such as they were. Circumstances forced Jeb to keep an open mind regarding the guilty party or parties.

The next day found the team at the main gate of Camp Ojhri just after sunup. The days had begun to be extremely hot, and both Jeb and the captain expressed concern about working in such heat. Less concern about the ability of the Americans to endure the harsh conditions and more concern about the known volatility of the UXO in the elevated temperatures. The fires were extinguished and the water turned off. The big hoses still crisscrossed the garrison and what remained was a muddy terrain. The hoses were pointing toward the stored ordnance. The closer they got to the middle of the garrison, the muddier the conditions became. Now that the water was shut off, the sun was baking the mud into hard dirt which presented yet another challenge—finding and removing the UXO.

The captain, the sergeant major, and Jeb realized the need to make an adjustment to their plan. First, their days would start earlier, and they would work for as long as they safely could into the morning before the heat presented a safety hazard. They would start their days at sunrise to maximize time on the garrison. The other adjustment was the suspension of render safe procedures inside the wire, except when necessary. Jeb asked his Pak counterparts to maintain the perimeter they cordoned off immediately following the blast. The team would blow in place any fuzed UXO they encountered—except for any 122mm rockets—remaining on the garrison.

Jeb informed the captain he believed he had sufficient intelligence on the ordnance contained in this shipment. There would be no need for any further technical exploitation, just destruction. For any UXO not already identified, a few Polaroids would be sufficient record before destroying it. Outside the 122mm rockets, the largest ordnance encountered was 82mm mortar rounds and the occasional recoilless rifle round. With no more than a quarter of an M112 block of C-4, they could be easily blown in place, which would allow them to stretch their supply. Sandbags could be used to minimize frag. The garrison was already in such sorry shape there was no real need to be concerned about property damage. The Pak Army brass considered Camp Ojhri a total loss. The only plan now was to clear the garrison and surrounding area of UXO.

With the Pak soldiers at least modestly equipped with some basic safety gear, the team could fan out and begin the UXO clearing operation on the garrison in earnest. There were a few, last-minute adjustments made to the plan. First, since there were still reports of UXO outside the garrison in and around the city, one team would be on call to run incidents outside the wire as needed. Second, since they would be engaged in demolitions of some of the UXO, they would confine operations to one quadrant of the garrison at a time as an added safety consideration, with the entire team working together.

Any fuzed ordnance the team collected would be marked for destruction in place. Any unfuzed ordnance collected would be stored for removal to the demolition range offsite for later destruction. Finally, the captain sent the sergeant major and Adams back to the embassy to address the administrative task of positively identifying the recovered ordnance and cataloging the collected data. The Polaroid photos were an integral part of the effort, and Scott was concerned they hadn't brought enough film to collect data on each item using a photograph. To conserve film, they took a photograph of the latest items found. Any time they recovered a like item, they recorded as much data as they could on that item—nomenclature, lot numbers, etc.—on paper. They kept a photo with the relevant paper log of that item, then submitted photos and data to Adams. Most of the team preferred the field work to the administrative tasks to which the sergeant major and Wiley were assigned, but they were enjoying much more favorable work conditions back at the embassy.

As they worked their way toward the center of the garrison, the team began to encounter far less fuzed ordnance. They did, however, start to see plentiful fuzes by themselves scattered about. This presented as much of a challenge as if the fuzes were attached to a piece of ordnance. A fuze contained a booster charge that would detonate the explosive content of the round to which it was attached. In fact, it was the fuze that was the most dangerous part of dealing with UXO. The booster material was much more sensitive than the explosive content inside the ordnance it was affixed to.

Mostly, they encountered basic fuzes. So far, they were all the point-detonating variety, meaning they were screwed into a fuze well at the nose of the projectile and would initiate a high order detonation when the round impacted its target. These types of fuzes were common on mortar rounds. Some point-detonating fuzes were quite simple. The impact of the round was sufficient to drive an internal pin into the booster thereby detonating the explosive contents of the round. Others were much more sophisticated in nature having intricate mechanisms activated in several ways. One way was called a mechanical time or mech time. Some mech time fuzes could be set almost like one would set an egg timer. For example, a mortarman could set a dial mechanism on the fuze to detonate at a specific distance traveled, or a specific time traveled, depending on the design. Some mech time fuzes were adjusted using a screwdriver-type tool to turn a set screw on the side of the fuze. Others were twisted to the desired setting. After the preset time or distance was achieved, a mechanism would release the firing pin allowing the fuze to function.

Another type of fuze encountered was called a proximity fuze, or variable time (VT). As the name implies, this type of fuze would function when it came within a certain proximity of its target. What made these fuzes so dangerous was the fact they could contain electronic sensors that detected its target relative to its own position. Back in school, EOD students often referred to these VT fuzes as "very touchy." They required careful handling. The best course of action was no handling at all. Just placing a charge next to a VT fuze was dangerous enough. Some fuzes of this variety could be so sensitive a sudden slight temperature change could be enough to activate them. For example, a fuze of this type sitting all day in direct sunlight, could detonate simply by having a shadow cast over it. These were the conditions the team found themselves in and so, the need to be abundantly careful.

Most of the fuzes recovered had their safety pins in place—that was the good news. The bad news was, in some cases, they were so damaged from the blast it was impossible to assess their condition. Even though the safeties were present, the blast could have been sufficient to have caused the mechanisms inside them to arm. This was particularly true with proximity fuzes. While the boosters in the fuzes the team was surrounded by were relatively small, they were sensitive and packed a punch. They could easily take off a hand. The safest option would be to blow them in place.

The next several days were spent beginning to cover every square foot of Camp Ojhri, scanning meticulously for UXO, marking fuzed ordnance for disposal on site and removing what could be safely handled for disposal off site. The team began to develop something of a rhythm amid all the devastation, but made it a point not to allow that rhythm to develop into tedium and complacency—perhaps the most dangerous things of all to an EOD tech.

The work at the garrison continued in much the same way as the team settled into the process. They removed the ordnance they could handle with minimal hazard and blew the remaining UXO in place. The interactions with the Pak soldiers became more friendly, despite the language barrier. The junior officers helped bridge that gap. They were almost all Western educated—primarily in the US and UK—and spoke English well, if not fluently. Working closely alongside each other, Will and Captain Abed developed a cordial rapport. Will learned he went to college at the University of Illinois and earned his baccalaureate degree in mechanical engineering. The Pak Army officer corps appeared to place a high value on engineering degrees.

Captain Abed became so casual with Will that he would chatter incessantly as they went about their work. He would address a variety of random topics he assumed Will would have an interest in. He talked a lot about his experiences back in Champaign, Illinois. He seemed to love American culture and his tone conveyed an almost wistfulness at having to leave it behind. He returned to Pakistan less than four years earlier, so his memories of Americana were still fresh. Such were his good-natured ramblings that Will became aware of the need to maintain a close attention to the task at hand.

"Do you like Stevie Wonder?" Abed asked Will absently one morning as they were sweeping for UXO. "I am particularly fond of 'Part Time Lover.'"

"Stop right there, Captain!" Will exclaimed.

He complied at once, turned, and looked at Will, his right foot still above the ground.

"There's a round about three feet in front of you, sir," Will said. "Just to your right, see it?"

"Yes, I see it," Abed replied as he turned to Will again with a painful expression.

It was an 82mm mortar round, but from Will's vantage point he couldn't make out whether it was fuzed, and if so, what condition it was in.

“Watch where you put your foot down, sir,” Will advised.

Captain Abed gingerly placed his right foot on the ground and breathed an audible sigh of relief.

The mortar round turned out to be unfuzed, and Will directed one of Captain Abed’s soldiers to remove it for later disposal off site.

“Thank you, Sergeant Will,” he said. “That was very observant.”

“Sure thing,” Will replied as respectfully as possible. “We have to be extra careful out here, sir.”

“Indeed,” Abed replied.

CHAPTER FIFTEEN

CAMP OHJRI
RAWALPINDI, PAKISTAN
APRIL 18, 1988—FIRST DAY OF RAMAZAN
1135 HRS.

A few days into the "garrison sweep," Tom Thiessen, Shane Hutchinson, and Will came upon a mosque near the center of the garrison. Captain Abed stayed behind in the safe area at the edge of the garrison that morning. "I will join you later," he told them. "I am awaiting instruction from Major Omar," he added with a foreboding tone. *Uh-oh*, Will thought to himself. *That can't be good.* Major Omar was the surly Pak officer they met on their first workday on the garrison.

"I will be along directly," Captain Abed added, as the team set off.

The mosque in question was near the epicenter of the blast and sustained considerable damage. As they approached the once ornate place of worship, they saw some heads visible through holes caused by the explosive blast. The crumbling edifice was barely recognizable as a mosque. As they carefully flanked what remained of the structure, three men inside began to yell frantically at them. They were clearly distressed and all three of them raised their hands as if they were surrendering to the Americans. The team stopped and Hutchinson motioned for the three men to come out. They refused to move but continued to wail. Their wailings were heard beyond the immediate area and in just a few moments a squad of Pak soldiers arrived on the scene. The soldiers were providing security to the garrison and were armed with AK-47s.

While they obviously spoke the same language, the appearance of the armed soldiers did little to deescalate the situation. In fact, the three men in the mosque began wailing even louder despite the efforts of the Pak soldiers. Adding to the confusion was the fact none of the soldiers spoke English.

"Hell, I don't know what to do," Hutchinson said. "They're scared s**tless."

"I expect so," Will said. "We've been blasting our way in all morning, and then these guys show up with guns pointed at 'em. I guess I'd be scared too."

"Wonder what they're doing in that mosque?" Thiessen pondered aloud.

"Prayin' dips**t," Shane replied without missing a beat.

The wailing of the three men continued unabated and the response of the security squad only added to the din of confusion. The soldiers did, however, succeed in persuading the three men to lower their hands, but they would not be moved from the mosque.

"We got s**t to do," Hutchinson said. "We can't wait around for these assholes to calm down." As they considered their next move, Captain Abed arrived. With all the noise, he walked up on them almost undetected.

"What seems to be the problem?" Captain Abed inquired.

"You tell me, sir, and we'll both know," Hutchinson said.

Abed didn't reply. He walked over to what looked like a ranking Pakistani soldier, issued a command in Urdu, and the soldiers quickly lowered their rifles in unison. He then turned to the three men in the mosque and began speaking to them in a quiet way as he approached them. The wailing stopped, and he engaged them in conversation. A few moments later, having successfully diffused the situation, Captain Abed returned to the team.

"What the hell, sir?" Hutchinson inquired curtly.

"These men are quite frightened," Abed said, stating the obvious.

"Clearly," Will said. "What are they doing in that mosque, sir—why won't they come out?"

"It appears they were in prayer when the blast took place," Abed explained. "They are afraid to come out of the mosque."

"It's a wonder it didn't kill them," Thiessen said. "It looks like someone dropped a bomb directly on it."

"That is the problem," Abed continued. "They believe Allah spared them and now they don't want to leave the refuge they believe he provided them."

"Well, having those AKs pointed at 'em didn't help any either," Hutchinson said.

"You are correct, Sergeant," Abed replied.

"Well sir," Will said. "We've still got quite bit of work ahead of us. What would you suggest we do?"

"For the time being, these men will not be moved," Abed replied. "They are not soldiers. They are peasants who work here on the garrison."

Hutchinson, Thiessen, and Will exchanged looks and raised eyebrows. They were all taken aback at Captain Abed's use of the word "peasant" to describe the three men.

"I am going to suggest we adjust our course and continue the sweep," Abed advised.

They were on a southwesterly course and adjusted to continue due south. As they prepared to move out, they caught sight of Captain Halstead, Morgan, and Chad Campbell approaching on their right flank.

"I think we'll just wait here for a minute or two, Captain, if that's alright with you," Hutchinson said. "Here comes the rest of our team."

"Certainly," Abed replied.

Captain Halstead was in high spirits on this morning. He was able to get a call in to his wife the night before and hearing from her always improved his mood. Not that he had been in an unusually bad mood, but none of the team were able to communicate with family back home since their arrival, and that was starting to affect the overall demeanor. General Wassom approached the captain after dinner the night before and instructed him the team would now be permitted to make a call back home—just one call—and embassy staff would help with the calls. They fanned out after dinner so Captain Halstead being the only member of team still around after the evening meal, availed himself of the opportunity and was able to speak to Renee for about ten minutes. He told the team that morning they could set up calls back home later in the afternoon, and this improved everybody's disposition.

"What's up?" Captain Halstead inquired as Hutchinson, Morgan, and Campbell approached. He paused briefly to take a drink from his canteen as Hutchinson began to relate the events of the last few minutes.

"Well sir," Hutchinson began. "We got a little situation here. See them fellas in that mosque over there. What's left of it anyway. Well, they ain't movin'."

"Somebody want to tell me what the hell is going on," Captain Halstead reiterated, with a look clearly indicating he was not satisfied with Hutchinson's feeble attempt at explaining the situation. Captain Halstead was beginning to show signs of irritation.

"It's like this, sir," Hutchinson began again, speaking loudly, before being interrupted.

"If I may, sir," Will interjected, "I'm sure Captain Abed here could fill you in on all the particulars."

Hutchinson's initial reaction to Will's interruption was to shoot him a hard look. He clearly didn't appreciate Will cutting him off like that. But before he could verbalize his displeasure, Captain Abed spoke up.

"Right you are, Sergeant," Abed said. "Captain, this is a most unfortunate circumstance."

He gave Captain Halstead a detailed outline of the situation.

"So let me see if I understand this," Captain Halstead said. "Those poor guys have been hunkered down in that mosque for, what, a week now?"

"That is correct, Captain," Abed replied.

"No food, no water?" the captain asked.

"Correct," said Abed. "There has been water close by due to the fire hoses," he explained. "Although it's not very clean water, and I fear it has made them sick."

"'Bout as clean as the water at our hotel," Hutchinson said under his breath.

"Shut it, Hutch," Morgan said quickly.

"Well, I don't know how they survived the blast, we're pretty close to ground zero," Captain Halstead said. "There's not much left of that mosque. But a week without food and clean water? That's a wonder, I guess God WAS looking out for them."

"Indeed, sir," Abed replied. "That is why they do not wish to leave the safety of the mosque."

"Well, they won't last much longer if they don't get some fresh water pretty quick," Captain Halstead said. "Will they drink after us?" he inquired.

"Come again?" Abed replied.

"Will they drink from our canteens?" Captain Halstead asked.

"Oh, I'm certain they will refuse," Abed replied.

"Hmm," Captain Halstead replied, clearly perplexed. "That's too bad. They really need to hydrate."

"They will refuse because Ramazan began at sunrise this morning," Captain Abed explained. "These men are strict adherents of Islam."

"Oh hell, that's right," Captain Halstead said, frustrated at his own oversight. "Pardon my language, Captain," he said.

Captain Abed nodded affirmatively, unperturbed.

"One moment, Captain," Captain Halstead said. He turned and stepped toward Morgan to confer privately. When he thought he was safely out of earshot of the Pak Captain, he spoke.

"I'm not going to beg these guys to drink," he began, "but s***t, they look like they're about to drop," he added. "Any suggestions?"

"Sir, I would venture that Captain Abed would have to order them to drink," Morgan said. "Worst thing they can say is no, though. Might as well ask."

"Well, they damn sure won't listen to me," Captain Halstead said. "This Abed fellow seems pretty agreeable by comparison. Let me see if I can appeal to his good nature."

Turning back to the others, Captain Halstead said, "Captain Abed, I wonder if I could prevail upon you to strongly urge these men to drink. They're very near dehydrated, and I'd feel a hell of a lot—pardon me—I'd feel a lot better about things if I knew they'd be willing to take water."

"I understand your concerns, Captain," Abed replied. "Your compassion is most admirable. I shall make the inquiry."

He walked over to the mosque and spoke briefly to the men. From where Will stood, some twenty yards away, he couldn't hear Captain Abed, but whatever he said was persuasive to the weary men. One man in the group looked respectfully at the captain, placed his hands together as if in prayer, and nodded affirmatively without saying a word. Will assumed him to be the leader among the three. He had red hair, which stood out in that part of the world. The other two men nodded in unison.

Captain Abed turned to us with a smile and raised his hand as a sign of success.

"Break out your canteens, boys," Captain Halstead said. "These guys are thirsty."

Morgan, Thiessen, and Will were the first to offer canteens to the thirst-stricken men. Each readily accepted the offer and began to drink voraciously.

The men began to guzzle the water and Captain Abed quickly ordered them to slow down. At least Will assumed that was his instruction as the men began to slow their drinking considerably after he spoke.

Standing close to them, it was clear these men were in terrible shape. Morgan and Will exchanged looks but said nothing. Morgan must have read Will's expression of concern. He approached Captain Halstead and discreetly said, "Sir, these guys need more than a drink of water."

"That's a fact," the captain said. "They're in tough shape."

"I wonder if anybody has bothered to call an ambulance," Morgan said. "They're going to need some IV fluids pretty quick."

"Let me get with this captain and see about that," Captain Halstead said.

He turned from Morgan and gestured to Captain Abed. "Captain, a word?" Captain Halstead asked.

"Of course, Captain," Abed replied. He was calm and affable throughout this episode and remained so with his American counterpart. He walked over to Captain Halstead and the two of them turned slightly and walked a few steps away to talk privately.

"Captain, these men are in dire need of medical attention," Captain Halstead began. "They need much more than a drink of water."

"Indeed, Captain," Abed replied. "I dispatched one of my soldiers earlier to summon an ambulance," he said. "It should arrive directly."

"Well, that's good news," Captain Halstead said. "I guess we'll just need to give them as much water as we can until it arrives."

"Very good, sir," Abed replied. As he responded to Captain Halstead, Captain Abed turned, and saw two vehicles moving slowly toward them. "Ah, that appears to be our ambulance."

The first vehicle was a Pak Army truck, the kind the team rode in with their assigned squads a few days earlier. Immediately following was a small white SUV. As the two vehicles drew closer, Will could make out that Jeb was driving the little white Suzuki.

They pulled up near the mosque, and Jeb got out of his vehicle. The driver of the big truck stayed in the cab and left the engine running. A small squad of Pak soldiers jumped out of the back of the truck moved toward the three men, who were drinking water and resting. The soldiers approached the three men in a menacing way, and the team was concerned it could re-ignite a situation they just ended. Sensing the potential for a setback, Captain Abed quickly intervened. He spoke firmly to the soldiers who backed off at once, then calmly addressed the three men. They were hesitant to move, but with Captain Abed's reassurance, the three acquiesced and reluctantly went with the soldiers to the truck. Severely dehydrated and exhausted, the men were close to delirium. They still needed help just getting into the back of the truck, but the water made them more reasonable, and they got in the truck without further incident.

"They are on their way to hospital," Captain Abed said.

"I was expecting an ambulance," Captain Halstead said. He wasn't convinced they would receive any medical attention.

"Of course, Captain," Abed said. "The traffic is so bad in the city it was more expeditious to transport these men by one of the trucks we have at our disposal."

"If you say so, Captain," Captain Halstead replied, still unconvinced. "I'm sure they'll be fine," he added, although he clearly had doubts what would happen to the three men.

Jeb watched the events unfold since his arrival but said nothing until the truck carrying the three men cleared the area.

He pulled Captain Halstead to one side. "What's the story?" Jeb asked.

Captain Halstead gave Jeb the full brief on the situation. He seemed less than surprised.

"S***t," Jeb said. "I forgot to mention Ramazan," he added when Captain Halstead mentioned how difficult it was to convince the three men to take water. "That's going to slow us down considerably."

Ramadan—or Ramazan as it was referred to in Pakistan—was just one more item to add to the list of complicating factors frustrating this mission so far. The Pak soldiers were out in the field with the team, but they were forbidden from taking food, or even water, between dawn and dusk during the observation of this religious period. There was concern about their ability to withstand the rigors of the work in the excessive heat without proper hydration, but they proved up to the task.

"We damn sure didn't expect to run into anybody out in this mess," Captain Halstead said. "Not alive anyway."

"From the looks of them," Jeb replied, "they just barely were."

Jeb scratched his head and looked thoughtful for a moment. Something occurred to him. "They were in there praying when the blast happened?" he asked.

"That's what that captain there said," Captain Halstead replied referring to Captain Abed, who maintained his position near the mosque when Jeb and Captain Halstead stepped away to speak privately.

"That tracks," Jeb said. "The blast occurred fairly close to prayer time," he added.

"He said they weren't soldiers," Captain Halstead said. "My guys tell me he referred to them as 'peasants.'"

"Well, that's probably the best way to describe them, at least by their standards," Jeb explained. "They're kind of like orderlies or something," he said. "They do menial tasks like cooking and cleaning and things, mostly for the officer corps."

"Okay," the captain said, not sure how to respond.

"Yeah, it's a different world over here," Jeb said, his tone indicating he was ready to move on from the explanation of Pakistani peasants. "I'm gonna need to follow that truck," he said. "Those guys might be able to help me piece a few things together."

Jeb believed the three men had valuable information that could shed light on what happened the day of the blast. He would have to be quick though. White Beard was undoubtedly aware of the incident by now and would be anxious to question the men too. Jeb had to catch up with that truck before White Beard did if he was to extract any intelligence at all. If White Beard got to them first it would be too late.

CHAPTER SIXTEEN

Captain Halstead walked back over to the mosque. The team was availing themselves of the meager shade the mosque provided. The shade was leaving as the late morning sun rose to its highest point of the day.

"Let's gear up," the captain instructed. "We can still get in an hour or two before we knock off," he added.

Will wanted to look inside the mosque. He had never been in a mosque before—or seen one at all. He was in synagogue once though. He was working on a State Department detail during the UN conference in New York City a couple of years before. He was assigned to the Israeli delegation and the foreign minister was speaking at a synagogue in Manhattan. Jackson and Will were part of the advance team and assisted in providing technical security for the foreign minister's visit. Will wondered how a mosque compared to a synagogue or a church for that matter. He peeked inside to satisfy his curiosity only to find little more than rubble.

"We'll need to pace ourselves," the captain said.

"Pace ourselves, sir?" Morgan inquired.

"This is the first day of Ramazan," the captain explained. "These Paks can't eat or drink, we don't want to overwork them in this heat. We don't need any Pak soldiers falling out on our watch."

"Hell, they look fine to me, sir," Hutchinson said. He could rarely be prevented from offering comment on any given topic, whether his input was solicited or not.

"Be that as it may," the captain replied, "we're going to take it light, Sergeant." His tone clearly conveyed his patience was wearing thin, and Hutchinson's comment only worsened the situation. For once, the tone was not lost on Hutchinson who simply responded, "Copy that, sir," and said nothing more.

Despite the deliberate pace, the team seemed to be making steady progress. Nearing the end of the day, Hutchinson encountered a fuzed 82mm mortar. He identified the fuze as a VT and prepared a shot to blow the UXO in place. The team remained a safe distance from the round in question as Hutchinson proceeded downrange to place his shot. They heard him holler "fire in the hole," and expected his return quickly. They waited a few minutes, and he still hadn't returned to the safe area. Morgan checked his watch, and just as he did, the shot was heard. Their "safe area" consisted of a truck, parked some 150 yards up range of the site where Hutchinson was working. The team all popped up and began to run toward the blast.

"Stop, stop, stop!!" the captain screamed. "Nobody moves! "Keep cool. Morgan, you and Carter go check it out. And for *****'s sake, be careful."

"Roger that, sir," Morgan replied. He turned and motioned for Will to follow. "Let's go."

Will followed dutifully but didn't speak. His heart was pounding, and he assumed everybody else's was too. He looked back briefly at the team, who were all ghostly white. Even the accompanying Pak soldiers, who were lounging near the truck when the blast occurred, were drop-jawed, not knowing what to expect—having lived through these experiences with several of their own comrades before the Americans' arrival. Captain Halstead had a grave look on his face as Morgan and Carter turned to walk downrange.

Morgan and Will proceeded at a brisk pace while still watching every step. They wanted to get to Hutchinson as quickly as possible but needed to be careful not to injure—or worse, kill—themselves in the process. As they approached, they saw the smoke rising from the small shot and caught the unmistakable scent of freshly blown C-4 in their nostrils. Morgan and Will stopped and took a 360-degree look around seeing no sign of Hutchinson. They looked at each other, and although Will couldn't see his own expression, he imagined it was as grim as Morgan's.

"Well, s**t," Morgan said quietly as he cast a solemn look downward, fearing the worst. They were the only words he could muster.

An instant later, they both caught a glimpse of something moving to their right. They looked intently as a most relieving sight came into full view—Shane Hutchinson stepping out from behind a tree and walking their way as casually as if he were taking a stroll through a park. Morgan and Will sighed audibly.

"Hello, ladies," Hutchinson said, nonchalantly as he approached them. "Why the long faces?"

He was unaware the team assumed he was dead, and that Captain Halstead sent Morgan and Carter downrange to recover his body or body parts. Morgan struggled to reconcile his relief at the sight of Hutchinson unharmed, with his anger at Hutchinson's typical lack of situational awareness.

"You asshole!" Morgan exclaimed. "What the f*** just happened?!"

"What?" Hutchinson replied absently.

"We thought you were dead, dumbass," Morgan said. "Why didn't you make it back to the safe area?" he demanded, his anger rising.

"Well s**t," Hutchinson began. "I walked up on that 82mm with the VT, you know the one."

"Yes, dammit," Morgan said, confounded by Hutchinson's lack of awareness. "Get to the point!"

"Alright, alright—geez," Hutchinson said. "So, I'm walking up on this 82, and I set my shot right next to it, just like you're supposed to, right," he added making sure Morgan was aware he did everything by the book. "This thing's got a VT fuze in it, so I'm being real careful, ya know?"

"Yes, yes, yes, we know about the VT fuze," Morgan exclaimed. "For the love of God, will you please get to the damn point!"

"Well, I set my shot like I said," Hutchinson said, "and I pulled my igniter, and just as I did, that f***er armed."

"Oh crap," Will exclaimed. He had been hanging on every word, but Hutchinson was telling this story as if he were sitting at a bar back home. Will was almost as aggravated at this point as Morgan.

"It armed?" Morgan asked. "What do you mean, 'it armed'?"

"Well, it made a whirring sound, and a click," Hutchinson explained.

"Did you touch it when you placed your charge?" Morgan asked.

"Hell no, I didn't touch it," Hutchinson shot back, a little agitated at the suggestion he might have done something wrong. "I know better than to f*** with those VT fuzes."

"Alright, alright," Morgan said, in a tone meant to soothe Hutchinson's ruffled feathers. "Then what?"

"Well, I dove as far as I could dive in the other direction, that's what," Hutchinson said. "Then I low-crawled about twenty yards as fast as I could, jumped up, and beat feet over into those trees over there."

"I'll be damned," Morgan said quietly, as much to himself as anyone else. The feelings of urgency, anger, and frustration gave way to genuine relief that his teammate was all right. "Well, it must have been a shadow then," Morgan surmised.

"What are you talkin' about—a shadow?" Hutchinson replied.

"Well, it's over a hundred degrees out here, and that thing has been laying out here all day in direct sunlight," Morgan explained. "You probably cast a shadow on it without meaning to and that's what made it arm."

"Whatever," Hutchinson replied.

"Well, let's get back to the safe area," Morgan said. "And when you tell this story to the captain—and you will—make it a quick story, huh?"

"What do you mean?" Hutchinson asked.

"I mean get to the point as quickly as possible," Morgan said. "The captain isn't in any kind of mood for a long-winded account of what just happened."

That much was true. Captain Halstead started the morning feeling a lot better having had the opportunity to talk to his wife the night before, but the events of the day were wearing his patience down to a nub. Morgan, Hutchinson, and Carter walked up to the safe area where the rest of the team was anxiously awaiting their return. Even from a distance they could see the relief on their faces of their teammates when they saw three of them walking back instead of just two.

"What the hell, man?!" Campbell inquired. He was glad to see Hutchinson back, uninjured. They had become good friends and he was happy to see him in one piece.

"Yes," Captain Halstead demanded, "what the hell, Sergeant?" The truth is, Captain Halstead was as relieved as everyone—perhaps more so—to see a soldier he assumed was most likely dead, walking back to the safe area unscathed.

"Well sir, it's like this," Hutchinson began, at which point Morgan cleared his throat loudly and shot Hutchinson a hard look.

Hutchinson got the message. "Yes sir," he began, and then delivered a succinct report with uncharacteristic brevity that surprised everyone.

"Very good, Hutchinson," the captain replied, taken aback by the professionalism of Hutchinson's delivery of the report, and the cool manner with which he handled himself. It was clear there was more to Hutchinson than the captain thought. Hutchinson was a blowhard most of the time, but when the need arose, he proved to be a more than capable NCO. The captain had no desire to press for more information, at least not at that moment. He was confident if there was a need for anything more, Morgan would have said so. As Hutchinson finished, Morgan nodded toward the captain, a sign nothing further was required.

"I think this would be a good time to head back to the embassy," the captain suggested, as he turned toward Captain Abed. "It's been quite a day."

"Indeed, it has," Captain Abed replied.

The vans that transported them from the hotel to the garrison would arrive shortly, so they had time to take a brief rest while they waited.

"Check these out," Will said to Thiessen who stood next to him, and he elbowed him lightly.

Thiessen turned to see two fuzes, one in each of Will's hands. They were point-detonating fuzes that had their booster cups sheared off. Will picked them up earlier in the day, and after conferring with Morgan, placed them in a pouch on his tool belt.

"Did you remove the boosters?" Thiessen inquired of Will. It would have been a reckless move if he had, but Tom didn't say anything.

"Heck no," Will replied. "I found them this way. I guess the boosters got knocked off. I thought they'd make cool souvenirs." The two fuzes were Egyptian copies of Soviet models used in 84mm recoilless rifle rounds.

"I'm not sure the captain will go along with that," Tom said, not knowing the captain was walking right up behind him.

"Go along with what?" Captain Halstead inquired.

"Uhhh . . ." Tom stammered. He didn't want to get a teammate in trouble, so he hesitated to answer.

"Sir," Will replied, "would it be okay for me to keep these? The boosters have been knocked off so they're inert," he explained as he held the fuzes out for the captain to see. "I thought they'd make good souvenirs," he added.

The captain picked up one, then the other, giving each close inspection. "Hmm, these would make good souvenirs."

Will smiled, but only for a moment. The captain had other plans for his souvenirs.

"Sergeant," the captain said, "I'm afraid I can't let you keep these." The smile fell from Will's face.

"Crap," Will said, before he could catch himself. "Oh, um, sorry sir—I, uh . . ."

"Relax, Carter," the captain responded before Will got any further tongue-tied. "I've been wondering what we might be able to take the general and the ambassador, and these will be just the thing."

The explanation didn't really clear anything up for Will. He had no clue as to why the captain would need to take the general and the ambassador a souvenir.

Reading his expression of consternation, the captain explained further. "Turns out we've been invited to the ambassador's residence for dinner, sometime in the next few days. It's good manners to bring the host a gift. Usually, you bring a bottle of wine or something like that, but I doubt there's a liquor store anywhere around here close," he added with a slight chuckle. "We have to be creative, I guess."

"Yes sir," Will replied. "I see," he said, even though he still wasn't sure what the captain planned to do. "So, you're going to give these to the general and the ambassador then?"

"No," the captain said. "You are."

"Me, sir?"

"Well, you're the one who found them. Besides, you're the junior man, Carter, and that means you get the s**t detail," the captain added, smiling.

By this time, the entire team had walked up and heard most of the conversation about souvenirs. They laughed heartily when the captain gave Will the assignment of presenting the souvenir fuzes.

"Oh, that's precious," Hutchinson said, derisively. "Little Willy's gonna make the big presentation to the brass. I can't wait to see this."

"I'll hang on to these fuzes for now," the captain said.

CHAPTER SEVENTEEN

The vans arrived and the team loaded up to leave. They were almost back to the embassy and in addition to the prospect of swimming—something they were all looking forward to—Captain Halstead informed them they could make a call home if they wanted. When they arrived at the embassy, they all filed into an office and got instructions from one of the staff there. Each of the team wrote down the name and phone number to be contacted. The staff scheduled everything out so the office would not be jammed full of people trying to communicate with their loved ones back home. Will gave them his dad's name and number, and a staffer said she would notify him when the call went through. As it turned out, he was the only one of the team not making a call to the Eastern time zone. Consequently, they put him at the back of the line to allow the others to go first. With an eleven-hour time difference, he estimated he would be talking to his folks in Kennett, Missouri, by about six a.m. their time.

Embassy staff notified Will his call was on the line just after 5:00 p.m., Islamabad time. Expecting his call to be close to that time, he was already out of the pool and dried off. He causally made his way to the office where a phone awaited. He picked up the phone, pressed the flashing button as instructed and said, "Hello," unaware his dad had been on the line waiting for almost ten minutes. Ordinarily, that would be little more than irritation for him, but in this case, it proved to be maybe the longest ten minutes of his dad's life. What Will didn't know was the only thing his dad knew at this point was he answered a call from someone identifying himself as "the operator from the United States Embassy in Islamabad, Pakistan." If that wasn't bad enough, the operator simply instructed him to "please hold the line for an important call."

"Will, Will?! Is that you?!" he asked, near desperation is his voice. "Yeah, Dad, what's up?" Will replied, oblivious to the hellish ten minutes his dad just endured. Will could hear his mom in the background, crying. He had no idea what was wrong.

"Are you okay?" his dad asked frantically.

"I'm fine," Will replied. "What's wrong with Mom?"

"Hang on a sec," he instructed. "Ruth Anne! Ruth Anne!" his dad shouted. "It's Will—he's fine, he's fine."

"What's going on, Dad?" Will asked, his concern mounting.

"Well, we got this call from the embassy in Pakistan," he explained. "Obviously, we were more than a little surprised to get a call from somebody in Pakistan," he continued. "I didn't know what was going on, and they just told me to hold. We haven't heard from you in a while, so I was getting a little concerned."

"Well, what was Mom crying about?" Will asked.

"You know how your mom is. I told her who was on the line, and she panicked. We just talked to your brother three days ago, he was in port in Argentina, so we knew this call had to be about you. Of course, she feared the worst when I told her where the call was from. It didn't help that we were on hold so long—that operator wouldn't tell us anything. That made us a little anxious for sure."

As a veteran who spent twenty-four years in the military and endured multiple deployments, Will's dad knew notifying next of kin in the event of a soldier's death didn't take place over the phone with the embassy in a foreign country. Still, the call caused great concern and sent his mother into a blind panic. His dad had his hands full trying to calm her as they awaited what they assumed would be news about their son, and prayed together that the news wouldn't be bad.

Adding to their fears was their own recent experience in Turkey. Will's parents were serving as missionaries in Izmir and returned to the United States the year before. They went to Izmir mostly to minister to the American GIs at Incirlik Air Force Base, but they attracted a following of local Turks, many of whom converted to Christianity. Eventually, the Turkish government took notice and expressed their desire for Will's parents to leave Turkey "for their own safety." If Pakistan was anything like Turkey, they assumed they had cause for concern.

"Well, I'm fine," Will reassured him.

"What in the world are you doing in Pakistan?" his dad asked.

"Well, I can't tell you that, Dad, but everything's okay."

"Your mom wants to talk to you, here she is."

"Will?!" she asked. "Is that you?"

"Yes ma'am, it's me."

His mom began to cry at the sound of Will's voice. She had convinced herself he was dead, and they were waiting for embassy confirmation. Now, she was crying with relief. Nevertheless, his dad was impatient with what he considered to be undue drama.

"Mom, Mom, I'm fine," Will said, trying to calm her as much as he could.

"Ruth Anne, give me that phone," his dad insisted. "He's fine, calm down."

"She'll be alright," his dad said, picking up the phone to continue the conversation. "You know how she gets."

"Yes sir, well, I can't tell you much about what's going on here. What's going on in your world?"

They talked a little about the latest goings on back home—grandparents, aunts and uncles, his mom's job, his dad's job—but before long an embassy staffer walked in and said, "one minute."

"I'm going to have to get off."

"Alright, hang on for your mom."

"Will," she began. "You be careful over there, you hear me?"

"Yes ma'am. I'll be careful."

"When are you coming home?"

"I don't know, Mom. We've got a lot of work to do over here. Besides, I couldn't tell you even if I did know when we were coming home."

"Well, you just get yourself back here quick," she said. "And in one piece."

"Okay, Mom, I will. I gotta go now, Mom." The staffer was now standing in the door.

"Alright then, I love you, and make good choices, hon," she began to sob again as she handed his dad the phone.

"She'll be alright. You take care of yourself, son," doing his best to keep his own emotions in check. "And remember who you are, and whose you are."

"I will."

"See you when you get back."

"Yes sir. Love you."

"Love you too, son, bye."

Will hung up the phone and looked up at the staffer.

"I'm so sorry to rush you, sir," she said, sincerely. "They give us very strict time constraints on international calls"

"Yes ma'am. I understand."

After the call home, Will vacillated between the feeling of relief at having spoken to his parents—at least now they knew where he was and that he was all right—and the worry of knowing the fear the call induced. As he was walking back to the pool area, the captain intercepted him and inquired about the call. "Folks doing okay?" he asked, seeing Will's hangdog expression.

"Oh, yes sir," Will replied respectfully, but absently. "They're fine." He was always inclined to shed tears whenever he saw, or heard, his mom cry. He was doing his best to hold them back now and the captain knew it.

"Well, I know they're worried about you," he said. "That's just natural. But you'll be fine. Besides, right now you've got bigger problems."

"What's that, sir?" Will asked, snapping to, assuming there was something serious to address.

"Your team's getting their asses kicked by the Marines," he said, pointing to the volleyball court. "You better get out there."

"Roger that, sir," Will said, and broke into a trot as the team hollered for him to hurry up.

The sergeant major was filling in for Will, and he was motioning for him as he began to step off the court. Will wasn't sure how long they'd been playing, but clearly the sergeant major was winded and ready for a break.

"Get your ass out here, kid," the sergeant major said. "I've been covering for you, but I'm done."

As he passed by the little bleachers, Will heard a familiar and friendly voice. "I was wondering when you'd show up." It was Tara, and he wasn't sure he'd be able, or even want to play after hearing her dulcet voice.

"You better get out there," she said. "Your boys have already lost two."

Will paused just long enough to smile at her. He looked over at the team, who were all yelling at him by now, and then looked back at her.

"We can talk later," she said, seeming to read his mind. "Now go on before they lose another one."

"'Bout time, Romeo," Morgan said, as he put his arm around Will's neck and pulled him toward him. "Sergeant Major really stunk it up out here," he said in a very discreet tone, being careful the sergeant major didn't hear. "He may like playing volleyball, but that doesn't mean he's any good at it."

Will joined the game, and they played for a while until their hunger got the best of them. The rest of the team headed for the dining room, but Will was more interested in spending time with Tara.

"You coming, Carter?" Campbell asked, knowing full well what the answer to that question would be.

"Hell no, he's not coming," Hutchinson interjected. "At least not if he's got any sense."

"Nah, y'all go ahead," Will said. "I'll be along later."

"Yeah, probably five minutes later," Hutchinson replied, laughing loudly.

"Lock it up, Hutch," Morgan instructed. He knew Will was enamored with Tara and didn't see any need to allow Hutchinson to make sport of his feelings or impede his progress. It was clear to even the casual onlooker Tara and Will were smitten with each other.

"Out front at 2030, Carter," Morgan said, referring to the time the vans would leave the embassy to take them back to their hotel. "See you then," he added with a wink and a smile.

"Copy," Will said, as he stood waiting for the team to get safely out of earshot. He was ready to spend some time alone with Tara, who sat patiently on the lowest row of the small bleachers beside the volleyball court.

"Could I take you to dinner?" Will asked anxiously. He wanted to sit down by her but was conscious of the fact he just finished playing volleyball with five other EOD techs and six Marines. Not to mention having been in the field most of the day. He needed a shower.

"Well, I was going to ask you the same thing," she said.

"Sure," Will said. The invitation surprised him. A woman never asked him to dinner before, to his knowledge, and if she had, certainly not one as beautiful as Tara. "Let me grab a quick shower, and we can head over to the dining room," Will said, assuming the dinner would be at the embassy dining room.

"That's not really what I had in mind," Tara replied. She had a seductive smile and her eyes—beautiful as they were—had a twinkle in them Will had not seen before. "I was thinking of something a little more private."

"Okay," Will replied. He knew what she was thinking but was careful not to assume anything.

"How 'bout I cook you dinner up at my apartment," she said. "How's that sound?"

"Oh, you cook?" Will replied, teasingly.

"Yes, I cook, Will Carter," she said. "And I'm pretty good too."

Will had to admit he loved the sound of her voice and the way she talked. Her slight accent stopped short of being a drawl but had the most elegant, almost musical lilt that gave her away as a pure Southern girl. Adding to her charm was the way she addressed him by both his first and last names when she was making a point.

"Sounds great," Will said, gathering his things. "Let me run over to the locker room and take a quick shower."

"Don't worry about that—you can shower at my place," she said.

"Are you sure?" he asked. "I can just run over there; I won't be but a minute or two."

"I'm sure," she said. "Besides, that locker room is probably pretty nasty anyway."

She was right about that. It wasn't the cleanest, but the team had been using it now for close to a week without complaint.

Tara had a little apartment to herself. The embassy offered housing to unmarried or unaccompanied staff right there on the compound. Living at the embassy had to be a lot like living on a college campus, Will thought, although since he hadn't yet been to college, he could only speculate.

"Come on," Tara said, motioning for Will to join her. He was self-conscious and tried to keep a little space between them so as not to offend her with the smell of the day's work still on him. Despite his best effort, Tara reached for his hand and held it as they walked. There wasn't a word spoken on the short walk to her apartment. She held Will's hand tightly, her fingers interlaced with his, occasionally placing her other hand on his wrist as they walked slowly.

CHAPTER EIGHTEEN

When they arrived at the door of her small apartment, Tara released Will's hand and reached for her key. She opened the door and walked in as he followed closely behind her. When she turned to close and lock the door behind them, she brushed against him. Will could feel the supple curves of her body touching his as she leaned in toward him. She put her hand on his face and placed her lips on his. It was the most exhilarating first kiss he ever experienced and set the stage for a perfect evening.

After a moment or two, Will prevailed upon her to let him shower before dinner. He showered quickly, not only because he was anxious to resume what Tara started, but because his family taught him to be respectful to his host. A quick shower was respectful to a host—or in this case hostess—who was generous enough to offer one.

Tara's apartment was small, neat, and tastefully decorated. It smelled of floral potpourri. Another feature of her apartment was since it was a one-bedroom, the bathroom was in the bedroom. Her small bathroom had a variety of sweet-smelling soaps and haircare products from which to choose. It was a sharp contrast to the barracks that was Will's home for the past few years. Well-provisioned as it was though, he noticed after his shower there were no towels on the towel bar.

"I guess I forgot to ask for a towel," Will hollered from the bathroom, loudly enough to get Tara's attention, but not so much it might be heard by her neighbors.

"It's out here," Tara replied. Will opened the bathroom door, and sure enough, there was a towel neatly folded by the nightstand on the edge of the bed. Tara also sat on the edge of the bed wearing nothing but a loosely fastened silk robe and a smile. Will was a bit startled when he walked out the door toward the towel and saw her sitting there. So much so he retreated briefly behind the door, his head still visible. “Oh, I’m sorry,” he stammered. “I didn’t realize . . .”

Tara giggled and smiled her beautiful smile. “It’s okay,” she reassured him. “Come here.”

Stunned, Will gingerly walked out of the bathroom stepping toward the bed. Tara stood reaching for the towel, and when she did, the silk robe she was barely wearing slipped from her shoulders revealing her stunning body. “Don’t be bashful. Here . . .” she said, holding up the towel with both hands. “Let me help you.” Will stepped to her, and she placed the towel around his back with one hand. She reached for the other end with her free hand and pulled him to her with the towel.

Their lips met, and they spent the better part of the evening, bodies intertwined, enjoying the pleasures of two young lovers, which a war in Afghanistan and massive explosion in Pakistan had strangely brought together. At one point Will, still hungry, absently asked, “What about dinner?”

“Dinner can wait,” she replied, smiling sweetly. It did.

It was like a dream until Will happened to glance over at the clock. He was oblivious to time in Tara’s bed, but the clock shocked him back to the here and now. “Oh no,” he said. “It’s 8:15!”

“I guess you better get going,” she said, unfazed.

“Yep,” Will replied, urgently. “I hate to leave so soon, sorry about dinner.”

“Oh, that’s okay,” she said. “No big deal,” she insisted. “Besides, I’m going to send some home with you.”

She stood, donned her robe, and went into the kitchen to prepare dinner-to-go while Will dressed. She made lasagna, garlic toast, and a salad. The salad wouldn’t travel well, but she wrapped up the lasagna—which was still piping hot—in some aluminum foil, along with the bread. “That’s still pretty hot,” she said, as Will walked into the kitchen. She produced a stack of paper napkins and placed the hot, foil-wrapped package on the napkins. “Carry it like that so you don’t burn yourself.”

“Well, thank you for the dinner,” Will said. “And . . .”

"And what?" She inquired with a wry smile.

"Well, uh, well . . ." he stammered.

"Well, thank YOU," she said, giggling. "You are a cutie. It's been a great evening."

"Yes, it has," Will agreed.

"Now you be careful out there, okay?" She had never let on she knew exactly what Will was doing, but she knew it involved explosives, and it was dangerous. "I want to see you again."

"I always am," he replied. "I'll be back tomorrow. We'll probably knock off around 2:30 or so."

"Alright then," Tara replied. "I'll see you tomorrow," she said and sealed the deal with a passionate, send-off kiss.

She opened the door, and as he walked out, he turned to get one last look at her before leaving. She was breathtaking. He waved and she responded with a broad smile and a girlish goodbye wave.

Will practically floated back to the awaiting vans at the front of the embassy. He had his tool belt in one hand and was carrying the warm foil package in the other when he walked up. Morgan, the captain, the sergeant major, and of course Wiley Adams—who was never far from the sergeant major—were already there.

"Here he is," Morgan said. "How was dinner?" he asked, smiling devilishly, and putting a facetious emphasis on the word "dinner."

"Oh, it was good," Will said coyly.

"Good?" the sergeant major inquired, incredulous. "Hell, son, I saw what was on the menu. I hope it was a damn sight better than good."

"Yes, Sergeant Major," Will replied, his face flushing. "It was a damn sight better than good."

"That's what I'm talking about kid," Scott said chuckling. "Good answer.

The rest of the team—Hutchinson, Campbell, and Thiessen—walked up at just that moment.

"What are you blushing for, Carter?" Campbell asked, smiling.

"Yeah," Thiessen added, "and what's in that foil?"

"That," Will replied, "is my dinner—lasagna."

"Damn, son," Campbell said.

"Wait a minute," Hutchinson interjected in his usual blustering tone. "Let me see if I got this straight. You get laid, and then *SHE* sends *YOU* home with dinner—how's that work?"

"Lock it up, asshole," the sergeant major demanded. "There's a time and a place for that bulls**t, and this ain't either one!"

The sergeant major didn't necessarily dislike Hutchinson, but he was becoming increasingly frustrated with his inability to discern when and where "locker room talk" was appropriate. Hutchinson had proven to be an asset in the field, cool headed, and capable. The sergeant major knew this, and mostly overlooked Hutchinson's frequent lapses in judgment. However, standing within earshot of the embassy's front door demanded a level of decorum Hutchinson was prone to forget. The sergeant major's verbal reminder, accompanied by a harsh look was sufficient to subdue Hutchinson, for the time being anyway.

Will didn't appreciate the casual, if not vulgar way, some members of his team referred to the experience he just had with Tara. But he knew it was his own fault for allowing it to happen in the first place. Any attempt to protest at this point would only make matters worse, so he kept quiet. The truth was, Will was feeling guilty. The last words his mother said to him on their phone call earlier that evening—"make good choices"—reverberated in his mind. On that score he had certainly failed. He was raised in a Christian home and knew better, yet he allowed himself to get carried away in a moment of unexpected passion. He would have to be careful not to let that happen again.

The two white vans arrived just at that moment. One of the drivers was a Pakistani named Khali Khan. He was a pleasant, older gentleman with whom Will had struck up somewhat of a friendship. He was always amiable, particularly to Will; mostly because Will made more of an effort to be cordial to him more than the others. The other team members weren't rude to him, but they had other things on their minds—home mostly—and didn't talk much to him. They were all married and were growing increasingly disconsolate missing their wives and the comforts of home. Chad Campbell had become downright moody and was prone to snap at junior team members, Carter and Thiessen, for no apparent reason. The usually easy-going captain and the sergeant major were also showing signs of irritability and growing more intolerant of shenanigans, particularly Hutchinson's humor. For his part though, Hutchinson continued as usual, undaunted by criticism or chastisement. And of course, there was Wiley. He was as constant as a clock, oblivious to most everything around him.

For Will, it was more of an adventure. He was doing everything he could to enjoy himself and learn as much as he could. That was the reason Will made a point of riding with Khali Khan, and this evening was no exception. "Good evening, Mr. Khan," Will said.

"Ah, good evening, Sergeant Will," he replied, in a most congenial tone. "And how was your day today?"

Will sat directly behind Khan in the van, and they chattered away as he drove through the streets of Islamabad. Over the past few days of riding with Khali Khan, Will learned he was an Army veteran. In fact, he was a sergeant major and served in, as he put it, "many wars." It turned out the wars in question were all with India, a perennial and persistent adversary of Pakistan. Sometimes he liked to talk about cricket, a topic Will knew just enough about from his boyhood in England to hold a conversation. Mostly, he enjoyed Will's willingness to talk idly.

The vans pulled up to the hotel and the team got out and walked to their rooms. Will was getting hungry for the lasagna. Finally, in his room, he laid the package on the dresser and carefully peeled the foil back. It was still warm and looked great. At that moment, Will realized he overlooked one important detail, he didn't have a fork. Undeterred, he reached for his tool belt and secured his Kabar knife. In the absence of a proper utensil, his knife worked well, and he ate the lasagna quickly along with the bread. That night he got the best sleep he'd had in a long time, satisfied with a great dinner and the fresh memory of a wonderful evening spent with a beautiful young woman.

CHAPTER NINETEEN

CAMP OHJRI
RAWALPINDI, PAKISTAN
APRIL 19, 1988
0530 HRS.

The next morning began with the team meeting as usual in the lobby and then being transported to the garrison to continue their work. But Jeb wasn't with them this morning. He would come later. It was the first time Jeb didn't start the day with the team. Will was by now used to seeing him in the mornings and had even developed a good rapport with him. Jeb being from Texas, spent his share of time on horseback, and he was impressed with Will's cowboy background. They talked a lot, and Will found his extensive experience in this part of the world reassuring. While Jeb's absence was conspicuous, Will didn't think anything about it at the time. They ate on the fly as usual and arrived at the garrison as the sun began to rise.

The captain advised that the team would be separating. They had been making excellent progress, amassing a huge amount of unexploded ordnance awaiting destruction at the demolition range north of the city. Morgan, Hutchinson, Campbell and Thiessen proceeded to the range to begin destruction of the stockpiled UXO. The captain and Carter remained on the garrison to continue operations there. Will was dispatched to the northeastern quadrant of the garrison to resume the sweep for UXO accompanied by Captain Abed and his squad. The captain stayed behind at the gate. "I'm waiting for Jeb," the captain said. "I'll be along as soon as I hear from him."

Will was glad to hear Jeb was planning on being in the field with them and went about his business as he had for the last several days.

Captain Abed and he, along with his squad of Pak soldiers, began their sweep. Everything was progressing in a routine manner. A couple of hours into the morning, Will was feeling thirsty in the torrid heat. He grabbed the canteen affixed to his belt, but before drinking, offered it to one of the soldiers who appeared thirstier than he was. The soldier placed his hand over his mouth, gestured upward, and turned his eyes toward the sky. Will looked at Captain Abed, perplexed.

"He is fasting," the captain reminded Will.

"Oh yeah," Will said. "I forgot—Ramazan, right?"

"Correct, Sergeant," Abed replied. "He will not drink until sundown," he explained. "You may certainly drink though, Sergeant, as you are not bound by the observances of Islam," Captain Abed added, reading Will's expression of concern.

Will returned the canteen to his belt. "I'm good, sir," he said. Although he was parched, he couldn't bring himself to drink in front of these men. If he absolutely had to drink later, he'd find a spot somewhere out of sight of these soldiers.

Just then, a Pak "jeep" pulled up. The driver remained in the camouflage vehicle as a Pak officer got out and walked toward the working squad. It was Major Omar. Will's observations of him were unfavorable, and today was no exception. Omar walked up and stood next to Will, uttered a few words to Captain Abed, and then, without asking, took the canteen from Will's belt and drank liberally. He finished his long draught with an audible "ah," and then casually handed the canteen back to Will.

That this officer would casually drink in front of his men with a cavalier disregard for their health—it hovered around one hundred degrees—not to mention their religious observances, stunned Will. Worse was the disrespectful manner with which he helped himself to Will's canteen. Visibly dismayed by Major Omar's actions, Captain Abed, as a junior officer, could say nothing.

The major left as quickly as he arrived, returning to his awaiting jeep and speeding away. Captain Abed seemed to be relieved by the major's departure. "He was merely checking our progress," the captain explained. He was clearly embarrassed by the conduct of his fellow officer. Although he said nothing further about the incident, he didn't need to. His expression offered more than words.

Captain Abed was an anomaly among the Pak officer corps. From the top down, most of them showed little regard for their soldiers—or anyone else for that matter—evinced by their willingness to send soldiers downrange to upend unexploded ordnance with a stick, or to drink in front of them when the soldiers were forbidden from drinking. Abed, on the other hand, had an affinity for his soldiers and they responded with a high degree of respect, so visible in their faces when he spoke to them.

No sooner than the major departed, another vehicle approached—a white SUV driven by Cory Leftwich, Planning and Outreach. He stopped and quickly got out. He stood behind the door of his SUV and hollered, "Carter!" He motioned for Will, who hurried over.

"You got all your stuff?" he asked.

"Yes sir," Will replied.

"Well hop in," he said.

Will stood there momentarily, not sure why he was there. "Come on," Leftwich said. "We gotta move—now."

"Roger that," Will said, still unsure where they were headed, or why.

"Do I need to say anything to Captain Abed?" he asked.

"No—he'll be fine," Leftwich replied. "I need to get you to the hotel ASAP."

"What's going on at the hotel?"

"Nothing. You just need to get checked out as quick as you can."

Leftwich was clearly in a hurry, and he was deliberately evading Will's questions. He looked over at Will briefly and read the expression on his face.

"I know you've got questions," he said. "I'm going to get you to the embassy after the hotel, and we'll let you know what's up when we get the whole team assembled."

That was as much as he offered, and Will had to be content with it for now. They wheeled up to the front of the hotel and got out of the SUV. "Gotta be quick," Leftwich instructed. "Get your s**t and get back down here. I'll take care of getting you checked out."

Will went quickly up to grab his stuff. As a matter of course, he did his best to keep his luggage as neat as he could every day, and on that day, his penchant for neatness paid off. He was in his room for little more than a minute or two, and back downstairs quickly.

"All set?" Leftwich asked.

"All set," Will replied.

"Alright—let's get going."

They made it back to the embassy faster than usual. Will wasn't sure if it was lighter than usual pre-lunch traffic, or Leftwich's aggressive driving. Leftwich seemed visibly relieved to be back, although he offered no explanation for the abrupt halt to the work on the garrison and the unexpected checkout at the hotel. "You might want to go ahead and grab some lunch," he suggested. "The rest of the team will be along shortly."

"Are they okay?" Will asked.

"They're fine," Leftwich replied. "You'll get a brief shortly. I'd go ahead and get a bite while you can."

"Okay," Will replied. There was little else he could do. Clearly that was all the information Leftwich was going to provide. He decided to head to the cafeteria and found his timing was fortuitous. Seated with a colleague, Tara was having lunch too. She was a welcome sight and the memory of the evening before filled Will's consciousness. He walked over to her table and she turned and looked up at him. "Well, there you are," she said with a big smile. "Were your ears burning? We were just talking about you."

"Well as a matter of fact they have been burning," Will replied. "Along with the rest of me. This sun is brutal."

"Oooo—you do have a nice little sunburn going, don't you?" she said, gently touching Will's arm as she said it. "This is my boss, Margie," she said, introducing him to the lady sitting at her table. Will guessed Margie to be in her early fifties. She had a very pleasant appearance, and though he would never have said it, she reminded Will of his mom a little.

"It's nice to meet you, ma'am," Will said—smiling as much at Tara as Margie. He didn't extend his hand for a handshake—he was taught by his dad years before that a gentleman should only shake hands with a lady if she offers her hand, and then it shouldn't be an aggressive, overly firm handshake.

"Well, it's nice to meet you, Will," she replied, extending her hand. "I've heard a lot about you."

Will met her handshake with just enough grip to match hers, as his dad instructed. He didn't want to come off like a brute, but he was careful not to appear meek either. His was an old-fashioned upbringing with training in respect for women and elders. In this case, Margie was both. He also wanted to make a good impression on Tara, who clearly talked about him enough to Margie she knew his name without him mentioning it.

"You're right, Tara," Margie said, her hand still in Will's. "He is handsome," she added, patting his hand with her left hand before releasing it.

Will felt his face flush at the compliment, and both ladies giggled. "Oh, look at him blush," Margie said, smiling.

"I was going to grab a quick bite before my team gets back," Will said. "Is your lunch break over?"

Margie stood and pushed her chair back under the table. "You've got time," she said, addressing Tara. "I'll leave you two alone."

Will turned to let her pass and when he did, caught sight of the rest of his team headed into the cafeteria for lunch.

"Well here comes my team," Will said, bracing himself for the requisite ribbing, most likely from Hutchinson. To Will's relief, his famished colleagues focused only on their hunger. Ignoring Will, they got straight in line.

"Which one of them is your commanding officer?" Margie asked. "I've got a question for him—what's his name?"

"Captain Halstead, ma'am," he replied. "He's the last one in line—in the blue shirt."

"Captain—Captain?" Margie called, practically hollering across the dining room. She was holding Will by the arm as she tried to get the captain's attention.

Captain Halstead turned and saw Margie's hand raised. "Yes ma'am?"

Margie didn't wait for the captain to come over. She inquired loudly from a good thirty feet away, "Captain, what's the idea bringing this young man to a place like this?" she demanded, still holding him by the arm. "Why, he can't be more than sixteen years old."

"Sergeant Carter," Captain Halstead said loudly, putting an emphasis on the word "sergeant" to make a point. "How old are you?"

"I'm twenty-two, sir," Will replied, mortified.

"There ya go, ma'am," the captain said, matter-of-factly. "Sergeant Carter is twenty-two." He didn't want to be rude, but he was as famished as the rest of the team and didn't want to waste time with idle conversation about the age of his junior team member.

"Well forgive me, Sergeant," Margie said, releasing Will's arm. "I didn't realize you were twenty-two, and a sergeant too," she said facetiously.

"Now Ms. Margie," Tara interjected respectfully, but embarrassed. "You know I told you he was twenty-two. I told her you were twenty-two," she said, turning to Will with a smile.

"Oh, I know you did," Margie said. "I just wanted to see if I could make that cute baby face turn red again," she added with a big grin. "Enjoy your lunch, Sergeant," Margie said. "See ya later, hon," she said to Tara, with a wink. Then she turned and walked away.

"Well, she's something else," Will said, when Margie was safely out of hearing.

"Yes, she is."

Sergeant Major Scott walked by at that moment carrying a tray of food. "You better eat something if you're going to, Carter," he said. "We've got a brief in ten minutes."

"Roger that, Sergeant Major."

Tara stood up and said, "I better let you eat."

"Yeah, I'm going to have to hustle, I guess."

"I'll just plan on seeing you tonight then?"

"Absolutely," Will said. "I'm not real sure where I'll be though."

"Well, if you're anywhere on the embassy, I'll find you," she said. "See you later, babe," she added quietly. They both knew it would have been wildly inappropriate for any public display of affection at that point, so she discreetly touched Will's arm as she said good-bye.

Will went through the cafeteria line quickly and sat down at the table with Morgan and Tom Thiessen. "Hurry up and eat, Will," Morgan said. "We gotta roll." Will wolfed down a cheeseburger and fries just in time to fall in behind the team as they headed out of the cafeteria to their brief, not sure what to expect.

CHAPTER TWENTY

The team entered the room where they received their first brief. Just like that day, a selection of soft drinks and snack cakes were placed neatly on a side table.

"Well hell, if they're gonna keep puttin' 'em out," Hutchinson said, "I'm gonna keep eatin' 'em." He helped himself to a Twinkie and a Coke.

One thing about Hutchinson—there were times when it wasn't all that bad to have him around. He was a consistent icebreaker. It wasn't always good, but in this case it certainly was. One by one the entire team stepped up to avail themselves of the snacks and drinks left for them. Even the captain indulged.

They sat around the table for a good ten minutes, waiting. As it turned out, Jeb and Leftwich arrived at Camp Ojhri at the same time to meet with the captain. Leftwich was dispatched to collect Will from his area of operations, and the captain went with Jeb to get the rest of the team at the demolition range. None of them had any idea why the brief was called, except the captain, who clearly knew more than he was saying.

Jeb, Brad Miller of Planning and Outreach, and General Wassom walked in as the team was finishing dessert. "Afternoon, boys," the general said, to which the entire team responded in unison, "Good afternoon, sir," as they came to attention.

"At ease, gentlemen," the general said. "Take your seats."

They sat and prepared for the news. Jeb wasted no time, dispensing with any small talk. "Yesterday at approximately 0820 hours local time, U.S. military forces launched an attack on multiple Iranian targets in and around the Strait of Hormuz," he began. "The attack was in response to the illegal mining of the strait and other areas of the Persian Gulf, one of which was struck by the USS

Samuel B. Roberts as it escorted oil tankers to protect them from Iranian attacks."

There was a pregnant pause. In that moment, the team pondered what this meant. They assumed the U.S. was now at war with Iran. It was no surprise. Iran had been a constant thorn in America's side since the 1979 Islamic Revolution.

The USS *Samuel Roberts* incident must have been the last straw for President Reagan who authorized Operation Praying Mantis in response. Just then, Will remembered his Navy teammates from the USS *Enterprise*. He recalled Senior Chief Sonberg telling him they were doing mine countermeasures in the Gulf when they were sent to Pakistan. Since they returned to the *Enterprise*, Will had no doubt they were now right in the thick of things.

Jeb continued. "So, what does this mean for you, here and now?" he asked rhetorically. "Here's what we know—Brad," turning to Miller and yielding the floor.

"Thanks, Hawkeye," Miller said. "In what we assume is a response to the attacks Hawkeye just outlined, there has been a threat issued against your team. The threat has been vetted through multiple sources, and we have every reason to believe it is credible and actionable."

The captain and sergeant major looked solemn, and the rest of the team sat there aghast at what they heard. It was clear to Will now why Leftwich was in such a hurry for him to check out of the hotel and rush back to the embassy.

"We have been discussing the options available to us," Miller said. "We'll discuss those in a minute. Right now, it looks like you might have some questions."

The soldiers looked around at one another, none of them wanting to be the first to break the silence. Even Hutchinson had nothing to say, which was saying something. The captain was the first to speak. Curiously, he didn't ask a question. Instead, he suggested to Brad Miller he should give greater clarification. That indicated to Will the captain had a full brief and just wanted his team to know more.

"Perhaps you could give a little bit of background and detail about the nature of the threat, so the team has a better understanding of what we're up against."

Miller began to provide more details. “Specifically, the threat named each one of you individually. If you recall from your initial briefing you got when you landed, we knew there was a release of your names—still tracking that by the way. So, they’ve known you were here from the start.”

“You keep saying threat,” Morgan said. “Define ‘threat.’”

“What we know—the verbiage used,” Miller replied, “was ‘the termination of the American EOD team operating in Pakistan,’” he answered, using air quotes with his fingers as he said it.

“Who, specifically, are ‘they’?” Morgan inquired. “And just how capable are ‘*they*’?” he asked.

“There’s a significant Iranian diaspora here in Pakistan,” Miller explained. “We’ve seen the numbers escalate in the last couple of years particularly. We’re not altogether certain why there has been such an increase in those numbers, but there is a war going on between Iran and Iraq—it’s possible they are primarily refugees. They are mostly concentrated down around Karachi, but we are starting to see a few more of them around here—just not as significant in number.

“As to their capability,” Miller went on, “there may be some veterans among the Iranian diaspora in country, so we don’t want to discount or underestimate what they may or may not be capable of. We aren’t aware of any particular groups in country—Iranian-backed, that is—that may have a better developed capability, but we’re more concerned about the source of the threat. That’s what gives us the most heartburn.”

“What do you know about the source?” Thiessen asked.

“Yes,” Miller began. “The threat came from Iran—verified by HUMINT and SIGINT,” he added, referring to human intelligence and signals intelligence. “Then, this morning, we found at least one of the English-speaking papers here in Pakistan that published the threat.”

“Make it four,” Cory Leftwich said, laying a stack of newspapers on the table in front of Brad Miller. Leftwich walked in a few minutes earlier and was standing behind Miller with the papers. “One of them here in Islamabad.”

“So are we at war with Iran now?” Will asked.

"No, not yet anyway. In fact, it's my understanding there has been considerable de-escalation on our part after we inflicted some heavy damage and casualties on Iranian targets," Miller explained. "That's why they're so mad, and that's why we have to take this threat seriously."

"Maybe we could discuss our options," Captain Halstead suggested.

"Of course," Miller replied. "Our initial thought was to evacuate the team—we have an aircraft on alert. We were going to send you to the *Enterprise* which would have been our quickest option to get you out of the country."

Will had to admit, at that moment, the option Brad Miller described sounded great to him. Not because he was anxious to leave, but the thought of getting to land on an aircraft carrier was extremely appealing. Of course, getting *ON* the carrier was one thing—getting *OFF* the carrier would be the real fun! The only way off would be that catapult shot they use to assist the planes taking off, and that would be something to experience. Just as quickly as that thought passed through his mind, the image of Tara popped into his head. Will wasn't in any hurry to leave her behind despite the chance of seeing action on an aircraft carrier.

"Hawkeye tells me you guys have been making some great progress out there," Miller said, "but you've still got a lot of work to do, I understand. That brings us to plan B."

"We could send you to the *Enterprise* if we had to, but they've got their own problems—it's still pretty hot there with the Iranians. We'll keep that option open though.

"What we need to do is keep the team here so you can finish up," Miller continued. "But that has some complications too."

"Complications?" Morgan asked.

"The threat mentioned a specific timeline," Miller explained. "Specifically, May 5," he added cryptically.

"What's May the 5th?" the team all murmured.

"Well, there was something about it being a birthday present for the Ayatollah," Miller explained. "But that's not right, his birthday is September 24. And it's not Eid al-Fitr—that's not until the

17th of May. We don't know what the significance is, but we know they specifically mentioned May 5."

"What's that 'Eid-whatever' it was you mentioned?" Hutchinson asked. The sergeant major rolled his eyes, looked down and shook his head. He knew it was a legitimate question but was embarrassed by how Hutchinson asked it.

"Well, that marks the end of the fast—Ramazan," he replied. "But Ramazan just started and that's still a ways off. What we're proposing is that we give you guys a little break."

The team looked around at each other wondering what he meant by that. Jeb could see the consternation on their faces, and he added, "We're going to hide you in a safe house for a couple weeks and then see about getting you back into the field after the 5th." He was growing tired of the back and forth and preferred to address of the situation directly.

Miller took the cue from Jeb to be more direct. "That's pretty much it. You're going to cool your heels until May 5, and we'll reevaluate then. If we assess at that time that we can get you back in the field to finish up, that's what we'll do. If we don't think we can make that happen, we'll have an alternate plan and make a decision at that time."

At first, it all sounded intriguing to Will. A safe house? This was the stuff of movies and spy novels. *How exhilarating*, he thought. But then it occurred to him this must be serious—urgent enough to go into hiding. His thinking quickly changed. He had never been a target before and wasn't sure how to react.

"Here's how this is gonna work," Jeb began. He was ready to get this meeting done. His frustration was visible. He knew it wasn't the team's fault and was trying not to appear hostile to them or anyone else for that matter, but this stalled operation was already delayed from the start. *They were finally making real progress*, he thought, *and now this*. "You guys will go out to the safe house and hunker down. It's nice. It's got everything you'll need, and there's even a cook there for you, he'll fix you whatever you want, you'll love it. In a day or two, we may let you come back to the embassy and hang out here during the day. We'll be continually monitoring and assessing the situation," he continued. "We'll let you know when you can get out of the safe house, and where you can go, mostly likely just back and forth from there to the embassy."

Nobody said a word. There was an awkward silence before Jeb turned to the general. "Anything to add, sir?"

"I think that's just about got it covered," General Wassom said. "This is just temporary, boys—these guys'll take good care of you." The general had been quiet but attentive throughout the briefing. He knew he had to rely heavily on the judgment of Jeb and his colleagues. He had a high degree of respect for them, particularly Jeb, and he was comfortable with their decision. Still, what Jeb shared bothered him about White Beard, the ongoing delays he caused—deliberate, they seemed, to confound their efforts—and now this latest information about the three men in the mosque. He hadn't had a chance to digest that fully and felt he needed more time to discuss it with Jeb to get a better handle on it. That would have to wait. For now, he knew he needed to see to the security of the team. General Wassom smiled reassuringly and exited the room.

"We're gonna wait until after dinner before we move," Miller said. "So do what you want until then. The vans will depart at the usual time—2030. Any questions—good," he said, without giving anyone time to ask one. "See you at 2030."

As the team began to exit, Miller added, "One last thing—don't forget you guys are having dinner at the Ambo's residence day after tomorrow. See you guys later."

CHAPTER TWENTY-ONE

The team filed out and headed down to the pool. Will was starting to get bored with lounging by the pool and said as much to Morgan.

"Yeah, I'm getting tired of this layin' around too," Morgan agreed. He was starting to feel guilty about being so idle, but he knew there was little he could do about it. "Let's go," he said, as Will fell in behind him not sure what Morgan had in mind.

As they headed back inside, Morgan suggested they stop at the cafeteria for some ice cream. "They have soft serve in there," he said. "Chocolate-vanilla swirl—mmm," he added.

That sounded good to Will, so he didn't argue. They walked into the cafeteria to find Jeb sitting alone at a table with a cup of coffee and what was left of a slice of pie. He appeared lost in thought, and after they got their ice cream, they walked up to his table.

"Oh, hey guys," Jeb said. "Have a seat."

"We don't want to bother you," Will said politely, although he very much wanted to pick his brain a bit. He was wondering about the three men in the mosque, and what Jeb could say, if anything, about what happened the day they found them.

"Not at all," he said. "Sit, sit."

Morgan and Will ate their ice cream and Jeb began making small talk, which was unusual for him.

"So how you guys doing?" he asked.

"Well, we're fine," Morgan responded. "But I've got a question."

"Shoot."

"Whatever happened to those three guys we found in that mosque the other day?" Will almost choked on his ice cream. Partly because it was precisely what was on his mind, and partly because of the blunt way Morgan asked the question. Morgan understood, though, that Jeb was very direct and would be highly likely to appreciate a direct question as opposed to beating around the bush.

"Funny you should ask," Jeb said. "I was just sitting here, thinking about that very thing."

"Anything you can talk about?" Morgan asked. "I'd sure like to know what was going on with those guys. I'm not sure they were there by accident."

Jeb raised an eyebrow at Morgan's speculation. He was impressed Morgan had the ability to read people—and situations for that matter.

"Well, I couldn't talk about it here," Jeb said. "But if you were to show up in that SCIF up on three in about ten minutes or so, we might be able to visit a little," he added, referring the Sensitive Compartmented Information Facility on the third floor.

With that, Jeb got up from the table and left the cafeteria.

"Well, that's a conversation worth missing out on volleyball for," Morgan said. "You up for it?"

"Of course," Will said. "I was hoping to find out more about those guys. I kind of had a weird feeling about that whole deal myself."

It wasn't so much the interaction with the three men that raised their suspicions. It was Jeb's response to their presence and the fact he was in such a hurry to follow them that got Will's attention.

"This ought to be interesting," Morgan said. "Finish your ice cream and we'll head that way."

As Will sat there finishing his chocolate-vanilla swirl, he thought about the unusual friendships forming among members of the team since their arrival. He was sitting there with Morgan who was fifteen years his senior and outranked him by two pay grades. Chad, Tom, and he were all the same rank, so it was natural they would gravitate toward each other. And of course, Tom and Chad were from the same unit back home, so it made sense for the two of them to be friendly. But Hutchinson and Campbell seemed to be forming a close connection. When they worked in two-man teams, Hutchinson would often pair up with Campbell as his team member. Morgan became Will's de facto team leader, although Thiessen would join them if he and the captain weren't paired. Will had occasion to join the captain once or twice, as he had that morning briefly before a halt in work. And to no one's surprise, Sergeant Major Scott and Wiley were joined at the hip as they were from the start.

The captain was comfortable allowing this structure to form naturally. He never questioned it or tried to force members of the team to rotate or mix it up just for the sake of change. He was very observant and brought a no-nonsense approach to his leadership. Will's dad occasionally used phrases like, "if it ain't broke, don't fix it," or "no need to reinvent the wheel," and in that regard the captain reminded Will a lot of his dad. Both were level-headed, cool in a crisis, with an abundance of common sense. Admirable traits characteristic of good leaders.

In Will's view, the entire team was performing very well as a whole, and just as well when they broke out into two- or three-man teams. The captain and the sergeant major must have agreed, or they would certainly have let them know.

Before his mind could wander any further, Morgan stood up from the table. "C'mon," he said. "Let's go get the lowdown on those dudes from the mosque. This should be good."

Will followed along, anxious to hear who they might have been. He was shocked to hear Captain Abed describe the men as peasants. But as Jeb pointed out, it was a different world in Southwest Asia. The caste system was still prevalent in places like India and Pakistan. It was a little hard for Will to fathom, although when he thought about it, there were some similarities to that system in his country. Will was only a generation removed from sharecroppers and bootleggers. If there were a cycle to break, his dad certainly did it. He left the farm, spent a career in the military, earning a commission and a master's degree—the first in his family to attend college—before retiring and starting a second career in public health. The three men Will and Morgan were to learn more about were unlikely to ever get such an opportunity.

Will was standing behind Morgan when he knocked on the door of the office/SCIF. Jeb opened the heavy door and motioned them in. "Come on in," he said. "Have a seat."

Jeb took his seat at the head of the table. There was a stack of documents on the table in front of him. Will had no idea what the documents were related to, but they were clearly important, marked with a "TOP SECRET" cover sheet.

They sat down and waited for him to begin.

"Now I'm going to share some things about those three guys that I wouldn't ordinarily, but you guys were there, and you saw what was going on, so I'm going to read you in. This absolutely doesn't leave this room—clear?"

"Yes sir," they replied in unison.

"Okay," he said. "One of those guys works for me—that red-headed son of a b***h," he said, referring to the one who appeared to be the leader of the three. "The problem is, I'm pretty sure he works for White Beard too."

"Oh, now that's interesting," Morgan said.

"Yeah, we can get some good intel from him," Jeb explained, "provided we get to him first. The problem is, he's kind of a whore. He'll just give it up to anyone with money—including White Beard—which is why we have to get to him first."

Jeb shared more details. He reiterated how these arms shipments usually passed through Cherat, the outpost above the Peshawar Valley. "When I found out this shipment was coming through Ojhri, and the arrangements were made without consulting me—that raised some red flags. I've been doing this s**t for a while now, and this is the first time anything has come through this way. And being left out of the loop was deliberate. That red-haired b*****d—Apu is his name—has been a fairly useful source at lower levels. He fits in with the peasants as they're called, like those two he was with in that mosque. So, I put him on the garrison to keep eyes on some of the officers coming and going."

"What about the other two—what's their deal?" Morgan asked.

"Well, that's his team," Jeb answered. "They really are peasants, and they do whatever Apu says. It makes for good cover to get these guys into places we have trouble getting into, like the garrison. They've been orderlies out there for a few weeks now. They basically just do whatever the officers tell them to do—laundry, cooking, polish their boots, rub their feet—menial s**t. Hell, there's no telling what those sick f***ers ask those poor b*****ds to do," Jeb said, referring to the Pak officers who kept orderlies around. "They really do treat them like s**t—below second-class citizens—way below.

"The Paks don't vet these orderlies at all though—hell, they're just orderlies, right?" Jeb said. "They just come and go pretty much unnoticed, which is really good for us."

Will was hanging on every word, utterly fascinated. Morgan was too; and he was asking some excellent questions.

"So what was the deal out there the other day?" Morgan asked. "You went after those guys pretty quick."

"Well, I had to get to Apu first," Jeb said. "If White Beard got to them first, they wouldn't have given us s**t."

"So when White Beard introduced himself, he said he was with the engineers," Morgan said. "I'm guessing he's more than that?"

"Oh yeah," Jeb said. "He really is an engineer, that's true, but he's also the deputy director of ISI—their intelligence service."

"Interesting . . ." Morgan said, intrigued.

"Look, there's no reason in the world a general officer—an agency deputy director, no less—should be so hands-on with an operation of this nature," Jeb said. "Under normal circumstances, that is. Hell, a general looks over the situation, maybe takes a windshield tour just to get a better feel for what's going on, or to cover his ass politically—then tells a colonel to handle it and keep him posted, who delegates the operation to a major. S**t, White Beard has been physically on the garrison since day one, literally directing the operation for ******'s sake.

"Now, that tells me something's up," Jeb continued. "I've been moving Stingers into Afghanistan for two years now. I know what the f*** I'm doing. The fact that suddenly a shipment of arms—particularly this big—comes through an installation in the middle of a major metropolitan area makes no sense whatsoever. Cherat has been the primary waypoint for over two years. I get the need to mix it up a little for security purposes—that's why we have a couple of other places we've used occasionally, but not Ojhri."

As it turned out, Camp Ojhri did have an interesting history dating back to WWII. Currently serving as the Pak Army

Headquarters, it was once used as a supply depot, complete with a rail spur, to help move materiel and men. But the infrastructure was aging and deteriorating, and most of its buildings were little more than mud brick structures with thatched roofs from WWII. Ojhri was certainly not the best choice to store a large cache of weapons bound for Afghanistan—a shipment with an estimated value north of 100 million U.S. dollars—the largest single shipment bound for Afghanistan so far. In addition to its poor state of repair, it had become increasingly difficult to secure the installation owing to its location between two major metropolitan areas, one of which was the 1960s planned capitol city, Islamabad. The capitol city was growing steadily and encroaching on the decrepit installation. Operations as sensitive as moving large shipments of weapons bound for Afghanistan would be more secure using other transit routes.

Complicating matters further was the concern by U.S. Department of Defense officials of ongoing pilferage of the weapons shipments by Pakistani "handlers." This was a charge the Pakistanis flatly denied. The Pak Army was notified some weeks earlier by DoD officials that there would be a team dispatched to inspect the shipment. That may have been the reason they routed such a large shipment through Ojhri for ease of access. The Pakistanis were making at least a pretense of transparency and wanted to offer easier access to the weapons provided by the Americans.

The Pakistanis weren't acting altruistically. They were getting financial aid from U.S. taxpayers for their efforts, and always wanted more in "commissions." Pilferage of arms shipments bound for Afghanistan became routine in Pakistan. The DoD was tired of it. Of course, any pilferage would require someone who had access, some technical knowledge, and the capability to turn the stolen weapons into cash. Not just anyone could meet those criteria, but White Beard certainly could.

Whoever executed the sabotage on Camp Ojhri—and it was now clearly sabotage—may have been engaging in preemptive action meant to dissuade American inspectors from coming to Pakistan. Their plan worked. There would be no DoD inspectors, at least not right away. Whatever information the DoD—or any other U.S. agency—could glean from this attack, would come from the American EOD team and Jeb. It was too early to tell just how this act of sabotage was executed and by whom, but no one believed the intent was to cause a high order detonation amid two major population centers. Poor storage was the catalyst for the explosive, unintended chain reaction.

"So let me see if I understand this," Morgan said. "You think White Beard stole the Stingers and blew the rest?"

"I'm pretty sure White Beard stole the Stingers, in fact, I'm certain of that," Jeb said. "But I don't think he blew the shipment, at least not on purpose."

"What do you think happened?" Will asked.

"I think his plan was to stage an accident to make it look like the Stingers were destroyed," Jeb speculated. "But he made a few mistakes. First, he should have left a few behind to make it look legit."

"Well, why didn't he?" Will inquired.

"Stingers are extremely valuable on the arms market and they're hard to get a hold of," Jeb explained. "That asshole got greedy—probably started seeing dollar signs and didn't want to sacrifice a single one, even to validate his story."

"What was the other mistake?" Morgan asked.

"He didn't account for the poor storage," Jeb said. "They had that s**t packed in there way too tight."

"And the whole thing sympathetically detonated," Morgan said.

"Exactly," Jeb replied. "Y'all have seen the ordnance. Pretty standard stuff. With the exception of the Stingers, all the s**t we've been sending them is basically commercially available. The Afghans get ahold of a captured Soviet BM-21, and we send them the Egyptian knock-off ammo to load 'em with, same with mortars and 'reckless' rifles, but it's the Stingers that have been making the difference. And how many Stingers have y'all recovered?" Jeb asked, knowing the answer.

"Zero," Morgan said.

"Zero," Jeb said, holding up his hand in the sign of a zero. "But I've got a manifest that shows we put more than two hundred

Stingers with this shipment before it left Egypt—my guys in Cairo assured me of it, and they don't f*** around."

"So back to our buddies in the mosque," Morgan said. "What do they know?"

"These orderlies come and go, they're treated like property," Jeb explained. "These officers don't pay any attention to them other than to tell them to press their uniforms, or shine their boots, or whatever."

Jeb explained in greater detail how this minority community, from whence the three men hailed, was treated in Pakistan, and how they could be so effective without really having much of an idea what they were doing. While the caste system persists in varying degrees to this day in India, it's not part of traditional Islam. That, in and of itself, may have been as much to blame for the enmity over the years between the Indian Muslims and the Hindus from which they sought liberation. In the Punjab region of Pakistan, and other areas of the country, there is a minority population with historic roots in Indian Dalit Hinduism. To escape the caste system, many Dalit Hindus converted to Christianity and sought refuge in the far western reaches of India—the Punjab region—where that community was more prevalent. When the Pakistanis liberated the region from India and it became part of Pakistan, many of those Christians converted to Islam to assimilate into what was now their new country. The conversion did little to elevate their status in their new country, and their persecution continued. They are known as Muslim Shaikh and reside primarily in the Punjab Province of Pakistan. There is another community with similar roots known as Khyber Pakhtunkhwa, who live in the North-West Frontier Province. That's where Jeb met and recruited Apu and his friends. While Pakistanis don't routinely practice the traditional Indian caste system, their cultural similarities to India make them tolerant of the type of persecution Apu and his friends were accustomed to.

As an orderly on Camp Ojhri, Apu had unfettered access to the officer corps of the Pak Army. They paid him no mind. He was clever though and used his two friends to do the actual orderly work while he just looked busy and listened. Jeb found him to be a fairly reliable source when it came to monitoring the movements of certain officers of interest. After all, Camp Ojhri was the home of the Pak Army, so it was obviously a target-rich environment. And Apu was slick: Jeb became aware of how Apu came into direct contact with White Beard on more than one occasion. He also assumed, since White Beard was also very clever and the deputy director of ISI to boot, Apu was working for White Beard too. It wasn't a foregone conclusion, but Jeb chose to err on the side of caution. He treated Apu as a double agent, taking what intelligence he could, and handling him with great care.

"I managed to get to Apu before White Beard got to him," Jeb said. "Lucky for him I did."

"Why's that?" Will asked.

"His cover was blown," Jeb said. "Apparently White Beard knew he'd been working for me. That's why he didn't want to come out of that mosque as much as anything. I will say that blast did scare the s**t of 'em though—that's a fact."

Morgan and Will chuckled lightly.

"He's no good to me now," Jeb said. "We had to hide all three of them. We'll figure out something to do with them later, but in the meantime, they did give us some good intel."

"White Beard's the ringleader of course," Jeb began. "We figured that much. Apu ID'd Major Omar too."

"He's the guy who grabbed my canteen this morning," Will said.

"Little sawed-off piece of s**t, that's him," Jeb said.

Will smiled at the thought of Jeb referring to Major Omar as "sawed-off" since Jeb himself was barely five feet, seven inches tall. But Major Omar was at least two inches shorter than Jeb, and Will had to agree Jeb's assessment of Omar's character was spot-on.

"Apu named off two or three others they saw that night around the shipment, but they've made themselves scarce. One of them is that little pissant at the airfield when you guys landed—the one who was giving your guy s**t when he was offloading the plane—Lieutenant Bhatti."

"I heard about him from Campbell, but I never saw him," Will said.

"Just as well. He probably would have tried to steal your watch. He was sent out there to monitor the transfer of explosives from the plane to the trucks," Jeb explained, putting a sarcastic emphasis on the word *monitor*. "That means he was sent out there to steal whatever he could get his hands on—the man is a pure thief."

"How'd you know about him being sent out to the plane?" Morgan asked. Will sensed Morgan already knew the answer to the question and was only asking for validation.

"Apu tipped us," Jeb said, as Morgan and Will nodded.

"That's what I thought you'd say," Morgan replied.

CHAPTER TWENTY-TWO

Will would not have characterized their deployment to Pakistan as "routine." Of course, deployment was new to him, so he had no real frame of reference. But at the outset—wearing civilian clothes, handing over dog tags, switching aircrews, pre-dawn landing—he had the sense the term "routine" clearly didn't apply. They were deployed mostly to help in a cleanup operation of an ammunition supply point, but it quickly became clear the primary focus shifted. Now this information from Jeb was adding another element of intrigue.

Since their arrival in Pakistan, Will never felt endangered or threatened—until today. The people they worked with, although not particularly friendly, were not overtly hostile either. *Aloof* was a better word to describe the rank-and-file soldiers with whom they interacted. The same could not be said for at least a few of the officers they encountered though, whose behavior clearly indicated they disapproved of the very presence of the Americans. It was becoming increasingly clear why.

White Beard did little to conceal his disdain for the Americans. He was a high-ranking officer and deputy head of the ISI, so if he hadn't wanted Americans in Pakistan, he was senior enough to throw up roadblocks. The fact they were there, however, suggested he lacked influence in critical areas. Worse, his superiors may not have told him the Americans were coming, which could have only added to his frustration. Given the sum of U.S. military aid to Pakistan, and how important the operation in Afghanistan was, DoD may have demanded of the Pakistan president that the EOD team be there. That was the most probable scenario, which would also explain Jeb's behavior. He conducted himself as though he had a clear mandate. He remained sharply focused, even though the mission abruptly changed from recovery of Stingers to solving the riddle of their disappearance. If anything, the shift of the mission made Jeb even more intent on finding answers.

Morgan and Carter left the SCIF with a better understanding of why they were there, and a greater appreciation for Jeb and the job he was doing. They didn't discuss it any further, and when the rest of team asked where they had been as they arrived poolside, Morgan quickly mentioned a visit to the Seabees shop, skillfully dodging their questions.

After dinner, the team loaded up to go to their new quarters—a safe house at an undisclosed location somewhere in Islamabad. Their usual white vans were replaced by armored versions of similar vehicles. That's when the reality set in for Will that they were in a dangerous situation. Although they were in different vehicles, they had the same drivers. Will jumped in the first van and sat behind Khali Khan as he had been doing the last few days. Khan spoke courteously as he always did and inquired about Will's day. They made the usual chitchat, but Khali Khan made no mention of the new vehicle or the new destination. The drive was no different than all the other trips to the hotel. They drove through town arriving finally at a house in a quiet neighborhood.

SAFE HOUSE–UNDISCLOSED LOCATION
ISLAMABAD, PAKISTAN
APRIL 19, 1988

Will had no concerns about his safety at the safe house as armed guards patrolled it. There was also a wall around the property with turrets on four corners manned by more armed guards. Finally, a heavy steel gate protected the entry, with even more armed guards. So while safety was no longer a major issue there, discretion was. It struck Will as odd this structure was in such a benign setting. It stuck out among the other homes in a presumably peaceful, upper middle-class neighborhood.

As they approached their new accommodations, Khali Khan drove straight up to the gate and matter-of-factly addressed the guards. He had to open the door to speak to them since the bullet-proof glass in the windows could not be rolled down. The guards performed a cursory check of the vehicle and glanced inside. One guard gave a wave to another, and the heavy steel gate began to roll clear of the driveway to reveal the house that would serve as the team's quarters for the next several days or weeks. They had no idea how long they'd be staying.

A butler-like man greeted them at the door. He was wearing a white shalwar kameez with a smart black vest over it. His shirt had a banded collar, buttoned to the top. He addressed the captain formally and saw him to his room first. As there were only five guest rooms, the team would need to double up. The man put the captain and the sergeant major in rooms of their own. Once they were attended to, the "butler" showed the rest to their rooms. Will bunked with Thiessen; Hutchinson and Campbell shared a room; leaving Adams and Morgan together.

"I guess I drew the short straw," Morgan said. The comment floated right by Wiley but drew a light chuckle from the rest. Although Morgan had little regard for Wiley, he didn't see any point in making an issue of the sleeping arrangements. Besides, the rooms were nice and well-appointed. Each had a bathroom complete with shower. Morgan knew there was little to complain about, so he didn't.

The "butler" gave the team a few minutes to settle in before summoning them to the main room, what one would consider a living room in an American home. In fact, the house layout was like what you might find in a traditional American home. There was a sizable dining room adjoining the living room, and the kitchen was visible off the dining room. Once they were all in the living room, the "butler" introduced himself.

"Gentlemen, I am Aziz, the house manager," he said. "I will be seeing to your needs here. Cook has already departed for the evening, but he will return in the morning to prepare your breakfast. If you have any special requests for breakfast, we will make every effort to accommodate. Kindly tell me before you retire and I will instruct Cook."

"If you wish to have a snack or beverage before you retire, we have crisps and snack cakes and other treats available in the kitchen,"

Aziz explained. “If you would like tea or a fizzy drink, I will gladly prepare them for you.”

Nobody said a word as Aziz spoke. They were all taken aback at the formality of his presentation. He clearly spoke with a Pakistani accent, but there was an elegance to his command of the English language.

“Allow me to prepare your rooms,” Aziz said, before he disappeared down the hall and began turning down the beds.

The team stood silently in the living room waiting for Aziz to return, which he did quickly.

“Gentlemen, your rooms are prepared. Before you retire, I should like to point out more amenities for you. Here we have a very nice television and a video cassette machine,” he said, as he opened the two doors of a large armoire. “And there is a selection of video tapes for your viewing pleasure as well.”

Aziz then pointed out a sideboard against a wall under a big mirror. “Here you will find numerous American magazines as well as playing cards and a chess board—do any of you play chess?”

“I do,” Hutchinson responded, to which the sergeant major gave an overt eye roll.

“You play chess?” Morgan inquired, incredulous.

“Sure I do,” Hutchinson replied, tapping his finger against his temple. “This ain’t just a hat rack.”

“Well, I guess we’ll just have to see about that,” Morgan said.

“Alright,” the captain interjected. “That’ll do.”

“Thank you very much, Aziz,” the captain said. “You’ve been very kind—is there anything else we should know before we retire?”

The captain heard all he needed at this point and was about ready to call it a night. He didn’t want to appear rude to Aziz but felt the need to go ahead and curtail the orientation. He had no idea how long they’d be here and felt that anything further they needed to know they could just learn later.

“What time would you like breakfast, sir?” Aziz inquired.

The captain didn’t see any need to get up as early as they had been since they would just be holed up at the house anyway. He looked over at the sergeant major. “Eight o’clock?”

“Works for me, sir,” the sergeant major replied.

“Eight o’clock it is,” the captain said.

“Very good, sir—eight o’clock. Goodnight, gentlemen,” Aziz said, bowing slightly at the waist with both hands together and backing up two steps before turning and proceeding through the dining room toward the kitchen.

“Wow—this is nicer than the hotel,” Will said as they walked down the hall to their rooms.

CHAPTER TWENTY-THREE

Will slept peacefully and awoke at about 5:30 the next morning. Even though they were in a residential area, he could still hear the faint call to prayer emanating from a mosque somewhere in the distance—not as loud as it was at the hotel—but still audible. He was becoming accustomed to the sound in the early morning, and his own internal clock was prepared for it by now. His eyes opened, not abruptly, but alertly, close to same time as the call began.

Thiessen, on the other hand, was unfazed. He continued sleeping soundly in the other twin bed next to the nightstand between their two beds. Will took the opportunity to take a quick shower and prepare for the day. He appeared to be the only one up by the time he quietly emerged from his room and went into the living room. It would still be two hours until breakfast, so he took the opportunity to peruse the collection of videos Aziz mentioned the night before.

It wasn't exactly a treasure trove of cinematic achievement. Whoever curated this collection clearly had a penchant for action films. *Death Wish I*, *II*, and *III*, the *Dirty Harry* franchise, *First Blood*, among others. One caught Will's eye—*Uncommon Valor*—a story about a rescue mission of forgotten American POWs in Vietnam. It was only six o'clock in the morning, so it would have to wait, but that was a movie he thought he'd like.

Will was trying to be as quiet as possible but looking for a way to pass the time. He found a deck of cards in the sideboard and began to play solitaire. He passed the time for better than a half hour before Hutchinson walked in.

"Playing with yourself again, Carter?" he inquired facetiously, chuckling at his own wit.

"You know it," Will replied. He saw no reason to give him any further material to work with and continued his game.

"I could use some coffee," Hutchinson said. "Where's that butler?"

"I haven't seen him."

"Good morning, gentlemen," Aziz announced loudly as he entered the living room, surprising Will and startling Shane who had his back to him.

"What the f***?!" Hutchinson exclaimed, unnerved. He turned to see Aziz standing close behind him.

"I am so sorry, sir," Aziz said, effusively. "Very, very sorry. I did not mean to alarm you, sir."

"Oh, you're fine," Hutchinson said, attempting to mask his own embarrassment as much as assuage Aziz. "Kinda snuck up on me there."

"Yes sir," Aziz replied. "Very sorry."

"Breakfast will be served at eight o'clock this morning," Aziz said. "However, I can offer you some coffee or tea now if you like."

"Hell yeah," Hutchinson said. "I need some coffee."

"Very good, sir. And for you, sir?" he asked, looking at Will kindly.

"Last night you mentioned fizzy drinks," Will said. "Do you have any Coke?"

"Ah, sadly no, sir," Aziz answered. "However, I can provide you some Pepsi Cola."

"Maybe I'll just have tea this morning," Will said. He was a Coke drinker, and saw no need to compromise, even in a foreign country.

"Very good, sir. Tea for you, and coffee for you, sir," he said looking at Hutchinson as he turned toward the kitchen.

"Tea? I suppose you'll order up some quiche for breakfast too," Hutchinson said with a grin. "You might check the medicine cabinet in your bathroom for some maxi pads while you're at it."

"I'll check," Will said, resuming his solitaire game. In the brief time he had been around Hutchinson, Will learned it was best to just play along when he decided to start teasing. It had the effect of diffusing the situation, taking some of the fun out if it for him.

Will's game was short lived. Sergeant Major Scott walked in looking disheveled and unhappy.

"What are you two assholes doing? It's 6:30 in the f***ing morning!" he said, his voice rising.

"It's actually closer to 6:45, Sergeant Major," Hutchinson said, looking at his watch.

"Don't push my buttons this early in the morning, asshole!"

"Well, Sergeant Major, I got up early and was in here in the living room playing cards, and Sergeant Shane came in looking for some coffee," Will explained. "When Aziz showed up and asked us if we wanted coffee, he kind of spooked Sergeant Shane here."

"Shut up, dips**t," Hutchinson said. "He didn't spook me. He just snuck—"

"Coffee?" the sergeant major inquired, before Hutchinson could finish his explanation. "Hell, I could use some coffee myself."

"Of course, sir," Aziz said. "I shall bring you some coffee as well."

"What the hell?!" the sergeant major exclaimed, turning to see Aziz the house manager standing behind him.

Aziz walked up behind the sergeant major in just the same way he surprised Hutchinson. And the sergeant major responded just like Hutchinson, startled and embarrassed.

"A thousand apologies, sir," Aziz said contritely. "I did not mean to startle you."

"No problem," the sergeant major said. "Maybe next time just don't sneak up on me like that."

"Of course, sir, very sorry. Gentlemen, your coffee and your tea," Aziz said, placing a tray on the coffee table.

"Damn, somebody ought to put a bell on that sumb***h," the sergeant major said, after Aziz left the room.

"That's what I was trying to tell you, Sergeant Major," Hutchinson said. "That damn butler sneaks around here like a cat."

By now, the whole house was awake. The captain straggled in looking for some coffee, and before long, everyone but Wiley was in the living room either asking about or contributing to the early morning noise.

"Hell, if I'd known everybody was going to be up this early, I'd have ordered an earlier breakfast," the captain said. "I would take some coffee though."

At that moment, Aziz took the opportunity to announce himself while he was still in the dining room. He acted like he didn't want to risk startling us by sneaking into the living room. He wasn't really sneaking earlier, he just had light steps which gave the appearance of sneaking. Coupled with a very loud voice, the effect—as evinced by the sergeant major and Hutchinson—could be startling.

Aziz placed the sergeant major's coffee on the sideboard. "Your coffee, sir."

The sergeant major grabbed the cup and took a careful sip, with a slight slurp. "Ahh, thank you," he said. "Just what the doctor ordered."

"Certainly, sir," Aziz replied. "I shall return with more coffee for the rest of you. Would any of you care for anything else before breakfast—some fruit juice perhaps?"

A chorus of affirmative responses met the offer of juice, and in short order Aziz returned with an ample supply of both coffee and orange juice.

"Sir, everyone appears to be awake now," Aziz said, addressing the captain. "Perhaps we could expedite your breakfast? Cook is working on it now."

"That sounds like a pretty good idea," the captain replied. "Thank you."

"Of course," Aziz replied. "I shall see to it. It won't be long, sir."

Shortly, there was an impressive spread waiting for them on the dining room table. They all sat and unceremoniously dug in. Just then there was a knock on the kitchen door and a familiar voice spoke to the cook. In a moment, Jeb walked into the dining room dressed like they never saw him before. He was wearing a dark shalwar kameez with a khaki-colored vest, and a brown Pakol—a hat commonly worn in Afghanistan and Pakistan. Pakistanis referred to it as a Chitrali cap, but it was the same thing. The hat looked like a big donut with a pizza laying on top of it, Will thought.

"Morning, gentlemen," Jeb said. "I see everyone made it through the night. But you're light a man. Where's Adams?"

"Here I am," Wiley said, walking into the dining room and rubbing the sleep from his eyes. "Why didn't anyone wake me up?

"You're a full-grown man, Wiley," the sergeant major responded, shortly. "You ought to know when it's time to get up."

Wiley had been around the sergeant major long enough to know not to say anything further. He sat at the table and filled his plate without speaking.

Jeb was still standing at the kitchen door, and since Will finished eating—and Jeb was a superior officer—he stood and offered him his seat at the table. At the same time, Aziz appeared with another chair. "For you, sir," he said, motioning for Jeb to be seated at the table. "Would you like some tea or coffee?"

"Coffee, please," he said. "Keep your seat, Sergeant Carter," he added. Will took that to mean he wanted him to stay put for some information he may share.

"So how are things going?" Jeb inquired, looking at the captain.

"Well, sir," the captain began, "we've been here for less than twelve hours and we're all about ready to kill each other. What does that tell you?"

Jeb chuckled. "Mostly that tells me you're normal. Cabin fever—been there."

"Well, we've got it," the captain replied.

"I just thought I'd drop by and check in on you," Jeb said. "Nothing really new to report. I'll be out of pocket for the next few days. Miller and Leftwich will be by to look in on you."

"Out of pocket?" the captain asked. "That sounds ominous."

"Well, I've got a meeting across the border," Jeb replied.

"Ah, that explains the outfit," the captain said.

"Yeah, it never hurts to go native," Jeb explained. "Blend in—low profile."

"Well, we're going to keep y'all hunkered down here for a while," Jeb said. "But the good news is we've made arrangements to provide transportation back and forth to the embassy. That way you'll be less likely to kill each other before I get back. These guys can find a few things to occupy their time at the embassy, I'm sure," he said. "You'll have to hang here today, and we'll send out the vans to get you tomorrow around 1000 hours."

"Sounds good," the captain responded.

"Don't forget—you've got dinner at the Ambo's residence tomorrow evening," Jeb reminded the captain. "I more than likely won't be back for that, but the general will be there." Jeb stood and pushed back from the table. "You'll leave for the Ambo's residence directly from the embassy, so take some fresh clothes with you. I know how your guys like their volleyball, so have 'em knock off early enough to clean up and get ready."

"Will do," the captain replied.

Jeb turned and made his way through the door into the kitchen preparing to leave through the back door. Will was seated next to Jeb near the end of the table closest to the door to the kitchen. Will got up and discreetly followed Jeb into the kitchen.

"Got room for one more, sir?" Will asked Jeb. He was standing at the door with his hand on the doorknob. Will knew the answer would most likely be "no," but he thought he'd ask in the off chance he might consider letting him tag along. Will wanted to see and do as much as he could and going across the border into Afghanistan at that time, seemed to him the educational opportunity of a lifetime.

"I wish I did," Jeb said. "But I'm not sure I could get away with bringing you along. And I'd have a hell of a time trying to blend you in with that yellow hair and those green eyes.

"Just sit tight for another week or so," Jeb said. "I'll get you out and show you a few things."

"Roger that," Will replied.

CHAPTER TWENTY-FOUR

Will was intensely intrigued by the idea of getting out and seeing a few things, as Jeb suggested they might do. In an earlier conversation, Jeb mentioned the refugee camps around Peshawar on the Afghan border. Will was anxious to see them. No one knew for sure how long they'd be confined to the safe house and the embassy, but he was excited at the prospect of getting out beyond the twin cities area to see what the countryside looked like.

Since Will had already showered, shaved, and prepared for the day, he settled into the living room after breakfast. He had the honor of making the first choice of movies and took a minute to scan the video selection. He found a couple of classics—*Dr. Zhivago* and *Lawrence of Arabia*—but didn't have much interest in either of them. And Will was certain this crowd wouldn't either. The titles jogged his memory though, and it occurred to him he might have a little fun.

"Come on, Carter," Hutchinson chided. "What's it gonna be?"

Will held up two videos, one in each hand. "*My Fair Lady* or *Breakfast at Tiffany's*?" Of course, he wasn't holding either one of those movies, but Hutchinson didn't know that, and the response was entirely predictable.

"You gotta be s**ttin' me!" Hutchinson exclaimed. "Is this guy for real?!—come on!"

Morgan wasn't in on the joke, but he could clearly see Will was holding *Uncommon Valor* in one hand, and *First Blood* in the other. That made it even funnier as far as he was concerned. Hutchinson was far enough away he couldn't make out what the videos were, but it was clear he wasn't pleased. The captain seemed to get a kick out of it too, and openly laughed. True to form, Wiley asked, "What's so funny?"

"Never mind," Morgan said, dismissively.

"You better pick something else, Carter," the captain advised. "Looks like Hutchinson's about to wet himself over there."

"Lighten up, Hutch—damn," Morgan said. "He's got a couple of good ones there—play one, Will, before he loses it."

"*Uncommon Valor* it is," Will said.

"Oh, that's good," Morgan said. "I've seen it."

"You never know with Carter," Hutchinson said.

The team spent the day watching movies, playing cards, and eating. The food was good, but it was never good to eat out of boredom. If this is what safe house life was going to be like, they'd all be twenty pounds heavier before they ever got out of confinement if they weren't careful. To his credit, Campbell spent about as much time doing pushups and sit-ups as he did eating, which wasn't unusual for him. Will decided that was a wise decision, given the amount of food that they had access to, so he joined in. Will was in decent shape, but Campbell was a beast, and it was difficult to keep up with him.

Not to be outdone, Hutchinson joined in, competitive as ever, never liking to be left out of anything. Before long, Thiessen joined as well. Morgan had no interest at all in participating in any calisthenics not absolutely required. He was nearing retirement and didn't feel the need to do anything extraneous at this point in his career. Wiley busied himself playing solitaire and ignored the pushups and sit-ups going on. He was a wiry guy and managed to stay very thin without much effort at all. In fact, no one could recall having ever seen Wiley do a pushup or a sit-up—or run for that matter—and yet he managed to stay skinny as a rail.

The captain watched without comment, mostly sipping coffee, or occasionally stepping outside for a cigarette. He was usually sociable but felt the need to maintain a little distance under the circumstances. Sergeant Major Scott had not emerged from his bedroom since he sequestered himself after breakfast.

As the late afternoon gave way to early evening, a savory aroma began to waft in from the kitchen. Before long, Aziz walked into the dining room where the team was playing cards. "Have you enjoyed your card game, gentlemen?" he asked. While polite, it was clear the inquiry was meant to prompt them to leave so he could prepare the table for dinner.

"We just finished," Morgan said. "Thank you, Aziz—what's for dinner?"

"Yeah, something smells good," Will added.

"Cook has prepared a variety of dishes for your dinner this evening," Aziz replied. "I'm certain you will be quite pleased."

"Well, it smells damn good," Hutchinson said. "I can tell you that much."

"Thank you, sir," Aziz said. "Dinner will be served shortly."

"Let's get out of Aziz's way," Morgan said.

Aziz nodded and smiled as the team left the room.

The dinner was a feast. A variety of meats, vegetables, curries, rice, breads, and sauces filled the table. Beef was Will's preferred meat and he spotted some on a big platter.

"Pass some of that beef this way when you get a chance, Tom," Will said. Thiessen passed it over and Will placed a generous portion on his plate. It was a very lean cut.

Aziz was standing to the side of the dining room near the door to the kitchen watching as the team passed the platters around the table. "Actually sir, that is not beef, it is buffalo," Aziz said.

"Buffalo?" Will responded, pausing slightly. "What kind of buffalo?" he asked, not that it mattered. He was just naturally curious about such things.

"Water buffalo," Aziz replied. "Very important here in Pakistan, sir. We get most of our milk from buffalo as well."

"Well, how 'bout that," Will replied. "Was that buffalo milk we had at breakfast?"

"Indeed, it was, sir."

"I thought it seemed a little heavier than what I'm used to."

"Oh yes, sir. Buffalo milk is much richer than cow's milk."

"Try it, sir," Aziz said, motioning to the meat on Will's plate.

Without reservation Will took a bite and found the taste and texture to be very comparable to beef. It was a little tougher than beef but had a very satisfying flavor.

"That is good," Will said.

Aziz smiled and nodded.

"Yeah, I don't care what it is," Hutchinson said between bites. "It's damn good."

Aziz took great satisfaction in knowing the team was enjoying the food. He motioned from the kitchen door for the cook, who appeared in the dining room doorway a moment later. The cook was wearing a tan shalwar suit with the shirt sleeves rolled up to the elbows, a white apron, and a white brimless cap on his head—a kufi. He was a short, older gentleman with a well-worn face. He peered around the door to look in at the Americans and his face lit up. He was obviously delighted they were enjoying the food he prepared.

If all that wasn't enough, Aziz brought out dessert as they were finishing their meal. He placed a big tray of square treats at the center of the table. They had the appearance of rice crispy treats, except they were a darker brown—as if made from Cocoa Crispies instead of Rice Crispies. As it turned out, they were not rice. They were habshi halwa squares—a common dessert in Pakistan. They were sweet, rich, had a nutty flavor and texture and were quickly consumed by the hungry team, along with the coffee Aziz provided. The strong coffee helped offset the sweetness of the habshi halwa. In just a few moments, the big platter of treats was empty.

"Well, that was a hell of a meal," Hutchinson said, as he began to make his way into the living room. He rubbed his stomach as he said it as if to emphasize the point.

"That was a lot better than anything they serve at the embassy," the sergeant major added.

If the last twenty-four hours were any indication of what they could expect each day, safe house life wouldn't be so bad, Will thought, though he missed Tara already. He would no doubt see her tomorrow. Will had to admit he was growing fond of Tara and enjoyed her company—a welcome relief from the coarseness of his teammates. They were obviously missing their wives and homes; seeing Will with a beautiful young woman was unlikely to make them any happier in Pakistan.

The team passed another evening in the safe house without incident. Breakfast was earlier the next morning, and they anxiously awaited transportation to the embassy. If nothing else, they could get out of the house and lounge by the pool.

Will wondered if Jeb's trip across the border was routine or prompted by the events leading to the sequestration of his team. He posed the question to Morgan. As their time in Islamabad went on, Will found he could talk to Morgan without worrying about being dismissed or ridiculed.

"I was wondering the same thing myself," Morgan responded. "I guess we'll just have to ask him when he gets back. Without knowing his routine, it's hard to speculate. Of course, guys in his line of work try to steer clear of routine."

"Steer clear of routine?" Will repeated. "What do you mean?"

"Well, these guys can have a lot of eyes on them," Morgan explained. "They don't want to get into habits or patterns that could make it easier for an adversary to get a bead on them. Patterns can reveal things about you. It may be as simple as helping to confirm who you work for. These guys have to be very careful about that. The last thing they want to do is give themselves away. They vary their routes when they're going somewhere they go to frequently. They do that to protect sensitive destinations that could be potential targets. They might make abrupt turns when they're driving to see if they can detect someone following them. They do all kinds of stuff to make sure they don't inadvertently give up any information through their daily behaviors. They call it tradecraft. Of course, that term applies to a lot more than just how they travel and move around."

"That's interesting," Will replied. "How do you know about 'tradecraft'?"

"Well, my brother's in the business. I've picked up some of that from him. And I like to read a lot—spy novels, you know, stuff like that."

"Your brother is in the business?"

"Yeah, he works for the agency," Morgan replied. "He's a case officer."

"A case officer?"

"Yeah, like these guys Miller and Leftwich. I'm pretty sure they're case officers."

"Is Jeb a case officer?"

"I don't think so. I'm not sure what he is. I know he's a Green Beret, and I know he's an intel guy. My guess is he probably works *for* DIA, but he's definitely working *with* CIA. It's possible he's attached to CIA in some capacity. Either way, he sure seems to know what the hell he's doing."

That much was clear. Will was fascinated by what Jeb was doing, even though he wasn't entirely sure of the breadth of his mission, and specifically what he did when he went over the border. Will wasn't certain, but hearing Jeb talk about the Stingers, and the intensity he showed regarding their disposition because of the blast, he came to believe Jeb may have been the one responsible for recommending Stingers be provided to the Mujahideen in the first place. Whether he was or wasn't, it was clear Jeb was certainly a key enabler when it came to placing Stinger missiles in the hands of the Afghan freedom fighters.

As far as Will and Morgan knew, this was Jeb's first trip across the border since the blast at Camp Ojhri. Undoubtedly, his contacts in Afghanistan would know about the incident by now. As primitive as Afghanistan may have seemed at the time, the people there had access to a variety of newspapers—among other media sources—and would certainly have heard the news by now. Jeb had the unenviable task of breaking the news to his Afghan colleagues personally that the Mujahideen would not be receiving any Stingers in this shipment.

CHAPTER TWENTY-FIVE

GOSHTA, NANGARHAR PROVINCE, AFGHANISTAN
APRIL 21, 1988
1935 HRS.

Jeb's primary contact in Afghanistan was a young man named Muhammadin. He was just twenty-seven years old but was a seasoned veteran, made so not only by the Russian invaders who wreaked havoc on his homeland, but the internal strife with Afghan communists going on since at least his early teen years. Forced to fight or die in many cases, Muhammadin was involved with internal tribal squabbles since he was a boy—which were common in his country—but it was in his first encounter with the Russians the young Afghan lost a sister, a brother, and his grandfather, among many more of his extended family and fellow villagers. His father was killed in the 1978 Saur Revolution that saw the Afghan communists come to power leaving Muhammadin as the head of his household, and the communist People's Democratic Party of Afghanistan in control of his country. He developed an intense hatred for the communists as Afghanistan descended into civil war.

Muhammadin rose through the ranks swiftly. The fight against the communists, now aided by the Soviets, quickly decimated the number of fighting-aged men and took a heavy toll on their senior leadership as well. Muhammadin demonstrated a knack for staying alive. He was a quick study and applied what he learned about the Russians in an efficient, strategic manner. He was tactically proficient and a proven battlefield leader.

Although he was a fierce fighter, he was also affable. He had a natural political ability, which may have accounted for his quick rise into the upper echelons of leadership as much as his skill on the battlefield. And he was Pashtun, which helped him quickly foster relationships in Pakistan along the Afghan border. There was a significant Pashtun population in the western reaches of Pakistan. His contacts with Pakistan's Special Services Group—who were mostly responsible for training the Mujahideen—introduced him to Jeb. Over the last three years, Jeb and Muhammadin developed a close friendship. Each knew they could trust the other.

When Jeb arrived at Muhammadin's camp near Goshta on the Kunar River, he was greeted gleefully by Muhammadin and others in the camp. Jeb had become something of a celebrity among the Afghan freedom fighters under Muhammadin's command, and they always turned out to welcome him. Jeb enjoyed being in camp among the Afghan soldiers. The sights, the sounds, and the smells became familiar to him. He particularly liked hearing the horses nicker and snort as they milled about in the pens near the camp tents. It reminded him of his youth in Texas where he spent summers on his grandfather's ranch in the hill country north of San Antonio.

Muhammadin's first order of business was to feed his weary American friend. Jeb had been traveling all day. He left Islamabad by helicopter, then drove the rest of the way from Peshawar. He could usually make the trip to Goshta in under six hours, but a flat tire on the rough road slowed his progress. Still, he managed to arrive in camp just in time for dinner.

Jeb assumed Muhammadin heard the news of the blast by now. He always tried to allow Muhammadin to do most of the talking—he found he tended to learn more that way—though the subject of Camp Ojhri never came up throughout their dinner conversation. It wasn't until after dinner when they stepped outside to have a smoke that Muhammadin brought it up. Jeb knew Muhammadin was fond of American cigarettes, so he tried to bring him a carton or two whenever he could. This trip he packed two cartons of Marlboro Reds, and Muhammadin wasted no time indulging.

"I should like to meet your new American friends," Muhammadin said in Pashto, as he lit a cigarette. Although Jeb was progressing on his Pashto, he preferred to speak Russian with Muhammadin, a language in which they were both fluent. However, Jeb knew Muhammadin took it as a great compliment that he was working so hard to improve his Pashto.

"Of course," Jeb said, in Pashto. "I will arrange it very soon." He was a little surprised Muhammadin would so casually mention his "new American friends," but it was a clear indication Muhammadin was aware of the Camp Ojhri blast. Of course, he knew Muhammadin was referring to the EOD team since there were no other American military working in Pakistan at the time.

"Your Pashto is improving, my friend," Muhammadin said, continuing to smoke one of the Marlboros Jeb had given him. "Soon you'll sound like a natural-born Pashtun," he added with a friendly laugh.

"That's my goal," Jeb replied, smiling.

Jeb began speaking in Russian as he explained the situation. He would have to speak in more technical terms, and he was more confident he could offer much greater detail in a language in which he was more proficient. Muhammadin understood and listened attentively without expression. Jeb refrained from including his suspicions about who might be responsible.

Muhammadin was very perceptive though and soon began to posit theories of his own, although Jeb never confirmed any of them. Muhammadin's most plausible theory closely matched his. He was amazed at how quickly Muhammadin could piece this scenario together and arrive at almost exactly the same conclusion. Even though he trusted Muhammadin, Jeb was careful not to give too much information away.

Although he had been working with the S.S.G. for some time now for the purpose of training his men, Muhammadin had little regard for Pakistanis. Even though there was a sizable Pashtun population in Pakistan, there was a long history of enmity between the two countries. It wasn't until the Soviets entered Afghanistan at the request of the communist President Taraki that tensions began to ease between the Pashtuns and the Pakistani government. It was necessary for Muhammadin to work with the Pakistanis, but he didn't like them, and he didn't trust them. Jeb's news came as no real surprise to Muhammadin.

"I thought it would only be a matter of time before something like this happened," Muhammadin said. "Every trip I've made to Pakistan over the last three years, I've sensed they have been using our struggle to enrich themselves. God only knows whose hands our weapons will end up in now."

Jeb was constantly amazed at how astute the young Afghan commander was. It was no wonder how quickly he had ascended in the ranks. Although Muhammadin had never been far outside his home country, he was well read and highly intelligent. He had a natural intellectual curiosity and keen analytical skills.

Although the Soviets were in the initial stages of winding down their occupation of Afghanistan, there were still battles being fought in various locations around the country, even as the Russians were drawing down. "We still need our weapons and ammunition," Muhammadin said. "The war is not yet over. Even after the Russians leave, I fear the fighting will continue."

That seemed a dire pronouncement, Jeb thought. He had been working with Muhammadin for three years and he still felt at somewhat of a loss when it came to fully understanding the inter-tribal dynamics, centuries in the making in this enigmatic country. Throughout history there were tribal wars in Afghanistan. They were a warring people. There was honor in it, it seemed. In Jeb's mind they were much more like some of the Native American tribes than anyone back home seemed to recognize. They were a horse culture, much like the bands that comprised the greater Apache tribe. And like the Apache, when the bands weren't fighting a common adversary as a tribe, they oftentimes fought amongst themselves acting on intra-tribal rivalries and disputes.

Still, Muhammadin's ominous observation gave Jeb pause. What did Muhammadin know that would make him believe the fighting would continue?

"What's makes you think so?" Jeb asked.

"I'm hearing talk even among my own people. There will be a struggle for power once the Russians leave. We all agree the

Russians must go—all the tribes hate the communists. We will not go back to communism. But the Tajiks and Pashtuns will not agree on who should lead the country. There will be a struggle between Sunni and Shia—even among my own Pashtun people. I'm afraid we will need your help for a long time, my friend. Even though I am Sunni, I do not trust the Saudis."

Muhammadin spoke candidly to Jeb because he knew he could trust him. Jeb found Muhammadin's suspicions of the Saudis alarming but unsurprising. Since the U.S. had been involved with supporting the Mujahideen, the Saudis had matched U.S. funding dollar for dollar helping to leverage American buying power. Despite that, there still seemed to be a Saudi agenda. As much as anything, Jeb believed their interests may have been to provide a counterbalance to the growing Iranian Shia influence in Afghanistan. It appeared from Muhammadin's foreboding tone though, it could be much more than that. Time would tell, and as far as Jeb was concerned, the situation bore close monitoring. Muhammadin had been forthcoming over the years—even opening his home to Jeb on multiple occasions. He generously shared intelligence with Jeb as well, and this added information specifically detailing the activities of a Saudi from an affluent family in Riyadh. The Saudi in question was actively recruiting Mujahideen veterans for a cause that was still unclear. That was intelligence Jeb shared up the chain of command but was only considered ancillary to the bigger issue of continuing to arm the Mujahideen.

CHAPTER TWENTY-SIX

U.S. AMBASSADOR'S RESIDENCE
ISLAMABAD, PAKISTAN
APRIL 21, 1988
1930 HRS.

About the time Jeb was sitting down to dinner with his Mujahideen hosts, the team was sitting down to dinner at the U.S. ambassador's residence. It was a beautiful home and Will felt self-conscious about his appearance. He was wearing jeans and jungle boots with the cleanest of the polo shirts he could find in his duffel bag. They were told the dress code was casual, but except for the captain—who was wearing khakis, a nice button-down oxford shirt, and loafers—they were all wearing jeans and combat boots. Despite the dress code, the ambassador walked into the large great room of the residence wearing a suit and tie adding to Will's self-consciousness. He couldn't say the same about the rest of the team. Mostly, they seemed oblivious to any degree of formality, showing no concern about their state of dress.

While the captain and sergeant major made the cursory small talk with the ambassador, the junior team members made short work of the hors d'oeuvres circulating around the room. Will got the impression this would be a short evening. While the ambassador was standing there making small talk with the captain, the sergeant major, and the general, he repeatedly checked his watch as if he were waiting on a bus to arrive at any moment. I'm sure he could have thought of a dozen other things he would have rather been doing at that time, and his near constant watch-checking made that abundantly clear.

The general stood among the ambassador and the two senior team members for just a few minutes before slipping away. He came over to the rest of the team, and Morgan quickly stood up and discreetly got their attention. He didn't think it was appropriate to call them to attention, but his throat clearing signaled they should all stand up in the general's presence. As General Wassom approached, he genially urged them to keep their seats. He came over to talk casually and didn't want any formalities to constrain the team from speaking candidly.

Nobody took their seats until the general sat down, at which point he engaged Morgan. General Wassom was curious to know how they were progressing, some of the things they encountered in their work, and the assessment of their Pak counterparts. Morgan gave the general a thorough technical brief about the nature of the work they were doing and some of the ordnance they found among other things.

Wassom was knowledgeable about ordnance having been an artillery officer and listened attentively, asking only the occasional technical question, but otherwise mostly absorbing the information Morgan shared. It wasn't until the general directly queried Morgan about their Pak counterparts that Morgan showed any hesitation in forthrightly answering his questions.

"It's alright, Sergeant. I know you don't want to speak ill of our hosts. We were afraid they might be difficult to work with."

"Oh, no sir," Morgan said, respectfully. "The Pak soldiers have been great. It's just . . ."

"Just what, Sergeant?" General Wassom asked.

"Well, sir."

"Speak freely, Sergeant."

"No disrespect intended, sir," Morgan began, "but these Pak officers . . . well, they have little, if any, regard for their men, sir."

"Well, that's been our observation too. My main concern is that y'all are being treated appropriately."

"Well, sir, Jeb's been doing a pretty good job keeping the officers off our a—um, out of our hair."

For just a second, the general raised an eyebrow and Morgan felt the need to qualify that statement.

"Of course, I mean the Pak officers, sir."

General Wassom chuckled. "Well, that's what Hawkeye gets paid for, and I knew you meant the Pak officers."

"What about you, Sergeant, Carter?" the general inquired, as he turned toward Will. "I hear you're the horseman of the bunch. What do you think of the horses you've seen here in Pakistan?"

"Uh, well, sir," Will began. "The horses I've seen so far have been pretty small and pretty poor. I'm used to a lot bigger than these. And we feed 'em a little better back home, sir."

"Same here. I've always had gaited horses myself. They're generally pretty good size, and we kept 'em pretty heavy too. They tell me you're a cowboy—is that true?"

"Yes sir, I mean I was before I joined the Army, that is. I cowboyed on some ranches out in New Mexico when I was in high school, and I worked for a couple of horse trainers too."

"Well, once a cowboy, always a cowboy. That's the way I see it anyway. Ever play any polo, Sergeant?"

"No sir, but I've always wanted to."

"I know a few of these Pak officers who play polo. They keep a string of polo ponies that are a little short, but they are stocky son of a guns—I guess they get fed a lot better than these poor nags you see around town. In fact, I bought myself a polo saddle not too long ago. Nothing more than a souvenir really—I don't play polo myself. Just thought it would be neat to have, and it was dirt cheap, so I figured what the heck."

"I wouldn't mind getting my hands on one of those, sir."

"I got it at a little shop in Rawalpindi—they have all kinds of saddles and tack. I'll tell your driver where it is and maybe you can go see for yourself when things settle down a bit."

"Thank you, sir."

Will's teammates had long since tuned out the conversation about horses, none of them having any interest at all in the topic. They set about consuming more hors d'oeuvres as they waited for dinner to commence.

The general's comment about things settling down a bit brought issues back into focus. Will was enjoying the conversation—he always liked talking horses—but he snapped back to reality when General Wassom indirectly reminded him why they were there.

One of the house staff walked in as they were finishing their conversation and announced dinner being served. All proceeded into a large dining room where a card marked each place setting. The ambassador sat on one end of the table with the captain immediately to his right, and the general on the other end with Sergeant Major Scott seated on his right. The rest of the team was placed around the table randomly, except for Will who was seated next to Morgan. The captain instructed Morgan to sit next to Will in case he needed a little coaching.

"See those two boxes on the table back there?" Morgan asked, motioning to a sideboard behind their chairs. "Those are your fuzes. The Seabees made 'em into plaques. The captain had them boxed and wrapped. Probably after dessert, the captain is gonna say a few words to the ambassador and then turn it over to you for the presentations. The general's is the one with the little star on the front of the box—see it?—don't mix 'em up."

The panicked look on Will's face prompted Morgan to offer some kind words of encouragement. "You'll be fine. Just don't overthink it."

Will had no idea what to say or how to say it and spent most of the meal going over what he might say to avoid looking like a fool when the time came to make the presentations. When the staff began to clear the dessert plates, Morgan leaned over and whispered, "You're up, slugger."

Right on cue, Captain Halstead stood and tapped his wine glass with a dessert spoon to get everyone's attention.

"Mr. Ambassador, General," the captain began, looking at each of the two men in turn as he spoke. "On behalf of our team, we'd like to thank you for your support of our mission, and your gracious hospitality. To show our appreciation, we would like to present each of you with a special gift to commemorate this mission—Sergeant Carter."

"Thank you, sir," Will said, as he stood, and began his presentations. As Will later remembered it, he said, "On behalf of our team, we would like to present you with a token of our esteem to commemorate the Camp Ojhri blast." In reality it was more like he only managed a few sentence fragments and handed the plaques to their recipients.

Will's worry aside, the ambassador and the general were genuinely appreciative.

With the dinner over, Will was glad to be getting back in the van to return to the safe house. The captain slapped him on the back as he passed. "Good job, Carter."

Morgan was seated behind him in the van. Will turned and asked him, "How do you think that went?"

"Blah, blah, blah plaque," he said with a chuckle.

"Really?" Will asked. "Oh man, I was afraid I would mess that up."

"Nah, you did fine, Will. You scored some big points with the general. He really likes you—I can tell."

That was reassuring to hear. Just two days later Will received a handwritten note from General Wassom, thanking him for the gift and for the work they were doing in Pakistan.

CHAPTER TWENTY-SEVEN

Several days passed as the team whiled away the hours intermittently watching videos, lounging by the pool, and even playing a little tennis on the embassy's clay courts. Despite the amusements at their disposal, the team was getting antsy. They were ready to get back to work. Will was fortunate to have the added diversion of female companionship. He was careful not to mention Tara to his teammates though, conscious of the fact they were getting homesick as well as stir crazy. Besides, he saw no need to kiss and tell, and didn't want to subject himself to any undue persecution at the hands of Hutchinson.

One day while Will was at lunch, the general walked into the cafeteria. He was looking for Will, who sat by himself drinking a Coke, hoping Tara would be down soon. Will noticed the general was casually walking toward his table, so he stood and came to attention.

"Afternoon, Sergeant."

"Afternoon, sir."

"Go ahead and have a seat, son," he said, as he pulled out a chair for himself. He sat at the table, and Will followed suit.

"How are enjoying your time in Pakistan?"

Will wasn't sure where this was going, but he got a feeling it was more than small talk.

"Well sir, I'm really enjoying it. I mean, this is a great experience, sir."

"It is that. How would you feel about sticking around awhile?"

"Sir?"

"I've enjoyed having soldiers around these past few weeks. Nothing against the Marines or the Seabees for that matter, but I've missed having soldiers around. We speak the same language. I could use an aide, and I think you'd be just the right soldier for that job—what do you think?"

Dumbfounded, Will struggled to reply. The general read his expression. "Give it some thought, Sergeant. We'll talk later."

With that the general stood, pushed his chair under the table. Ordinarily, Will would have come to attention when an officer stood, but he was so taken aback by the offer he just sat there trying to figure it out. The general took no offense at the oversight and made no correction. He simply smiled, patted Will on the shoulder, and left the cafeteria.

Will sat at the cafeteria table lost in thought, pondering the potential opportunity the general proposed, when Tara joined him. He was almost startled when he heard the chair scooted from under the table.

"Little jumpy aren't ya, babe," Tara said, smiling. "Where'd you go?" noticing the faraway look in Will's eye.

"Oh, hey—hi," Will said. "I was just a little zoned out."

"I can see that. Anything in particular on your mind?"

"Nah, nothing really. How's your day going?" He didn't want to share the exchange he just had with the general. He thought it would only complicate things with Tara.

The redirect worked. Tara began telling Will about her day which was sufficient to divert his attention from his own concerns. He enjoyed hearing her talk, and she seemed genuinely appreciative of the fact he listened. They spent lunch together and made plans to see each other again after work that evening.

Aside from the time spent with Tara, the days at the embassy were becoming mundane and increasingly tedious for Will. In fact, the whole team was tiring of the inactivity, and were all anxious to get back to work.

"This s**t's getting old," Chad Campbell said one afternoon while they were lounging by the pool. "I'm about ready to get back in the field or else go back home." Chad rarely spoke, but on this point, everyone agreed.

There was a general murmur of agreement among the team. Morale was on the cusp of sharp decline and the captain knew it. He just happened to be outside by the pool with the team that day, which was rare. The captain tried to make it a point to maintain some distance between himself and the men—mostly for appearances—but he decided to join them that afternoon.

"Just a few more days, boys," the captain said. "We'll get back in the field soon and wrap this up pretty quick. Hell, I'm as anxious as you guys are to get back home. My dogs have probably forgotten who I am by now."

The captain made the comment about his dogs as a joke, but the truth was he was starting to miss home—particularly his wife—more than he expected. He had only the one opportunity to call home a couple of weeks before and would have loved to speak to Renee again. He had to be careful to guard against allowing his absence from home to affect the overall morale of the team. He knew the team would certainly cue off him, and the last thing he needed was a team of malcontents. Mostly, he did a stellar job of keeping a positive attitude.

"I don't know what anybody has to complain about anyway," Wiley chimed in. "We get to lay around by this pool all day, the food is good—what more could you ask for?"

"Well, for starters I could ask you to shut the f*** up!" Hutchinson shot back. He had no regard for Wiley at all and felt any input he offered demanded swift and sharp rebuke.

"Hey, whoa dude!" Morgan said, attempting to intercept what could turn into a prolonged argument, or worse, if it weren't shut down quickly. Morgan was also aware that morale was starting to slip and didn't want to see it erode any further with an internal squabble. "Lighten up, man. He's just making an observation that's all. Besides, I know this is getting a little boring, but you have to admit this is pretty good duty."

"Yeah, it's not bad," Hutchinson agreed. "But I will say this: a man can get tired of chocolate cake if he eats enough of it."

"What's that supposed to mean?" Thiessen asked.

"Well, dumbass, what it means is—"

"What I think he means is," Morgan quickly interjected, "that even something really good—like chocolate cake, for example—can get old if you have too much of it."

The captain and the sergeant major went inside while the rest of the team dove into the pool.

The timing was fortuitous for the captain and the sergeant major. As they were grabbing a cup of coffee from the cafeteria, Jeb walked in.

"Gentlemen," he said, nodding and acknowledging them both.

"Well, you're back," the captain said.

"Yep, got in late last night." How are you boys holding up?"

"I think our guys could use a change of scenery," the captain answered. "They're not exactly at each other's throats just yet, but getting there."

"I figured they might be getting a little punchy. I was just talking to Miller and Leftwich and we think maybe they could get out for a little excursion."

"Excursion, sir?" the sergeant major asked.

"Yeah, they're going north tomorrow. They said they could roll out in a van if your guys wanted to ride along."

"North?" the captain inquired.

"They weren't specific. Not sure what they're up to—maybe just stretching their legs a little—but they said y'all could come if you want to. I guarantee you the scenery up that way is worth the ride."

Captain Halstead didn't know if "stretching their legs" was a cryptic CIA euphemism, but he didn't think it would be a bad idea to give his guys a chance to stretch their own legs too. He wasn't sure what the Planning and Outreach guys were up to, but he figured it must be safe enough if they were asking the team along.

"I'm sure they'll want to go," the captain said.

"How 'bout you, Captain?" Jeb asked.

"I think I'm going to stick around here and go over some of our notes and pictures," the captain said, referring to the intel they collected on some of the ordnance found so far. "We've run into a fuze or two I'd like to get a little more familiar with."

"Copy that. Sergeant Major?"

"Think I'll stick around too. Sometimes the captain needs a little help understanding all this technical stuff," he added, smiling. The captain rolled his eyes and smiled.

The truth of the matter was Captain Halstead had it in mind to try and arrange another call home. Sergeant Major Scott was thinking the same thing but didn't say anything. He knew the captain was up to something though. They had gone over the intel several times by now, there being little else to do since they weren't in the field. Looking over the intel again didn't exactly track, but the sergeant major withheld further comment until he knew what the captain was thinking.

"We're going to get you back in the field in just a few more days. Tell your guys to hang in there and be ready," Jeb said.

"Will do," the captain replied.

Later that afternoon Halstead went outside to let the team know about the planned trip north. They were all excited at the prospect of getting out of the city and seeing the countryside. All except Wiley. He had it in mind it was his duty to stay behind and attend to the sergeant major's every need. His pronouncement that he intended to remain at the embassy was not well received by the captain.

"Well, I guess I'll just hang back here," Wiley stated matter-of-factly, as though it was essential he accompany Sergeant Major Scott.

"That won't be necessary, Sergeant," the captain replied.

Wiley looked downcast at the captain's rebuke. "Well, sir, I just thought I might be able to help out if you and the sergeant major needed anything." He looked around hoping the sergeant major would walk up and weigh in on his behalf, but on that score, he was disappointed. The sergeant major remained inside, and Wiley had no one to advocate for him. The truth was, the sergeant major felt he needed a break from Wiley. He liked Wiley, but his undying loyalty could sometimes be a little annoying and tedious.

"We'll be fine," the captain said. "You'll travel with the team tomorrow," he added, leaving no doubt about how Wiley would be spending the next day.

The captain stayed just long enough to inform them of the plans for the following day. He was anxious for a call back home and returned inside to make the arrangements and grab a bite of dinner.

With the captain safely out of earshot, Hutchinson started in. "I swear, Wiley. If the sergeant major ever stops short, your nose is probably gonna snap off. Damn, son."

The comment was particularly funny given the fact Wiley had an unusually large nose.

"I don't know, Hutch," Thiessen said. "With that schnaz of his, he'd probably do more damage to the sergeant major than he would to himself."

A general laugh ensued.

"I don't want to picture that," Campbell added, chuckling. "S**t."

"What's your deal with the sergeant major anyway?" Hutchinson inquired.

"There's no deal," Wiley replied. "He's just been my boss for a long time. I like to stay close in case he needs anything, that's all."

"Whatever," Hutchinson said. "I'm hungry." And without further comment, he went inside to find a meal.

"I think I could eat too," Morgan said. With that, they all made their way inside to the dining room.

Over dinner Morgan and Will discussed the prospect of going north. "What do you think's going on up north?"

"No clue," Morgan replied. "But it beats hanging around here."

The entire team shared that sentiment. An opportunity to get away from the safe house and the embassy was worth it, wherever the excursion might take them. The captain mentioned it was supposed to be scenic up that way, so Will was anxious to see what lay in store.

After dinner, Leftwich came by to let them know they'd be leaving from the safe house the next morning at 0500. "We've got a lot of driving ahead of us," he said. "You guys are gonna want to get plenty of sleep."

Since they had been at the safe house, the general agreed to allow them more time at the embassy, so they were used to leaving at 10:00 p.m. instead of the usual 8:30. But with a long trip planned for the next day, it was decided the team would leave the embassy at 7:00 p.m. to allow more time to sleep. That was disappointing to Will as he had gotten used to spending time with Tara in the evenings. For tonight at least, there would be a temporary hold placed on their amorous activities.

CHAPTER TWENTY-EIGHT

SAFE HOUSE–UNDISCLOSED LOCATION
ISLAMABAD, PAKISTAN
MAY 2, 1988
0500 HRS.

Five o'clock in the morning rolled around and the team prepared to leave the safe house. Their transportation arrived on time. Aziz was kind enough to provide them with some coffee, juice, and a kind of bread and honey. "For your journey," Aziz said, handing each of them a bag and Styrofoam cup filled with hot coffee. "Safe travels. Safe travels."

Will jumped on board the van, followed closely by Morgan and Tom Thiessen.

"Good morning, gentlemen," Khan said. "And how is everyone this fine morning? We have a long journey ahead of us today."

"I don't know how he can tell if it's a fine morning or not," Thiessen said. "It's pitch black out here."

"Yeah, yeah," Morgan said, feigning sympathy. "Just have a seat."

Tom took a seat in the back of the van pausing just long enough to place his coffee in the cup holder by his seat, and his breakfast bag on the seat next to him, before falling fast asleep.

Wiley Adams filed in and joined Thiessen in the very back. Hutchinson and Campbell occupied the middle row of seats.

Will took a seat behind Khali Khan next to Morgan and said "good morning" in Urdu. When he did, Khali Khan looked at him in the rear-view mirror, smiling broadly.

"Ah, Sergeant Will—you are learning Urdu." Very good, sed. And a good morning to you as well," he replied in Urdu. At least that's what Will thought he said. He caught the "good morning" part in there somewhere, but he had no idea for sure what the rest of it was. At any rate, Khan seemed genuinely pleased that Will was trying to communicate in his language. There was a worker in the cafeteria at the embassy who was helping Will learn basic phrases in Urdu, so he had a tutor Khali Khan didn't know about.

"Well, I guess we're ready, Mr. Khan," Morgan said, as he pulled the sliding door of the van closed.

"One moment, sed," Khali Khan replied. "We must wait for Mr. Cory."

At that moment, Cory Leftwich jumped on board. "All set," he said, as he closed the door. He made a quick trip to the bathroom in the house knowing it might be a few hours before he had the opportunity to do so again.

"Gee, sed," Khali Khan replied, and proceeded out the safe house gate.

"Notice anything about this vehicle?" Morgan asked quietly, leaning in closer so Will could hear him.

"Yeah, I do. This is one of our old vans—it's not armored."

"Bingo," Morgan said. He was being quiet, but Cory Leftwich, who sat in front next to Khali Khan could easily hear their conversation.

"Those armored vans are way too heavy," Leftwich said. "We've got some steep roads to navigate where we're going. They'd never make it."

"Okay—mountains," Morgan said. "This ought to be fun. What's the mission today?"

"Well, not so much a mission today," Leftwich replied. "Just checking on a couple of things up north." That was as close to any details as the team was going to get from Cory Leftwich for now as far as the purpose of the trip. He did offer a little information about what they might see along the way though.

They drove for close to an hour without hearing even one comment, which was unusual with Hutchinson in the mix. He boarded the van without saying a word and went straight to sleep. Will dozed off as well, but when Khali Khan swerved to avoid hitting something, he awoke abruptly. He muttered something under his breath angrily, and then looked up in the rear-view mirror.

"What the hell!?" Morgan exclaimed Also being startled awake.

"Very sorry, men," Khali Khan said. "There was a monkey in the road."

"Well hell," Hutchinson said, coming to and rubbing his eyes. "If I was driving there'd be one less monkey on this road—damn."

"Very sorry, sed," Khali Khan added, again.

With the team now fully awake due to Khali Khan's monkey dodge, they could see the mountains becoming visible on each side of them—a stark contrast to what they left behind in Islamabad.

"We've got about two and half hours yet before we stop," Leftwich said. "Unless one of you needs to take a piss. We're headed for Muzaffarabad. It's a pretty good size town—we can get out and stretch our legs there for a while before we move on."

"They've got this bazaar up there," Leftwich said. "It's a good place to do some shopping if you want to grab some cheap trinkets or souvenirs."

They slept through the checkpoint at Murree—a key waypoint on the road to Muzaffarabad. The terrain changed as they proceeded northward. No one said much of anything as the sun began to rise higher in the sky, bringing the panoramic mountain vistas into clear view.

MUZAFFARABAD, PAKISTAN
MAY 2, 1988
0955 HRS.

After a steady climb into the mountains north of Murree, the van descended into the southern outskirts of Muzaffarabad nestled in the Neelam valley at the confluence of two rivers—the Neelam and the Jhelum. Leftwich said they were at around twenty-four hundred feet. Muzaffarabad was a fairly good size town, and the increase in traffic the closer they got to the city bore that out. By ten o'clock they were in the center of the city with the bazaar Leftwich mentioned, their first stop.

Once afoot, the team mostly meandered around the bazaar seeing the sights. Leftwich hadn't verbalized any agenda and he never specified a departure time either. He just followed along—somewhat nervously—and frequently checked his watch. Khali Khan acted as a tour guide answering questions and directing them to booths and shops of interest. Will grabbed a trinket or two to take home to his mom and dad, with one find he was particularly proud of. It was an ornate brass stirrup from an antique saddle. He found six small woven rugs that fit nicely inside the stirrup—they looked like miniature prayer rugs. Will snatched up the rugs and the stirrup thinking it would make a nice coaster set for his mom's coffee table. Khali Khan helped with the transaction and no doubt negotiated a better deal than Will could have on his own. "You must bargain, sed," Mr. Khan said with a smile after they left the shop.

Chad Campbell happened upon a vendor who was selling bootleg cassette tapes out of a handcart. He had quite a collection. Each tape was a copy of an actual album with the title and the songs listed on the insert of the case in beautiful handwriting. The vendor, a young man close to Will's age, seemed immensely proud of his wares.

"I have all the latest music from America," he said, as he began to rattle off names. "I have Whitney Houston, Madonna, Lisa Lisa, Chicago, Kenny G, Randy Travis—"

"Whoa," Campbell interjected. "Did you say Randy Travis?"

"Oh, yes sir," the young man replied. "'Always and Forever,' I have it right here," he said as he filed through his collection producing the tape and holding it up for Chad to see. The young man spoke English well, which was unexpected.

"What'll you take for it?" Campbell asked, taking the tape from the vendor to give it closer inspection.

The young man looked thoughtfully for a second and then answered, "One thousand rupees."

Campbell scoffed and handed the young man his tape back. "You must be crazy," he said and turned to walk away. Morgan was watching the exchange with great delight.

"That's less that ten bucks, man," he said discreetly to Campbell, chuckling.

"S**t, I ain't payin' no ten bucks for this bootleg knock-off. I can get the real thing at home for less than that."

Morgan just laughed. “Haggle with him a little,” he advised under his breath. “He wants to make you a deal.”

Campbell approached the young man again. “Tell you what, I’ve got five bucks here,” he said, reaching into his pocket and producing a five-dollar bill. “That’s the deal.”

“No, no, no,” the young man replied. “No dollars—only rupees,” he said, waving off Campbell’s proposal.

“Fine with me,” Chad responded, as he folded the fiver and placed it back into his pocket.

“Wait, wait,” the vendor said, holding his hands up as if in surrender. “You give me five American dollars,” the young man said reluctantly, looking both ways when he said it, “and I give you Randy Travis.”

“Deal,” Campbell said, handing over the five-dollar bill and in turn, receiving his bootleg Randy Travis tape.

“Hell, he probably still made twice as much money as he expected to,” Morgan said with a chuckle, as they walked down the street to the next shop.

“Probably so,” Campbell admitted. “I just wanted to see if I could get him to take American money.”

Further on down the street, Leftwich—who had been bringing up the rear—abruptly overtook the team and stopped. “About time to get going. We’ve still got quite a bit of driving to do.” He instructed Khali Khan to get the van and meet them. Khali Khan went in the opposite direction at a good clip while the rest of the group continued down the tight lane of the market to a broader street some one hundred yards to their east at the edge of the bazaar. They would await Khan’s arrival there.

“You guys sit tight right here if you don’t mind,” Leftwich instructed them. “I’ll be right back.” He went ahead up the street for a short walk and disappeared into a shop. There were a variety of signs on the shop, most of which were in Urdu, but the one that stuck out was a Western Union sign. Will wondered if Leftwich was going to wire some money somewhere or receive some. Who knew? *No matter*, he thought to himself and gave it no further mind.

Morgan spotted a coffee shop right across the street, so he and Will decided to run in quickly and see what they had to offer. They each grabbed a drink—Will was delighted to find they had Coca-Cola—and a flaky pastry of some kind and returned to the designated spot to wait. Hutchinson and the others followed suit, each buying a beverage and a snack of their own for the road.

While the rest of the team was in the coffee shop across the street, Morgan asked Will an odd question. "Anything about this trip seem strange to you?"

Will had to admit he found it unusual that Leftwich brought up the rear as they walked through the bazaar, and he seemed to be checking his watch quite a bit. He didn't talk much either. Morgan agreed. He found Leftwich's behavior odd too.

"Something seems off, but I can't quite put my finger on it," Morgan said. "He's acting a little nervous. Let's see how the rest of this day plays out."

They were finishing their drinks as Khali Khan drove up. He jumped out of the van and quickly opened the door. "Hurry, hurry, gentlemen," he said, politely, but urgently. "We must be on our way."

The team jumped in and quickly shut the door as Mr. Khan drove down the street directly across from the shop Leftwich entered just a few minutes earlier. Leftwich was visible from the street. He was talking on a pay phone inside the shop. As the van approached, he abruptly ended his conversation, hung up the phone, and quickly jumped in the front seat of the van next to Mr. Khan.

"Let's go," he instructed. Khan wasted little time. He seemed to know the city well. Quickly, he had them moving toward their next, unknown destination. Soon, they were out of the city headed east on a very steep and curvy road.

CHAPTER TWENTY-NINE

"Damn, it's a good thing I finished my coffee," Hutchinson said. "I'd be wearing it by now."

"Yeah, this is a hell of a road," Morgan said. "You guys probably want to keep your heads up. Otherwise, you might get car sick."

Adams already looked a little green around the gills.

"For ******'s sake, don't puke back here, Wiley," Thiessen said. He sat in the back next to Wiley and saw it coming.

"There's a straightaway up ahead," Leftwich said. "We can pull over up there if we need to. We don't want anybody getting sick in here."

"I'll be alright," Wiley said unconvincingly.

"Probably best if we pull over first chance we get," Morgan said.

"Pull over up there," Leftwich instructed, pointing out a spot on the shoulder of the road where Khali Kahn could easily stop.

Mr. Khan dutifully pulled over and quickly opened the door so they could get out. Seated in the back, Wiley was the last one off. He exited the van and quickly got down on one knee. He started to spit but was able to avoid vomiting, although his mouth watered profusely.

"You must be some kind of surfer if you get car sick like this," Hutchinson said sarcastically.

"Well, that's different," Wiley protested, trying to collect himself. "When you're surfing—"

"Enough of that," Morgan interrupted. "We don't have time for the finer points of surfing right now. You alright?"

"I'm good."

"Well, take a few deep breaths and walk around for a minute," Morgan advised.

"Okay," Wiley answered, lamely. He knew he would take tremendous ribbing over this incident in the future, but right then he was more concerned about not throwing up.

"There's a cooler up there toward the front," Leftwich said. "Grab something to drink and let's get loaded up," he said, anxiously.

Morgan and Will exchanged looks when he said it, but they said nothing.

"We've got a little over an hour before we get there," Leftwich said. "There's a good place to eat up there too."

"Up where?" Hutchinson asked.

"Sudhan Gali is where we're headed, it's a really scenic little town way up there. It's over seven thousand feet elevation. Gorgeous country, I thought you guys might like to get a look at it."

Khali Khan had them back on the road and they continued the tortuous trek up the mountain.

"Sounds good," Morgan said. "One question: Are we still in Pakistan?"

"Well, yes and no," Leftwich replied. "This is the Kashmir region we're in now. It's still contested between India and Pakistan. The Indians say it's India, and the Paks say it's Pakistan. There's actually not a border; it's called a 'Line of Control.' Even though this place we're going is in India, as far as India is concerned, it's under the control of Islamabad."

"It is Pakistan," Khali Khan interjected. Will could tell by the look on his face in the rearview mirror, Khali Khan was itching to comment, but he held his tongue as Leftwich explained the geopolitical lay of the land. Khali Khan had, as he told Will before, been in "many wars," and it turns out most of them were fought over the land they were currently traversing. He was from the region and knew it well. Sudhan Gali and the surrounding area were Muslim with few exceptions, and there was little doubt Pakistan governed it. Still, the border remained contested, hence the "Line of Control." Tensions were still high between India and Pakistan, and every now and then would come to a boil. Khali Khan said nothing further, but it was clear to all this was a sensitive subject for him.

"Is it safe for us to be up here?" Will inquired

"Oh sure," Leftwich replied. "They get Western tourists up here all the time. Not unusual at all."

"Hmm," Morgan said, quietly, almost to himself.

"What?" Will asked.

"Oh, nothing," Morgan answered.

Little was said on the rest of the journey as they simply took in the scenery. Occasionally, they held their breaths when they saw shear drop-offs from the almost nonexistent shoulders of the road, and a sizable number of 180-degree switchbacks as they ascended the mountain.

SUDHAN GALI, PAKISTAN
MAY 2, 1988
1305 HRS.

Finally, they arrived at Sudhan Gali five minutes after one o'clock, just as Leftwich projected. Khali Khan wasted no time getting them to the little tea house where they would eat lunch. The men expected fare like what they had been eating at the safe house, and that was close to what they received. It was a rustic place with stunning vistas in every direction. To the north, they could see snow-capped peaks, and to the south, vast valleys, lush and green. Tiny colorful cottages dotted the landscape below them. Visible to the east and west were thick stands of tall pine trees that had stood, by some estimations, for hundreds of years, like the Rocky Mountains back home. Or as Hutchinson claimed, the Smokies.

"I gotta say, this looks a lot like home," Hutchinson said.

"We have a lot of pines back in Wisconsin too," Thiessen said casually.

"Well, you damn sure don't have nothin' like the good ole Smoky Mountains," Hutchinson said.

"The timber industry in Wisconsin is very significant," Thiessen said. He felt the honor of his home state had been slighted and was not about to let that go unchecked. "I'll have you know that loggers in Wisconsin are some of the biggest contributors to our state's gross domestic product. Just last year—"

"Alright, alright," Morgan said. "At ease, for ******'s sake. We're just having a nice lunch here—geez." Thiessen was highly agitated and Morgan felt the need to deescalate before the debate got out of hand.

"Yeah man," Hutchinson continued. "What's your deal? You runnin' for Congress or what? Damn, son," he added, which elicited laughs around the table.

"That'll do, Hutch," Morgan said, as Hutchinson leaned back in his chair smiling and eating.

A waiter came out to clear the table and another followed closely behind to lay dessert plates and spoons in front of each of them. Leftwich, Khan, and the team were the only patrons present, so the staff at the little tea house could pay a lot of attention to their group.

"Excuse me," Leftwich said, pushing his chair back from the table. "I'm gonna hit the head before dessert." The entrance to the kitchen was down the hall just a few steps beyond the bathrooms. Leftwich passed the bathroom and went through the kitchen door. Will nudged Morgan and gestured in the direction of the kitchen. Without drawing attention, he and Morgan watched what was about to unfold.

They had a clear view of the kitchen door. Leftwich was standing in the doorway with his back to them. Directly, a man stood in front of Leftwich. They couldn't quite see the man Leftwich was talking to, but he was tall—they could see the top of his head above Leftwich's—and he had red hair, unusual for this part of the world. Leftwich reached into his vest to retrieve an unknown object, and then placed the item on the counter to his left. The two men talked for a minute or two longer and then Leftwich turned and walked back toward the table, but not before ducking into one of the bathrooms in the hallway, giving a clear view of the kitchen door. The man who was talking to Leftwich was none other than Apu! The last time they saw him he was loaded into the back of a Pak Army truck with his two confederates, ostensibly en route to a hospital.

"Well, I'll be damned," Morgan said, astonished.

Apu looked at Morgan and Will briefly, and his expression indicated he remembered them, despite that episode being very traumatic for him and his cohorts. For a just a second, he smiled with a slight nod in their direction, before reaching for the item Leftwich left on the table. It was a folded manila envelope. He quickly tucked the envelope inside his vest and retreated from view.

Leftwich returned to his seat and two waiters began to serve coffee and dessert. Neither Will nor Morgan had paid much attention to the waiters earlier as they served lunch and cleared the table. Now when they placed the bread pudding before them, Will saw the two waiters were Apu's wailing Mosque colleagues. The three men were now working at the Sudhan Gali tea house.

Except for Wiley and Leftwich, the rest of them were present the day they encountered the three men in the mosque. Yet no one recognized them at first in the Sudhan Gali tea house. Leftwich, nervous for most of the day, now seemed more relaxed, like a heavy burden was lifted off his shoulders. "One last cup of coffee and we'll be on our way," he said lightly. "We've got about five, five and half hours back to Islamabad. Probably ought to roll into the house about eight-ish."

With nothing much more to see or do in Sudhan Gali, they loaded up and left the town at around two-thirty. The roads were every bit as treacherous on the descent. Khali Khan rode the brakes and was extremely cautious. He was taking a different route back, making something like a loop back to Islamabad.

After about an hour and a half of winding roads and sharper drop-offs, Khali Khan informed Leftwich they would need to stop soon. "We are low on petrol. There is a village just a few kilometers ahead. There is a filling station there."

Khali Khan assured the team the worst of the winding roads was behind them. They descended a lot, and the terrain was beginning to open some. Still, the views were spectacular, and the rustic village was very inviting, even though there wasn't much to it.

"Mind if we take a little walk?" Morgan asked Leftwich. Morgan thought it might be smart to help Wiley walk off more car sickness. He held it together managing not to puke thus far, but even though the roads were beginning to straighten out a little, Morgan thought a little fresh air would be good for all of them before continuing.

"Sure," Leftwich replied. "Go ahead. In fact, Mr. Khan, why don't you go with them, so they don't get lost. I'll see to the van."

"Gee, sed. Let us go, men," Khali Khan said, gesturing with his arms to move them forward.

The team fell in behind Khali Khan and began walking up the road toward small houses and a couple of shops. Vibrant colors adorned the houses. There were a few people walking up and down the road, mostly women and small children. The men must have been working away from the village, there were so few in sight. They passed a mother carrying a child with a toddler, and yet another small child, in tow. The older child—Will guessed around five or six years old—pulled on his mother's shirt frantically and pointed at Will, his eyes wide.

Will looked at Khali Khan hoping for an explanation. He read Will's expression accurately. "It is your hair. It is most likely the first time that child has seen a man with hair as blonde as yours. These people are mostly peasants. Very few of them will ever leave this village. That child has probably never seen anyone like you before."

Will let that soak in for a moment as they continued down the road. That was the second time he heard Pakistanis refer to their countrymen as "peasants." As he considered the differences between their cultures for a moment, Will's eyes were drawn to a beautiful young woman walking alongside the road. She was stunningly beautiful, accompanied by three older women. It wasn't just her beauty that set her apart. She was wearing an ornate shalwar kameez, much different than the muted colors most of the women were wearing. She must have been someone special, Will thought. Khali Khan quickly informed him that was, indeed, the case.

"No sed, no sed—you must not look!" Khali Khan said, insistently. "Avert your eyes, sed."

Will complied quickly, not knowing what was going on but trusting Khali Khan did. They walked on further and when the young beauty passed, Khali Khan explained himself.

"She is the daughter of the village chieftain. It is forbidden for men to look upon her. The Chieftain could have you arrested or worse, Allah forbid. We should go. Come, come."

They proceeded down the road to the van, wasting little time loading up and leaving to avoid an international incident.

"What kind of s**t are you getting us into, Carter?" Hutchinson pressed, as Khali Khan sped away from the village. "We probably ought to just leave your ass behind."

"I just looked up and there she was," Will explained. "I didn't know what was going on."

"I probably should have mentioned that," Leftwich said. "Some of these villages up here are really primitive. Ultra conservative. Good thing you had Khan with you, that could have turned bad quick."

"Gee, sed," Khali Khan said. "You must be very, very careful."

Thankfully, they never saw the chieftain, and Khali Khan's quick departure was a wise move.

A few hours later, they rolled up to the gate of the safe house at the same time Leftwich estimated. He had obviously made this trip before. It was a long day and most of the team was content to go straight to bed. Not knowing for sure when they would return, Aziz did not have an evening meal prepared, but he did offer a variety of snacks and drinks. Morgan was the only one to eat. Everyone else went to bed. Wiley was still wrestling with car sickness, and the rest were just dog-tired.

After initially retiring to his room, Will began to think about the events of the day. He was certain he would not be able to fall asleep quickly, so he returned to the living room hoping to engage Morgan about everything that happened on the trip.

Will found Morgan seated on the couch with a can of Diet Pepsi and a bag of potato chips on the coffee table in front of him. He thought Will might come back out.

"Well now that was a hell of a day," Morgan said.

"Ya think?"

"We're going to have to visit with our buddy Jeb about this. He's got some 'splainin' to do."

CHAPTER THIRTY

U.S. EMBASSY
ISLAMABAD, PAKISTAN
MAY 3, 1988
1125 HRS.

The next day at the embassy, Will had the good fortune of meeting Tara at the cafeteria during lunch. "I thought I'd find you here," she said. "How was Kashmir?"

"It was beautiful up there. Gorgeous country, but a lot of driving."

"Yeah, it's a haul. What all did you do?"

Will began to talk about the drive up into the mountains, dodging the monkey on the road north, the bazaar at Muzzafarabad, and lunch at Sudhan Gali. He didn't go into any detail, and it was better he didn't. It dawned on him at that moment he never mentioned they were going up north. The night before he left, Will simply dropped by Tara's apartment to let her know he had to leave earlier than usual that evening. It was curious. Tara acted like she'd heard this story before.

"How's your day been going?" Will asked Tara.

She began to chat casually about the goings-on at work. No elaborate details, just some of the routine tasks she had in front of her that day.

"What exactly do you do here anyway? I mean, I know you said you work in the office of protocol, but I don't really know what that means."

"Well, we assist the ambassador with official visits, coordinate guest visits to the embassy, things like that."

"We?"

"Well, our office. You met my boss, Margie—remember?"

"Sure."

"Why do you ask?"

"Just curious. I guess, I just wanted to get a better understanding of what you do."

As Tara spoke, Will began to reflect on what he knew about her, returning to their first meeting when she was giving the embassy orientation. He never introduced himself, and yet she knew his name and rank. She seemed unsurprised they went to a safe house. Will had not mentioned the term "safe house" to her, but she knew where the team was staying. In fact, nothing Will mentioned surprised her. She always seemed to know where he was, whether at the embassy or elsewhere. And then there was the fact she spoke Russian or at least she told him she did. Why would she claim to speak Russian if she didn't? Will didn't know what a protocol officer did in Pakistan, but speaking Urdu seemed more important than Russian. Unless, of course, Tara's concerns were further north and east in Afghanistan, where people spoke Russian. Lost in his own thoughts and worries, Tara noticed.

"Will?—Will? Are you okay?"

"Oh—uh, yeah. Sorry about that."

"Lost you there for a second. Is everything alright?"

"Yeah, I'm sorry about that. I guess I kind of zoned out for a minute."

"I guess I should get back to work."

"Sure."

"See you after," Tara said, with a playful wink. She patted his hand as she left the table, and he smiled as she walked away.

Will sat there alone, the smile gone. Could Tara be what she said she was, a small-town girl from Tennessee? Instinctively, he knew there had to be more to her than she told him. But then again, what difference would it make? He would be going home soon, so why not enjoy the adventure?

Just then Hutchinson dropped his tray on the table, interrupting Will's thoughts.

"What's your problem?" Hutchinson inquired, brusquely.

Campbell was following close behind with Morgan bringing up the rear.

"Yeah," Campbell said. "You look like someone just shot your dog."

"Nothing wrong with me," Will said. "Just finishing up lunch."

Campbell was a fast eater and quickly left the table for the pool area. Will was obviously lingering over lunch, thinking about Tara. Morgan recognized Will had something on his mind.

"Alright, what's going on in that head of yours?"

Will related his concerns about Tara to Morgan who had a straightforward way of looking at things.

"What difference does it make?" He was not trying to be flippant, but he recognized the situation was temporary.

"You're not planning on marrying this girl, are you?"

"Well, no."

"This is a fling, man. Look, I'm not trying to be insensitive, but this relationship can't have much of a future, you know that, right? I mean she's not going to give up her career and follow you back to Indiantown Gap. And that's just where you're gonna be before too long. My advice is just live in the moment, have a good time, and don't overthink things. I will say though, I can understand how you could get attached, she's hot."

While Will reached that conclusion on his own, hearing it from Morgan confirmed to him he was correct.

"What do you think she does here?" Will asked Morgan.

"Your gal—well, protocol of course. You heard her."

"I still don't know what that is for sure."

"What it probably means is she doesn't really work for State at all. It's probably cover."

"Cover?—Cover for what?"

"Well, these Agency types use a bunch of different embassy positions for what's called 'official cover.'"

"Agency? You mean she works for the CIA?"

"Well, I don't know. But it's entirely possible. You said she spoke Russian, right?"

"That's what she told me."

"Well, think about it. This close to Afghanistan, where they speak Russian and there's a bunch of Russians runnin' around, that's a pretty good skill to have, don't ya think?"

"I'd say so," Will answered. Morgan was pushing Will to be less emotional.

"You said your brother was a case officer, right?" Will asked.

"Yep."

"You think Tara is a case officer."

"I doubt that. My money is on 'analyst.'"

"So she could be analyzing the intel these case officers collect?"

"Now you're getting it. Maybe you have a future as an analyst yourself."

"Well, I doubt she'd tell me if she was working for the Agency."

"Of course not. She's not going to blow her cover. You know who'd know though—Jeb."

"You think he'd tell us?"

"Hell no," Morgan replied. "But we're going to ask him anyway—just so he knows we're paying attention. Besides, I think that whole trip north yesterday was just cover, and I want to ask him about that too."

"Cover? Cover for what?"

"Why would Leftwich need us to tag along if he had some business to do up there? First off, there's a checkpoint at Murree, which we slept through. A van, driven by a Pak, full of Westerners that early in the morning would attract less attention than one white guy driving in a car by himself at that hour, don't you think?"

"I don't know, why's that?"

"Hell, we probably just looked like a bus load of tourists. Then there's that stop at the bazaar. What do you think that was about?"

"I just assumed he was giving us a chance to do some shopping and sightsee a little," Will speculated.

"Well, sure he was. But he was acting a little nervous, don't you think? And what was up with that Western Union shop? And we got outta there pretty quick too, wouldn't you say?" Morgan added.

"Yeah, that did seem a little strange," Will acknowledged.

"And the real question—what are the odds we'd run into those dudes from the mosque in that village in the mountains? No way that was just coincidence. I think he used us as cover to get something up to those guys without being detected. I think we walked around the bazaar long enough that if anybody was following us, he'd have been able to make them. Then, when he was sure we weren't being followed, he could ease over to that Western Union shop to either pick something up or drop something off—you saw him on the phone in there, right?"

"I saw him."

"Right. And he didn't waste any time getting out of there and on the road either."

"Yeah, that's true."

"Hell, Jeb told us they were going to have to hide those guys, remember? He said they were blown; they were no good to him anymore. And he damn sure laid something down on that kitchen counter, I saw that red-haired guy pick it up."

"Yep, I saw it too," Will said.

"What was that sucker's name?" Morgan asked.

"Apu," Will said.

"Apu, yeah, that's him."

Morgan seemed to have pieced it all together. It made sense to Will.

"S**t man, this was an op—plain and simple. I'd just like to have been in on it, that's all," Morgan said. "I want to see if Jeb will confirm any of this or not. It's worth asking him."

The more Will thought about the trip, the more it made sense. It was highly unlikely a coincidence they ran into those three men. And Leftwich just happened to have a conversation with a guy Jeb said was one of his assets. Will didn't feel used or endangered. He was happy to help, if that was the plan. Jeb and his colleagues may have believed it would be better if the team were unwitting accomplices in an intelligence operation. But it certainly looked like an op in retrospect. At least there was an element of plausible deniability. It was sure to come up in conversation the next time Morgan and Will had an opportunity to speak to Jeb.

CHAPTER THIRTY-ONE

Lounging by the pool later that day, Will began to think about how Hutchinson likened their mission to chocolate cake. It was true—too much of a good thing could grow tiresome, like lounging by the pool, for example. The team was anxious to get back in the field or else go home. Will was concerned he might need to be a little more cautious around Tara. He wasn't getting tired of her to be sure—not by a long shot—but that was the problem. He needed to be careful he didn't get too attached to her. And added to the uncertainty with Tara, there was the general's offer for Will to be his aide.

With these thoughts swirling around Will's head, Captain Halstead plopped down in a chaise lounge next to him. As time went on, the captain grew less concerned about mixing too closely with his men. He was as anxious as they were to complete the mission. If they were going to stay holed up in a safe house or at the embassy, he might as well take advantage of the amenities.

"Afternoon, sir," Will said.

"Whatta ya say, Carter? You doing all right?"

"Yes sir," Will replied.

Campbell and Thiessen were swimming, and the rest of the team was scattered about the embassy. The circumstances provided a degree of privacy, and it occurred to Will he might not have a better opportunity to discuss General Wassom's offer with the captain than that moment.

"Sir, I was just wondering if you knew that the general offered me—"

"That he offered you a job here at the embassy? Yeah, that's not happening. He told me he made you the offer."

"Yes sir."

"Look, I'm not trying to be difficult, but I'll tell you what I told him. The Army's got way too much money invested in you to waste you over here in *BFE* bringing coffee to a general. I will say as far as generals go, he's a pretty good one and I can see why you might like to stay. But if he really needed an aide, he'd be better off to get a lieutenant to come and see to his needs, you're overqualified. Besides, I want you to come to work for me," he added, smiling.

"Sir?"

"You're up for re-enlistment pretty soon, right?"

"Yes sir."

"Well, I need a new training NCO at Meade. I could use you. Think about it—it's an E-6 slot, so I'll put you in front of the board right away. We'll talk later," Halstead concluded, as he closed his eyes and positioned himself better to absorb the Pakistani sun.

The thought of going before an E-6 board so early in his career was appealing, but Will wasn't sure he'd stay in the Army. He had plenty of time to make a decision about his future, but he had no doubt the decision to stay in Pakistan was made for him. *Just as well*, he thought. He had so little of his stuff with him. It would have been a headache to try and figure out what to do with his truck and other possessions. Besides, if Will didn't re-enlist, he'd be getting out of the Army right about Christmas time and going home. It was nice to think the general thought highly enough of him to make the offer, but Will was content thinking this worked out for the best and didn't agonize any further over it.

A few minutes later Sergeant Major Scott appeared with Adams who was as usual a step behind him. The two of them walked toward the pool. The sergeant major walked up to Will and quietly asked, "Is he sleeping?" pointing toward the captain, who placed a towel over his face to block the sun, occasionally snoring as he dozed.

"I'm awake," the captain said. "What's up?"

"Just ran into Jeb, sir."

He removed the towel from his face and sat upright. "What's on Jeb's mind?"

"He said he wants to see us for a few minutes."

"Where is he?"

"Cafeteria. He was drinking some coffee and eating pie."

Will smiled when the sergeant major informed the captain of Jeb's whereabouts. That's where he was when he and Morgan inquired about the three men in the mosque.

"I guess Jeb really likes his afternoon coffee and pie," Will said. He blurted that out without thinking, and immediately regretted it. He didn't want the captain and the sergeant major to think he was listening in on their conversation, even though it would have been hard to avoid listening. They were sitting and standing right next to him.

"Coffee and pie?" the captain inquired casually. He didn't seem bothered at all with Will's contribution to the conversation.

"Yes sir. Me and Sergeant Morgan ran into him in the cafeteria a week or so ago and he was drinking coffee and eating pie and it was right about this time of day too."

"Well, I guess you're right, Carter," the captain said, standing up as he spoke. "He must like his afternoon coffee and pie."

"Ready, Sergeant Major?"

"After you, sir."

"Maybe I'll just have some coffee and pie myself," the captain said, as they walked toward the embassy for their impromptu meeting.

Wiley fell in behind the captain and the sergeant major as if it were his business to participate in the meeting with Jeb, which seemed to annoy the captain. "You can stand fast, Sergeant," the captain said to Adams as he headed toward the gate. Wiley cast a look of defeat at the sergeant major, who tried to discreetly gesture for Wiley to stay behind as he followed the captain to avoid just such an occurrence. Wiley either didn't see the gesture or didn't understand it. But, after the captain's pronouncement, it was clear he wasn't invited. Once out of earshot, the captain remarked to the sergeant major, "Hell, my dogs don't follow me around that closely."

"Yes sir. He's very loyal." Scott made no further comment, but he did feel Wiley—although replete with a collection of annoying habits—was a good soldier overall, and often had scorn unduly heaped on him.

As the captain and sergeant major walked out of the gate from the pool area, Morgan walked in. They passed with only a brief acknowledgment before Morgan sat down on the chaise where the captain had been lounging. He was eating an ice cream cone and was hurrying to consume it before it was lost to the heat. It was approaching one hundred degrees at that point in the afternoon. The chocolate and vanilla swirl dripped down to his wrist and he was doing his best to at least eat the ice cream down to the top of the cone so he could speak before losing the rest of it. He clearly had something interesting to share with Will and tried to speak as he wrestled with his ice cream cone.

"So—um—I just ran into—" Morgan began, before pausing to slurp some ice cream from the back of his hand. "—Jeb."

"Let me guess," Will replied. "He was having pie and coffee in the cafeteria?"

"Mm hmm—" Morgan grunted as he switched the cone to his left hand and wiped the ice cream from his right hand on his pants leg. "How'd you know that?"

"Me and Sergeant Major Scott saw him in the cafeteria earlier and he asked us to come out and find the captain," Wiley interjected. He had taken a seat in the chair next to Will after the captain's rebuke and was silently brooding over his exclusion. Although Morgan was obviously talking to Will, Wiley couldn't control his impulse to join the conversation.

"Why don't you go take a swim, Wiley. I need to talk to Carter here."

Wiley took the hint. Without another word he stripped down to his shorts and dove in the pool.

"He bugs the s**t outta me," Morgan said, to which Will just chuckled.

"Where you been all afternoon?"

"I got bored, so I went out to the Seabees shop for a while. They have so much cool stuff out there. They were unpacking some kind of new industrial lathe that just arrived. No idea what they're gonna do with that. Those guys could build any damn thing you want."

Morgan could tell by Will's expression he had no interest in the Seabees at that moment, despite their stellar capabilities. "So what's up with Jeb?" Will inquired, hoping to get him back on topic.

"Right, right—Jeb," Morgan replied. "Ran into him while I was getting my ice cream. He wants us to go with him tonight."

That got Will's immediate attention. "Go where?" At that moment he was ready to go anywhere.

"Apparently there's a part of town where a lot of Afghan refugees hang out. He wants us to go eat with him and meet some of his Afghan friends."

"Shoot yeah. I'm in."

"He says we'll leave straight from the embassy around 1800."

"Did you talk to him about our trip up north?"

"Nah, I was going to, but there were a lot of people around, and I didn't want to get into it with a bunch of ears that close by. I know the captain and sergeant major are in there talking to him right now anyway. I'm going to give it few minutes and see if we can go upstairs and talk to him a little, with nobody else around."

"What do you think they're talking about?"

"Probably just getting the latest update. Three days would be the earliest we could get back in the field if they haven't learned anything more than they already told us. I'm ready."

"Same here."

Holed up in the safe house for two weeks, they settled into a routine that could be better described as a boring rut. The trip north certainly helped break up the monotony, but the back and forth between the safe house and the embassy was tiresome. The most pleasant diversion Will had was the company of Tara, but even that had its limits. Even if she could have visited Will at the safe house, there was even less to do there than at the embassy. The only real cure for their collective lassitude was a resumption of their mission.

"Carter, get in here," Campbell shouted. "Let's play some polo."

Will jumped in the pool and Morgan followed close behind. The team was engaged in a spirited game of embassy water polo when the captain and the sergeant major reappeared poolside. They had important news to share, and as the team climbed out of the pool, Sergeant Major Scott inquired as to whether they needed to assemble in a more secure setting.

"There's nothing classified about this," the captain replied. "All I need to say is that we are a *go* to get back in the field in three days. I just wanted everyone in one place when I gave you the news."

"Roger that, sir," the sergeant major said. "You jokers got any questions?"

No one asked any questions, but there was a general murmur of excitement at the news. They were all anxious to get back to work.

"I've had about enough of this embassy for today," the captain said. "I'm headed back to the house in a few minutes if anybody wants to go. Otherwise, you can catch the van at the usual time, and I'll see you in the morning."

"I'm with you, sir," the sergeant major said.

"Me too," Wiley said, to no one's surprise.

As the captain, the sergeant major, and Adams turned to leave, Hutchinson turned toward the cafeteria.

"I'm thirsty," Hutchinson said.

"Cafeteria's closed, man. Try the commissary."

"Whatever," Hutchinson replied. He headed toward the commissary as Campbell and Thiessen fell in behind him.

"Good," Morgan said, when everyone was out of hearing. "Let's go find Jeb now."

Carter and Morgan made their way up to the third floor where they met with Jeb and his colleagues several times before. Morgan hit the buzzer and the heavy door opened. Jeb appeared from behind the door.

"Afternoon, gentlemen."

"Afternoon, sir," they replied in unison.

"What can I do for you?"

"Well sir," Morgan began. "We were wondering if you had a few minutes to talk."

"Sure, come on in." He ushered them into the conference room. "Be right with you."

Morgan and Will sat there a few minutes awaiting Jeb's return.

"What are you going to ask him?" Will asked in a whisper.

"All kinds of s**t. I'll start with that trip to the mountains."

Just then Jeb walked in. "You boys ready to get back to work?"

"Yes sir," Morgan said. "Absolutely."

"What's on your minds?"

"Well sir, if I may," Morgan began. He knew Jeb was direct and would appreciate directness from him. "It's about the trip up north the other day. We ran into those three men in a little coffee shop in a mountain village, the ones we found in the blasted mosque on the base. That can't be a coincidence, sir."

"Ya caught that, huh? I thought you might. I never told Leftwich about our conversation, so he doesn't know y'all know anything. What about the rest of your team—did they recognize any of them?"

"No sir, I doubt they were paying much attention," Morgan answered. "If they did, they haven't mentioned it. And there's very little this crew wouldn't mention if they were aware."

"Sir, just curious," Will said. "Are they safe up there?"

"Well, we think so—as safe as they can be anyway. Keep in mind this is Pakistan, and this is a dangerous game. But they knew that going in. As long as they keep their mouths shut, they should be fine. They're still on our payroll—for now anyway. Apu has a tendency to talk too much. But we made sure he knows we know he's been working both sides. And if WE know, he knows White Beard knows too, and he's scared s**tless of White Beard."

"So you're done with them then?" Morgan asked.

"For now, at least. We'll give them a little money occasionally just to keep them close. Apu did give us a little bit of new information we're going to try and vet pretty soon, but other than that, they're not very valuable to us where they are now."

"So that trip up north?" Morgan inquired. "That was an op, wasn't it?"

"Hell yeah. Y'all looked like a bunch of tourists on a road trip. From what I understand, it all went pretty damn smooth too, except for Carter flirting with a Chieftain's daughter?" Jeb added chuckling. "C'mon, son, these sons o' b*****s will cut your arm off—or maybe your short arm. Gotta be extra careful."

"Yes sir," Will replied sheepishly. "Only I wasn't flirting, I—"

"Oh hell, I know, I'm just giving you s**t, son."

"One more thing, sir," Morgan said. "This girl Tara—who works for State?"

"Over in Protocol? That Tara?"

"Yes sir, that's her," Morgan said. "I—I mean we—were just wondering what she does here."

"Well hell, son, she works in Protocol," Jeb said, with a broad smile and a wink. "She assists the ambassador with official visits and s**t like that."

"Good copy, sir," Morgan said.

"You boys planning on joining me tonight?"

"Yes sir," Morgan answered.

"Anybody else coming with you?"

"Well three of us are already back at the house," Morgan said.

"We're taking a van, so we'll have room if anybody else wants to come along. Rolling out at 1800."

"Roger that, sir," Morgan said.

With that, Morgan and Carter left the secure space and headed back out toward the pool. As they descended the stairs, Morgan noted what Jeb said about Tara. "Did that clear anything up about your gal pal?"

"I guess."

"You guess? You know damn well he was as much as telling us she's one of theirs."

"Yeah, I suppose that's right."

"Why are you letting this bother you? Are you worried she's more of a badass than you?" he asked chuckling. "Is that it?"

"Yeah, it kinda is, I guess. I had it mind she was just a small-town girl-next-door type."

"Whatever, man. You need to lighten up and go with the flow. She knows exactly what she's doing, and that's fine. Besides, she's probably not gonna kick your ass anyway, unless you keep walking around looking like that. Relax dude," he laughed.

Morgan wasn't trying to be coarse, but Will didn't appreciate the casual way he addressed his relationship—if you could call it that—with Tara. He had a high opinion of her and didn't want her image tarnished by a bunch of loose talk. What bothered Will most was knowing that if there was any damage to her reputation, he had certainly made a large contribution to it.

U.S. EMBASSY
ISLAMABAD, PAKISTAN
MAY 3, 1988
1730 HRS.

By the time Carter and Morgan arrived poolside, not surprisingly, Hutchinson, Campbell, and Thiessen were intermittently swimming and sunning.

"Where the hell have y'all been?" Hutchinson asked.

Rather than answer the question, Morgan merely replied by asking if either of them would like to come along to dinner tonight. Hutchinson declined at once. "The less time I spend around Jeb the better."

"Anybody else want to go?" Morgan asked.

"I've got a call home scheduled tonight," Thiessen said. "I can't go."

"Hell, I might as well go," Campbell said. He didn't feel like going back to the house knowing there was little to offer there. And he was as sick of hanging around the embassy as everyone else.

"Sounds good," Morgan said.

At a few minutes before six o'clock, Morgan, Campbell, and Carter assembled in front of the embassy entrance awaiting Jeb's arrival. At precisely six, a white van wheeled up driven by Khali Khan. The door slid open, and Jeb hollered, "Hop in, boys."

Without hesitation, the three of them jumped in the van and it quickly left the embassy. Jeb informed them their destination was an area on the outskirts of Rawalpindi. The area was home to a significant population of Afghan refugees. It was also a favorite location for freedom fighters to spend some rest and recreation time—a respite from the ongoing war in their home country.

"We're having dinner with a friend of mine," Jeb explained, as Khali Khan sped through the busy streets on a southwesterly course. "This is a guy I've worked with for a few years now. He's young, but he's a sure enough veteran. He's been fighting these commie sons of b***hes since he was a teenager—even before the damn Russians invaded. He's a tough b*****d."

"Is this the guy that helps you out across the border?" Morgan inquired. Will wasn't sure he should be asking questions of that nature in front of Khali Khan, but Morgan was direct, and Jeb had already talked openly about the subject in front of Khali Khan. Morgan outranked Carter so there was little he could do anyway. Besides, Will was as curious as Morgan, so he just kept his mouth shut and listened.

"Yeah, he's been my primary contact for a while now. He's what you might consider equivalent to a battalion commander in our Army. He's got as many as four company-sized elements under him at any given time. That's his conventional mission, if you could call it that."

"Conventional?" Morgan asked.

"Well, he does some unconventional stuff too. He's had quite a bit of training from these Pak S.S.G. guys—that's their special ops unit. That's how I met him. They recommended him."

Jeb was sitting in the passenger seat next to Khali Khan and had turned to the right, craning his neck to converse with Morgan. Campbell and Carter listened intently.

"I don't agree with these Paks on much, but this recommendation was a good one. He knows what the hell he's doing."

"Does he know about Camp Ohjri?" Morgan asked. Will had to hand it to Morgan. He wasn't afraid to ask pointed questions. Will thought the same thing but was afraid to ask. He was discovering if he listened more, eventually Morgan would get to the questions he had in mind, and it was better they come from him.

"Well, I briefed him the last time I was at his camp. He already knew about it though. Not surprised—nothing much gets past him."

"And that was last week?" Morgan continued his questioning. "After you stopped by the safe house?"

"Yep, that's where I was going. I was pretty sure he already knew, but I needed to go over and talk to him personally. He appreciates that kind of thing."

Jeb seemed unbothered by the peppering of questions he was receiving from Morgan. In fact, he appeared eager to share the updated information. Campbell though, had not been privy to any previous conversations with Jeb, so Will was attempting to discreetly bring him up to speed while closely monitoring the back-and-forth between Jeb and Morgan.

As the conversation wound down, the streets began to narrow and the people in them became more abundant making passage more difficult. Khali Kahn made frequent use of the horn, occasionally yelled loudly, and gestured to obstinate pedestrians when they didn't move quickly enough for him. Soon, they pulled up to a kind of café. "We have arrived," Khali Khan announced.

CHAPTER THIRTY-TWO

RAWALPINDI, PAKISTAN
MAY 3, 1988
1825 HRS.

The entrance to the cafe was full of passersby, dressed the way Jeb was the morning he stopped for coffee at the safe house. As far as Will could tell, they looked unarmed but also had the look of hardened fighters, like Jeb described his Afghan counterpart.

"Let's eat, boys," Jeb said, as he exited the van.

Will threw open the door of the van and they followed Jeb to the cafe. He brought along his aviator's helmet bag which served as his "didi" bag—the olive drab variety common among GIs of every branch—and was carrying it as he got out of the van. "Hang on a sec, I don't want to carry this around all night."

"Well chunk it in the van and let's go—damn," Campbell said. He was easily perturbed and not particularly patient.

"Mr. Khan, will you keep an eye on this for me?" Will asked.

"Of course, sed."

As Will placed the bag between the two front seats next to Khali Khan, he noticed the EOD badge pinned above his name tape just below the handles of the bag. He quickly unpinned the black badge and tucked it into his pocket. Campbell saw and just shook his head, unsure what Will was doing, or why.

Khali Khan drove the van a few yards down the street. He parked and awaited their return.

The three soldiers stood behind Jeb in the vestibule of the cafe. Jeb peered toward the back of the big dining room from their position close to the door. When he caught sight of a familiar face, he waved, and the man waved back. The man proceeded immediately in their direction. He wasn't a particularly large man, but he was striking. He had a long, brown beard almost sandy in color, dressed as they expected with one notable difference, he had bandoliers strapped over both shoulders. The bandoliers held what appeared to be 7.62mm rounds, which made sense that being the caliber of the AK-47 Kalashnikov rifle, the preferred weapon of the Mujahideen. He wasn't armed, but the bandoliers gave him a menacing appearance. As he got closer his eyes became visible. They were a light brown, which was a sharp contrast to the dark features of most of the people Will and his teammates encountered in Pakistan. This was undoubtedly Jeb's contact in Afghanistan. He hugged Jeb when he approached and the two exchanged a few words in a language Will had never heard, before turning toward them and beginning introductions. Jeb pointed to each of the three in turn, speaking in what sounded like Russian to Will's inexperienced ears, enunciating their names in English. The man smiled congenially to each of them and said in English, "I am Muhammadin."

Muhammadin shook hands with each of them but held onto Will's hand as he turned to Jeb. He said something in what must have been Pashto, to which Jeb smiled and nodded. Will had no idea what he said to Jeb, but one word came out decidedly clear, "buckaroo." Will assumed Muhammadin was asking if he was a cowboy, and when Jeb responded in the affirmative, the Afghan freedom fighter added his left hand to their handshake and shook even more vigorously. He smiled broadly and spoke to Will. He seemed genuinely delighted to meet Will even though he didn't understand a word he said.

"Well, cowboy," Morgan said. "Looks like you've got a fan."

"I guess so," Will replied. He never had a "fan" before and wasn't exactly sure what to make of it. No matter, he thought. He was hungry and let the thought pass as he anxiously awaited food.

Muhammadin and Jeb turned and headed toward the back of the dining room. Muhammadin gestured for them to follow. There was a large table in a back, dimly lit corner of the cafe. Will could see an interesting tapestry hanging on the wall above the table. The closer he got to the table, the more intrigued he became. Will stopped momentarily to view the tapestry, which depicted several horsemen in what looked like some form of mounted combat. Jeb noticed Will taking an interest in the tapestry and commented.

"That's buzkashi," Jeb said. "It's an important sport they play in Afghanistan."

"Sport? Looks more like a battle."

"Well, it kind of is," Jeb replied. "Have a seat and we'll tell you about buzkashi."

Muhammadin took his seat with his back to the wall, beneath the buzkashi tapestry. Jeb sat to his right, and there was another Afghan seated to his left. Will assumed he was either a translator or a bodyguard, or both. He sat at the table earlier, and when they approached, he stood until Muhammadin was seated. Muhammadin pointed at a chair directly across from him and gestured for Will to sit there. Morgan sat to Will's left and Campbell to his right. It was a large round table with room for more, but there were only six of them seated. There were two more men standing close by. Dressed much like Muhammadin, their look suggested they were battle-hardened freedom fighters providing security for Muhammadin. While Muhammadin had a friendly face and liked to entertain, the two men were stolid and remained expressionless throughout the dinner.

After everyone sat, Muhammadin motioned to a waiter close by, and within just a few moments they began serving beverages. He leaned over to Jeb and spoke in what sounded like Russian while gesturing discreetly toward a table in a dimly lit adjacent corner of the dining room. There were three men seated at the table with only a pot of tea between them. Dressed conspicuously, they were not wearing traditional Afghani or Pakistani garb, which was out of place in this part of town and this restaurant. Their clothes looked European. In fact one man was even wearing a Real Madrid track suit jacket but they were of Middle Eastern descent. They stuck out like sore thumbs.

The three men were clearly watching the Americans too, although trying to appear nonchalant as they occasionally sipped their tea. Will caught a brief glimpse of the men as he passed by them going to Muhammadin's table but thought no more of them.

"Is there a problem?" Morgan inquired quietly.

"No problem," Jeb said. "Just some eyes on us, that's all."

"Should we be worried?"

"No—they should be worried," Jeb said. "This is not a friendly place for them."

"Who are they?" Morgan remained very calm and discreet but was clearly concerned.

"Not sure just yet," Jeb said, "but I bet we find out by the time they serve us our dessert. Don't worry about those assholes. Muhammadin's boys are on them. And his guys are not to be f***ed with."

Campbell and Carter stayed quiet and still, both doing their best not to appear alarmed. Morgan was on alert but did not seem distressed.

Jeb didn't appear unduly concerned over the men either, which calmed Will. He knew Jeb could handle himself. As the wait staff began to place platters of food on the table, the tension eased. Muhammadin spoke and gestured for his guests to eat.

"What did he just say?" Will asked.

"That's Pashto for 'dig in,'" Jeb replied with a smile.

"Just what I wanted to hear," a famished Campbell said.

"Buzkashi," Muhammadin said. Buzkashi was buzkashi in English or Pashto.

"That's right," Will said. "Y'all were gonna tell us about buzkashi."

Muhammadin began the conversation about buzkashi with Jeb intermittently translating for him.

"First off," Jeb began. "You have to understand these are horse people—a horse culture. In Muhammadin's village, in most villages in fact, if you haven't mastered horsemanship by the time you're thirteen, you got a real problem."

"What's that?" Morgan asked.

"Well, it's a very macho kind of culture," Jeb replied. "If you're not a master horseman, they think you're queer, or feeble-minded, or something like that. You're not a man though. And that's the attitude they bring when they play buzkashi."

"Well dang, that's tough," Will said. "What if you don't have access to a horse growing up?" He thought about his own experience as a child. Will never had the opportunity to get on a horse until he was twelve. Of course, this was a different world, but he still made the comparison in his mind.

"That's not an issue in Afghanistan," Jeb said. "They've got plenty of horses all over the place. It's a rite of passage."

"There's a big city or two in Afghanistan, right?" Morgan asked. "I'm guessing that's not such a big deal for city folks?"

"Well, yes and no," Jeb said. "Buzkashi is the national sport of Afghanistan, and they play it a lot in places like Kabul and Kandahar, but it's a spectator sport for them. Hell, they even have rich guys who will sponsor a team or a player. Usually, it's landlords who own the horses and sort of put together teams of their own for matches in the cities. But in the hinterlands—the tribal areas, it's everything to them."

As they asked questions, Jeb continued to serve as the interpreter. Occasionally, Muhammadin would try to steer Jeb into Pashto, but Jeb was more comfortable with Russian, so the bulk of their dialog was conducted in Russian.

"Over in Kazakhstan and Kyrgyzstan and places like that, they actually have organized teams, and sort of leagues where they play their version of buzkashi," Jeb said. "In the tribal areas in Afghanistan—outside of the big city tournaments—it's purely village against village."

"So how do they play?" Morgan asked.

"Yeah, it seems pretty brutal from the looks of that tapestry," Will added.

Muhammadin chuckled as Jeb interpreted their comments, and he looked briefly over his shoulder at the tapestry. He looked back at them and nodded, then began to speak to Jeb again.

"Well, it's basically medieval blood sport polo if you can imagine that," Jeb began. "They play on a big ole field—about twice the length of a football field and maybe twice as wide—with goals on either end. They take a calf carcass or sometimes a goat but they don't hold up as long, and the object is for each team to try and drag this dead calf across a baseline I guess you'd call it, and then drop it into the goal. The goal looks kind of like a big donut. Only it's about three feet high and six feet in diameter."

"That's a BIG donut," Morgan said with a chuckle.

"It doesn't seem so big when you're at a dead run with a bunch of other guys beating on you with a buzkashi whip," Jeb said.

"Whip?" asked Morgan.

"Yeah—Carter, you've probably seen a quirt before, right?" Jeb asked. "Hell, probably even used one."

"Oh, yes sir, I got one at the house."

Jeb turned to the others and explained, "The buzkashi whip is like what an American cowboy would call a quirt, only it's more like a weapon with poppers wrapped in wire."

"Dang," Will replied. "Ouch."

"Ouch is right," Jeb said. "Guys die all the time in these village buzkashi matches. It's rough."

They talked a little more about the finer points of the game and as the conversation wound down, Jeb and Muhammadin fell into a good-natured disagreement. It involved Will, as both Jeb and Muhammadin gestured toward him, and Muhammadin uttered the word "cowboy" more than once.

"What's being said?" Will asked.

"He's inviting you to come to his village and play buzkashi," Jeb explained.

Will's heart jumped. "Oh, yes sir. That would be great—I'm in."

"No, that would not be great. You'd probably get killed and you've got a job to finish here," Jeb said.

"Yes sir," Will said, though disappointed. "I hope Muhammadin isn't insulted."

"Already thought of that, and I've got it covered. He understands you've got to complete your mission. He's a military man and he knows mission comes first."

"Roger that, sir," Will replied.

At that point Muhammadin stood and pushed his chair under the table. The Afghani seated next to him, undoubtedly Muhammadin's aide, gestured to one of the men standing by the table. The man moved toward the door with Muhammadin and Jeb following closely. Muhammadin's aide fell in behind the group with the final Afghan.

The three American soldiers stood as Muhammadin and Jeb began leaving. Muhammadin shook hands with Morgan, Campbell, and Carter. At that moment Will remembered the EOD badge he had tucked away in his pocket. He quickly retrieved it and handed it to Muhammadin. His eyes opened wide, and he smiled broadly. Muhammadin took the clutches off the back of the badge and immediately pinned it to his vest over his left pocket. He placed his hand over it and then reached out to hug Will, first to one side and then the other. He nodded graciously, then turned and made his exit.

"Y'all sit tight for a minute, I'll be right back," Jeb instructed.

"What was that about?" Campbell inquired, looking at Will.

"What?"

"What's up with giving that guy your EOD badge?"

"Well, I was just trying to be courteous to our host," Will answered.

"That, my friend," Morgan interjected, "was called diplomacy. Well done, Will. That was smooth."

The three of them returned to their seats at the table as Jeb instructed, awaiting his return. They were quietly talking amongst themselves when they were abruptly interrupted by the three Middle Eastern gentlemen who were seated in the far corner of the dining room.

Campbell was the first to spot them as they approached, and his eyes locked on them. Morgan and Will knew something caught Campbell's attention as he looked past them at the three advancing men. Morgan and Carter turned their chairs just in time to be verbally accosted by one of the three.

"Americans?" the man inquired brusquely and with obvious hatred. "Americans?"

Morgan looked at me and Campbell before standing to reply, "Yeah, we're Americans," he said. "What about it?"

Campbell stood as well and gave the men a hard look, awaiting a response from the interlopers.

"F*** America!" the man said.

Will quickly jumped up and stopped Campbell, who in a blind rage, looked bent on immediate retribution after the unexpected insult was hurled their way. "Chad, Chad—wait, hold on, dude!" Will pleaded. He felt the same way Campbell did but paused to consider the consequences of a brawl in a Rawalpindi backstreet cafe. Morgan saw Will had his hands full trying to contain Campbell's fury and quickly turned toward them to try and prevent any further escalation. Campbell began hurling a flurry of expletives at the three men.

"Campbell, Campbell!" Morgan said sternly. "At ease, at ease! Settle down!"

The man who did the talking stood fast, while his compatriots began to discreetly retreat. They perceived that if Campbell were released, it would pose a serious threat to their safety. Obviously, they had no desire to risk a fight with the enraged American. They began to step back toward their table, unbeknownst to the agitator who was standing defiantly, but now alone.

"Excuse me?!" Morgan replied, turning from Campbell toward the Middle Eastern man. "You wanna say that again?" looking beyond the man toward the table where his two comrades were now seated. The man glanced back and became acutely aware that he was standing alone in the presence of three angry Americans whom he gravely insulted, deserted by his countrymen. His expression quickly changed. His manner was less threatening, and he took a step or two back.

Before the situation could escalate further, Jeb appeared and stepped between Morgan and the man who instigated the incident.

"Y'all have a seat," Jeb instructed. "I'll handle this."

They complied at once but positioned their chairs to respond quickly should the need arise.

Jeb never laid a hand on the man, but his presence proved sufficiently intimidating. It was amazing to see how this diminutive Texan could so quickly and easily assert his dominance over a man who stood at least four inches taller. The man retreated to his table quickly and sat with Jeb following. Jeb stood at the table for a few moments, talking. As the conversation appeared to wind down, Jeb sternly tapped on the table a couple of times as if to drive home a point, then turned and walked back to his table.

"Let's go," Jeb said.

"Who the f*** are those guys?" Chad asked.

"I said let's go!"

"Move out," Morgan added. He knew Campbell was geared up for a fight and wanted to make sure they were safely out of the cafe before anything more could happen. Walking out of the dining room, Morgan positioned himself between Campbell and the table of the three men as an added precaution.

Campbell complied, but not before shooting a defiant sneer at the three men as he passed by their table.

No one spoke as they quickly climbed back in the awaiting van and sped away.

"What the hell was that about?" Morgan asked, now that we were safely in the van. "Who were those assholes?"

"Iranians," Jeb replied. "Probably draft dodgers."

"Iranians, huh?" Morgan said, almost to himself. "How 'bout that?"

"Draft dodgers?" Will asked, incredulous.

"Well, maybe," Jeb said. "They were trying to come off like patriots or some s**t," he explained. "They were acting like they were all upset about Americans attacking them in the Gulf. Then I asked them why they weren't back home fighting the Iraqis and they shut up real quick. That tells me they're either draft dodgers or they're working for somebody."

"Working for somebody?" Morgan asked. "Who, the Soviets?"

"Could be," Jeb replied. "More likely Iranian Intel. Hell, they could be working for ISI."

"So what now?" Will asked.

"Well for now, we're gonna head back to the house. But we're gonna take the long way home, if you know what I mean."

Morgan smiled. He knew that meant a circuitous route back to the safe house to ensure they weren't being followed. Jeb kept a watchful eye as Khali Khan meandered through the streets of Rawalpindi and back to Islamabad and the security of the safe house.

The extended return trip did provide an opportunity to ask a few extra questions. Jeb clearly wasn't convinced those Iranians just happened to be at that cafe.

"So you think those guys were operatives?" Morgan inquired.

"Well, I think we're going to find out pretty quick," Jeb replied. "Those waiters at the cafe weren't just waiters. Plus, Muhammadin's guys were on them as soon as they walked in the door—before we ever got there, in fact. Whether they just happened into that cafe, or they were there for us, it was a bad decision to go in there. All I can say is they better hope to Allah that Muhammadin's boys don't get to them first. Like I said before, they don't f*** around."

"Muhammadin's boys?" Morgan asked.

"Yeah, he had a couple of guys at a table in the other corner. Did you not see them?"

"Well, it wasn't very well lit in there," Morgan replied.

"You probably wouldn't have noticed them anyway. Those guys are good at blending in—they just looked like a couple of guys drinking tea. I spotted them when we walked in, but hell, I wouldn't have known who they were if Muhammadin hadn't told me."

"Wait a minute," Campbell interjected. "What about the waiters? You said they weren't just waiters."

"No, they're ours."

"Ours?" Will asked.

"Well, we put those guys in there to sort of keep an eye on things. You have to understand, that part of town is a hangout for Mujahideen fighters. Anyone who might want to stir s**t up with the Mujahideen—well, that would be a good place to start."

"What kind of s**t?" Morgan asked.

"It's a recruiting hotbed," Jeb replied. "These freedom fighters come over here for some R&R, and the mercenaries hang out over here and try to recruit them. A lot of these Mujahideen fighters have years of experience. Hell, if they're still alive after fighting this long, they must be pretty damn good, right?"

"Recruit them for what?" Will asked.

"H**l, there's s**t going on all over the world, son," Jeb said. "The Russians are f***ing around in Nicaragua, you've always got something going on in the Middle East, there's sub-Saharan Africa—places like Somalia, Sudan, Ethiopia—there's Libya, Lebanon, South America, you name it. There's always a market for experienced fighters."

"In fact . . ." Jeb paused briefly as if he was considering the propriety of what he was about to share. "In fact, last time I was across the border, Muhammadin told me about some rich Saudi who was spending money over there. He's some kind of religious zealot building schools and recruiting for God knows what. We'll have to watch him, especially after the Russians un-ass the AO (area of operation). He's probably got guys over here recruiting too."

"What about these Iranians?" Morgan asked. He found the information about the rich Saudi fascinating, if somewhat foreboding, but wanted to keep Jeb on the topic of the Iranians.

"Those Iranian a**holes would be a good example," Jeb replied. "I have no idea what they're up to, but they damn sure don't have any legitimate reason to be hangin' out there."

"So, you said those waiters at the cafe are 'ours,'" Will said. "'Ours' meaning, they work for Muhammadin?"

"Oh, hell no," Jeb said. "Those guys work for us—well, *me*, I guess you could say. They're kind of like those three boys y'all met in that mosque out on the Ojhri garrison."

"Does Muhammadin know about them?" Morgan asked.

"I don't tell Muhammadin everything. It's better that he doesn't know everything we know. Besides, I'm pretty sure he doesn't tell me everything either. That's just sort of how this game is played, ya know."

It turned out "Muhammadin's boys" were following these guys most of the day or longer. Muhammadin discreetly pointed them out when they sat for dinner at the cafe. When Jeb stepped outside with Muhammadin as he prepared to leave, he learned more—as much as Muhammadin could share in that unsecure environment. It would only be a matter of time before the Iranians would be in the custody of the Mujahideen commander. Muhammadin appeared to be a friendly young man—to the EOD team anyway—but according to Jeb, he was a fierce warrior and would show the Iranians no quarter. Jeb would not intervene. He knew Muhammadin would take his time and extract what information he could from the three Iranians. There would then be a swift and discreet end to the questioning, after which Muhammadin would undoubtedly share any useful intelligence with Jeb.

Jeb knew he could trust Muhammadin's intelligence, but in this case, it could take a few days before he knew more about the Iranians. Jeb thought it best to return the three teammates to the safe house as quickly as he could so he could get back to work. He was anxious and it showed. As they wheeled up to the gate of the safe house, he hurried them along saying only, "See you guys later." With that brief courtesy, he sped away.

"Well, that was interesting," Morgan said, facetiously.

"Remind me not to go out with Jeb anymore," Campbell said. "Damn."

"You mean you didn't enjoy dinner," Morgan said with a chuckle.

"Oh, dinner was fine," Campbell replied. "It was all that other s**t I didn't much care for. That sumb***h is gonna get us all killed."

Morgan laughed out loud. Campbell's expression indicated he didn't see the humor.

"I don't think you have to worry about Jeb getting us killed," Morgan reassured him. "And I think he's probably the smartest 'sumb***h' we've run into over here."

CHAPTER THIRTY-THREE

Back at the safe house they were digesting the events of the evening, along with their meal, while Jeb made a quick return to the embassy. He knew he could continue no further with Khali Khan's assistance. Khali Khan was supposed to be only a driver—vetted though he was—and his active involvement in what Jeb might be about to get into, could be viewed as reckless. Khali Khan drove Jeb back to the embassy. Jeb thanked him for his help and dismissed him for the evening. He would secure his own transportation and go ahead alone.

As Jeb walked out to his little Suzuki SUV, he ran into his colleague Leftwich. Leftwich was about to call it a day, when he noticed Jeb moving at a hurried pace toward his vehicle.

"What's up?" Leftwich inquired. "You look like you're in a hurry."

"I am." It occurred to him running into Leftwich at that moment might prove fortuitous. He knew he could use a little help. Perhaps he could persuade Leftwich to come along.

"You busy?" Jeb inquired.

"Not particularly, what's up?"

"Get in. I'll brief you on the way. On second thought, you drive," Jeb said, tossing the keys to Leftwich.

"What the hell have I got myself into?" Leftwich asked rhetorically, as he quickly entered the vehicle and fired up the engine. The truth was, Leftwich was always a willing hand, and he had high respect for Jeb. Agreeing to go with Jeb was not a tough sell.

The two quickly drove away from the embassy while Jeb gave his colleague the rough coordinates of the cafe. Leftwich went there once before and thought he knew the route. They sped to the cafe hoping Muhammadin's intelligence officers were still there. When they arrived at the cafe, they were disappointed to find the officers were long gone. Jeb's two "waiters" were still there though, cleaning up and preparing to close the cafe. They followed the situation and shared valuable information with Jeb.

Mujahideen intelligence officers who had been seated at another corner table while the team dined there earlier wasted no time taking the three Iranians into custody. According to the "waiters," Muhammadin's men took the three Iranians into a back room just off the kitchen, shortly after the Americans left. There were three other Afghans waiting in the back room: Muhammadin; one of his guards stationed beside the table at dinner; and the aide seated to Muhammadin's left. His name was Ghulam and, as it turned out, he was also an "intelligence officer," a euphemism for what they really were. By American standards, they weren't intelligence officers. They were assassins or brute squads. Jeb used the term intelligence officer or IO to show respect to Muhammadin. But he knew who they were and was certain Muhammadin knew he knew.

The Mujahideen had no real intelligence capability to speak of. Not along the lines of American capabilities or the Soviets, for that matter. That didn't mean they couldn't collect and, when necessary, extract information from high-value targets with great efficiency. The information they provided Jeb and his colleagues over the years, in its raw form, was used to provide a broader intelligence picture of the situation in Afghanistan. But their tactics were brutal, to say the least.

The Iranians now in custody were undoubtedly aware of their dire situation. The Mujahideen's reputation was well-known. It was borne from the atrocities they suffered at the hands of the Soviets. They responded in kind to the brutalities inflicted by the Soviet troops on Afghani men, women, and children—rape, torture, and worse. The Soviets were indiscriminate in their cruelty.

For their part, the Mujahideen were no strangers to dispensing their own medieval brand of torture. Their methods were developed, perfected, and deployed as far back as the days of Genghis Khan. For centuries, Afghanistan seemed to be at the center of conflict. It was no surprise they should be so adept at dispensing gruesome varieties of pain. Generations of experience honed their skills. In fact, Soviet soldiers became all too familiar with the Mujahideen's barbarous capabilities. They knew if they were ever in a situation where they could be captured by the Mujahideen, the best move they could make would be to end their suffering first. "Save the last bullet for yourself" was the standing order.

The only thing that could make the Iranians suffer more at the hands of the Mujahideen "IOs" would be if they were affiliated with the Soviets. If the three men were working for the Soviets, they'd suffer immense and prolonged pain before death alone could end their anguish.

Ghulam was the chief interrogator. He was skilled in the black art of extracting information. In situations like this, after instructing Ghulam, Muhammadin simply observed. The first order of business for Ghulam would be to find out for whom the Iranians were working. The three Iranians sat together at a small table. Ghulam took a seat across from them while Muhammadin and his bodyguard stood next to the wall to Ghulam's right. One of the Iranians, aware of the severity of the situation, offered everything he could in an effort to save his own skin before questioning. Before he could say much though, one of the Iranians stood and struck his countryman in the face so hard he began to bleed profusely from his nose. The three men were shackled together at the wrists with two sets of handcuffs. The man in the middle was the first to try to talk. It was the man to his right—the same man who had confronted the Americans in the cafe dining room—who struck his colleague. He had his right hand free and used it to pronounced effect against his babbling compatriot.

"Shut your mouth, you sniveling coward!" the man exclaimed in Farsi. "Not another word or I'll kill you myself!" As he shouted at his countryman, he attempted another blow but was intercepted. Before he could throw another punch, Ghulam simply gestured to the man standing against the wall next to Muhammadin.

Muhammadin's bodyguard quickly responded with a punch to the face sufficient to quiet the Iranian. The man began spitting blood on the table and said nothing more.

Muhammadin had some concerns about attracting attention to the cafe. Although this part of town had many displaced Afghans, he saw no need to draw undue scrutiny. "Perhaps this interrogation should be continued elsewhere."

"As you wish, sir," Ghulam replied. Muhammadin was in charge—there was no doubt about that—but he showed a great deal of respect to Ghulam. He treated Ghulam like a trusted uncle, mostly deferring to him in matters such as this.

As Muhammadin and Ghulam discussed an alternate location to continue the interrogation, Ghulam shared an important detail with Muhammadin. As the Iranian man began spewing forth information, he mentioned something important before his colleague was able to shut him up with a punch to the face. Ghulam understood Farsi. Muhammadin's Farsi skills were minimal, so the Iranian man's frantic babblings were meaningless to him without Ghulam.

"It appears our friends are working for the ISI," Ghulam informed him.

Muhammadin raised both eyebrows on that stunning revelation. The two were keeping their voices low while conversing in Pashto. They moved over toward the door of the back room they occupied, turned their backs, and spoke very softly, continuing their conversation.

"This would have been much less complicated if they had simply been working for the Russians," Muhammadin said.

"Agreed, sir."

Just then, there was a knock on the door. Muhammadin gestured for his bodyguard to check it, and when he opened the door slightly, he saw Jeb standing there. Of course, he recognized Jeb, but he did not allow him in the room at first. He looked at his boss instead and informed him who was standing on the other side. Muhammadin nodded to indicate it was safe for Jeb to enter.

"Well, my friend," Muhammadin began, speaking softly in Russian. "It appears these three gentlemen are under the employ of ISI."

*Son of a b***h*, Jeb said to himself. "White Beard is f***ing us." Jeb made the comments in English, and under his breath, so Muhammadin had no idea what he said, but he could tell by Jeb's response he clearly wasn't happy.

"What's that?" Muhammadin asked.

"White Beard," Jeb replied, in Russian. "I knew he was up to some dirty stuff. I never thought he'd hire these Iranian bastards though."

"This does not surprise me. The Iranians have been very active lately, as far east as Kandahar, and beyond."

"Well, this complicates things," Jeb said.

"My thoughts exactly," Muhammadin agreed.

Why couldn't it just be Russians, Jeb thought to himself. He knew this situation would end quickly if that were the case. The Mujahideen worked closely with the ISI over the years, so this situation would need deft handling. If White Beard learned Muhammadin had three of his assets in custody—Iranians or not—there could be serious issues.

Jeb needed to make the three Iranians believe these "Muj IOs" were ready to start cutting them up. The trick would be convincing them the Mujahideen thought they worked for the Russians. If they believed they would suffer a similar fate as the hated Russians, Jeb thought the Iranians would cooperate.

"Have you started questioning them yet?" Jeb asked.

"Ghulam began his preliminary examination," Muhammadin replied. "But one of the men was attacked as he started to speak."

"Attacked?" Jeb said, surprised. "By who?"

"The fellow on his right."

"That figures," Jeb said. "That's the bastard who squared off on my boys earlier tonight."

"Squared off?" Muhammadin asked, unfamiliar with the term.

"Yes, he just verbally confronted them in the cafe after dinner while you and I were outside. If I hadn't come in when I did, I'm afraid my team would have taken them apart. That little guy is a bulldog," Jeb added, referring to Campbell.

"Yes—lucky for them you intervened," Muhammadin said with a chuckle.

"How about I take a run at them?" Jeb asked.

"You?"

"If I can convince them that you believe they're working for the Russians. I bet we can get more out of them." Jeb saw no need to mention the Muj reputation for brutality to Muhammadin—it was well known, and he certainly didn't approve of those methods—but he thought he could leverage that reputation at the very least.

"Let's separate them for now," Jeb suggested. "Divide and conquer."

"Indeed," Muhammadin replied. "The one in the middle seemed the most anxious to talk. Perhaps you'll start with him?"

"Sounds like a plan. If you'll take those other two out and seclude them somewhere, I'll start on this guy. I have one favor I would ask of you."

"Of course," Muhammadin replied affably.

"I'd like to question him in private, if you don't mind."

"Oh, I do not know about that, my friend," Muhammadin replied. "Ghulam is usually present for these proceedings."

"Yes sir," Jeb replied respectfully. "I know Ghulam is very effective." Indeed, Jeb knew Ghulam and his methods well. He also knew if he hadn't arrived when he did, Ghulam would undoubtedly be employing some of those methods right now. "I'd like to work on his mind a little first before I turn him over to Ghulam."

"Very well. I will inform Ghulam and we shall defer to you on this gentleman—for now. But we should like to interrogate the other two ourselves."

"Of course," Jeb agreed. "But could you wait a few minutes to get started? I'm going to put the fear of God in this bastard."

"Sounds 'like a plan,' as you say," Muhammadin replied with a smile.

Muhammadin and his bodyguard removed the handcuffs from the man in the middle, then placed the cuffs on both the wrists of the men on his left and right. Ghulam instructed the man in the middle to remain seated as Muhammadin and his bodyguard "helped" the other two men to their feet.

"You should hope to Allah they finish you before I get a chance to, you traitor!" the man on the right growled to his seated countryman as he passed him, spitting on him for good measure.

As Muhammadin, his bodyguard, Ghulam, and their two Iranian captives cleared the room, Jeb closed the door behind them and casually lit a cigarette. He didn't usually smoke, but he always kept a pack of cigarettes on him in case he needed to offer a smoke to a friend out of courtesy. Most of the Paks and Afghans he worked with liked American cigarettes. He found it often ingratiated him to his counterparts to offer them one. He also found it made him look casual and relaxed, and in situations like this, that pretense could be useful.

He took a drag or two before taking a seat across the table from the scared, beaten, and bloodied man. At this point it was clear the man who hit him was their leader. Jeb estimated the young Iranian to be in his early twenties. He shook a cigarette out of the pack of Winston Reds, and the young man reached for it with a trembling hand. Jeb reached across the table with his lighter, but the Iranian's hand was shaking so much Jeb had to use his other hand to steady the cigarette to get it lit.

"You speak English?" Jeb inquired.

The young man nodded.

"Good," Jeb replied. "Cause my Farsi is not great. What's your name, son?"

The young man looked down. He didn't want to answer. He continued intermittently to puff nervously on his cigarette, coughing lightly.

"Surely you can tell me your name. What's the harm in that?" Jeb added, blowing smoke across the table in a passive aggressive manner. "This could be a long night if you won't even tell me your name."

"Farrokh."

"Good, good. Let me ask you something, Farrokh—do you know who these guys are?"

The man nodded.

"You've heard about them, yes?"

He nodded again and swallowed hard.

"Well, then you know it's a blessing for you that I'm the one in here talking to you right now, and not them—right?" Jeb said.

"Yes."

"That guy that punched you in the face—is he your boss?" Jeb asked.

"He is not my boss."

"Well, if he's not your boss, then who is he? Why are you with him?"

"He is my cousin's friend."

"Your cousin? Then the other guy is your cousin?"

"Yes."

"Well, this other guy looks like the boss," Jeb said. "Are the three of you working together?"

"We were in the Army together. We came to Afghanistan looking for work."

"Looking for work—in Afghanistan?" Jeb replied, incredulous. "What kind of work?"

"We heard they were looking for men with fighting experience. We were in the Army, so we came."

"Who are 'they,'" Jeb asked.

"Come again?"

"Who are 'they'? You said 'they' were looking for fighters, who are 'they'?"

"I do not know. I just came along."

"You said you came to Afghanistan looking for work, is that right?" Jeb asked.

"Yes, yes." Farrokh was clearly unnerved.

"Well, this is Pakistan. Are you working now, or are you on vacation?"

"No, no, I am here with my cousin."

"Yes, you said that already," Jeb said. "Your cousin. I'll ask you again—you know who those guys are on the other side of that door, right?"

Farrokh nodded. Tears began to spill from his eyes. As if on cue, he heard a body slam up against the door and the voice of his cousin wailing "no, no, no!" Someone was administering a severe beating to his cousin.

"My friends tell me that right before 'your boss' punched you in the nose, you mentioned the ISI—is that right?"

"ISI? I do not know anything about the ISI."

"Is that right? Well, then you must work for the Russians," Jeb said. "You know who hates the Russians more than anything? Those guys on the other side of that door. And they do bad things to the Russians when they catch them. And they do bad things to people who work for the Russians when they catch them. Do you follow me, Farrokh? Do you understand what I'm telling you? Now I'm about to open that door and tell my buddies you work for the Russians. Unless you tell me what I need to know. Now one last time—who do you work for?" Jeb demanded.

"Okay, okay. We were hired to come to Pakistan to follow the Americans," Farrokh replied desperately.

"Hired by who?"

Just then an ungodly shriek emanated from the other side of the door. Farrokh knew it was his cousin screaming, and he began to sob.

"You want to tell me who hired you?" Jeb asked again.

"It was a Pakistani soldier—an officer. We met him in Kandahar. We did not know he was ISI when we first met him. We found that out when we arrived in Islamabad."

"And what was this officer's name?" Jeb asked.

"He was not wearing a uniform."

"That doesn't mean s**t to me—I want to know his name!" Jeb insisted. He knew the young man was stalling but was confident he could get the needed answers with enough pressure.

"Did you hear that screaming out there?" Jeb asked. "That sounded like your cousin, I think. Was that your cousin? It doesn't sound like they're being very gentle with him. Maybe I open that door and invite Mr. Ghulam in. Would you like to talk to Mr. Ghulam, Farrokh?"

"Bhatti, his name is Bhatti," Farrokh revealed, as he continued sobbing.

*Well, that little son of a b***h*, Jeb thought to himself. This was disturbing news. Lieutenant Bhatti was certainly one of White Beard's "go to" guys. That confirmed Jeb's suspicions about White Beard. He paused his interrogation just long enough to share that latest information with his Afghan colleague. He stepped out of the room for a moment to confer with Muhammadin.

"This information is not surprising in the least," Muhammadin replied on hearing Jeb's news. "I have had my suspicions of the ISI for some time now. I knew they were not to be trusted."

"Where's the other man?" Jeb inquired. He noticed there was only one man in the hall. The man was beaten badly and bleeding profusely from one side of his head. Muhammadin's bodyguard held him to his feet. Ghulam was standing by, unfazed by the proceedings.

"He will require further interrogation. He is being prepared to travel just now."

"Okay." Jeb chose not to press any further knowing there would be time later to discuss the man's fate. For now, Jeb needed to get back to his own charge.

"I'm going to continue with this other young man. I'm making good progress with him."

"Very well," Muhammadin replied mildly.

Jeb returned to the room with Farrokh and resumed his questioning.

"How long ago did Bhatti hire you?" Jeb asked.

"I've said too much—they will kill me," Farrokh sobbed.

"You've got two choices, Farrokh. Tell me what I want to know or I open that door and let those guys go to work on you."

"Two weeks ago. It was two weeks," Farrokh said. He favored the idea of talking to Jeb rather than the Mujahideen.

"You've been following the Americans for two weeks? The same guys in the cafe tonight?"

"Yes, yes," Farrokh answered.

"Where have you followed them?"

"No, no—please! I cannot!" Farrokh begged.

"Your only way out of here in one piece tonight, Farrokh, is for you to tell me what I want to know."

The wailing from beyond the door continued. Farrokh knew he would suffer an even worse fate if the man opened the door. He decided his best bet was to tell him what he knew.

"We followed them up to Muzaffarabad, but we lost them in the market and came back to Islamabad," Farrokh said.

"How did you find out they were going to Muzaffarabad?" Jeb asked.

"Bhatti."

Jeb knew he had an even more serious problem on his hands now. How would Bhatti know his guys were going to Muzaffarabad?

"Just follow—that's it? Just follow the Americans?" Jeb pressed.

"Yes, yes."

"Just follow and report back to Bhatti—that's it?"

"Please, please, that's all I know," Farrokh begged.

"When are you supposed to report back to Bhatti?"

"No, no, I cannot, please . . ."

"When Farrokh, when?!"

"Tonight, tonight. We were to follow them tonight and report back to Bhatti."

"Okay, tonight. Where are you supposed to meet Bhatti?"

"I do not know where. Nouri knows where."

"And Nouri is . . .?" Jeb prodded.

"The one who struck me. He is the leader."

"Okay Farrokh, you just sit tight here for a minute." Jeb turned to the door.

"No, no, no, please, no . . ." Farrokh wailed.

Jeb knocked on the door and Muhammadin stepped in. His presence prompted even more sobbing from Farrokh. Just when he thought things couldn't get worse, Muhammadin's bodyguard appeared, dragging Farrokh's cousin by the arm. He looked like he had just walked off a battlefield. Farrokh continued sobbing and proceeded to lose his bladder. "Hassan!" Farrokh cried (in Farsi). "What have they done to you?"

"You must tell them what they want to know," Hassan replied, struggling to breathe, exhausted. "They have taken Nouri. If you cooperate, they have promised to take us home."

Hassan was holding his left ear, which was bleeding profusely. It was not completely severed, but it was cut deeply, and Hassan was doing his best to hold it in place. Farrokh looked down at Hassan's right hand and shrieked. His index finger was missing at the second knuckle and the nails on his remaining fingers were all missing as well—and bleeding profusely.

"There is a warehouse near Camp Ojhri," Farrokh began. "We do not know the address, but we know how to find it."

"Well boys," Jeb said. "We can't take you home until you show us where that warehouse is."

"If we show you," Farrokh asked, "you will take us home?"

"That's the deal."

"We will show you," Farrokh agreed.

Ghulam entered the room and directed Hassan to sit next to his cousin. The two began conversing in Farsi.

"No talking!" Ghulam instructed. Hassan complied at once. The beating he received at the direction of Ghulam was sufficient to command Hassan's complete submission. He didn't say another word. Hassan knew he had been fortunate. Had he been associated with the Soviets, he knew he would have suffered even greater pain—and most likely death. Ghulam quickly deduced that Hassan and his cousin Farrokh were little more than travel companions for the real instigator, Nouri.

Nouri was defiant with Ghulam from the outset. He and Muhammadin knew Nouri would need to be separated from his companions and moved to a place better suited for rigorous interrogation. However, before he was bound, gagged, and masked for his journey over the border into Afghanistan, Ghulam was able to find out Nouri was more than an ordinary Iranian soldier like his companions. It wasn't exactly clear yet who Nouri was working for, but he was adamant about not working for Pakistan intelligence.

"I have nothing to do with ISI," Nouri contended, when pressed. "I am here for the Zionist Americans, they must die. I will avenge the lives of my people taken by the vile Americans who occupy our waters."

Ghulam knew he would have to be much more creative in extracting information from Nouri and chose to send him to a camp in Afghanistan. There, Ghulam could employ his methods, unimpeded by too many potential witnesses in a heavily populated area.

⁂

CHAPTER THIRTY-FOUR

Jeb wasn't exactly sure what he expected to find or even where he expected to find it, but he knew there was more to this story than just three Iranians hired to follow his EOD team. While Farrokh informed him they were to meet Bhatti, Jeb thought it best to bring Farrokh alone, and leave his cousin, Hassan, to await their return. Hassan remaining in the custody of Ghulam would also help ensure Farrokh's cooperation. Besides, Jeb only needed to find the location where they were supposed to meet. Beyond that, he didn't have much use for Farrokh. Once the location was found, he would return Farrokh to Ghulam, and he and Muhammadin could do with him and his cousin as they saw fit.

"Shall I accompany you?" Muhammadin asked, as Jeb prepared to leave the cafe with Farrokh.

Jeb paused for a moment, long enough to consider how not to insult Muhammadin with his response. After all, Muhammadin had a personal stake in what was going on, and Jeb knew he might benefit from having someone like him along who could assist if necessary. Then he considered the optics of potentially being caught by an ISI officer in the company of a Mujahideen commander, with an ISI asset in their custody. There would be a lot of explaining to do. He would have to handle this much more discreetly.

"I'd like nothing better than for you to accompany me, my friend," Jeb began. "But I think I'm going to have to play this one alone. I hope you understand."

"Of course," Muhammadin replied. "I shall await your return," he said. Muhammadin knew that Jeb had made the correct choice. In fact, he would have been surprised had Jeb agreed to his request. He mostly asked just to see how Jeb would respond.

"Besides," Jeb continued. "I've got Leftwich waiting for me outside. He'll watch my back."

"Indeed."

"This shouldn't take long," Jeb said. "With any luck, I'll be back in less than an hour."

"Very well," Muhammadin said, nodding. "I shall be here."

Jeb proceeded out the front door of the cafe and immediately climbed into the awaiting SUV unceremoniously pushing Farrokh to the back seat.

"Where to?" Leftwich asked.

"Camp Ohjri."

"Copy that," Leftwich answered. He executed a quick U-turn in the middle of the street and took a direct course to the garrison. The traffic had abated considerably—both cars and people—and he was able to drive much faster than earlier in the evening. As they approached the garrison, Farrokh began to get his bearings. He guided them around to the south side of the camp and gave them further instructions to the exact location of the building.

EN ROUTE TO CAMP OHJRI
MAY 3, 1988
2225 HRS.

"Turn right," Farrokh instructed, as Leftwich quickly complied. "Turn left. Up ahead on the left. About one hundred meters," he added, pointing down the dark street paralleling the southern edge of the camp.

"Stop here," Jeb said, and the vehicle came to a quick halt on the edge of the road. "Where is it?"

Farrokh pointed up the road to what looked like a building with a pair of large overhead doors. There was a walk-in door to the right of the overhead doors, and there was an alley on either side of the building. There were several other buildings, many of which appeared to be homes and shops of one kind or another. This area was remarkably close to the blast and there was obvious damage, much of it severe, to many of the buildings lining the street. There was even a school just across from what Farrokh called a warehouse. Most of the buildings were evacuated, and this area was cordoned off after the blast. Although the cordon was since removed, residents and merchants in the area were slow to return due to the continued blasting taking place on the garrison.

About the time Jeb began to suspect Farrokh may have led him on a wild goose chase, two men appeared from an alley on the far side of the building Farrokh pointed out. In the shadows of the building, it was difficult to make out much detail until one man lit a cigarette and held the match out to his comrade to light his cigarette. In that brief five seconds or so, Jeb could clearly see these two men were Pak soldiers, both of whom had AK-47s slung casually over their shoulders.

The two men walked by the front of the building—which Jeb now suspected was a garage rather than a warehouse—and turned down the alley on the near side of the building.

"That's the warehouse?" Jeb asked.

"Yes," Farrokh replied.

"Where's Bhatti?" Jeb demanded.

"I do not know," Farrokh answered.

"Is he inside?" There were no windows on the building, but there was a window on the door. Jeb saw no light shining from the inside, but it was possible the window was painted or boarded over. It was difficult to tell from that angle.

"I do not know," Farrokh said again. "I have never been inside. Lieutenant Bhatti is usually in a car in front of the warehouse."

"What about those guards? Are they usually here when you meet Bhatti?"

"I have never seen guards here before."

Jeb waited a few minutes and the guards passed again. They were still smoking their cigarettes and seemed oblivious to their surroundings, engrossed in conversation. A few more minutes passed, and the guards appeared in front of the building yet again, pausing just long enough to crush out their cigarettes on the ground in front of the building before resuming their patrol.

The soldiers were clearly guarding the building for some unknown reason. Jeb quietly watched as the soldiers continued their patrol. He pondered his next move as he watched.

"When is Bhatti supposed to be here?" Jeb asked, looking at his watch.

"I do not know. He only talked with Nouri."

Jeb looked at Leftwich and gestured for him to get out of the vehicle. The two moved toward the back of the vehicle to talk privately, several steps beyond where they parked.

"I'm curious why these two Pak soldiers are guarding this building," Jeb said.

"Yeah—strange," Leftwich agreed. "The cordon's been down for almost a week now."

Under normal circumstances, it would not have been unusual to see soldiers patrolling the area around Camp Ohjri at any time of day or night. That was particularly true in the immediate aftermath of the blast. After all, this was the headquarters of the Pak Army. People in this part of town were quite accustomed to seeing armed soldiers in the vicinity. After the area was evacuated and cordoned off, there were even more soldiers patrolling the perimeter of the camp. In fact, the perimeter at one point was extended well beyond the street on which Jeb and Leftwich now stood. But this street was two streets south of the fence line of the garrison, and these two soldiers seemed to being paying particular attention to this one building.

"You mind taking this kid back to the cafe by yourself?" Jeb asked. "I think I'm gonna stake this building out for a while longer. I want to see if that bastard Bhatti shows up."

"Sure, no problem. I just need something to tie him up with since I'll be by myself."

Jeb walked toward the vehicle and opened the rear lift gate. He rifled through a tool bag he had in the back and produced two large zip ties.

"Here you go," Jeb said, handing the zip ties to Leftwich.

"You think of everything, don't you," Leftwich said with a smile.

"Never hurts to be prepared."

The two moved around to the side of the vehicle and opened the back door of the passenger side. Farrokh shrieked as they opened the door, certain he was in for a beating or some type of harsh treatment. He had no reason to fear though. Despite the volume of information he was able to extract from the young Iranian, Jeb never laid a hand on him. A sharp contrast to the treatment his cousin received.

"Quiet. Turn around and put your hands behind your back," Jeb ordered. Farrokh complied at once. Even though Jeb never used any violence against him, Farrokh feared the milder treatment he received up until now was about to change.

Jeb secured the young man's hands behind his back with the two zip ties. He then positioned him on the seat and belted him in. He jerked on the shoulder strap of the seatbelt to lock it in place as an extra security measure. Farrokh showed no aggressive behavior toward Jeb at all. On the contrary, he was mostly submissive. Jeb knew that could change in an instant though, and he wasn't about to send his colleague off with a prisoner who might be able to get free and become violent.

"That'll hold him. If you'll run him back to the cafe, I'll just wait right here for you. Park a couple hundred yards up the road there and flash your lights twice when you get here. I think I'll see if there's a good vantage point in that schoolhouse across the street."

"Copy," Leftwich replied.

Before Leftwich drove away, Jeb stuck his head in the door and gave Farrokh a final look. "Now you behave yourself, Farrokh, understand? I'd hate to have to tell Mr. Ghulam you got out of line." Farrokh said nothing, though he swallowed hard and nodded affirmatively. Jeb treated him very kindly by comparison, but Farrokh was deathly afraid of him, nevertheless. Jeb possessed an unconscious ability to buffalo men—some quite fearsome themselves—who were larger than he was.

"See you in a bit," Jeb said, as Leftwich set off to deliver his captive to the awaiting Mujahideen commander.

Jeb estimated he had around an hour before Leftwich returned. He slipped off behind the school and looked for a way inside. He came across an unlocked door. Hastily evacuated because of the blast, the basic security measure of locking doors behind them appeared to have been overlooked. Jeb quietly opened the door and carefully walked in. He entered through the back but was looking for a room that would give him an unobstructed view of the garage across the street. From his position on the street, he spotted a room on the second floor he felt would be ideal. Once inside, he found a stairwell leading to the second floor. In just a moment or two, he was standing at the door of a room he believed to be the one he spotted from the street. He carefully opened the unlocked door revealing a science lab classroom. He quietly made his way inside closing the door behind him. He stepped around one of the tables to get a better view out the window of the classroom. The view was perfect. He could clearly see the garage across the street and had an unobstructed view to the west, the direction from which Leftwich would be returning soon.

Jeb moved a chair slightly back from the window so as not to be seen from the street. The chair was more like a barstool that students used at one of the several lab tables positioned around the room. There was an array of beakers, test tubes, and even Bunsen burners at each table. He perched himself on the stool and peered outside.

Although the street was not very well lit, Jeb could see surprisingly well. There were several streetlights lining the street, but only two of them worked, and they were further down the east end of the street. Jeb assumed the blast from Camp Ohjri caused the unserviceable streetlights, but it was also likely they burned out long before the blast and the city had not bothered to replace them. The Paks were not exactly meticulous in their infrastructure maintenance, particularly in this part of town. Jeb attributed the good visibility as much to the three-quarter moon, which was now high in the sky.

Jeb could clearly see the soldiers continuing their patrol around the garage. About ten minutes passed and the two soldiers paused for another smoke break in front of the building. They scarcely got their cigarettes lit before a speeding car approached from the east. The two soldiers continued smoking and nonchalantly looked up the street observing the oncoming car. The driver slammed on the brakes directly in front of the garage, startling the two soldiers, who were too surprised to even draw the rifles slung over their shoulders. Two men quickly got out of the car. Jeb had never seen the driver before. He was wearing a Pak Army uniform, and he could make out sergeant stripes on his sleeve. The other man was also wearing an Army uniform and was familiar to Jeb: Lieutenant Bhatti.

*There you are, you mother f***er*, Jeb thought to himself. *What are you up to?*

Bhatti immediately laid into the two patrolling soldiers, who promptly extinguished their cigarettes, straightened their uniforms, and came to attention. His verbal berating continued as he pointed down the street. The two soldiers saluted smartly and proceeded in an easterly direction at a quick pace.

As the two soldiers disappeared down the street, Bhatti and the sergeant stepped to the front door of the garage. Bhatti looked up and down the street before opening the door and walking inside. The sergeant remained outside on watch. As Jeb suspected, the window on the door was painted over. But he could tell there was a light on inside the building. Bhatti was inside for less than five minutes before emerging. He turned off the light inside and he double-checked the door to ensure it was locked before motioning to his sergeant to get in the car. The two quickly sped away to the west.

Wonder what he's checking on in there, Jeb wondered. *I best just have a look see myself.*

Jeb knew it would only be about half an hour or so before Leftwich would return, so he chose to hold his position and wait. He might need some help anyway. He used the time to think about what happened over the last three hours or so. What started out as an innocent dinner with his Mujahideen counterparts quickly took an unexpected turn. In a hurry to respond, he hadn't fully absorbed the underlying reason for all this activity. Three Iranians were tracking his EOD team, and his ISI "friends" were underwriting the operation.

Jeb pondered the situation as he sat alone in the silent darkness. At least two of the Iranians were more than willing to share what they knew, the result being Jeb's current stakeout of a nondescript garage from the vantage point of an abandoned school. The wildcard was Iranian number three. He seemed prepared to stick to his guns, defiantly sneering even as Muhammadin's bodyguards bound, gagged, and masked him. Jeb was curious to learn if Nouri's stubborn resolve held out under Ghulam's methods. To Jeb, the Iranians seemed of little value to the Mujahideen against the Russians; but whatever information Ghulam got from Nouri could be beneficial to the United States. He was confident Muhammadin would share what he learned. For now, he stayed focused on the garage just across the street.

CHAPTER THIRTY-FIVE

CAMP OHJRI STAKEOUT
RAWALPINDI, PAKISTAN
MAY 3, 1988
2345 HRS.

A few minutes later, Jeb saw a pair of headlights on the street approaching from the west. He watched as the vehicle slowed, coming to a stop some two hundred yards or so from his position. The headlights flashed twice before the driver turned off the engine and turned out the lights. That would be Leftwich.

Jeb left his perch in the school and cautiously walked toward the vehicle parked up the street. He was certain it was Leftwich, but to be on the safe side he approached stealthily so as not to startle him or give himself away if, God forbid, it wasn't his colleague. Leftwich wasn't known to be particularly jumpy, but Jeb didn't want to leave anything to chance. In his experience, even some of the most capable men he worked with could react badly under unexpected stress. As he neared the vehicle, Jeb could see it was the white SUV Leftwich had been driving. Just the same, he gave a little whistle to alert Leftwich, who casually exited the vehicle.

"That was quick," Jeb said just above a whisper.

"Traffic was light. What's the verdict?" Leftwich asked, as he carefully and quietly closed the door of the SUV.

"Well, our friend Bhatti showed up. He sent the guards down the road, and he went inside the garage for a couple of minutes. He came back out and hit the road."

"Was he alone?"

"Nah, had a driver with him. He stood watch while Bhatti was inside."

"Hmm, what do you think's in there?"

"Let's go have a look."

The two approached the garage and carefully walked the perimeter before entering. Around the back of the building there were two fuel tanks, one gas and one diesel, confirming Jeb's suspicion that it must be a garage. The back of the building had another pair of large overhead doors much like the front, along with another walk-in door. The two agreed the back of the building would be the best location to enter. The front was better lit, and they would be more vulnerable for viewing by potential passersby—even nonchalant Pak soldiers, if they resumed their patrol.

Jeb surveyed the immediate area and spotted a piece of angle iron laying under one of the fuel pumps. At four feet in length, it was the leverage he needed. Jeb was able to get one of the overhead doors to move enough that he and Leftwich got their fingertips underneath. With a concerted effort and a little sweat, the two were soon inside.

"You didn't happen to bring a flashlight with you, did you?" Leftwich asked, half expecting a "no."

"As a matter of fact," Jeb said with a smile, producing a mini-mag flashlight.

"Of course. Why doesn't that surprise me?"

"Let's go ahead and drop this door so we don't throw any light outside," Jeb said. "You stand watch and I'll have a look inside."

"Copy that," Leftwich walked back and forth at the rear of the building between the alleys, keeping an eye in every direction while Jeb surveilled the inside.

Once inside, Jeb shined his flashlight around and didn't see anything out of the ordinary—nothing you wouldn't expect to see in any American garage—except for the fact that there weren't any cars. Usually, you would see a car or two inside a mechanic's shop. *Curious*, Jeb thought. The structure was certainly large enough to accommodate several cars. If the shop were abandoned quickly due to the blast, as the school looked like it had been, they would have left behind several cars under repair.

Jeb continued to scan the interior of the building when something caught his eye. Along the east wall of the building there was a pile of something covered by several tarps. Jeb approached the tarps and estimated the pile to be near four feet high. He pulled back the corner of one of the tarps and shined his light. He couldn't believe his eyes. It was a stack of Stinger missiles.

"What the f***?!" Jeb said to himself. He pulled the remaining tarps from the stack to reveal twenty-four Stingers. The cases were stacked three high, two deep, in four rows.

"Well s**t. I'm gonna need some help."

He quickly walked outside to brief Leftwich.

"You're not gonna believe this s**t." Jeb proceeded to tell Leftwich of his discovery.

"That's about 10 percent of what they were supposed to get, right?" Leftwich inquired.

"Just about."

"How do you want to handle it?"

"There's about to be a big f***in' accident here."

"Whatcha got in mind?"

"Well, before we do anything, we're gonna need to record those serial numbers and lot numbers. I wish I had one of them Polaroids those EOD boys carry. This'll have to do," Jeb added, as he pulled a pen and notepad from his vest.

"We'll have to be quick," Jeb said. "Let's get after it. I'll read off the numbers and you write 'em down."

"Copy. I'm ready."

The two proceeded back inside and went quickly to work. Once the task was completed, Leftwich returned the pen and pad to Jeb.

"Now what?"

"There's some gas cans over there," Jeb replied, pointing toward a corner next to one of the big overhead doors. "Grab a couple of those."

Jeb and Leftwich grabbed two gas cans each and headed outside. The folks who ran this garage must have been in a big hurry, having left both pumps unlocked. That was good luck. Jeb filled two cans with diesel and two cans with gas.

"Why the diesel?" Leftwich asked. "Why not just gas?" By now, it had become clear to Leftwich Jeb intended to destroy the missiles, but he wasn't sure exactly how yet.

"The gas gets the fire started good," Jeb replied. "But the diesel will help it burn a long time, longer than just gas alone, and that's what we want."

"Will they detonate?"

"They shouldn't detonate."

"Shouldn't?"

"I don't give a s**t if they do. What we really want is to disable the launchers anyway. The missiles are no good without the launchers. Besides, around here nobody's gonna think a thing if they do go high order, s**t's been blowing up out here so long they're used to it by now."

That much was true. In fact, the area was so desensitized to the explosions on the garrison, it would be unlikely the local fire brigade would even be notified once the fire started. At least that's what Jeb hoped when he quickly hatched this scheme. He wanted to send a message. He wanted White Beard to know his pilfering was discovered. This should do the trick. White Beard would be in no position to do much of anything in response. To do so would be to acknowledge he stole the Stingers and that was the last thing White Beard wanted to admit. Jeb also knew this was little more than a moral victory. It was only about a tenth of the total number of Stingers—who knew where the remaining 90 percent were—but there was at least some satisfaction in essentially proving the Stingers were stolen.

Before Jeb set about soaking the missiles in diesel fuel, he decided to take one with them in the small SUV. One would be sufficient to convince his superiors he had at least proven his theory, even if he couldn't recover all the stolen missiles. He and Leftwich opened every case and doused each with diesel. He noticed a stack of tires in one corner of the shop and they placed them on top of the Stinger stack to make the fire burn longer and hotter. He then poured the gas over the top and continued out the overhead door leaving a trail behind him, before pouring the last bit of gas as he exited the building.

"Ready?" Jeb asked.

"Ready," came the reply from Leftwich.

"Grab one of those tarps over there. We'll need it to cover that Stinger case." Jeb pulled out his notepad and tore out a blank page. He wadded the paper and grabbed his lighter.

"Let's get ready to run. Here goes."

Leftwich positioned himself on the northwest corner of the building and prepared to run. He had one hand on the handle on one end of the Stinger case, with a tarp in the other. Jeb lit the paper and dropped it in front of the overhead door. The gas ignited with a loud *whoosh*. Jeb grabbed the handle on the other end of the missile case and they began to sprint to their vehicle. They reached the SUV drenched in sweat and loaded the Stinger, concealing it under the tarp. From the time they entered the building to the time they reached their vehicle, a little over twenty minutes elapsed. They paused long enough to ensure the building was burning in earnest. Leftwich started up the vehicle and turned around to make their escape. As they reached the end of the road, Jeb looked back and saw a heavy column of black smoke wafting skyward.

CHAPTER THIRTY-SIX

RAWALPINDI, PAKISTAN
MAY 4, 1988
0015 HRS.

En route to the cafe, Jeb and Leftwich discussed their next move. They would certainly need to secure the missile in their possession. The best place would be the embassy, but even that could be complicated. The only acceptable location would be the secure spaces occupied by station staff. Leftwich thought, humorously, if anything were to go ballistic it would most likely be the station chief when he walked in and saw a Stinger missile in the office.

Jeb knew they needed to get back to the embassy in a hurry, but he told Muhammadin he'd be back, hopefully within an hour. It was going on two hours now, but Jeb was confident Muhammadin would still be at the cafe. He said he'd wait, and that was good enough for Jeb.

"When we get to that cafe, you just keep the motor running and hold fast." Jeb reached behind his back and pulled out a pistol from underneath his vest. He handed the pistol to Leftwich as they pulled up to the cafe and stopped a few yards from the door. "Keep this handy. I'll be in and out."

Jeb knocked on the door of the closed café and one of his waiter friends quickly let him in. When he walked in the cafe, Jeb was not disappointed. Muhammadin was waiting patiently, seated at a table in the dining room drinking tea with his bodyguard seated on one side and Ghulam on the other.

"Ah, my friend has returned," Muhammadin said in a friendly tone. "Come—have some tea."

"I'm afraid I can't stay. I'm due back at the embassy and I'm already late."

"Yes, I was expecting you earlier. Something must have delayed you." That was the only pressing Muhammadin would do at the moment. "What did you learn?"

"Well, I wanted to wait long enough to see if Bhatti was going to show up. And he did. Once I confirmed it was Bhatti, we headed back here. He took a while getting there though."

"Indeed." Muhammadin suspected there was more to the delay than just the tardiness of Bhatti but said nothing further about it.

"We're going to surveil that warehouse and try to see what's going on for the next few days. I'm pretty sure they're up to something." Jeb deliberately referred to the building as a warehouse. Had he revealed the fact it was a garage rather than a warehouse, as the young Iranian had called it, he was confident Muhammadin would have made the connection once the news broke, if it did, about a fire at a garage near Camp Ohjri. Muhammadin didn't miss much. Jeb saw no need, at this point, to share the information about the discovery of Stingers in the possession of the ISI.

"We will be departing soon for Goshta. I should like to see you again soon if you are agreeable?"

"Is tomorrow soon enough?"

"Of course. Perhaps by that time we will have procured some useful information from our Iranian friend," Muhammadin said with a smile.

"No doubt you will," Jeb answered.

"Very good then. I know you are in a hurry so I shall say goodbye."

"Goodbye, my friend. Travel safely."

Muhammadin smiled and nodded. The two shook hands and Jeb made his way toward the door.

Leftwich was anxiously awaiting Jeb's return. It was late, and while there were few people around at that hour, his cargo was so sensitive, he was apprehensive. Leftwich was young—just twenty-six—and Islamabad was his first station. He had been there close to two years and was preparing to rotate within the next few months.

Although he was still fairly green, Jeb found him to be a competent, reliable case officer and worked with him often.

Leftwich had his head turned when Jeb opened the door and jumped in the vehicle. "Oh s**t!" Leftwich gasped at being startled.

"Sorry about that, kid. Let's move."

"Embassy?" Leftwich asked.

"Yep."

As he drove, something foreboding occurred to Leftwich. "How the hell are we gonna get this through security?"

"I thought about that too. Even if they have dogs out, I doubt they'd be able to smell anything. That's a pretty heavy case, and all I can smell is gas anyway."

"Yeah, I got a little carried away with the gas can," Leftwich admitted.

"Well, they know us—we're not visitors. They'll probably just give us a cursory check and wave us through."

They drove on a little further. As the embassy came in sight, Leftwich said, "You know chief is gonna s**t a brick when he walks in and sees a missile in the office?"

"Hell, he oughta be glad to see it," Jeb said. "That's a valuable piece of intelligence. Besides, I plan on being there in the morning long before he gets there anyway."

Once they cleared security and got the missile inside, Jeb instructed Leftwich he would take it from there. "You probably ought to get along home."

"You sure? You don't need anything else?"

"Nah, I'm good. I'll see you in the morning."

"Copy," Leftwich said, turning toward the door. "Oh, by the way. Here's your bullet launcher," he added, reaching behind his back, and producing the Beretta M9 Jeb had handed him earlier in the evening.

"Thanks, I might need that. See ya."

Leftwich nodded and smiled, then left without further comment. It had been quite an evening and he looked forward to a good night's sleep.

Jeb decided to store the missile case in the SCIF. Office staff would start to trickle in as early as seven in the morning, and placing the item in the SCIF would help avoid undue attention. The gas smell was strong though, and even behind the heavy door of the SCIF, quite discernible. Jeb decided it would be better if he camped out in the office to be there before the chief arrived. The gas smell would undoubtedly arouse suspicion as people made their way into the office. To quell the concerns, he could bed down on the couch, grab a shower early in the morning, and be there to answer any questions that might arise. Jeb stretched out on the couch in the outer office. The heavy smell of gas lingered. Jeb sat up and realized it was his pants he splashed gas on that was the primary source of the smell.

Well, hell, he thought to himself. *It's a wonder I didn't set myself on fire.*

He had a change of clothes in his SUV, so he decided to grab the clean clothes, bag up the gas-splashed pants, and take a quick shower before heading back to the office. When he returned, the aroma of gas still lingered faintly. He looked under the sink in the break room and found some Windex. *This will have to do*, he thought. Jeb grabbed a roll of paper towels and headed into the SCIF. He gave the missile case a good soaking and wiped it down with paper towels. You could still catch a faint whiff, but you had to be close to the case.

"That'll work." He threw the paper towels in the break room trash can and returned the Windex. It occurred to him he saw a can of air freshener in the bathroom earlier, so he took the can of Glade and liberally sprayed the SCIF before settling back down on the couch for a much-needed nap.

"What's that smell?" the chief bellowed, as he walked into the office. Jeb bolted upright from the couch.

"And why in the hell are you sleeping on the couch?"

"Mornin' Chief," Jeb replied. "Just catchin' a little sleep."

"Yes, I can see that. But you didn't answer my question."

"Well, I—"

As Jeb began to answer, the chief interrupted.

"Before you answer. Let me ask you another question. I got a call first thing this morning about a fire out near Ohjri. Do you know anything about that?"

"Out near Ojhri?" Jeb replied, coyly.

"You've been working the Ohjri case. I figured you'd know about it."

Jeb knew it would be best to come clean with the chief and give him a full brief. He walked him into the SCIF and showed him the Stinger he recovered. Jeb began with the three Iranians at the cafe and continued from there. He gave the chief a detailed account of the evening and finished with an explanation of the smell in the office, which by now was a combination of Glade "Floral Whisper" and unleaded gasoline.

"That explains the smell. But you should probably know the building you burned was a maintenance facility for city trucks, or something like that."

"Well s**t."

"Yeah—no s**t," the chief said. "If it had been private property, probably nobody would have mentioned anything. Hell, they probably wouldn't have even noticed it out there. But this got their attention."

"Who's attention?"

"Your buddy White Beard for one. He's pretty pissed."

"He better mind he doesn't get too pissed," Jeb said. "If he's not careful, people are gonna start to wonder why he cares so much about a city maintenance facility." Jeb had the leverage he needed with White Beard. "Any word on the damage?"

"Burned to the ground is what they tell me. That area is still fairly deserted. By the time it was called in and the fire trucks got there, it was pretty well totaled."

"I'll probably head out there and take a look for myself." Jeb stood up and prepared to take his leave before the chief could ask any more questions.

"By the way. What about your EOD guys? Can they go back into the field yet?"

“Day after tomorrow,” Jeb answered. “I think they’re just about finished though, given what we learned last night.”

“You’re satisfied you know what happened with the Stingers?”

“I think we know all we’re gonna know at this point,” a mildly irritated Jeb replied. He knew the odds of finding the remaining missiles, numbering more than two hundred, were slim. “Finding those last night was mostly just dumb luck. We probably wouldn’t have found what we found if White Beard hadn’t f***ed up and sent those Iranians to track my EOD team. Too clever by half, I’d say.”

“How much longer you plan to keep them—your team, I mean?”

“Couple weeks ought to do it. I think I’ll go out to the safe house and have breakfast with ’em this morning. I’ll find out how much C-4 they have left, but I’d say we should be able to send them home fairly soon.”

“Sounds good. Just let me know.”

“Copy that, sir,” Jeb said, as he walked out the door bound for the safe house.

CHAPTER THIRTY-SEVEN

SAFE HOUSE–UNDISCLOSED LOCATION
ISLAMABAD, PAKISTAN
MAY 4, 1988
0610 HRS.

Will walked into the living room of the safe house hoping to catch Aziz early. Will was in the habit of getting up ahead of the rest of the team to enjoy a quiet cup of tea or glass of juice before the noise of the morning began. Aziz didn't appear to be about, but Will caught a glimpse of someone sitting at the dining room table. It was Jeb. He saw Will peering into the dining room and motioned for him to come in and sit down.

"Come have some coffee, Sergeant Carter," Jeb said, waving him into the room where he was sipping on a cup too.

Will would have opted for tea but thought it would have been rude to ask for something different since Jeb specifically offered coffee. Aziz appeared in the dining room walking through the kitchen door. He was preparing breakfast when Jeb arrived. Aziz was carrying an empty coffee cup and politely placed it in front of Will.

"Good morning, Sergeant," Aziz said. "I trust you slept well?"

"Yes, thank you."

"Very good, sed." With that, Will and Aziz completed their morning conversational routine.

Will was relieved to see Aziz had placed an ample supply of cream and sugar on the table. He liberally added both to his coffee to make it drinkable. Cook made the coffee extra strong, and even with the addition of a lot of cream and sugar, it was still bitter. Will winced slightly when he took the first sip. Jeb was happily drinking his coffee black and chuckled lightly at the sight of Will tasting the coffee.

"Little stout, huh?"

"Yes sir," Will said. "I guess I'm not much of a coffee drinker."

"Takes a little getting used to." It wasn't just Cook who prepared his coffee extra strong. A strong brew was clearly the preferred method in Pakistan. "These Paks like their coffee strong."

"It's almost like being back in cow camp," said Will.

"Mm-hmm. Well, last night was one hell of an evening, I guess," Jeb said.

"Yes sir," Will agreed. "I sure wasn't expecting to run into any Iranians."

"Yeah, that was a little bit of a surprise. But we got that handled."

"Handled, sir?"

"Hang on just a sec," Morgan said, appearing suddenly. He heard voices in the dining room and hated to miss anything. "I want to hear this, but I need some coffee first, if that's okay."

Jeb nodded in response. Morgan disappeared into the kitchen briefly and returned with a coffee cup in hand. He sat at the table and poured himself a cup, adding cream and sugar before taking a sip.

"Sorry, sir," Morgan began. "You said you got it handled?"

"That's right," Jeb said. "They're in the custody of the Mujahideen."

"That can't be good for those Iranians," Morgan said.

"No, it's not," Jeb said. "Muhammadin's boys can be pretty rough."

"Did you get any sense of why they were in there?" Morgan asked. "They seemed way out of place."

"That they were," Jeb agreed. "I'm sure Muhammadin will get to the bottom of it though. Is the captain up yet?" This wasn't the best time or place to discuss the events of last evening. Jeb came to meet with the captain, not to get bogged down in details of yesterday's improvised operation. Jeb was comfortable briefing Morgan and Carter on the three men in the mosque. Now, he felt it necessary to play it close to the vest on the Iranians. He wasn't sure what, if anything, he could share yet. What he did know was he could not share information on his discovery of the small cache of Stingers, and their subsequent destruction—yet.

"Let me go see if I can rouse him," Morgan said, heading off to knock on the captain's door. He'd get the chance to probe later, he thought.

Morgan knocked twice lightly on the captain's door. He waited a few seconds and got no response. He knocked once more, and the door opened abruptly before he could knock a second time.

"What the hell is it?" the captain demanded. He was standing at the door, dripping wet, with a towel wrapped around him.

"Sorry, sir," Morgan replied. "Jeb's here. Says he needs to speak to you."

The captain looked at his wrist as if to check the time, realizing he wasn't wearing his watch having just gotten out of the shower. "S**t. What time is it anyway?"

"Almost six-thirty, sir."

"Okay. Give me a few minutes. You better wake up the sergeant major too."

"Oh hell . . ." Morgan responded, before catching himself. "Sorry, sir. You want *me* to wake him up?" He would rather have poked a sleeping bear with a short stick than to wake up the sergeant major. He was in good spirits of late, the result of having had a recent lengthy phone conversation with his wife back home. Still, Morgan didn't want to risk aggravating him if he could avoid it.

"Dammit—go wake him up." The captain's patience was growing short, the disconsolate look on Morgan's face wasn't helping. "He'll be pissed if he thinks he missed something."

"Yes sir," Morgan replied dutifully and went to the sergeant major's door. He knocked very lightly and spoke just above a whisper. "Sergeant Major? Sergeant Major?" he said, barely audibly.

What Morgan didn't know was the sergeant major was already up and even showered and shaved. He dressed and was about to head to the kitchen for coffee when he heard Morgan talking to the captain in the hallway. He heard Morgan's apprehension about waking him and decided to have a little fun. He was in an unusual mood for a joke that morning. He let Morgan stand in the hallway for a little longer. Long enough he would have to knock again.

"Sergeant Major, Sergeant Major," Morgan said quietly again, as he tapped lightly on the door.

"What the hell do you want?!" the sergeant major bellowed, throwing his door open.

"Oh s**t," Morgan replied, with a gasp. "Sorry, Sergeant Major. The captain's meeting with Jeb in a few minutes. He wants you to join him."

"I know, I know. I heard y'all talking in the hall."

"Roger that, Sergeant Major."

"Sounded like you were scared to wake me up," Scott said, peering over the top of his glasses with a mischievous grin.

"Well, Sergeant Major, I . . ."

"Wimps**t," the sergeant major said, before breaking into loud laughter.

Morgan simply smiled, saying nothing further and walked back to drink his morning coffee in the dining room.

Morgan sat at the dining room table in the hopes of engaging Jeb in conversation. He had barely enough time to take a sip from his coffee cup before the captain and sergeant major walked in. The captain looked disheveled. He skipped his morning shave and heavy dose of Vitalis Hair Tonic to make his hair behave.

Jeb looked at Will and Morgan in turn. "Would you boys mind giving us the room?"

"Of course, sir," Morgan replied, grabbing his coffee cup before making his exit. Will fell in close behind him. They took a seat in the living room, and Will began to look through the video collection. He looked back and saw Jeb close the French doors between the living room and the dining room. Will hadn't even realized the doors were there.

"Must be some high-level s**t," Morgan said with a smile.

"Guess so," Will replied.

Jeb allowed the men to fill their cups and take their seats before addressing them.

"Looks like we'll be ready to get y'all back in the field day after tomorrow," Jeb said. "How's that sound?"

"We're ready," the captain replied. "These guys are bouncing off the walls."

"Now I know that's Friday, and we wouldn't ordinarily work on a Friday," Jeb explained. "But by God, we've waited long enough. The Paks will just have to live with it."

"That's fine with us, sir" the sergeant major said. "We've had enough time off."

"I'm going to check out the progress today at Ohjri and the demo range," Jeb said. "I'll have some details for you later today."

"Roger that, sir," Halstead answered. "Anything you need from us?"

"About how much C-4 do you think you have left?"

The captain looked at the sergeant major. "What do you think?"

"Not sure, sir. Morgan's keeping track of that."

"Get him in here."

Scott was seated with his back to the French doors. He scooted his chair away from the table, turned, and knocked on the glass door. Morgan heard the knock and craned his neck around to see the sergeant major motioning him to join them.

"Wonder what this is about?" Morgan jumped up quickly from the chair and went to the dining room.

"How much C-4 we got left?" Scott asked, as Morgan opened the glass door. "A full pallet?"

"Not quite a full pallet, Sergeant Major. Just under a thousand pounds I'd say."

The four pallets of C-4 were loaded at one thousand pounds each. An M-112 block of C-4 weighed one and a quarter pounds. Morgan kept close tabs on their C-4 inventory as the senior NCO in the field. By his count they had 745 M-112 blocks left. Of course, they hadn't been out to the demo range in more than two weeks or to their storage location either. It was quite possible their C-4 inventory could have dwindled considerably.

"At least that's how much we had left at last count," Morgan said. He added that qualifier knowing the Paks were inclined to pilfer and may well have already made off with the explosives.

"They haven't touched our s**t," Jeb said. "I guarantee that." He had the storage facility under constant surveillance.

"How long would it take for you to go through that much C-4?"

"We could go through that in a day, sir, if that's what you need," the captain answered. He wasn't sure where Jeb was going with this. "How fast do you need us to go through it?"

"Well, we think we're just about done. You guys have done some great work here, and we want to keep you around for maybe ten to twelve days or so before we send you back to the world."

"Yes sir," the captain said. "We can handle that."

"The Paks have been continuing operations on the garrison. Once you guys showed 'em how to do things, they made pretty good progress. They still have a whole lot of ordnance out at the range we need you to destroy though. There's a lot stacked up out there. If you pace yourselves, you think you could stretch that out over maybe ten to twelve days or so?"

"Absolutely, sir," the captain said. "Whatever you need."

"I'll catch up with you at the embassy this afternoon and let you know how things are looking." Jeb took a last sip of coffee and exited the safe house through the back door off the kitchen.

As Jeb left, Aziz entered the dining room announcing breakfast almost being ready.

"Thank you, Aziz," the captain said. "I could eat."

"Of course, sir. Only a moment."

"Well, that's some good news," the sergeant major said.

"Yeah, I'm hungry too," Morgan said.

"Not breakfast, dumbass," the sergeant major said. "I'm talking about us going home."

"Well, let's not get too far ahead of ourselves," the captain said. "Let's wait and see what Jeb has to say before we start packing our bags." He was as anxious as anyone to get back home but wanted to manage expectations and not get the team too excited about the prospect of an eminent departure. "We've still got a job to do."

CHAPTER THIRTY-EIGHT

CAMP OHJRI
RAWALPINDI, PAKISTAN
MAY 4, 1988
0750 HRS.

As the team was sitting down to breakfast, Jeb was driving out toward Camp Ohjri to assess the damage from the previous night's fire. As he drove, he considered the future of his EOD team. He could just as easily send them home. The remaining work could be carried out by the Paks. But sending them home would undoubtedly attract attention. The fire certainly got White Beard's attention. And Jeb knew it was only a matter of time before he would know of the disappearance of his Iranian assets.

As deputy director of ISI, White Beard would piece things together quickly. There was no way to pin it on Jeb, but the incident would undoubtedly add another layer of tension between the two. Jeb resolved that after a day or two in the field, he would announce to his Pak counterparts the American EOD team would be wrapping up and heading home in two weeks. He could play this up in several ways to insulate himself from potential connection to the fire. He decided he would heap praise on the Paks—lauding how fast and efficiently the Pak soldiers took to their training and commending them on their progress. That, he felt, should be sufficient to blunt any suspicions about the fire that White Beard and his cohorts might have about him or his EOD team. Besides, in two weeks, the work could be completed anyway.

Satisfied with his plan for the next couple of weeks, Jeb went to the garage he set on fire. He arrived to find the building smoldering. From his conversation with the chief earlier, Jeb learned the fire brigade was called to put out the fire. They must have decided against extinguishing the blaze. There was no evidence of water sprayed anywhere. The building must have been too far gone when they arrived, and they decided to let it burn. Jeb viewed this as fortuitous, as it gave him the opportunity to get an excellent, closeup look at the remnants. He could detect no evidence of any of the Stinger missiles. It was possible some of White Beard's people were there ahead of him to extract any incriminating evidence left behind, but that was unlikely given the extent of the damage. In fact, other than a few iron protrusions from the ground of the superstructure of the building, there was virtually nothing left but smoldering ash.

Jeb walked around to the side of the building to get a closer look at where the Stingers were stored against the building's east wall. He could see no trace of anything recognizable. The fire must have indeed burned extremely hot. He recalled having noticed several cases of motor oil stacked next to the missiles and thought to himself how that would also serve as an effective accelerant, but he had no idea at the time it would be so effective, enhancing the destructive power of this little inferno.

Just then a small gust of wind caused some lingering hot coals to ignite. He was far enough away he wasn't singed, but it was a reminder that he was too close. He decided to back off a little and continued to walk around the fire at a safer distance. He was convinced no evidence could have survived this conflagration and decided to move on before someone spotted him. He was too late. Just as he was getting into his SUV, a Pak Army Jeep came roaring up to the charred remains of the building. The driver slammed on the brakes. It was none other than White Beard. "S**t," Jeb muttered under his breath, as he waved politely to acknowledge the Pak general.

"Morning, sir," Jeb said.

"I see you heard the news about the fire," White Beard replied, offering no salutation in return.

"Actually, I was just coming by the garrison to check on the progress this morning when I saw the smoke. Thought I'd check it out." He knew that was a thin response. He would normally enter the garrison at the north gate, and the fire was two streets beyond the south gate, which was closed and cordoned off since the blast. White Beard decided to test Jeb's explanation.

"You are coming from the embassy?"

Jeb caught on quick. The embassy was north of the garrison. If he came from the north, as usual and arrived at the north gate of the garrison, the smoke would have been almost indiscernible from that distance. The flames had all but died, and the lingering smoke was not rising high and the wind was blowing it to the east.

"Uh, no, actually I was coming from the south."

"The south, you say?"

"That's right," Jeb said. "I had some business down that way. This must have been one heck of a fire, huh?"

"Indeed," White Beard said, not satisfied with Jeb's response, but pressing no further.

"What was this place anyway?" Jeb asked.

"This was a municipal vehicle maintenance facility."

"Hmm . . . damn shame," Jeb said, shaking his head. "Nobody hurt I hope."

"I have heard no reports of any casualties."

"Well, that's good news. Say, Brigadier, what brings you out here this morning?"

"This is my garrison," White Beard replied, in a slightly peevish tone.

"This is your garrison?" Jeb replied, pointing to the ground. "I thought that was your garrison," repositioning his arm to point to the north.

"It is in close proximity to my garrison, and therefore, it is my concern," White Beard responded, his indignation rising.

"Indeed." Jeb skillfully turned the tables on the Pak general, putting him on the defensive. "Well, you have a nice day now, sir." Jeb got in his SUV and sped away to the north gate of the garrison. He took great delight in knowing he burrowed under White Beard's skin. Jeb disliked him more every day and any opportunity to goad the Pak general was well worth the added effort.

An incensed White Beard said nothing incriminating. In silence, he seethed, watching the diminutive American drive away in the dust.

Jeb decided to make a cursory check of the garrison just in case someone was watching. He drove in the north gate and stopped about a hundred yards in. There was little to see, however, other than the destruction the blast left behind. It appeared the bulk of the ordnance was mostly cleared. There were still a few fire hoses left, but there were soldiers actively rolling those up for removal. The bulk of the work left to complete was to destroy the stockpile of ordnance out at the range north of town. He was confident that could fill two weeks easily. Yet he thought it best to see the stockpile to get a better sense of what was needed, so he jumped back in his SUV and headed north.

When he arrived at the demo range, Jeb was shocked to find such a huge stockpile of ordnance. The Pak soldiers had been busy. To his eyes, it appeared there may not be enough C-4 to finish the job. He decided the first order of business the next day would be to bring the team out to the demo range to get an idea how much C-4 and time it would take to make this ungodly pile of ordnance go away.

By the time Jeb returned to the embassy, it was approaching lunch time. He was confident he could locate one team member or all of them, at the cafeteria. He was almost correct. Everyone but the captain was going through the line getting lunch. He went through the line and sat at a table across from Sergeant Major Scott.

"Mind if I join you?"

"Sure, sir. Have a seat."

"The captain around?"

"He's getting a haircut. Anything you can tell me?"

"Yeah, I was just gonna lay out the plan for the next couple of weeks. I was just out at the demo range, and they've got ordnance stacked up out there like cord wood. I'm concerned y'all don't have enough C-4 left to finish all that."

"Well, we can be creative with C-4," the sergeant major assured him. "You'd be surprised how far we can stretch it if we need to."

Jeb was as concerned about stretching time as he was about stretching C-4. He wanted to be sure the team could make two weeks' worth of work out at the demo range. He was impressed with how fast and efficiently they worked the first day out at the range. Those were some big shots and yet they were just a fraction of what was awaiting them out at the range.

"There he is," Scott said.

Jeb turned to see the captain walking up to the table with freshly cut hair.

"Man, that is one hell of a barber," the captain said, taking a seat next to the sergeant major. "You ever use him?"

"Oh yeah," Jeb answered. "When I get my hair cut, he's the guy I use," he said.

"That head massage—damn," the captain said. "I'm about ready for a nap. He's got some kind of kung fu grip or something. I wasn't sure I could get out of the chair by the time he was through with me."

"Yeah, he's thorough," Jeb said. "Did he tell you the story of his favorite Marine?"

"Favorite Marine? No, he never mentioned that."

"Did you see that Marine's picture on the wall across from his chair?" Jeb asked.

"Oh yeah, I saw it when he turned the chair around. But I almost lost consciousness when he got started on that head massage."

"What's the deal with his favorite Marine?" the sergeant major asked.

"Well, back in '79," Jeb began, "when all that s**t went down in Tehran. The Iranians weren't just trying to start a revolution in Iran; they were trying to start a global Islamic revolution. So the Ayatollah sent out press releases all over the world to try and get the Muslims all fired up. Of course, they were successful in Tehran—we saw what happened there. Anyway, the press releases said 'the Americans had taken Mecca' and of course, that was a call to arms to all

Muslims. Most of the riots that took place around the world in Islamic countries sort of fizzled out pretty quick. But not here. A few hundred Paks rioted outside the embassy, and it got bad. So they sound general quarters, and all the Marines go to their 'battle stations,' you know. This thing gets out of hand quick. The rioters stormed the embassy and set fires and s**t. Anyway, right about the time they sound general quarters, this kid—this Marine—is sitting in the barber chair getting a haircut, and he jumps up and runs. Well, the barber—Asif is his name—he freaks out and he's yelling at the kid 'wait, wait, I haven't finished your haircut!' Hell, he doesn't know what's going on, but he doesn't want this kid running off with half a haircut. But with the alarm sounding he figures he better get somewhere quick, so he hides under his barber chair.

"Well, by this time," Jeb continued, "these asshole rioters have weapons and start shooting. So, this Marine—a nineteen-year-old kid from Long Island—is running for his post and gets shot. Right up under his helmet, poor kid. An Army Warrant Officer got killed too. I mean it was a mess, they trapped a bunch of people who ended up asphyxiating to death cuz of all the fires they set. Hell, a few of those folks were burned to death—and they were Pak nationals who worked here at the embassy. Anyway, they ended up evacuating over a hundred embassy personnel and there was a big diplomatic brouhaha and everything. But they didn't even find that Marine until the next day. They got a room down there named for him. The 'Crowley Room.' His name was Steven J. Crowley."

"I saw that placard down there close to the Det Commander's office," the sergeant major said.

"Yep, that's it," Jeb said.

"Well, I'll be damned," the captain said. "And that's why the barber has that picture up?"

"Well, I guess Asif took it pretty hard. He felt like he sent him into eternity with only half a haircut. I don't know, maybe it's some kind of barber honor code or something. Anyway, he put that picture on the wall to remember him."

By this time, the team had all turned and fixed their attention on Jeb as he told the story of Asif's favorite Marine.

"Well, that's a hell of a story," Hutchinson said.

"Yeah, no s**t," Campbell agreed.

"Yep," Jeb said. "Sad, but true."

There was an awkward, lingering pause—an impromptu memorial silence in honor of a fallen Marine.

"You boys ready to hit the demo range?" Jeb asked.

"Oh, hell yes," Hutchinson exclaimed, accompanied by a chorus of affirmative murmurings.

"Good deal. Y'all have a whole day to get rested up before we start back."

Jeb finished his lunch and headed up to the third floor without saying anything more. Morgan was watching, waiting for an opportunity to talk further with Jeb.

"Come on," he said, rising from the table with his cafeteria tray in hand.

"Hang on," Will said, choking down his last few French fries followed by a final gulp of Coke to wash them down.

"He's probably up on the third floor," Morgan said, dropping off his tray as he proceeded out of the cafeteria. Will followed suit and fell in behind him.

"Time to get the G-2 on those Iranians." "G-2" being the military reference to intelligence.

"You think he'll tell us anything?" Will asked.

"Oh, hell yes. He just won't tell us everything."

Will was as anxious as Morgan to learn more about the incident. The confrontation with the three Iranians could easily have escalated had Campbell not been controlled. They were fortunate Jeb walked in when he did.

They arrived at the secure space on the third floor just in time to see Jeb walking out.

"Where you headed, sir?" Morgan asked. Will and Morgan had just gotten off the elevator and Jeb was heading for a stairwell at the end of the hall. He had his back to them and didn't see them coming.

"Oh, hey there," Jeb said, turning around. "Anything I can help you boys with?" He never really stopped, just slowed a little, as he made his way to the stairwell.

"We were hoping we could talk a little about those Iranians. That is, if you have a few minutes."

"Actually, I'm a little tight on time," Jeb said as he pushed the door open. "But come on." He motioned for the men to walk with him. "I'll tell you what I can."

Morgan and Will followed Jeb down the stairs. He was clearly in a hurry. "Sir, you mentioned those three Iranians were more likely operatives of some kind than draft dodgers. Did you find out anything more about them yet?"

"Well, like I said, Muhammadin's got them with him. In fact, that's where I'm headed right now."

Morgan and Will exchanged vexed looks as they reached the bottom of the stairs on the first floor. Jeb clearly read their expressions.

"Tell you what. If I get outta here pretty quick, I should be back late tomorrow afternoon. How 'bout we hook up for dinner? We can talk then—sound good?"

"Sounds good, sir," Morgan said.

"Yes sir," Will agreed.

"Y'all just hang around the embassy. I'll see you tomorrow."

"Roger that, sir."

CHAPTER THIRTY-NINE

Before leaving the SCIF, Jeb took a few minutes to bring Leftwich up to speed. "My team is back in the field Friday. I'm gonna need you to see them out to the demo range and get them started."

"I don't know s**t about demolitions," Leftwich said.

"You don't have to know s**t. They know plenty. Besides, maybe they'll give you a little training. Never know—it might come in handy."

"So, what, I just go with them out to the demo range?"

"Yep, be at the safe house at zero six," Jeb said. "Right now I'm headed to Goshta."

"How long you gonna be gone?"

"Quick trip. Should be back in time for dinner tomorrow if all goes well."

His brief conversation in the stairwell with Morgan and Carter didn't delay him much. He made straight for his SUV with only a slight detour to change clothes. He would soon be airborne. He was confident he could catch a ride on a helicopter to Peshawar. He knew better than to make a formal request for a special flight from the Pak Army, which would only alert White Beard. Jeb was familiar with flight schedules between Islamabad and Peshawar. He flew on their helicopters so often it would not be unusual for him to show up unannounced and ask if they had room for one more. He developed such a good rapport with both pilots and crew they were always happy to see him. Such was the case today. He was able to jump on a Huey without any questions asked.

PESHAWAR, PAKISTAN
MAY 4, 1988
1545 HRS.

When Jeb arrived in Peshawar, there was a truck awaiting his arrival driven by a trusted associate. The truck—a beat-up quad-cab Toyota Hilux—had stock racks on the bed, and for good reason. Jeb peered into the bed of the truck and saw there was a half dozen goats contentedly munching on hay. He got in the cab of the truck without hesitation, and they were off.

"Nice touch with the goats, Mike." He meant that as a compliment. The goats added to their camouflage. They looked a lot less conspicuous in a beat-up truck hauling goats on the road to Goshta. They were unlikely to meet any Soviets on their drive, but if they did it wouldn't hurt to look as native as possible.

Mike was a Green Beret, a master sergeant with close to twenty years in the Army. He joined the Army right out of high school. He had an aptitude for languages, and it wasn't long before Special Forces recruited him. He spent time in Laos and Cambodia in 1972. He spoke German and Russian, so he was a valuable commodity in both the European theater and Afghanistan. Mike's first tour in theater consisted of embedding with the S.S.G. to help train Mujahideen fighters. He quickly learned Pashto and became an asset to the Mujahideen and the S.S.G.

Now on his third deployment, Mike was an old hand. He had only been back in theater a week or so, but already had a good beard going. He was dark-complected and dark-eyed, so he had no trouble blending in. He worked with Jeb before. His last tour overlapped briefly with Jeb's arrival by a few months. The two got along well, but they were an odd match. Mike was six foot three and towered over Jeb. He stood out on an Afghan horse too. Mike became a competent horseman, but the smallish horses he had to ride in Afghanistan made him appear unusually large. He was a good sport about it, despite the teasing he got from Jeb and Muhammadin, whom he had also gotten to know well over the years.

"Good to see you," Jeb said, as they drove west. "Tracy and the kids all doing okay?"

"Tracy's great. Girls are growing like weeds," referring to his ten-year-old twin daughters.

They engaged in a little more catching up and small talk before Jeb began to bring him up to speed.

"I could have used your help last night. It was a busy night." Jeb gave him the full brief, talking for thirty minutes straight before Mike commented.

"S**t, sir, you have been busy."

"Yeah, and this visit with Muhammadin should be interesting too. No telling what he got from these Iranian sons of b*****s. By the way, Muhammadin doesn't know about the Stingers I found last night—and he doesn't need to know. I mean s**t, I wouldn't be surprised if he already found out what went down last night."

"He damn sure doesn't miss much," Mike said.

"If he asks me about 'em I'll probably come clean. But I'm not volunteering anything."

"You think these Iranians were really tracking your team?"

"Oh, they were tracking them at the very least. That little piss ant told me as much. But I'm not sure if that smartass team leader, or whatever he was, was gonna try and hit 'em or not. I didn't interrogate him—Ghulam was dealing with him. Muhammadin saw right quick that he was going to be a tougher nut to crack, that's why they brought him over here."

"Time Ghulam gets through with him that sumb***h'll be giving up his mother's maiden name," Mike said with a chuckle.

"We know the threat was legit. We just don't know if this is the guy. He's young, could be a rookie on his first assignment, who knows? I guess we'll find out."

"Ya think he's still alive?" Mike asked.

"Hell, it's only been twenty-four hours or so."

"You know that doesn't matter with these guys, boss."

"We'll know soon enough," Jeb said, as they continued west down the bumpy road, the setting sun in their faces.

Jeb and Mike arrived at Muhammadin's camp just before dinner. As always, Muhammadin and his crew were happy to welcome them.

Muhammadin was particularly glad to see Mike, with whom he worked closely in years past.

"It is good to see you again, my friend," Muhammadin was smiling broadly and came over and immediately offered Mike a welcoming hug. "I did not know if you would ever return."

"I had to return to help my friends," Mike answered, in Pashto.

"Indeed—indeed."

The host wasted no time seating his guests around the table. Jeb always enjoyed breaking bread with his Mujahideen colleagues, and Mike found he missed these experiences too. It had been a couple of years, but his Pashto was coming back to him, and he was reconnecting well with Muhammadin and his men, despite the time gap.

Jeb extended the courtesy of waiting until after the meal to talk business. Muhammadin sensed an urgency from his American friend, and he knew Jeb was anxious to hear about what they learned from the Iranians.

As the three men walked outside to have a smoke, Muhammadin casually inquired about Carter. "Is the 'cowboy' ready to come for a visit?"

"No doubt he would love to come and visit. I just don't know when we'll find the time." Jeb saw that Muhammadin was still wearing the EOD badge on his vest, and he asked about it.

"Ah, yes. I am very proud of this badge. My men have asked me about it several times. Please tell the cowboy that my men are anxious to meet him, and that we would gladly receive him in our ranks."

"I'll be sure and tell him."

"Now, about these Iranians. We were able to ascertain that the two younger men are cousins."

Of course, Jeb knew that, but withheld comment until Muhammadin completed his report. He was getting frustrated at Muhammadin's casual pace but did his best to conceal it.

"We also learned they were in the Iranian Army."

Jeb knew that as well. Farrokh, the younger of the two cousins told him as much.

"On further examination, Ghulam was able to determine these men were not just in the Army. They are members of what they call the Quds Force. This means they are highly trained."

"Of course," Jeb replied. What Jeb knew was the Islamic Revolutionary Guard Corps recently established a unit tasked with special operations and intelligence. They could be likened to a hybrid of the U.S. Army Special Forces and the CIA. This also meant the capability to execute an attack on his EOD team. But the cousins cooperated with him, indicating a lack of discipline or commitment. Young Farrokh gave up considerable information with little coercion.

"That's interesting," Jeb said. "What about the other man? He appeared to be a team leader."

"You are correct, my friend. And he required a much more extensive examination."

Mike raised an eyebrow when he heard the term "more extensive examination." *Poor bastard*, he thought to himself, knowing exactly what that meant.

"What did you learn?"

"This man was an Iranian intelligence officer."

"Was?"

"Yes. Unfortunately, he succumbed to Ghulam's extensive examination."

"That is unfortunate," Jeb said, fearing that they had only limited intel from what could have proven to be a valuable source.

"Indeed. However, before he expired, we did extract a wealth of information."

"Well, that's good. Please continue."

"This man was a newly trained intelligence officer. He was tasked with attacking your American team. The two younger men were working with him—they were also newly trained."

"Sounds like this was their first op," Jeb surmised.

"I believe you are correct," Muhammadin said.

"The leader sort of broke his cover pretty readily in that café. Unusual for an intelligence officer to be so undisciplined, wouldn't you say?"

"We questioned him about that as well. It seems he was so overcome with hatred at the sight of the three Americans he could no longer control himself."

"Well, it cost him dearly, didn't it?"

"Sadly, yes."

"The younger one said they were recruited by ISI," Jeb said.

"They weren't exactly recruited. The operation was being facilitated by an ISI officer. You mentioned a Lieutenant Bhatti?"

"Yes. The younger one said they met him in Kandahar," Jeb said.

"Yes, they met with him in Kandahar. Bhatti helped provide them safe passage to Islamabad and connected them with a source for support there."

Jeb could tell by Muhammadin's expression there was more information.

"What else."

"I am sorry to inform you of this, my friend. It appears they had a contact inside of your embassy—a Pakistani."

The news angered Jeb, but it also didn't surprise him. While they did their best to vet local employees, every now and then, one would fall through the cracks.

"Anything specific about this embassy contact?"

"He mentioned he works in the 'motor pool'?" Muhammadin replied with a look of uncertainty not knowing if he used the term correctly.

"Well, that narrows it down. Anything else I should know?"

"Interestingly, the two young cousins have no desire to return to Iran."

"That is interesting. Any particular reason?"

"They are certain they will be executed when they return for having failed in their mission."

"Well, that's probably true," Jeb agreed. "So, what do you plan to do with them?" He found it odd and a little sad that the two Iranians felt their chances of survival were higher in Afghanistan than they were in their own country.

"I had hoped you might have a suggestion," Muhammadin said. "As it happens, these two young men only volunteered for Quds Force training to avoid fighting the Iraqis. It seems they hoped the war would be over by the time they completed their training, but of course it is not. They quickly volunteered for this mission hoping to slip away once they were out of the country."

Jeb thought about it for a minute or two. While the two men could offer some insights into the newly formed Quds Force, he was unable to manage the long-term detention of two Iranian defectors. And they wanted to be defectors, there was little doubt.

"I would drop them off at the border and let them fend for themselves."

"That is an option," Muhammadin said. "Or perhaps I could save myself the trouble of a two-day drive to the border."

"I'll leave that up to you, my friend. I'm sure you'll make the best choice." Jeb was sure the young Iranians had little hope of survival at this point.

GOSHTA, AFGHANISTAN
MAY 5, 1988
0920 HRS.

Jeb and Mike passed the night without event and were able to slip off early the next morning. They thanked Muhammadin for his help and his hospitality before their early departure. They decided to leave the goats to show their appreciation.

"Your generosity is most appreciated, my friends," Muhammadin said, hugging each of the two Americans in turn. "I hope to see you again very soon. Farewell."

Jeb was in a hurry to get back to Islamabad. He had to share this latest information with his colleagues back at the embassy. Some four and half hours later—stopping only twice to take a leak—he and Mike pulled into Peshawar. Their timing was near perfect. In less than an hour Jeb was able to hop a Huey back to Islamabad, leaving Mike behind at the Peshawar outpost. With any luck, Jeb would be walking into the embassy about suppertime.

CHAPTER FORTY

U.S. EMBASSY
ISLAMABAD, PAKISTAN
MAY 5, 1988
1825 HRS.

Will joined Morgan and Tom Thiessen for dinner. He developed the habit of spending his evenings in the company of Tara, but she made herself scarce on this day.

"Where's your girlfriend?" Tom asked, benignly. Morgan looked at him and shook his head as if to indicate that was not a good topic of conversation at that point.

"I actually haven't seen her today. I guess she's busy."

"Oh, I'm sure she's busy," said the unmistakable voice of Hutchinson. He and Campbell walked up at that precise moment and heard Thiessen's inquiry. "Busy trying to avoid your ass," he chortled.

"Lock it up, asshole," Morgan said quietly, trying to be discreet. They were in the dining room amidst several embassy staff, some with their families and Morgan was hoping to get through the meal with some degree of decorum. The effort was lost on Hutchinson.

"Oh, they know," Hutchinson said, not modulating his volume.

"Know what?" Morgan asked, again, quietly, in the hope Hutchinson would take the hint to tone it down.

"They know the hot chick is dumping little Willy here."

Morgan stood from the table. "A word, Sergeant Hutchinson," he said, motioning for Hutchinson to follow him out of the dining room. They stopped outside in the lobby. Morgan looked both directions before speaking.

"Okay, first, lower your voice, for ******'s sake. I'm sure they can hear you all the way out at the swimming pool. People are trying to eat their damn dinner."

"What else?"

"And second, stop being such a d**k all the time. I mean, enough already—s**t."

Hutchinson laughed heartily. "These assholes need to lighten up, man."

"See, that's exactly what I'm talking about. Time and place, man, time and place."

"All right, all right. I can tone it down a little."

"Evening, gentlemen," Jeb said. He walked into the lobby of the dining room as he anticipated, at dinner time, and right as Morgan was attempting to smooth some of the rough off of Hutchinson's wanton coarseness.

"Hey sir," Morgan replied. "How's it going?"

"Going good. Thought I'd grab a bite of dinner—mind if I join y'all?"

"Of course, sir. We've already got a table." Morgan paused for a second and turned to Hutchinson. "Will you be joining us?"

"Hell no," Hutchinson said, and he turned to leave without further conversation.

Jeb sat at the table, as Campbell stood to leave.

"Think I'll see about a call home," Campbell said.

"I think I'll look into calling home too," Thiessen said, and they turned to leave.

Little was said during the course of the meal and Morgan was beginning to get a little anxious.

"So you just got back from Afghanistan?" Morgan asked Jeb, as dinner began to wind down.

"Yep. Quick trip."

"What did you find out about those guys?" Morgan asked.

"We'll have to go upstairs to talk about that. Let me get some coffee and dessert in me and we'll head that way."

"Sounds good, sir."

They lingered over a slice of cheesecake while Jeb enjoyed a slice of coconut creme pie and *two* cups of coffee. Will could see Morgan was getting visibly anxious, but Jeb was hungry. He hadn't eaten since dinner at Muhammadin's camp the night before. He was in no hurry.

"You boys ready to hit the range," Jeb asked between bites. "Yes sir," Morgan replied.

"They got that s**t stacked up out there," Jeb said. "They've been busy."

"I'll bet," Morgan replied.

"Think you can you get it blown in two weeks?" Jeb asked.

"We can have it done in less than a week. Hell, without a range limit, we can move pretty fast."

"I need it done in two weeks. Can you stretch it out that long?"

"I imagine we could," Morgan said. "But we'll have to configure our shots differently. That means we might run out of C-4."

"I bet I can get some explosives for you if you need it. I just need you to pace yourselves and stretch this out to two weeks."

"Can do, sir. Can you tell us why?"

"Yep," Jeb said, sipping the last of his coffee. "But not here."

"Roger that, sir."

"I'll see you up on three in ten mikes."

"Good copy," Morgan said.

They gave Jeb ample time to get up to the third floor before joining him. Jeb took the precaution of camouflaging the Stinger missile he recovered from the garage, after he briefed the chief on the operation. They agreed the fewer people who saw it, the better. Jeb placed a lateral file cabinet on top of it with a lamp on top of that. He stacked a bunch of books in front of it as well to further obscure it. By the time he was through, it was hardly noticeable as anything more than an additional piece of office furniture. You'd have to be looking for it to know it was there. Safe where it was for now, Jeb knew he would have to remove it and blow it up soon. It seemed a shame to destroy such an expensive weapon and a formidable one too. But there was really nothing else he could do. Of course, he would have to wait until after his EOD team left so they would never know about the recovery of even a small percentage of Stingers.

Jeb pondered the irony of the situation—that he couldn't task his EOD team with destroying one of the very items they came to Pakistan to help him recover—when Morgan and Will arrived.

Morgan knocked on the outer door and Jeb quickly opened the heavy door and let them in.

"Come on in, boys," Jeb seemed to be in a good mood; not to say he was ever in a noticeably bad mood. But he seemed obviously less stressed.

"Have a seat." Morgan and Will sat at the long table and awaited Jeb's comments.

"So I guess y'all are curious about those Iranian sons of b*****s, huh?"

"Yes sir," Morgan replied. "That whole deal has been bothering me."

"Well, here's what we found out." He filled them in on the details, except for his discovery of the small cache of Stingers and their subsequent destruction. Jeb saw no need to share that information with the EOD team now or in the future. But since they were involved in the confrontation with the Iranians at the cafe, he saw no need to withhold the information on who the young Iranians were, and what they had were doing.

"So those guys were supposed to kill us?" Morgan asked plainly.

"That's right."

"And how were they gonna do it?" Morgan queried. "Did they have some help? They didn't look like much."

"Well, that's the thing. These guys were young, and we think this was as much a test as anything. This new unit, this Quds Force, is a new capability for the Iranians. We think that's why they set a date certain for the targeting, again, sort of testing their capability. Hell, it could have just as easily been an initiation for these young operatives."

Jeb also made the deliberate decision not share the bigger concerns he had about this incident. The first that ISI had underwritten the whole operation. And the second that there was at least one contact within the embassy working for ISI. He knew he would have to share this latest information with the chief of station very soon, first thing in the morning in fact. It also occurred to him he had been so busy over the last few days, he hadn't taken the time to update General Wassom on this recent series of events. He would make it a point to visit with him soon as well. The chief and the general would be the ones to update the ambassador. Jeb was certain they would recommend to the ambassador a much tighter vetting process for local employees. In the meantime, they had yet to identify the individual responsible for the security breach.

"So where are these Iranians now, sir?" Will asked.

"Well, the Mujahideen has them. I expect they'll be sending them back to Iran very soon."

"By the way, Carter. Muhammadin couldn't stop talking about his American cowboy friend and the EOD badge you gave him." Jeb shared this information to change the topic of the Iranians' fate.

"I don't think you could have made him any happier if you walked up and handed him a million dollars. He's proud of that badge—nice gesture."

"Thank you, sir," Will replied.

"Well, gentlemen," Jeb said abruptly, as he pushed back from the table. "I've got some work to do." Signaling that the meeting had come to an end.

"Yes sir," Morgan said. "Thanks for the time. One more quick thing though. You asked us to stretch out our demo for two weeks. Why the two weeks when we could have this done in two or three days?"

"We don't want your departure to coincide with the incident involving the Iranians. That would look like one had something to do with the other, and we don't want that."

"Roger that, sir. Thanks again."

"You got it," Jeb replied. "See you guys in the morning."

With that, Will and Morgan departed the secure space on the third floor and headed back downstairs. Once in the elevator, Morgan confided that he didn't think Jeb was telling them everything about the Iranians.

"That two weeks deal doesn't make sense to me," Morgan suggested. "There's more to that than he's telling us."

"I guess he gave us more information than we probably should have gotten though," Will replied.

"That's probably right. Still . . ."

There was a long pause as Morgan thought about it.

"What?" Will asked.

"Something happened after he dropped us off at the safe house. There's a reason he wants us to hang around another two weeks."

"Well, that's what he said. He didn't want us leaving to—"

"Yeah, yeah. He doesn't want our departure to coincide with the Iranian incident. I got that."

"Well, what then?" Will said lamely, not knowing what else to say.

"Well, he's never gonna tell us, that's what. And that means we'll probably never know."

CHAPTER FORTY-ONE

DEMOLITION RANGE
NORTH OF ISLAMABAD, PAKISTAN
MAY 6, 1988
0830 HRS.

Jeb was keenly aware the American team's first day back in the field was a Friday—the day of worship. He had been deferential up to this point, but under the circumstances he felt it was more pressing to get his team back in the field as soon as possible, so he dispensed with the observation and sent the team back into the field. Jeb was certain White Beard would raise no objections since he verbalized how far behind they already were.

The team began to pace themselves on the remaining demolition operations. Their first day back in the field entailed getting an inventory of remaining ordnance, and how they would configure their shots to finish in two weeks. White Beard questioned the pace of the operation and expressed his concern that they weren't working fast enough to suit him. The explanation was based on safety, and the extreme heat played a critical part in their pace as well.

"We still had a significant amount of white phosphorus munitions," the captain reminded him. "These WP rounds need to be segregated from the high explosive rounds and destroyed in separate shots."

"Why must these munitions be separated?" White Beard asked. "This appears to be a waste of time."

White Beard was not present that first day on the range and hadn't received the brief given to the other Pak officers explaining the different techniques used to destroy several types of ordnance.

There were a couple of Pak officers present as White Beard continued to voice his displeasure—among them Captain Abed, the team leader with whom Will worked closely, but they chose to remain silent, allowing White Beard to continue his rant.

Captain Halstead maintained his composure, but it was clear to Leftwich, who accompanied the team out to the range, he was losing his patience with the Pak general.

"If I may, Brigadier," Leftwich interjected at one point, to diffuse the situation. "These men are very highly trained and experienced, sir. I would suggest we let them do the job they were sent here to do."

"We are behind schedule by at least two weeks," White Beard exclaimed. "And now I'm being told that it will be another two weeks before they will complete this task—unacceptable!" the general bellowed.

"Any delays are the result of extenuating circumstances beyond our control, Brigadier," Leftwich reminded him.

"Extenuating circumstances indeed."

"Well sir, the other option is to send these men back to the embassy and we'll just let the ambassador address this issue himself. Would that be satisfactory?"

"That will not be necessary. Carry on." With that, the Pak general turned on his heel and proceeded directly to his Jeep. The last thing White Beard wanted was for the U.S. ambassador to be directly involved in this operation. That would certainly mean he would be talking directly to President Zia, and White Beard knew the fewer eyes he had on him with respect to the Camp Ohjri blast, the better. He didn't want President Zia to question him about anything relating to this operation if he could avoid it.

Leftwich and Captain Halstead watched as White Beard's vehicle disappeared over the hill to the west of the demo range.

"Good riddance," Leftwich said. "That son of a b***h is a real piece of work."

"I won't disagree with you," the captain said. "Well, we've got work to do . . ." After a long pause. "You wanna blow some s**t up?"

"Sounds good. I don't have any training in demolitions, so you'll have to school me, I guess."

"We'll give you a quick demo 101." Demo 101 in this case would consist of the team doing all the work, with Leftwich watching. He would also be pulling the igniter on at least one shot and yelling "fire in the hole"—an "honor" usually reserved for the junior member of the team, namely Will.

DEMOLITION RANGE
NORTH OF ISLAMABAD, PAKISTAN
MAY 15, 1988
0830 HRS.

They spent the next several days efficiently destroying the unexploded ordnance collected over a period of some eight weeks. Overall, they recovered and destroyed over nine tons of ordnance from the Camp Ohjri blast.

"Ya know, you boys have probably done more demo since you've been here than most EOD techs do in a career," Sergeant Major Scott observed as they were wrapping up one afternoon. "Wouldn't you say, Captain?"

"Oh, I'd say so."

"I don't know why we don't just finish this last little bit," Hutchinson said. "Hell, we could finish this s**t up right now in two shots."

"Cuz, we have orders to finish up tomorrow, that's why," the sergeant major replied. "And that's all you need to know."

"Roger that, Sergeant Major. Good enough for me," Hutchinson replied.

The team ran out of C-4 as they suspected they would and Jeb was able to procure some form of plastic explosives from his Pakistani counterparts. It was proving to be somewhat of a challenge to work with, particularly in the torrid heat, but they made do.

The explosive compound—black in color with a gritty texture not unlike C-4—was nitroglycerin based, which meant they had to wear gloves to handle it. If absorbed through the skin of a bare hand, nitro caused a severe headache. Wiley learned this lesson the hard way. He and the sergeant major were stationed back at the embassy for much of the operation, but decided to join the team on this day. Wiley didn't notice that the rest of them had donned surgical gloves, with a second pair of cotton gloves over them. He was intrigued by the black explosive compound and immediately picked up a handful for further examination.

"This stuff is really gummy," he said, as he worked the substance in his hand to get a feel for it.

"You better put some gloves on, dumbass," Hutchinson said. "This s**t's nitro-based."

"Oh man. Why didn't somebody tell me." He looked up and noted that everyone else was wearing gloves—including the sergeant major.

"Hurry up and get that s**t off your hands," the sergeant major said. His admonition came too late. By the time Wiley was able to get the black goo from his hands, the headache was setting in.

"My head is pounding."

"Why don't you just head back to the safe area and sit in the shade. That headache is probably gonna get worse before it gets better. You need to get out of this sun."

Captain Abed happened to be with the team and heard the conversation. He issued an order to a Pak soldier who was working with them, and the soldier ran back up range, secured one of the waiting vehicles and quickly returned.

"Perhaps you should ride back to the safe area," Captain Abed said. "It is a long walk back in this heat."

"Thank you, sir," Wiley said, who by now was in such pain, it was difficult to speak. The young Pak soldier opened the door of the truck and Wiley got in. The two disappeared as they resumed their work.

Hutchinson overcame his urge to deride Wiley for such an oversight, noting he was already in considerable pain, and that there was no need to add insult to injury.

"This s**t sucks," he said simply, as the work continued. No one disagreed.

Jeb drove up just as Hutchinson and the sergeant major completed their conversation about the idea of finishing the task. He was riding in a van driven by Khali Khan.

"Afternoon, boys. Looks like y'all have just about knocked this in the head." Hutchinson considered weighing in on the topic, but the sergeant major, anticipating such a move, shot him a foreboding look. Hutchinson remained silent.

"Yes sir," the captain replied. "Just about."

"Well, I've got some news for you. You're going home day after tomorrow."

There was a wave of exuberance among the team, as they looked at each other.

"Hot damn," Hutchinson exclaimed. "I'm ready."

Jeb looked over at the remaining ordnance, then checked his watch.

"How long would it take to finish—today I mean—right now?"

The captain and the sergeant major looked at each other. "Couple hours?" the captain said.

"I think we can get it done in two hours," the sergeant major agreed.

"Two hours, sir," the captain affirmed, as he turned to Jeb.

"Sounds good. Here's the deal. You guys finish up today, and I'm giving you tomorrow off. Hang around the embassy and relax a little. The Pak Army brass wants to take y'all to dinner tomorrow evening as a thank you, so we'll leave the embassy around 1800—cool?"

"Yes sir," the captain answered. He was excited as anyone to be leaving.

"Well, let's get to it then," Jeb said. "I've actually done quite a bit of demo in my time. Just tell me what to do, and I'll do it."

"Roger that, sir," the captain said.

The team was so excited to get the news they would be leaving soon that they worked with extra vigor. They completed the final two shots in an hour and forty-five minutes.

"Done and done," Morgan pronounced, as the last reverberations of the second shot evaporated to a null.

"Hell yeah," Hutchinson said. "Let's go."

CHAPTER FORTY-TWO

It dawned on Will that tonight would be his last opportunity to spend time with Tara. He was careful not to get too attached, but the truth was he had become quite fond of Tara. Will sensed the feeling was mutual, but what mostly kept his feelings in check was the thought that she was a spy. How could she have any genuine feelings for him anyway? It was just her job, even though he saw her as the sweet girl-next-door from a small town. It had been a pleasure to be with her even if there was little hope of a future together.

As he bounced along in the van on the way back to the embassy, Will became lost in thoughts about his Pakistan experience. In fact, despite the initial wave of excitement when Jeb first announced they would be leaving, a subdued tone fell over the entire team on the ride back to the embassy. Everyone was silent. Even Hutchinson.

When they arrived at the embassy, Will was pleasantly surprised to find Tara waiting for him. She came over and took his hand.

"I've prepared something special for our last night," she whispered in his ear as they walked to her apartment. He was taken aback at her public display. She paid no mind to any of his teammates. It was out of character given her usual level of professional conduct. As he was about to leave Pakistan, she must have felt like she could drop any pretense. Will didn't question it.

Will wasn't the least bit surprised she knew when he would arrive. She appeared to know every move he made, sometimes even before he made it. Will was happy though with her pleasant greeting. They walked into her apartment, and he was not disappointed. The table was impeccably set with candles lit and a savory smell wafting through the kitchen.

"Something smells good. What's for dinner?"

She leaned in and kissed him. "Dinner's going to be awhile yet," she said, before leaning in for another kiss.

"Maybe I should grab a quick shower," Will suggested. He certainly needed a shower, although the request was as much an effort on his part to de-escalate a potential scenario where he might again succumb to his own weakness. After their first night together, Will was careful to avoid such situations. What Will didn't know was that Tara had been feeling guilty as well. That behavior was out of character for her. In fact, the reason Will had been successful in avoiding compromising positions, is that Tara was making sure they did. She was exactly who Will thought she was—that "girl next door" who was brought up in a good Christian home. Her dad was a deacon in their church and her mother was her eighth grade Sunday school teacher. They certainly would not have approved of their conduct.

After their evening meal, the rest of the team—with one exception—prepared to leave the embassy and return to the safe house.

"I'm gonna hang around here and wait on the ten o'clock bus," Morgan said. "See you guys later."

Morgan felt confident he could find a way to entertain himself for a couple of hours while he waited for the next van to the safe house. And of course, he knew Will would be along about that time too. He was curious about how his evening went.

As ten o'clock approached, Will knew he needed to gather his things and be on his way. As he was half-heartedly preparing to leave, Tara asked, "Why don't you stay the night?"

Will hesitated. "I'd love to, but you know I've got to be out front to catch that van in about ten minutes."

"I wouldn't worry about that. Your bosses have already left, they never take the late van anyway." Will didn't even comment on how she would know that. "I doubt they would even know you were gone."

"If it makes you feel any better, I can get you back in the morning before anybody ever wakes up. How would that be?"

Will had to admit the offer was appealing. "Well, I probably need to go out and see who's waiting on the van. Let me do that real quick and I'll be back and let you know." He was taken aback by the suggestion. He had never stayed later than ten o'clock and wasn't sure he should now, but he knew he wasn't ready for the evening to end.

"Okay babe. Hurry back," Tara said.

Will jogged out front to see who was waiting on the van. He deliberately left his gear in Tara's apartment, so he'd have an excuse to return if he were told he couldn't stay—even if just for a final kiss goodbye. Morgan was sitting on the front steps alone. He heard Will coming and turned toward him as he approached.

"There he is," he said genially. "How's your night, studly?"

"Well, it's going pretty good so far."

"So far? Where's your gear?"

"Well, that's what I wanted to talk about. Tara asked me to stay the night."

"Oh hell. You know that's not happening."

"Well, we're not going in the field tomorrow. And you know everybody except you and me sleep as late as they can when we have a day off. She says she can get me back to the house in the morning before anybody wakes up."

"I don't know—"

"Just one last night."

"Fine. But I'm not sure I can cover for you if you're not back when the captain and the sergeant major wake up."

"Okay," Will said. "I'll be back before anyone wakes up—nobody will miss me."

"I hope you're right," Morgan said. "See you first thing in the morning. First thing."

"Roger that," Will replied, and quickly set off back to Tara's apartment.

Morgan knew this was probably not the best decision and his tacit approval of it could cause problems for him if the captain and sergeant major found out. Still, he didn't want to be the barrier between two young lovers who just wanted to enjoy each other's company as long as they could. *They're not hurting anybody*, he reasoned to himself. *What's the harm?*

Will arrived back at Tara's apartment and she was delighted to hear he would be staying the night. "Oh good. I've already made arrangements for a car to take you back in the morning. Is 5:30 too early? You'll be walking in the house before six, how's that?"

"Well, that's perfect," Will said, not questioning how she knew he was staying in a "house." He already knew. Nothing she said or did surprised him anymore. He had long since dropped the subject of her work, so as not to force her to continue her charade. He didn't want to make her uncomfortable. Besides, they always found plenty of things to talk about without the topic of work ever coming up.

The more time Will spent with Tara, the more it seemed to him that maybe—more than just company—he provided for her somewhat of an escape. She had an important job. And incredibly stressful too, he imagined. Maybe spending time with him talking about benign things from back home—music, movies, family—was a catharsis for Tara. Will may have been her "boy next door." When he thought about it in that context, he felt better about the nature of their relationship. It didn't feel cheap or tawdry, or wrong. At that moment in time, it felt right. They were there for each other. They were right for each other. And brief as it was, it was special. Will chose to ignore the fact his departure was imminent. Instead, he would revel in the final hours he had with this beautiful young lady. But another night of passion was not what Tara had in mind. On the contrary. She needed to come clean with Will—about everything.

"I'm glad you agreed to stay the night. I need to tell you something. I know you've probably figured this out already," she paused briefly, considering her words. "I don't actually work for State."

"You don't have to say anything. I don't want to make you feel like you owe me any explanations."

"But I do. I need you to understand that I haven't been working you. You or anyone on your team. I want you to know that I really do like you—I care about you, and I don't want you to think ill of me."

"Really Tara, it's okay. You don't need to—"

"Stop," she interjected. "Let me say this. We weren't watching you, or your team. We knew there was a threat, and we couldn't quite put our finger on where it came from, but we suspected it was internal. I wasn't watching you—I was watching the people around you and your team, the embassy staff, you know, the local employees. We needed to see who it was inside the embassy that was feeding information to the ISI, and the only way to do that without tipping them was to get close to you—and your team."

Will remained silent, just trying to process this information.

"I didn't count on you though. I mean, I never expected to get involved with you like this. I never intended to, but I did. And I just want you know that I'm really Tara—I never lied about that. I want you to know that I've really enjoyed this time we've spent together. But I have to be honest, that first night together—that should have never happened. I'm so sorry about that. That's not who I am, and now that I've gotten to know you better, I know that's not who you are either. It's just this place. I've been missing home so much, and then I met you, and you just made me miss home even more. I just got caught up in it and lost myself. I guess I just needed you to know it was real—my feelings, I mean. That I'm real. Can you understand that?"

The truth was she never really lied to Will about anything. She truly did have an official role at State. She never offered any more information than that about her job and he never asked. What he didn't know was that this whole experience with him had caused Tara to rethink her career. Maybe she wasn't cut out for this type of work, she thought to herself. Maybe she ought to just go home and teach school as her parents had. Perhaps she loved the thought of adventure more than the actual adventure itself. What Tara knew was she missed home terribly and she had a lot of soul-searching to do.

"Well, I want you to know that I don't think any different of you at all," Will assured her. "This doesn't change anything as far as I'm concerned or the way I feel about you. I respect you, and your job, and everything you do."

"Thank you for understanding," she said, as she sank into his arms. "I'm going to miss you." They talked most of the night simply enjoying each other's company.

U.S. EMBASSY
ISLAMABAD, PAKISTAN
MAY 16, 1988
0530 HRS.

Morning came much too early, as it always does when you're dreading something. And Will dreaded saying goodbye to Tara. He rose and prepared to leave. They said little. She walked him to the door and placed a slip of paper in his hand.

"This is my address. Not here—home—Tennessee, I mean. If you ever want to write to me, I'd like that."

She held his face in her hands and kissed him sweetly on the lips before hugging him tightly for what seemed like several minutes. As she held him, she whispered in his ear.

"You are a sweet, special man, Will Carter. You take care of yourself and be safe, okay."

As she released him from her warm embrace, she kissed his cheek one final time. Tears welled up in her eyes. "Goodbye, sweetheart, I'll never forget you." She turned and walked into her bedroom closing the door behind her.

Will walked out her door knowing he would never see her again. But he left with a sweet memory. It was the first time any girlfriend he'd ever had referred to him as a man—usually they would use the word "guy." It sounded different, and it felt different. He would never forget it.

Will found a car waiting for him out front, just as Tara planned. And just as she predicted, he walked into the safe house at about ten minutes before six. He found Morgan seated in the living room.

"Morning. How did everything go?"

"As good as it gets, I guess," Will answered in a subdued tone.

Morgan knew he was upset and didn't press or say anything that might add to his distress.

"It's always hard to say goodbye to a sweetheart," the sergeant major said, walking into the living room, stirring his coffee.

"Oh. Sergeant Major, I-I-I—"

"Relax, kid. I was young once too. I was just telling Morgan here, I was surprised you didn't try to shack up with her a lot sooner. That little gal would be hard to resist."

Will stood there in stunned silence. The sergeant major knew what he did. More shockingly, he didn't appear to care.

"You're a good kid, Carter. More importantly, you're a good soldier. You're going places—no doubt."

Will continued to stand in front of Morgan and Sergeant Major Scott not knowing what to say. Morgan read his consternation, winked, and discreetly motioned for him to go on about his business.

"He's a good kid," the sergeant major said, after Will left the room. "You probably need to talk to him about re-enlisting."

"I think the captain's already been working on him," Morgan said. "But I'll talk to him too."

CHAPTER FORTY-THREE

SAFE HOUSE–UNDISCLOSED LOCATION
ISLAMABAD, PAKISTAN
MAY 16, 1988
1800 HRS.

The team passed the day watching videos and preparing to leave early the next morning. There was little in the way of conversation. Everyone was anxious to leave, and there was a palpable tension throughout the house.

After a day that seemed to last forever, the vans arrived at the house to take them out to their "Thank You and Goodbye" dinner with the Pakistani brass. Strangely, the dinner took place at a Chinese restaurant in downtown Islamabad. To no one's surprise, White Beard was not there. What passed for "brass" consisted of Major Omar, Captain Abed, and Lieutenant Bhatti.

They were seated promptly and waiters began serving dinner immediately. There was little pomp and circumstance accompanying this dinner, supposedly to "honor" the team for all their work. At one-point Major Omar rose to offer a toast. Lieutenant Bhatti distributed gifts to each of them—a green velvet box containing a set of cuff links, a tie clasp, and a key fob—each bearing the seal of the Pakistani Army. The Pak officers were all wearing shalwar kameezes. It was odd seeing them out of uniform, and it added to the unusual nature of the proceeding. Except for Captain Abed, they seemed to be mostly celebrating the team's imminent departure more than any support they provided them. It made for an awkward occasion, and they were glad to have it over when they arrived back at the safe house.

Jeb accompanied them to the dinner and he bristled at the fact Lieutenant Bhatti was present. All Bhatti did, as far as Jeb was concerned, was try to steal their explosives and pilfer Stinger missiles. He had no regard for Bhatti—and now even less, if that was possible, after learning of his involvement with the Iranians. Of course, Jeb never mentioned this to anyone, but it was clear there was tension in the room throughout the dinner.

"I'll see you guys first thing in the morning," Jeb said, as they clambered out of the vans at the safe house. "Aziz will send you off with a good breakfast. We need to leave the house about 7:30—copy?"

"Copy that, sir," the captain replied. "We'll be ready."

Will awoke the next morning to the welcome smell of breakfast wafting through the house. He wasted little time getting ready and, after a quick shower, sat at the dining room table. Everyone sat within ten minutes of each other, and Aziz quickly served breakfast. Hastily consumed, they were ready to go when the vans arrived at 7:30 sharp. Each of them shook hands with Aziz and Cook and thanked them both for taking such excellent care of them.

"It has been our great pleasure to serve you," Aziz said effusively. "Farewell, gentlemen." Aziz and Cook placed their hands together and bowed. "Safe journey. Safe journey."

The EOD team arrived at Chaklala Air Base just before 8:00 a.m. where a C-5 Galaxy was waiting. "This is a pretty big plane for our bunch," the captain remarked.

"Well, y'all are just hitching a ride," Jeb said.

When the team entered the plane, they saw what the real cargo was, a UH-1 Huey helicopter. It was amazing to see an aircraft inside an aircraft. The C-5 had a cavernous cargo bay. It looked like it could have accommodated another Huey. Outside of the team, this single helicopter was the only cargo aboard the humongous plane that they could see. They also quietly noticed the black Huey was unmarked. Once they were finally airborne though, it became a topic of conversation.

They loaded onto the plane expecting to rack out in the cargo bay as they did on the flight over. As it turned out, there was a passenger deck in the front of the plane. It had comfortable commercial airline seats, enough to accommodate more than seventy passengers. With only eight of them on board, there was plenty of room to stretch out and make a nest for the long flight home.

Jeb boarded the plane with them. Will assumed he was just going to see they had everything before they left and see them off. It turned out to be a debrief.

"Gentlemen," Jeb began, once they were all gathered around at the front of the passenger cabin. "This whole operation is highly classified—top secret, compartmentalized information. That means you don't talk about it anywhere, any time—copy?"

"Yes sir," they answered in unison.

"You guys have done some great work over here. Very important work. I'm proud of all of you. You've done us all proud. The general and I appreciate all you've done."

No one spoke. They just looked at each other awaiting any further comment Jeb might have. Will hoped to see the general before they left. He was disappointed he wasn't there to see them off. Just then Jeb accounted for General Wassom's conspicuous absence.

"The general would be here, but he's over in the Punjab region scouting a tank demonstration that's coming up soon with the Ambo and President Zia."

The whole team appeared relieved to know the general hadn't ignored their departure.

"If there are no questions. I'll say goodbye." Jeb shook the captain's hand and said, "Great job, Captain—appreciate it."

"Thank you, sir."

Jeb made the rounds shaking hands and thanking each of them individually, starting with Sergeant Major Scott and concluding with Carter. As he shook Will's hand, he handed him a piece of paper folded tightly enough to fit in the palm of his hand. "You're a good soldier, Sergeant Carter. If you don't re-enlist, I want you to give this guy a call. Tell him I sent you."

"Yes sir. Thank you."

As he prepared to exit the passenger deck, Jeb turned to the group one last time. “Safe travels, gentlemen,” he said with a wave. “It’s been a pleasure.” With that, Jeb was gone. Ten minutes later the team was airborne en route to Dharan, Saudi Arabia, their first waypoint on the long journey home.

“What was that paper Jeb handed you?” Morgan asked.

Will placed it in his pocket immediately and hadn’t even looked at it until Morgan’s inquiry prompted its retrieval. He removed it from his pocket, unfolded the paper and read it. *Colonel Dennis Norton, University of Missouri – Columbia, ROTC.* Will would find out later Colonel Norton was not only an instructor of military science, he was also a close associate of Jeb’s—and all that implied.

“Just some guy’s contact information,” Will replied, offering nothing more.

Morgan raised an eyebrow but didn’t press further.

CHAPTER FORTY-FOUR

DHAHRAN, SAUDI ARABIA
MAY 17, 1988
0930 HRS.

The flight to Dhahran took four hours. As the team deplaned, a ground crewman suddenly stopped them and guided them back on the plane.

"Whoa, whoa—you guys are going to have to get back on the plane and get some long pants on. This airfield is shared with the Saudis, so we have to observe all the protocols. Once you get through that gate over there," he said pointing, "you'll officially be on our base. You can wear shorts over there."

They hustled back onto the plane and quickly donned long pants. As he walked off the plane, Will had a can of orange Fanta in his hand and the ground crewman stopped him again.

"Hold it, son. You're gonna have to leave that pop can on the plane. They don't allow Coca-Cola products in Saudi Arabia."

"What? You're kidding me."

"No joke. Welcome to Saudi Arabia."

Will quickly downed the remaining Fanta and discarded the can into a plastic bag one of the air crew placed near the door of the plane.

Morgan was waiting patiently on the tarmac. "Damn," he said as Will joined him. "I hope it's not as hard to get out of this country as it is to get in."

As it turned out, they stayed the night in Saudi Arabia before traveling to Frankfurt, Germany. Once in Germany, they had another unexpected delay. There was a mechanical problem with the plane, and they had to wait for a part. They stayed two nights in Germany. Overall, the trip home took four days, in stark contrast to the rapid deployment that placed them on the ground in Pakistan in just twenty-six hours. There was less urgency on the flight home and they were just hitching a ride, as Jeb noted.

DOVER AFB, DELAWARE
MAY 20, 1988
1425 HRS.

The team arrived at Dover Air Force Base on a beautiful Friday afternoon. Major Aquino was there to greet them. He thanked them for their "outstanding work" and shook each of their hands. He seemed genuinely pleased to be welcoming them home. They loaded up into two vans and headed for Fort Dix, but not before prevailing upon the major to allow them to make a stop at McDonald's, the first one they came to. *It's great to be back in America*, Will thought to himself as he savored that first bite of a Big Mac.

T.J. Combs was waiting for Will at the Control Center when they arrived at Fort Dix. He welcomed him with a hug. "You made it, buddy. Glad you're back."

There was little left to do other than say their goodbyes and hit the road. Will shook hands all around and everybody prepared to go their own ways.

"You think about what we talked about Carter," Captain Halstead said as he shook Will's hand. "I'll put you in front of the E-6 board right away. I want to keep you."

"Yes sir. I will."

Morgan took a little longer to say goodbye. His wife, Linda, and two daughters were there to greet him. He introduced Will to his family. They were thrilled to have him back home and seemed delighted to meet Will as well. His wife even gave Will a hug, which reminded him that he needed to get a hold of his own family as quick as he could.

"Now you're gonna come spend a weekend with us this summer," Morgan said. "We'll take out the boat, water ski, cook out, the whole deal—right?"

"Right," Will replied. Morgan gave Will a hug and patted him on the shoulder.

"Get outta here."

Will turned to walk out when the sergeant major caught sight of him. "Stand fast, Sergeant Carter," he said, loudly.

Oh no, Will thought to himself. *What did I do?*

"Get over here."

Will dutifully responded and walked over to Sergeant Major Scott, not knowing what to expect.

"Great job, son," he said with a big smile. He shook Will's hand and said, "I'm glad we had you on the team. We'll be talking soon, hear?"

"Roger that, Sergeant Major."

"You boys take it easy driving home," the sergeant major said. "Didn't come all this way just to get a speeding ticket on the damn turnpike."

"Roger that, Sergeant Major."

Two hours and fifteen minutes later, Will and T.J. pulled into the back lot at the 56th EOD, Fort Indiantown Gap, Pennsylvania.

"I know you're probably pretty tired. But we were planning a welcome home dinner for you if you're up for it."

It was a little after five o'clock and the only one still at the unit was MSG Steve Jackson. Will walked in the building and up the hall to the orderly room. Despite himself, Jackson smiled and said, "Welcome back."

"Thanks, Top."

"You can tell me all about it later. Right now, I'm going home to change for dinner."

"I was just wondering. I have a little leave time and—" Will began to say.

"You just got back, and you want to go on leave?" Jackson asked.

"Well, if it's possible."

"Nah, I don't think so." There was a long pause, and Jackson broke out in a big grin. "No leave. But I do have a four-day pass for you."

"Oh wow," Will said, not expecting such generosity. He went from deflated to elated. "Thanks, Top."

"Don't thank me. Sergeant Major called an hour ago and told me to give you a four-day pass. That works out good for you because tomorrow's Saturday and your pass doesn't start until Monday."

That meant Will had six days to do what he wanted. He quickly decided he would go home to see his folks, but that fifteen-hour drive would wait until after his welcome home party.

CHAPTER FORTY-FIVE

FT. INDIANTOWN GAP, PENNSYLVANIA
AUGUST 17, 1988
1905 HRS.

Will had a great visit with his folks, and soon he was back into his usual routine—if you could call it that—at Ft. Indiantown Gap. It was an election year, and since Will's unit was a designated VIP Support Unit, the Secret Service was keeping them busy. Despite the hectic pace, Will managed to meet a sweet girl from Lebanon, Pennsylvania. They had been dating steadily most of the summer.

Will was preparing for a date with her one August evening when he received some sobering news. The television was on as he got out of the shower. He wasn't paying particularly close attention to the evening news as his mind was mostly on Michelle, and where he would be taking her for dinner that night. Just then, Dan Rather said something that captured Will's immediate attention: reports from Bahawalpur, Pakistan indicated that President Zia Ul Haq was killed in a plane crash.

The phone rang.

"Will, are you watching the news?" the caller asked. It was none other than Morgan. "Turn on the news, quick."

Morgan was watching the same broadcast and though he remained on the line, he said nothing as the two of them watched together.

Dan Rather noted that in addition to President Zia, U.S. Ambassador Arnold Raphel and U.S. Army Brigadier General Herbert Wassom were on the plane—a C-130 Hercules—with the Pakistani president and were among the dead. They had accompanied President Zia to a demonstration of the M1A1 Abrams tank by the Pak Army near Bahawalpur, Pakistan, in the Punjab region. Details were scant at the time, but early reports attributed the crash to engine failure.

Will watched, stunned.

"Man, you are one lucky son of a b***h," Morgan said.

"Me? How am I lucky?"

"The general asked you to stay in Pakistan and be his aide—remember?"

"Yeah . . . I remember," Will answered, solemnly.

"If you'd stayed, you'd be right there with him."

Morgan was right. That was the primary reason the general asked Will to stay in the first place.

"God was looking out for you, buddy."

"No doubt," Will agreed. He was still in a minor state of shock not knowing what to say, or even think. "They said the crash was caused by engine failure."

"Engine failure, my ass. This was an assassination. That plane was blown out to sky just as sure as I'm standing here."

"You're probably right," Will said. "What do you think brought it down?"

"You already know the answer to that question," Morgan said emphatically. "Stinger."

ACKNOWLEDGMENTS

Outside of my wife, there's been no one so influential in the process of writing this book than my good friend, colleague, and fellow veteran, Congressman Chris Stewart. A *New York Times* best-selling author (many times over), I approached him with the story idea in the hope he would write it. He declined. When I asked him why, he simply said "Because you're going to write it. This is a story that deserves to be told," he said, "and nobody can tell it like you." He set me on course, coached and encouraged me. He believed I could do it when I didn't. You don't run into people like him everyday and I'm truly thankful for his mentorship and his friendship.

I must also thank my publishers at Fidelis Publishing—Oliver North and Gary Terashita. It started with Col. North actually returning my phone call. He was willing to take a chance. That's when Gary came into the picture. He played an integral part in fine-tuning the work, and more than that, his godly influence has made a major impact on me personally.

I also extend my thanks to Mack McLarty, former President Clinton's chief of staff and fellow Arkansan, and Elliot Ackerman, best-selling author and special ops Marine. They helped facilitate the call to Col. North that got the ball rolling.

I'm sure every author has a unique experience in getting their work published, but it's not often you hear about it. Writing is the easy part. Finding a publisher—that's when it gets tough. To any aspiring author I'll tell you what I learned back in EOD school—if it was easy, anybody could do it.

Never quit!

KEY CHARACTERS

FT. INDIANTOWN GAP

**MSG Steve Jackson—First Sergeant at the 56th EOD. A Vietnam veteran EOD tech with over twenty years service.

**SPC Dan Hildegard—EOD assistant serving at the 56th EOD. Mild mannered and friendly with everyone. Close friends with SGT Will Carter.

**SGT T.J. Combs—a second-term EOD tech. One of only two married soldiers at the 56th EOD. He and his wife often hosted unit gatherings. Close friends with SGT Will Carter.

ARMY TEAM

**Captain John Halstead—a Vietnam veteran EOD tech. Served as an enlisted man prior to going to college and earning his commission. Operations officer at the EOD Control Center at Ft. Meade, Maryland. Chosen specifically for his experience with a similar incident in Vietnam.

**SGM James Scott—a Vietnam veteran EOD tech with almost thirty years' service. Senior NCO at the EOD Control Center at Ft. Dix, New Jersey. Like CPT Halstead, was chosen specifically for his extensive experience.

**SFC Ed Morgan—experienced EOD tech with almost twenty years' service. Acting First Sergeant at the operational EOD unit at Ft. Dix, New Jersey.

**SSG Wiley Adams—experienced EOD tech with almost sixteen years' service. Training NCO at the EOD Control Center at

---

*Actual figures with real names.

**Actual figures with fictitious names.

Ft. Dix, New Jersey. A quirky individual who was often the butt of jokes from his fellow soldiers. An otherwise capable EOD tech.

**SSG Shane Hutchinson—second term EOD tech serving at the EOD unit at West Point. A big man with a blustery personality, known to be a joker.

**SGT Chad Campbell—second term EOD tech serving at the EOD unit at Ft. Devens, Massachusetts. Short in stature with a reputation as a scrapper. He broke a civilian's jaw in a bar fight—an unprovoked attack—while attending EOD school at Indian Head, Maryland.

**SGT Tom Theissen—another second term EOD tech also assigned to the EOD unit at Ft. Devens. A very analytical thinker seen as somewhat of a "nerd" by his fellow soldiers.

**SGT Will Carter—a first term soldier, second generation EOD tech. A military brat, he spent his teen years in New Mexico. Nearing the end of his first term of service, he was wrestling with the decision to re-enlist or leave the Army and go to college.

NAVY TEAM

**LT Dale Johnson—the officer in charge of the EOD detachment serving on the USS Enterprise, he had nearly ten years in service.

**SCPO Brent Sonberg—the senior NCO of the USS Enterprise EOD detachment. He was nearing retirement and planning to return to his native Montana to establish a fly fishing guide service with his brother.

**PO1 Tony Wyndham—a stocky navy diver serving on the USS Enterprise in the EOD detachment. He had almost fifteen years' service and was known to have the ability to hold his breath for extended periods of time.

U.S. EMBASSY–PAKISTAN

**Jeb or "Hawkeye" as he was referred to by the CIA station staff—A Special Forces colonel on detail to the CIA. He was a key enabler in moving munitions to and the training of Mujahadeen forces battling the Soviets in Afghanistan. A formidable figure, he spoke at least three languages and although diminutive in size, he was an imposing and influential figure among the Mujahadeen fighters and his counterparts in Pakistan.

*Brigadier General Herbert Wassom—United States Defense Attaché in Pakistan. A wiry Vietnam veteran, well respected by his Pakistani counterparts and a trusted advisor to the U.S. Ambassador. Very outgoing and friendly.

*Ambassador Arnold Raphel—a career diplomat with the U.S. State Department, he was the 18th U.S. Ambassador to Pakistan. He assumed his Islamabad post in January of 1987. Raphel was experienced in Mid-East affairs. In 1979, he was a key member of the State Department's Special Operations Group set up to free the American hostages seized by Iranian militants at the United States Embassy in Tehran. Raphel was killed along with Pakistan President Zia and U. S. Defense Attaché Brigadier General Wassom in an assassination attack in August, 1988.

**Brad Miller and **Cory Leftwich—CIA case officers both of whom were assisting "Hawkeye" with the Camp Ohjri incident.

Tara—officially assigned to the State Department's Office of Protocol in Islamabad, she was serving in her first foreign duty assignment. She was tall and particularly attractive, as well as quite charming.

PAKISTANIS

*Brigadier Javed Nasir—the director of the Pakistan Army Engineers. "White Beard" as he was called due to his long white beard—unusual among the Pakistan Army Officer Corps—was also the deputy director of the Inter-Services Intelligence, the Pakistan counterpart of the CIA. He took the lead in the cleanup operations immediately following the Camp Ohjri blast. He maintained a hostile posture toward the American EOD teams.

1LT Bhatti—a trusted associate of White Beard, he was openly hostile to the Americans. He was actively involved in operations designed to delay the progress of the American EOD teams.

Ironically, he received his engineering degree from an American university.

*Major Omar—another associate of White Beard, it was unclear what role he played in relation to the Camp Ohjri blast, but he displayed an open animus toward the Americans.

*Captain Abed—in sharp contrast to most of the Pakistani Army officers, he was very affable and welcoming of the American EOD team, developing a particularly good rapport with SGT Carter. He received his engineering degree from the University of Illinois and had an affinity for American culture.

*Khali Khan—a Pakistan Army veteran, he was a vetted employee of the U.S. Embassy and did most of the driving for the American EOD team. He was quite friendly and particularly fond of SGT Carter.

**Aziz—the house manager at the "safe house" where the EOD team was placed. He spoke English very eloquently and took great pride in providing a high degree of service to his guests.

Apu—the Pakistani CIA asset who had an unusual characteristic—red hair. While he collected intelligence for Jeb, it was later discovered that he was possibly a double agent.

AFGHANS

*Muhammadin—Jeb's primary contact in Afghanistan, he was trained by the Pakistan Army Special Services Group—the counterpart of the U.S. Army Green Berets. Although only in his late twenties, he rose quickly through the ranks of the Mujahadeen owing to his extensive experience in fighting the Soviets as well as his political savvy. He developed a close relationship with Jeb, sharing vital intelligence and assisting in the movement of munitions and materiel in support of the Mujahadeen forces.

Ghulam—Muhammadin's trusted advisor, he also served as the primary interrogator of opposition forces in Mujahadeen custody. He had a reputation for being particularly brutal in his interrogation methods.